JUSTICE BITCH
ISSUE 2:

FLIGHT OF
THE POLTERGEIST

WRITTEN AND ILLUSTRATED BY

COYOTE PARIA

ISBN-13: 978-0-578-62463-1

Table of Contents

—

Chapter 1:
A Girl and Her Butler

Harriet was glad to have The Ross Manor back, if only temporarily. Technically, the mansion still belonged to her dead father's lover, Reynolds, the former butler, but Harriet's attempts to get back in contact with him after her reacquisition of the property were frustrating. It made Harriet very angry to think that Reynolds the butler, who had once been like a second father to her, was now ignoring her. Like she was nothing—*like she was garbage.*

"It doesn't make any sense," Harriet muttered to Spencer through gritted teeth as she stared at the screen of her cell phone. Her expensive pearl necklace was askew and her long dark hair was disheveled. During the course of this one-sided conversation, her left eye had developed a subtle and dangerous twitch, "He's not responding to any of my texts! You'd think he'd at least return my calls if it meant getting the mansion back!"

"You sound upset," Spencer said. He was the new butler (technically Reynolds' replacement) and he was currently dressed in his butler's uniform, with a black bowtie, a black tuxedo, and his shaggy black hair slicked back behind his ears. He stood in an uncharacteristically rigid way, holding a silver tray, which contained Harriet's breakfast, in the flat palms of both of his hands.

Enraged by this casual observation, Harriet stood up and knocked the tray out of Spencer's hands with a casual flick of her wrist, scattering the tray's contents throughout the room.

"Go clean that up!" Harriet barked.

"Yes, ma'am!" Spencer said back spastically and then he got to work gathering the scattered bowls, glasses, and silverware.

While he was scurrying around, cleaning food out of the red carpets, and off of black onyx pillars covered in screaming skulls, Harriet stared at the screen of her cell phone. A text from Reynolds appeared on the screen: *Currently on a cruise in Italy. Very busy. Will talk later.*

Harriet threw the cell phone down in disgust.

"Very busy? *Talk later?*" Harriet repeated, incensed by the casual brush-off. *What the hell's wrong with him? Why is he acting like this?*

"You know, it's probably better if he doesn't answer your calls," Spencer pointed out, "If he doesn't claim the mansion, then you can just keep living here indefinitely. Maybe he's just too rich to care about this place."

"You know I can't afford the taxes on this place without my inheritance," Harriet said with a tone of exasperation.

"Huh...I honestly didn't think of that," Spencer said, slouching a bit and scratching the back of his head.

Harriet slapped him on the ass and he straightened up instinctively.

"Don't slouch," Harriet said, "Butlers need good posture."

"Yes, ma'am."

Harriet paced the room, glaring at the stained glass windows, which depicted contorted, emaciated sinners being tortured by demons in hell.

"I'll lose this place if he decides to not pay the bills...and I think that's what he's decided. I think he's letting this place go."

"It's just a house, Harriet."

"Maybe to you."

Harriet thought of happier times, when her family had been alive, together, and whole. All of those memories lived in this house together, along with her memories of Reynolds, who had been a part of her family, not off gallivanting on some extravagant vacation; refusing to answer her calls. She recalled a time from her childhood, when Reynolds had played tea party with her and a host of stuffed animals. She remembered the man holding a plump plush elephant in one hand and an empty plastic teacup in the other.

"Yes, I am the elephant from Pamelaphant," Reynolds had said raising his pompous British accent a few octaves to indicate that he was speaking as the elephant.

"But what kind of food do you eat in Pamelaphant?" the 5-year-old Harriet had chirped back childishly.

Reynolds had hesitated, perhaps attempting to think of something clever and then replied, beaming with fatherly pride: "Why, bamelaphants, my girl."

"That's silly! That's not a word!" the 5-year-old Harriet had said, laughing.

"No, I suppose it isn't" Reynolds had said, laughing as well; grinning from ear to ear.

Harriet was jarred out of her flashback by Spencer, who approached her suppliantly. Since agreeing to become Harriet's sex slave, he had sworn off villainy. Despite this, however, the man still looked very archetypically villainous, with pale skin, dark hair, and a deep battle scar sliced under one eye.

"Aw…you look sad," Spencer said taking a strand of Harriet's long, dark hair and brushing it behind one ear.

"Shut the fuck up, Spencer. Go get me a Danish," Harriet muttered, angry that he had noticed this.

"Your wish is my command, oh cruel princess," Spencer said with a grin and then he took her hand in his and kissed it on the knuckle.

Chapter 2:
The Sexy Rad Super Pals Ride Again

In anticipation of attending the next Sexy Rad Super Pals meeting, Harriet showered and then dressed in a sleeveless, knee-length black dress, black heels, a string of white pearls, and a pair of designer sunglasses. It was good to have access to her designer wardrobe again. She celebrated by admiring her choice of clothes in the mirrored wall of a walk-in closet bigger than most people's living rooms, and by doing this for a few minutes longer than was strictly necessary.

She left the manor with Spencer, and they drove off in a black Jaguar, to the coffee shop where Viola's vigilante superhuman team often met. As the black Jaguar sped across a steep, red, suspension bridge, Harriet sat in the passenger seat, and watched the city skyline roll by. She turned her head in Spencer's direction, and watched him for a while as he drove. He was still dressed as a butler, as he had been yesterday, but, now, with his stubbly goatee shaved, and his dark hair neatly slicked back, he looked more convincing in the role.

"It's nice to have the manor back," Harriet said with a yawn and a lazy stretch of her powerful arms.

"Uh...but, Harriet...didn't your father leave the manor to Reynolds Sanderland?" Spencer reminded her.

"Crap. I wanted to forget about that," Harriet said with a groan, "I guess I'll have to tell him to take it off my hands when I see him for lunch this Saturday. That is if he bothers to show up. He could just send me a text and refuse to show up again, like last time."

"You know you don't have to give it back to him. You could just keep it," said Spencer.

"It legally belongs to him," said Harriet with some bitterness, "And besides, like I said, I can't afford the taxes on it anymore."

Spencer shrugged: *"Well*...if that's what you really want, you *are* the boss. But you could just keep the manor and then just blame me for taking it, and tell them that you're just a hostage, if the cops somehow manage to get it back. I mean, that's what I would do, but then again, what do I know? I'm just the butler."

"Spoken like a true good guy," Harriet muttered with a suspicious groan.

"Heheheh...heh...heh...maybe I still need to be taught," he chuckled.

The black Jaguar pulled into the parking lot next to the diner. Harriet and Spencer got out of the car and walked inside.

The bell over the door jingled as Harriet opened it. She saw Viola sitting in the place where she usually sat, grinning cheerfully and accompanied by Benjamin, Lilly, and Finsveld. Viola, was a pretty black woman who liked to dye her hair different vivacious pastel and primary colors. Viola's hair was currently died orange and straightened it into half-dollar-sized ringlets. She was wearing a baby blue tank top with a Hello Kitty necklace and a pair of ripped blue jeans.

Viola waved at Harriet as she saw her approach. Harriet waved back, enjoying the shocked looks on everyone's faces, as they slowly noticed that she was accompanied by Spencer. Perhaps their belated reaction to his bewildering presence in their midst was due to his newly groomed and polished butler persona. He walked a few steps behind Harriet, with his hands folded, submissively helping her out of her black velvet jacket before she sat down at the table, in the booth next to Finsveld, and across from Viola and Benjamin. Then, he sat down next to her, without saying a word. Spencer's silence in this instance indicated his new status as Harriet's fashion accessory. Like her black velvet purse and the string of pearls around her neck, it was his job to frame her attractively, without drawing too much attention to himself.

5

Staring across the table at Spencer, Viola's grin spread wide over white, square teeth. This was the grin of someone who had been proven right, and the grin of someone who predicted the acquisition of a new Sexy Rad Super Pal team member in the near future. Benjamin stared at Spencer also, but with an incredulous scowl. Finsveld, glanced in Spencer's direction with a vague recognition, bordering on indifference.

"Haarriet," Viola nearly sang, still grinning. "Who's *this*?"

"He's uh...he's my butler," Harriet replied falteringly.

Viola laughed, slamming both of her palms down on the table in front of her, in a gesture of victory: "*Ha!* I knew it!"

"Ok, ok, so maybe I *did* think he was cute. You don't have to rub it in," Harriet conceded.

Spencer smirked: "You think I'm cute."

"*Shut up,*" Harriet said.

Spencer shut up, but his grin remained.

"You know he's too young for you, right?" Benjamin muttered incredulously. He was a skinny guy with curly brown hair and bright green eyes. Currently, those striking green eyes were narrowed into slits, as Benjamin shot Harriet a look of hateful disgust from across the table. Harriet and Benjamin had never gotten along and there was always some level of passive-aggressive tension between them.

"No one asked for your opinion, *Benjamin*," Harriet replied with annoyance.

Finsveld (a large, fat man who wore a very dirty and ketchup-stained T-shirt) belched and replied truthfully: "Finsveld is indifferent."

"You see, now there's a man who knows how to keep his nose out of my business," Harriet said pleasantly, though still glaring at Benjamin, who rolled his green eyes at her in disgust.

"Alright! Down to business, team!" Viola announced happily. "A local store owner has reported reoccurring acts of vandalism and graffiti on his shop front and on the asphalt on the parking lot outside. The graffiti has been sandblasted off several times, but always makes a reappearance the night after being cleaned. So, tonight, we're going to stake out the parking lot until the vandal makes an appearance, bring the vandal to justice. and then reap the reward from the store owner."

"What's the reward?" Benjamin asked, though it was clear by the tone of his voice that he was not expecting much.

"200 dollars and half-price burritos for life," Viola said.

"Lame," Benjamin said, crossing his arms with annoyance.

"We usually do this for free though...so isn't anything we get for it just a bonus?" Lilly whispered.

"Yeah, Benjamin, don't be such a money-grubbing whore," Viola said. She balled her hand into a fist and stuck it out over the center of the table. Everyone at the table placed their hands on top of hers, one by one. Spencer was last to do this, and he moved with a nervous, faltering, hesitance, as Viola waited, silently inviting him to put his hand on.

"Sexy Rad Super Pals!" Viola shouted.

"Let's rock and roll!" the other members of the team finished with an overdramatic flourish.

They all took their hands off. Finsveld snapped his fingers and, in an instant, The Sexy Rad Super Pals were all dressed in costume.

The chubby waitress wandered by murmuring and scratching her blond head: "Hey, where'd those freaks go?"

"You mean the people who were sitting here before us?" Viola said innocently, without missing a beat. "They had to leave. But we're heroes so we'll pick up their tab. Also, me and my sexy friends will each have a coffee, to go. It's going to be a long night."

Chapter 3:
Very Important Parking Lot Stake Out

Viola's van pulled into a parking space outside of the *Lucky Shop Mart* on Korea Street. A moment later, The Sexy Rad Super Pals emerged from the vehicle in full costume. Harriet was dressed as Justice Bitch in a long black leather coat and fishnet stockings. Spencer was dressed as Death Laser with a long red cape and black leather pants. Viola was dressed as Hawkette with a long yellow cape and a pink pleather belly shirt. Lilly was dressed as Ghost Gal in a short, white, semi-transparent dress. Benjamin was dressed as Green Lightning in a bright green tuxedo and a top hat. And finally, as always, Finsveld was dressed as Finsveld in a pair of crumpled jeans and an ill-fitting condiment-stained T-shirt.

The parking lot was empty and quiet. The *Lucky Shop Mart* was closed, and the inside was obscured by two sliding metal blinds, behind both glass windowpanes, on either side of the front door.

Benjamin stood close to Viola and whispered urgently in her ear, voicing his concern about the team's newest member: "Are you sure we can trust him?"

Viola stared at Spencer, who was now dressed as Death Laser and playing with a coil of Harriet's dark hair, while she scanned the parking lot with her eyes, tense and alert, waiting for a perceptible disturbance. He grinned stupidly at her as she did this, eyeing her with a look of fan-boyish, lust-drunk admiration.

"I'm sure he's harmless," Viola whispered back dismissively.

"Yeah, but he's known as a villain. Don't you think that people are going to freak out when they see him with us?" Benjamin said quietly, obscuring his mouth with his hand so as not to be overheard.

"I believe in second chances," said Viola. "And besides you use to be a villain too, remember?"

"Yea, well, frankly, I trust *myself* more than I trust *him*. What kind of superhuman vigilante dresses like that anyway?" Benjamin said, subtly motioning with his eyes toward Spencer's leather and metal studded disguise.

"The dark and edgy kind," Viola argued, "Some of the best superhuman vigilantes fit that classic dark and edgy archetype. You know, like, No One Understands Me Boy, Angst Dad, Bat Guy, Captain Copyright Infringement, Cease and Desist Man…"

"Ok, ok, fine. Whatever. Angst Dad is fucking cool. But this 'Death Laser' character, he's *no* Angst Dad. I'm keeping my eye on him."

Time passed. The Sexy Rad Super Pals circled the parking lot, waiting for the vandal to make an appearance. However, the parking lot remained empty and quiet. The buzz of intermittent traffic and the occasional flash of headlights did little to alleviate the stagnant, isolated feeling.

Time passed. Harriet walked over to Viola's van and leaned against it with one hand, quickly abandoning her intensity and alertness. Spencer stood next to her, yawned, stretched, and put an arm around her shoulder. Viola and Benjamin sat down on a cement parking block near the deserted shop entrance, and started playing I-spy like a couple of bored-out-of-their-mind kids.

"I spy something that is pink," Viola said.

"The van," Benjamin replied quickly and bluntly.

Spencer started experimentally whistling the tune to a song he had thought of.

"I spy something that is gray," droned Benjamin unenthusiastically.

"The parking lot," Viola replied quickly and bluntly.

After about ten minutes of this, Finsveld declared himself "bored" and started to walk home. Viola and Benjamin waved goodbye as his morbidly obese form waddled away into the night. Harriet and Spencer, who were now standing against Viola's van, with their arms wrapped

—

around each other and their lips locked, did not notice him leave.

Feeling the texture of his rough tongue against hers, Harriet leaned into Spencer and ran her hands through his dark, slicked-back hair. Then, her hands slid down his muscular back to the soft curve of his backside.

"Does it still hurt?" Harriet whispered. She smiled slightly, nearly imperceptibly, her mouth very close to Spencer's ear. Her hand lingered on his behind.

"Not much," Spencer murmured back groggily as though having just emerged from a dream. His eyes were half-lidded as they stared into hers.

Harriet smirked evilly and then gripped his sore bottom tightly with one powerful, long-finger-nailed hand. Spencer's eyes shot open and he let out an involuntary yelp.

"I spy something *disgusting*," said Benjamin to Viola with a roll of his eyes.

"Aw, I think it's cute."

"Yeah, that's the problem with you, Viola," said Benjamin with a bitter exhale of frustration. "You think that *everything* is cute."

"Well, you know me. I love love."

"...Is *that* what we're calling it?"

Harriet let go of Spencer's ass and started kissing him again, oblivious to her audience at the other side of the parking lot. Benjamin took off his hat and mimed vomiting into it.

Viola rose to her feet and stretched, cracking her knuckles.

"Where is this damn graffiti vandal, already?" she said.

Her question was answered only by silence. A car drove by, and the engine filled the night air momentarily. An owl perched on a nearby streetlamp bellowed a deep *whoooo*, and then, fluttered off into the night.

Then, Viola spotted him, a shadowy, hooded figure, holding a spray can up in front of him, as he stood before the deserted shop front. The hooded figure shook the can, and then, began writing the word "butts" on the front of the shop in large, pink bubble letters.

"Stop right there!" Viola shouted, pointing at the hooded figure.

The vandal completed the letter S, taking his time, with it, paying special attention to the contour of the hastily scrawled bubble letter. He turned slowly toward Viola, who raised her fists, preparing herself for a confrontation. The vandal stepped into the light of a nearby streetlamp. Beneath a red hoodie, half of his face was covered by a black ski-mask, the other half of his face was pockmarked and frowning boredly, unimpressed by Viola's bravado.

"I am —" the vandal announced grandly, he was interrupted by a man's shouting voice.

"Stop right there!" the voice shouted.

Viola turned her head in the direction of the noise. Benjamin rose to his feet. Harriet and Spencer dislodged their tongues from each other's mouths.

Stuart, Dressed as The American Eagle, in an American-flag-print unitard, emerged from the shadows. He was followed by The League of American Heroes, all striding dramatically in a v-shaped formation behind him. They were all in full costume.

"I am The American Eagle," Stuart announced to the vandal, who had grown bored of the conversation and was now spray painting the words "crush pussy" on one of the glass windowpanes of the storefront. "And this is The League of American Heroes."

"And The Sexy Rad Super Pals!" Viola interjected in protest.

The League of American Heroes all posed dramatically as they introduced themselves one at a time along with some kind of a patriotic catchphrase like "I Love America!" or "Flag burning is bad!" By the time Flago and Lady Liberty had said their shtick, the vandal had covered the entire shop front with a collage of colorful profanity, and drawings of erect penises.

"What the hell, Stuart!" Viola shouted. "We've been waiting here all night to catch this guy! Tell you're stupid army buddies to get out of here!"

"We have as much right as you to be here, Viola," argued Stuart angrily.

"Oh yeah, well we were here first!"

"Oh yeah, well we're here second."

"I am PTSD Bro! Support our troops!" A violently trembling man in full body green and brown camouflage spandex announced, about two minutes too late.

The vandal threw down an empty can of spray paint and turned toward them once more. Then, flamboyantly introduced himself as well as his hokey villain theme, which was, apparently, being a white boy gangster:

"I am Spray Boi Fresh! And there ain't a wall, bridge, office building, sidewalk or fire hydrant in this city that don't know how fresh I am! I crush puss all day and night! I be crushin' that puss and gettin' that paper! Smokin', crushin' puss, and gettin' that bling, yo! I be Representin' day 'n night! So if you wanna' through down then I'm gonna drop you bitches, 'aight?"

Benjamin put his top hat on and walked over to Spray Boi Fresh, staring him straight in the eye.

"Yeah, well, the guy who owns this store you keep vandalizing is going to give me 200 dollars and half-price burritos for the rest of my life if I turn you in to the police, and I'm bored of these stupid introductions so..." Benjamin said.

"Yo, I an't scared of you," Spray Boi Fresh scoffed. Benjamin was a head shorter than him and had far narrower shoulders.

Benjamin's eyes glowed acid green. Green sparks flew from his fingers and the spray cans in Spray Boi Fresh's backpack exploded onto the sidewalk, trailing shreds of dark blue cloth from the ruined bag. Spray Boi Fresh stumbled backward as his art supplies sprouted twisted limbs and disturbing faces. The cans of spray paint stumbled toward him with gaping, jagged mouths, violently scratching at the air and making a gargling *craaaugghhhh* noise as they approached.

"Yo, I'm outta' here!" Spray Boi Fresh shouted as the sentient art supplies began flinging themselves at him, chomping his ankles bloody with the torn metal of their gaping mouths. He tried to kick them off as he turned and ran.

"League of American Heros! Get him!" Stuart shouted.

"Sexy Rad Super Pals! Get him *first!*" Viola shouted louder, impeding her competitors' path by putting herself between Stuart and the vandal.

"Oh, man, do we have ta'?" Spencer groaned as The Sexy Rad Super Pals too off in hot pursuit of Spray Boi Fresh, and Harriet disentangled herself from his arms, leaving him by the side of Viola's van.

"We can't let Stuart win!" Viola shouted furiously, turning her head briefly to glare at Spencer, as she sprinted toward the fleeing Spray Boi Fresh. "Those burritos are mine, do you hear me!"

With a bored sigh and a shrug of his leather-clad shoulders, Spencer started running toward Spray Boi Fresh, his eyes lighting crimson. Now it was a race. The League of American Heroes and The Sexy Rad Super Pals, pushing and shoving each other, weaving around speeding cars and traffic lights, struggling to move past each other as they tailed the still-fleeing Spray Boi Fresh. Harriet grew winded quickly and slowed to a jog, panting and clutching her side. Stuart jumped into the air and started flying. Viola did the same. The two raced above their feuding team members, approaching the fleeing vandal, just as he tapped into some distance running super speed mode and bolted ahead.

Below, Lady Liberty tripped over the tail of Benjamin's long green jacket. Her pointy copper-green headdress wobbled and she fell, face-first onto the cement. She rose quickly and tackled him to the ground in retribution. What was visible of her masked face was a mess of red blood and green face paint as green sparks flew from his hands and made her spiked headdress sentient. It sprouted arms and began clawing at her face, sending gushing rivulets of crimson down her forehead. She shrieked and dropped to the ground, clawing wildly at the living headdress as it tore bits of flesh from her painted forehead with a lopsided mouth.

Flago ran toward lady liberty, his American flag sandwich board flopping against his stomach as he jogged awkwardly toward her. He bumped into Lilly, violently shoving her aside as she obstructed his path. Lilly responded by disappearing and then reappearing with her powder pale legs wrapped tightly around Flago's neck. She strangled him with her thighs as her sharp nails clawed at his face. He screamed as her nails grew dangerously close to his eyes and then threw her off, knocking Spencer and PTSD Bro to the ground, as Lilly's body collided forcefully with theirs. Now Lilly, Spencer, and PTSD Bro struggled to free themselves from the awkward tangle of limbs. PTSD Bro trembled violently, and screamed as this incident triggered a bloody war flashback. Severed chunks of flesh exploding in clouds of shrapnel filled his brain, overpowering his logic, as he entered into a super-powered berserker mode. The muscles in his arms plumped considerably and he rose from the confusing fray, swinging. Lilly vanished an instant before his powerful fist connected with her jaw and he swung a second time at Spencer who let the blow phase through him and then punched back quickly before ducking away.

Viola and Stuart flew faster, slowly closing the distance between themselves and the fleeing villain. They were neck and neck, speeding forward, melting the city into a disorienting blur of streaming lights. Then, Stuart gained a sudden burst of speed and shot ahead, pouncing on Spray Boi Fresh and tackling him to the ground.

In a flash, Lady Liberty grabbed a cell phone from her

green, torch-shaped purse and dialed the police. Soon, the sound of police sirens filled the deserted space as a squad car pulled up and Spray Boy Fresh was taken away. The owner of *Lucky Shop Mart*, who had been watching the fight from the apartment above the store, emerged with the promised two hundred dollar check, shook Stuart's hand, and enthusiastically invited him to visit the shop and have all of the burritos he could eat. Viola scowled indignantly, and retreated to her van, muttering.

In the van, as Viola drove around, dropping off the members of her team at their apartments, the radio blared and Viola was sullen and silent.

"Its just 200 dollars," Benjamin reasoned in an attempt at comforting her, "Split between us all, it would be almost nothing."

"You're right, Benji," said Viola. "But it was never about the check. Our team is better than his, I know it. He just got lucky this time."

"Yeah, that's the spirit," said Harriet, "We'll get him next time."

Spencer leaned into Harriet, so that his leather suit was pressed against hers, and his mouth was very close to her ear. He nibbled at the corner of it, softly, playfully, then, whispered: "Fun is fun but aren't you getting a little tired of this amateur hour stuff? You're way too strong for this. It's beneath you."

"Silence, butler," Harriet breathed back, turning her face toward his, glaring at him with playful sternness mixed with sadistic lust.

Chapter 4:
When Gary Met Harriet

For the first time in a long time, Harriet was truly happy. She spent her days in a lust-drunk haze of animalistic hormones, at times completely disoriented by her attraction to Spencer, who always posed as a butler in front of the manor's service staff. She'd fired a perfectly adept old International Butler Academy graduate to keep this ruse convincing. Of course, the staff was less than thrilled that Harriet had replaced an experienced and venerated old professional, with a 19-year-old incompetent, but that didn't bother Harriet even slightly. They worked for *her*, after all. Well, at least they did until Reynolds Sanderland decided to come back and claim his inheritance. But the days rolled by and Reynolds never bothered to make an appearance. So Harriet grew comfortable, and began to think of the manor as her own.

Harriet spent much of her time, lounging around the manor, teaching Spencer how to do his job, while he fed her grapes or braided her long, dark hair. At times he would do super obnoxious things, like pretend to accidentally break dishes, or "trip" and spill wine on her shirt. He was an ex-villain, after all, and he had some pretty disturbing masochistic tendencies, that didn't end with purposely fucking up the simplest of tasks and then begging on his knees to be punished physically. Sometimes, she'd catch him digging his nails into the palms of his hands until they bled, or scratching at the wood of his guitar until it splintered and stuck in his hands. She did not say anything about it though. If he was actually a crazy person, then that was none of her business. If his intense attraction to her was a symptom of some deep-seated pathological self-loathing, then, she figured, so be it. It did not matter at all, because he was very sexy, and could play the guitar. His very presence clouded her like a drug.

In the evenings he'd strip off most of his clothing and

sing to her while he played a slow and enchanting instrumental. He would sing about how she was beautiful and cruel; about how she was a Goddess of war, of rage, of death, and of love. He would call her a "black-winged angel from hell", and then compare her to a variety of other mythical beasts, such as a harpy, a siren, a unicorn that ate the souls of the innocent, and so on and so forth.

"Hey babe," Spencer would murmur through half-lidded eyes as he strummed his guitar, "You're like a many-headed hydra, you burn like fire and sting like ice...you're like a beast with a thousand eyes or whatever...but hot though."

"Uh uh," Harriet groaned with mock irritation (in truth she was very turned on by being told how great she was over and over again. "You might want to watch talking like that. People might look past those piercings and tattoos and figure out that you're just a big fucking dork."

Spencer grinned and slouched instinctively but the shaggy hair that used to fall over his face when he did that was now neatly trimmed and gelled back, so she still saw his blush.

He chuckled and made a show of pretending to tune his guitar so that he would have something to do with his hands. Then, he reached out and tucked a strand of his dark hair behind one of his flushed ears, while gazing at her with hormone-addled inebriation:

"Heh heh hehheh...burns like fire."

He wanted to go all the way with her. She could see it in his eyes, sense it in his radiating aura. Up until this point, their inappropriate activities had mostly consisted of her beating the hell out of him when he pissed her off, but there had never been any actual sex. Making *him* vulnerable was one thing, but making *herself* vulnerable by going all the way with him was quite another. After everything that Spencer had done while parading as his villain alter ego, Harriet just didn't trust him enough to engage in that level of physical intimacy. At least not yet. Still, at times like this, she was deeply tempted.

Spencer put the guitar down and knelt in front of Harriet, as he often did. Then he took her by the hand and kissed her on the knuckle.

"My cruel goddess," he whispered theatrically, flashing her a wicked grin, "I am unworthy of you."

Harriet bopped him playfully on the forehead with her still-closed knuckle and said:

"You can say that again."

The old-fashioned phone on the bedside table rang. Harriet picked it off of its stand and held it to her ear.

"Hey, Harriet. It's Gary."

Harriet fell backward against the black satin sheets of the nearby bed, and curled her index finger around the chord of the old-fashioned phone. She stared up at the gilded ceiling and pictured her old friend, Gary Goldstein. Gary was in his early 30's, and had the fanciest law degree that money could buy. He was attractive, broad-shouldered, and usually pretty stiff and serious in demeanor. Harriet pictured his short, conservatively-styled, auburn hair, thick-framed glasses, and designer suit as her continued silence prompted him to repeat himself:

"Harriet? Uh… Harriet…are you there? It's uh…it's Gary?"

"Gary who?" Harriet replied teasingly. There was something in that earnest familiarity of his voice that made her want to mess with him, as she had often done when they were children.

"Gary Goldstein," Gary clarified reluctantly. Maybe he could tell that she was messing with him because he added: "Come on, I know you remember my name, Harriet. We were dating not that long ago."

"Oh, were we? It's hard for me to remember these things. I date so many people," Harriet said.

"Come on, Harriet. I know you remember me," Gary

said again, this time sounding a little irritated.

"That's right because you're sooo...important," Harriet sighed condescendingly. She pictured the look of confusion on his serious face and grinned despite herself. "Gary Goldstein, your father might have been a multi-millionaire, but my father was a multi-*billionaire*...and that makes *me* better than *you*."

"Ha ha...very funny."

"I'm not being funny. I'm simply stating a fact," Harriet replied bluntly, working hard to force the grin on her face out of her voice. "You should know, so-called 'rich boy', that since we broke up I've been dating a homeless guy who used to sing for his meals and live out of his car."

"I don't believe you."

"Not that there's much of a difference between him and you, in the money department. You see, that's funny. Because millionaires are poor," Harriet said.

"Remind me to laugh."

"Laugh, damn it. It's funny."

"Harriet...lately...I've been thinking a lot about, you know...you and me..." Gary said nervously and his voice trailed off.

"Have you?"

"Yeah, so I was by the docks yesterday and that got me thinking about when we were kids. Remember Junior Yacht Club, Harriet?"

"I remember that my father's yacht was bigger than your father's yacht," Harriet said.

Gary laughed and then sighed:

"Yeah...it was, wasn't it?"

"Yeah, I remember that dopey-ass 5 million dollar yacht," said Harriet, remembering Gary's father's yacht with fondness. It had been one of the smallest and least expensive yachts to grace The Junior Yacht Club. "It didn't even have a wine cellar."

"Not that we should have been drinking anyway,"

Gary said with a laugh.

"Well, not if it was the rat piss that your father could afford," Harriet said.

"Well, if your discerning tastes steered you away from alcoholism, then perhaps they've served you well," Gary said.

"Jesus, Gary you're such a prude," Harriet scoffed, "But I guess, in a way, it's kind of sweet that you care. Hey, do you remember when the kids from yacht club stole your glasses and through them into the ocean?"

"Yeah, they used to do that like every week," Gary conceded with some bitter nostalgia.

"I remember," Harriet said.

"You know it's not like they liked you either, Harriet," Gary pointed out, "When you weren't around they used to say that you were a crazy, entitled, psycho bitch with no grounding in reality."

"That might be true."

"I think they were jealous of you," Gary said.

Or, maybe they were just right, Harriet wondered privately. Then she changed the subject:

"Hey, remember when Ellen Propropolous stole your swim trunks and tied them to a rock, and then threw them into the ocean with your glasses and laptop?"

"God, don't remind me. Those kids were always so shallow and stuck-up," Gary said.

"Not me though?"

Gary paused for a moment as though contemplating this question.

"No…you were always different," Gary said and Harriet could hear the reluctant little grin in his voice, "I…I remember when you stabbed Ellen Propropolous with a salad fork and then set her hair on fire."

"That was an accident."

"Was it?"

"Heh…*no*…I did that for you, you know," Harriet admitted, remembering Ellen Propropolous' screams as she flailed her arms, in a vain attempt to dislodge the silver salad fork from her hand. She pictured the bleach-blond heiress stand up abruptly and trip over one of the catering tables, into a lit 18th-century candelabrum. Then, she remembered her screaming: "My father is going to *sue* your father!" while she tried to scrape gold leaf guacamole dip out of a designer dress made almost entirely of diamonds.

Harriet came to the sudden and disturbing realization that a trace of her violent and anti-social behavior might have predated her exposure to the radiation. Yet, in truth, this recovered memory brought her no shame or displeasure. How dare that stuck-up bimbo pick on Gary, just because he was a little awkward and not as rich as the other yacht club kids? As far as Harriet was concerned, Ellen Propropolous had gotten exactly what she deserved.

"Thanks for sticking up for me, Harriet," Gary said with some fondness, "I don't care if you *are* a crazy, psycho bitch. You're alright."

"Hmm…but maybe don't go spreading that story around…it could be bad for my image. You know…people might not understand. They might think that I'm a little…"

"…Unstable?" Gary finished.

"Yeah."

"Well, I don't think you have that much to worry about. If she brings it up at a party, she'll probably just come off sounding like a nut," Gary said.

Harriet laughed.

"And I remember how when we were in your dad's limo, Reynolds would call the limo driver "Jack" even though that wasn't his name," Gary said, "It drove him nuts. Do you remember that, Harriet?"

"Yeah I do," said Harriet, remembering how the limo driver would scowl and grimace every time that Reynolds referred to him dismissively as "Jack." She smiled when she recalled the memory of the cheeky old butler as she always did.

Upon their arrival to the theater, the young limo driver with the dark hair had extended his hand as though anticipating a tip from Reynolds. But after an hour of listening to the limo driver prattle on and on about his failed career as an actor, Reynolds was not having it.

"You want a tip, ay? Here's a tip, Jack. Leave the acting to the pros," Reynolds had quipped, high-fiving the limo driver's open hand. The look of shock on the limo driver's face had been priceless. And then, together, Reynolds, Harriet, and Gary had all had a good, hard laugh at the limo driver's expense.

Harriet was jarred out of her nostalgic flashback by the sound of Spencer accidentally (or possibly on purpose) knocking over a tall white vase while he dusted. The vase shattered, prompting Harriet to turn her head in Spencer's direction and shout viciously: *"Moron!* Pick up that broken glass before I make you *eat it!"*

Harriet put her mouth back up to the receiver of the phone and nonchalantly continued her conversation with Gary:

"Those were some good times," Gary recalled, "Haha. Poor Jack… he was a good sport though."

"Do you remember what that guy's real name was?" Harriet asked.

"Um…no, I don't think I ever bothered to ask," said Gary, "I just called him *the limo driver."*

"Yeah, I just called him Jack," Harriet confirmed with an indifferent shrug.

"You know, Har—" Gary started again. Then, the connection dropped. Harriet's ears were filled with a terrible electronic noise followed by silence. Her eyes shot to the phone chord just in time to catch Spencer casually snip it in half with a pair of scissors.

Harriet sat up abruptly and shouted: "Spencer, what the hell!"

Spencer dropped the scissors and feigned innocence

unconvincingly.

"What? What'd I do?" he replied, casually adjusting the black bowtie of his butler's uniform. It somehow came off as an aggressive gesture; kind of theatrical and abrupt, like a pro wrestler ripping off his shirt before he enters the ring.

"You *know* what." Harriet growled, her cold brown eyes, narrowing into angry slits.

Spencer arched an eyebrow and grinned mischievously:

"Yeah, so, what're you gonna' do about it?"

Harriet grabbed her purse and rooted around in it for her cell phone, grumbling to herself as she did so. The grin slipped slowly off of Spencer's face, as he came to the realization that he was being ignored.

"Harriet…"

"Shut up. I'll deal with you later," Harriet muttered. She retrieved her cell phone from the bag and searched her contacts for Gary's number.

"Harriet…"

"Spencer, I order you to go clean every toilet in the manor! Now, leave me alone for five seconds!" Harriet exclaimed with exasperation. It occurred to Harriet that Spencer might take her command super literally. Much like an evil genie. So she added as an afterthought: "But not literally 'five seconds.' Just go…go do butler things. Or something."

"Yes, mistress," Spencer replied with a slight bow. Then, he retreated sullenly from the room.

Harriet dialed Gary's number again and they resumed their conversation. Harriet walked past onyx pillars engraved with screaming skulls, and old paintings of sinners burning in hell, as she listened to him talk. His voice filled her with warm, familiar feelings of childhood. Gary was so important, and serious, and older than her…at times, it was easy to forget the awkward boy with the big glasses that she remembered; the boy that couldn't handle any challenge without having a panic attack; the boy who had depended on her; who had leaned on her like a crutch. That boy could never see himself as anything more than a disappointment to his God-like father. He had lived in the shadow of his powerful older brothers, perpetually tortured by his impossible quest for their approval.

But no one could have guessed that today. Gary was so well disguised now, smiling in TV commercials for his family's firm; appearing in the news on the arm of some beautiful actress or model. He was the kind of man that people respected and admired; the kind of man who could run for president and actually have a real shot of winning. Knowing this bothered Harriet a lot. She knew it was selfish, but she preferred the boy who needed her to the man who didn't.

Harriet walked down one of the spiral staircases into the foyer. She listened to Gary talk, and thought about the day she had met him. It had been years and years ago, when they were both very small. Foggy memories of their early alliance competed for Harriet's attention, and she battered them away with determination, reminding herself as she did so that things were different now, and that the past may as well have never happened.

"Hey, Harriet, you'll never guess where I am now," Gary said.

"No, where?"

"I'm in Ransburry, by the docks," Gary said.

"Right, you said you were near the docks," Harriet replied. "*Why?*"

"This is where The Ross Foundation is doing a lot of its off-shore drilling. I'm working with their legal team to try and combat some of the environmentalist protestors that want to put a damper on that. So, yeah, it's my job to talk to the press and make the company sound good."

Harriet could hear some shouts in the background. Gary seemed to be in a crowded, noisy place.

"Yuck, having a job is for poor people," Harriet teased.

"Come on, Harriet. I think it's really exciting. I mean, they chose me to be their TV guy, even though I'm their youngest guy and their newest hire. That must mean that I'm like their best guy, right?" Gary said, clearly very proud of himself. Harriet could hear the grin in his voice, and the uncharacteristic child-like euphoria. He seemed pretty excited that he and he alone had been chosen for this very important task.

"They chose you because you're pretty," Harriet observed frankly.

"What? No, that can't be true," Gary replied, "It's because I came up with the best line to feed the press. You see, drilling for oil in shallow water is actually *good* for the environment and tourism…because accidental oil spills will only kill off clouds of invasive jellyfish species."

"Yeah, ok," Harriet groaned, rolling her eyes, "But they actually chose you because you're their youngest lawyer, and you probably have the best hair."

"Well…I guess that's true," said Gary, "But the invasive jellyfish species will kill native species and drive off tourists…so accidental spills as a side effect of shallow-water oil drilling… are actually highly beneficial. I've written an entire pamphlet about it. It's very informative."

"Oh really? What's your next pamphlet going to be about? How burning down the rainforests will save the ocelots?" Harriet said.

The background noise around Gary rose in intensity, so that he had to shout in order to be heard above the din.

"Oh, ha, ha, Harriet! That's very funny!" Gary said very seriously, "This is important work I'm doing here! Very high profile work! And if I didn't do it, someone else would!"

"What's all of that noise in the background?"

"Just a bunch of protestors! I should probably get out of here! They're getting pretty rowdy!" Garry shouted.

Harriet could hear the angry background noise explode

into a barrage of full-blown screams. The aggressive protestors were now very audible over the receiver:

"Stop poisoning the water, Ross Foundation *scum!*"

"Hey, hey! Ho, ho! The radiation's got to go!"

By now, Harriet imagined that a bunch of the protesters were crowding around Gary, getting in his face. Their rage was palpable, so intense, in fact that she could feel it like an intense flashing wave, radiating through the receiver. She did not need to listen to what they were saying to know it. Gary was certainly in danger.

"Excuse me, gentleman, but the press conference is *over*, and we are no longer taking questions," Harriet heard Gary tell them. His voice was a little faint, like his mouth was far away from the speaker. "No, no more questions....if you have more questions please refer to our website....here...take a pamphlet...No, that's not...Well, you've never met my mother and...that's no...that's very rude. I'm not going to dignify that with a response...No. Well, the invasive jellyfish species...."

"Invasive jellyfish species *this*, asshole!"

"*Agh!*"

Harriet heard Gary make a noise like he'd been punched in the gut. Then, some loud clanking, like the phone was dropped. Harriet could feel the emotions of the people involved in this conversation over the receiver, they mixed together in a confusing ball of fear, rage, righteous indignity and murderous intent. There was yelling and confusion and chaos, a struggle, perhaps. In her mind's eye, Harriet envisioned a wave of protestors take Gary down. The image was brief and vivid, like a psychic vision. But perhaps Harriet had only imagined it.

Harriet held onto the phone and listened, her heart pumping in her chest. After a few seconds of silence, a chorus of unfamiliar voices spoke:

"We are *Greenhouse Mob!*"

"*Cactus Man!*"

"Poison Oak!"

*"*and I'm *Flytrap!"*

The three men spoke together now as one. Their voices were eerie and identical. For an instant, Harriet was overcome by a mental image of red-headed triplets dressed in green, which was hallucination-like in its intensity. Again, she dismissed this as her imagination.

"Our mission is to save the world *by any means necessary!* To cleanse the sky and the seas of man's contamination! To preserve all endangered species and their natural environments! Our enemy is the hunter, the logger, the polluter, and the callous businessman! For this is the enemy of the Earth, that we are sworn to protect! This is our sacred mission, and in order to accomplish it, we are fully prepared to exercise *deadly force!"*

"Don't waste my time with your idiotic mission statement," Harriet whispered dangerously. She could feel that dangerous anti-social rage building inside of her, "Just tell me where you're taking him."

"To his death, love," one of the men replied in an eye-twitchingly condescending tone, "Best alert the news. We want an audience."

"I'm not your *love*, asshole. And if you hurt him...I'm going to make sure all three of you *die*."

"All three of us...how did she....kn—"

"Shut up, Flytrap!"

"We're taking these Ross Foundation henchmen *out!* Hahaha...good riddance, I say!"

"I said, SHUT UP!" another of the three men shouted. They all sounded exactly the same and when they were all talking to each other, it was easy to get confused about who was saying what to whom.

"We're taking them to THE GREENHOUSE! Call the police and the *news!* We want an audience!"

"Don't you dare tell her where it is!"

"Biotech University, behind the Ecology building!"

Harriet pictured one of the triplets wrestle the cell phone out of Flytrap's hand. Then, the line went dead with a *click*.

Chapter 5:
The Team Assembles

Harriet stood there for a moment with a horrified expression on her face. A strange combination of confusing emotions flooded her.

Gary was in danger, and after everything that had happened between them, she wanted to pretend like she did not care. But the fact was that she did care. She felt a pang of nostalgic protectiveness toward him, then fear for his safety, quickly overpowered by a tidal wave of hot swirling homicidal rage. Greenhouse Mob's threat to employ "deadly force" in the elimination of their enemies was a threat on Gary's life, and Harriet wasn't going to stand for it.

The black onyx door creaked open and Spencer returned to the room, inclining his head in supplication.

"I've returned from performing my butlerly duties, oh mistress," he said.

"Well, good for you," Harriet said abruptly, "Gary's in trouble."

"Oh no. Too bad for him," Spencer replied with a bit of mock concern and then he shrugged indifferently.

"I'm going to call Viola and assemble the team. Are you in?"

"To save ol' what-is-face...I don't know...maybe we could just stay here, then, I could prepare you a meal and a hot bath...and then...maybe...who knows...I've been really good lately...maybe you could *reward* me?"

"You're a pig," Harriet growled as she quickly began dressing herself in the black leather pants, midriff shirt, and long coat of her Justice Bitch outfit.

"And you're a bitch," Spencer said, crossing his arms and scowling with frustration, "What am I supposed to do with this boner, huh?"

Harriet glowered at him and he took a nervous step backward, instinctively putting his hands up to protect his face.

"I'm sorry," he said quickly. He almost tripped over a red velvet footstool, as Harriet advanced on him with murder burning in her eyes. She pinned him against the wall, stared him straight in the eye, and hissed:

"No you're not."

He chuckled nervously, a slight blush tinting his pale cheeks. This reaction enraged her. Still, she didn't know what reaction she had been hoping for. She knew by now that Spencer's masochistic tendencies made him pretty hard to intimidate. Still, it bothered her that no matter how hard she tried, she couldn't seem to legitimately frighten him. This was a constant infuriating reminder that what they were doing was just a game. That she really wasn't in complete control.

"My God, you're beautiful," he whispered, never breaking the eye contact; never shying away from her hateful gaze, "…Hurt me…please."

Harriet withdrew with a disgruntled sneer and finished lacing up her boots. Then, she put the black mask on over her face.

"I've no time for such a horrible waste of my energy," Harriet said, pulling on the sleeves of her long black coat and turning to leave, "Eco Mob is about to execute Gary."

Harriet exited the room. She picked up her cell phone and started dialing Viola. She darted down a grand corridor and hastily descended a spiral staircase.

"Yeah, Hello," Viola's voice answered as the phone picked up.

"Eco Mob's going to execute Gary Goldstein and possibly a bunch of other lawyers too," Harriet said quickly, "Assemble the team and have them meet me at Biotech University, behind the ecology building."

"Alright, this is going to get interesting!" Viola exclaimed. This was the battle cry of a woman who didn't have a personal relationship with the person at stake and who was more interested in getting her team on the news than she was in preventing his grizzly end. There was no fear in her voice, and no grimness, merely a desire to do battle for battle's sake and an eagerness to demonstrate her power.

"Alright, see you there," Harriet said. Then she put the phone down and darted toward the door. Just as she was about to leave, however, she heard Spencer call her name:

"Harriet, wait!"

Harriet turned around and looked at him.

"...I want to help save ol' Mr. Perfect," Spencer said, "...But only because he sucks and I'm amazing."

"I'm not asking you to help," Harriet said.

"Then, command it."

"I'm not commanding it either," Harriet said, "I imagine you'll be more trouble than you're worth."

"Oh, come on, you could use my help. I'm good. I'm a good guy now," Spencer said.

"Yeah, you keep saying that but I still don't believe it," said Harriet, "But fine. I guess, whatever. I guess you can come."

Chapter 6:
The Birth of Greenhouse Mob

After his father's suicide, Kerry Radcliff, or Flytrap, as he is now called, spent the evenings alone in his family's greenhouse, silently tending to the plants. The carnivorous plants, in particular, brought him comfort. They fascinated him with their alien strangeness.

In the darkness, Kerry watched a Venus Flytrap close around the piece of meat at the end of his tweezers. Then, he watched a few desperate insects struggle to free themselves as they were dissolved in the acid of a tall and spotted pitcher plant. He remembered his father, before the man had been swallowed whole by the carnivorous plant that is soul-sucking depression, and dissolved, like those trapped insects, slowly before his eyes.

"Kerry, my boy, you and I, we have the power to save the world," his father had told him, years ago, before he had become so broken and beaten down by the inevitability of his failure, "This factory, our clean energy...it'll spark a change in the culture that will preserve our planet for years to come."

Kerry's father's dream had been to stop global warming, by making clean energy cost-effective and readily available to the world. The factory that had produced his ground-breaking inventions was once boisterous and promising but now it lay abandoned and in ruins. Big business with financial stake in the continued use of fossil fuels had seen to that.

Kerry's twin brothers, Terry and Jerry, had also grieved their father's untimely passing, and they had done so in a twin-ishly similar fashion. Each of them collected a certain type of plant that they tended to in the greenhouse, Terry being particularly fond of things with spikes, and Jerry being particularly fond of things that were itchy or poisonous. They would dub themselves "Cactus Man," and "Poison Oak" after their eventual exposure to the radiation.

"Brothers, this is the anniversary of our father's death!" Cactus Man proclaimed. He was dressed entirely in green now and surrounded by rows of massive, genetically-altered cactuses with spikes the size of sharpened daggers, "On this day, he was *murdered* by big business! But through our actions we keep the mission of father's now defunct company, Greenhouse Inc., alive!"

Three Ross Foundation lawyers sat in a row, gagged with duct tape and bound to wooden chairs with rope. The assortment of hostages contained a plump, balding man, an elderly woman with short, grey hair, and a handsome young man with big glasses. They all watched fearfully as Cactus Man paced back and forth, dramatically brandishing a potted succulent, as he spoke with theatrical fervor about his gripe with them all.

Cactus man's very green eyes peered out at the hostages from behind a very green mask. He drew closer to the elderly woman, holding the succulent out menacingly, as though it were a weapon.

"But like a cactus, I protect myself with spikes. If you strike me, your hand will be impaled," Cactus Man said.

"And if you strike *me*, your hand will sting and sear and inflate with boils!" Poison Oak chimed in when he sensed that it was his turn to speak. Cactus Man was the alpha twin and he always spoke first. He made the plans, he executed them, and he directed them. Poison Oak was merely a yes man that went along with everything his brother told him.

"And if you strike me, you will pull back a bloody stump!" Flytrap chimed in last, even though his heart wasn't truly in it. Flytrap may have aligned himself with the carnivorous plant, but it was Cactus Man who had acquired the taste for blood over the years. Cactus Man's tendency to delight in impaling his victims disturbed Flytrap quite a lot.

"You will suffer as my father has suffered, and as the earth suffers. But maybe, if you're lucky, we'll leave one of you alive to tell the tale, just barely…as a warning to the others," Cactus Man said. His face was now very close to that of the elderly woman's. He ran a hand through her short silver hair and then rested it on her shoulder menacingly, as if to say, "I am in total control of you now." She shivered and attempted to withdraw from his touch.

Cactus Man smirked and then walked over to the young man with the glasses. He recognized this hostage from his television appearances as The Ross Foundation's PR man, Gary Goldstein. Cactus Man ripped the duct tape off of Gary's mouth and Gary gasped, instinctively attempting to withdraw.

"You leave her alone! If you want to exact your bloody vengeance on somebody, start with me!" Gary shouted.

"Why how very sexist of you, Mr. Goldstein. The old bitch is just as guilty as you," Cactus Man chided, brandishing the succulent he was holding threateningly.

"What do you think that this I-speak-for-the-tree bull crap is going to accomplish, huh? No one's going to sympathize with your cause just because you make a few terroristic threats! If anything, you're hurting your cause!" Garry argued more aggressively than was probably wise.

"Mr. Goldstein, I have warned you that if you strike me with your silver tongue, it will be *impaled*," Cactus Man warned.

"You can't hurt me with that succulent, genius," Gary pointed out.

Cactus Man lifted the succulent swiftly upward, and then, broke the flower pot that it was planted in over Gary's head. He went limp and a few trickles of blood spilled down his forehead.

"Oh, I really think I can," Cactus Man countered with a sadistic smirk.

Gary was too groggy from the head trauma to even attempt talking back. His vision blurred and his head pounded. He shivered from pain and from fear.

"Whoa, what the hell, Terry! I thought we agreed that

we're dialing back the violence a little bit!" Flytrap shouted, wrestling the cracked flower pot out of his brother's hands.

"Don't say my real name, asshole!" Cactus Man shouted back, "Why do you always have to undermine me?"

"We're not the bad guys here. So, I'd sure appreciate it if you didn't try to act like one!" Flytrap shouted in exasperation.

"Hey we're Greenhouse *Mob*, Flytrap. Not Greenhouse Sparkly Rainbow Sunshine *Daycare*!" Cactus Man shouted back.

"Yeah!" Poison Oak agreed enthusiastically.

"So if you're my fucking twin, then act like it! Are you my fucking twin, or aren't you?" Cactus Man said, advancing on his brother menacingly. Sharp cactus needles sprouted from the palms of his hands and he brandished them as though prepared to strike the other man across the face and imbed them in his flesh. Flytrap took a step backward and cowered, holding his hands over his face protectively.

"That's what I thought," Cactus Man said.

Through the walls of the massive Greenhouse, Cactus Man spotted a team of heroes approaching from the distance.

"Looks like we have company. Good thing they won't be able to see us through this one-way glass," commented Poison Oak, upon noticing these unusually dressed people.

"Alright, you know the plan," Cactus Man announced commandingly, "Poison Oak, Flytrap, go get them!"

Poison Oak and Flytrap nodded obediently, and then, they turned and darted away.

Chapter 7:
Venus Hawk Trap

The greenhouse was vast and maze-like with many winding corridors, which were very whimsical and disorienting in their layout. Surely it would take these costumed challengersa while to reach Cactus Man and his three hostages.

In the meantime, Flytrap was very adept at blending in with the greenery. It was his style to wait and to watch, luring his victim with a false sense of security, and striking when they least expected it. Unlike his brothers, he only killed when it was absolutely necessary for his survival, mostly he just liked to watch potential challengers without their knowledge and listen to their stupid conversations.

Flytrap's skin changed colors as he walked, matching the plants behind him almost perfectly. It was as though he had turned invisible. His brother, Poison Oak, who possessed a similar power, did the same.

"There's a chance that they'll split up to search the place faster, so we should too," Poison Oak said, "You take the east corridor and I'll take the west one."

Flytrap nodded in agreement: "Ok."

The two brothers split up. Flytrap crept quietly down the east corridor of the Greenhouse. This was his favorite corridor; the one filled with solely carnivorous plants. Massive pitcher plants grew from the myriad of thick, leafy vines that snaked up the walls. Pots of Venus Flytraps and spotted corpse lilies lined the floors and the rows of low tables. Up ahead, Flytrap could hear people talking. Still camouflaged, he crept quietly forward so that he could spy on the intruders and hear what they were saying.

"Alright, team," a young woman announced spiritedly. Flytrap recognized her as Hawkette, the leader of The Sexy Rad Super Pals. Her long talons, paired with her pink and yellow outfit made him think of a colorful bird. "There's a split in the path up ahead, so we should probably break into two groups to cover more ground and find the hostages faster."

"Great idea," a man in black replied. Flytrap recognized him as the notorious villain, Death Laser, and wondered vaguely what he was doing with this particular group. He looked sinister, and out of place, and kind of like he didn't want to be there. "I'll go with Harriet."

"Oh no you fucking won't," a man in green retorted indignantly, stepping between Spencer and Harriet aggressively. "Viola, if you let them be in a group together, their nausea-inducing relationship is going to jeopardize this mission."

"That's actually an excellent point," Hawkette said, "Justice Bitch, you go with Finsveld and Green Lightning. Death Laser and Ghost Gal, you come with me."

Justice Bitch, Green Lightning, and a fat guy in a mustard-stained T-shirt, who was apparently named Finsveld, went down the west corridor. Hawkette, Ghost Gal, and Death Laser went down the east corridor.

Flytrap watched the three as they walked. Death Laser slouched slightly and shuffled his feet, sticking his hands in his pockets. He started whistling.

"Shut up," Hawkette whispered, "You'll warn them we're coming."

"Sorry," Death Laser replied and he fell obediently silent, straightening up slightly.

"This sure is a big place," Death Laser said quietly as they continued walking.

"Biotech's known for its bioengineering plant life program," Hawkette said, "This is the world's largest collection of military-grade deadly plants."

"Wow," Death Laser said, eyeing the pitcher plants with interest, "Some of these pitcher plants are as big as me!"

"That's kind of the point," Hawkette said, "You can submerge a man into one of these and he'll be dissolved to the bone."

"Heheheh…wish I had some of these when I was a villain," Death Laser chuckled, "They make my piranhas look like goldfish."

"Have you ever killed a man, Death Laser?" Hawkette asked, her voice bore an uncharacteristic grimness as she said this.

"Well, yes. But I'm not proud of it. The piranhas were for show mostly," Death Laser replied simply.

Hawkette did not pry for details. She merely nodded and continued walking.

"But can I ask you something, Hawkette?" Death Laser said.

"Sure, ask away."

"Do you ever get exhausted from being so perky all the time?" Death Laser asked, not in an aggressive way but in a tone that was genuinely curious.

"Uh, excuse you? Where the fuck do you get off, accusing me of being 'perky' all the time?" Hawkette replied angrily.

"Wow, my question took the perk right out of you. Would you look at that?" Death Laser said, far from alarmed, "It's just, to me, it seems like you're trying really hard. You know, like, you pretend to be happier than you really are because you want everyone to like you."

"You know, I don't think I like you," Hawkette said.

"And that's ok," Death Laser said, "Lots of people don't like me."

"It's not wrong to be diplomatic, you know. If a smile and an encouraging word is what people need to come together, then that's what I'm happy to provide, whether I'm feeling it or not," Hawkette said.

"So, say something encouraging about me."

"Encourage yourself, dipshit."

"Ooh, Viola, you don't sound like yourself. Have I struck a nerve?" Death Laser teased.

Viola exhaled with exhaustion.

"Fine, she said. I suppose you do deserve a second chance, and I believe in second chances...I will say this about you...it seems like you have what it takes to survive a relationship with Harriet," Viola said.

"Interesting choice of complements," Death Laser said, "I'm intrigued. Please elaborate."

"I've known Harriet for years and even though she's insanely rich, she drives men away like rats fleeing a burning building...I mean...but, it's no wonder why, what with her yelling, and breaking shit, and insane need to have complete and total control over everything. It's not her fault really. She's lived such an extravagant life. She's very out of touch with the everyday struggles of everyday people...I mean, don't get me wrong, I believe that she's a good person, really I do. But you need a lot of patience to see that, and most people just don't have that. So yeah, I see you as someone with a lot of patience. Your relationship is probably the second longest one she's ever had," Hawkette said.

"The second longest? And who was the longest one with?"

"Gary Goldstein," said Hawkette, "But they're always breaking up and getting back together so I'm not sure if that counts."

"What happened to being quiet?" Ghost Gal whispered, "Someone might be listening."

Hawkette and Death Laser jumped as though they had forgotten she was there.

"Right, I'm sorry, Hawkette. I didn't mean to dick up your mission by talking your ear off," Death Laser said, lowering his voice considerably.

"It's fine."

"And for the record, I actually do think you're kinda' cool."

"Aww, thank you."

Flytrap watched as they turned right and then left

again, down a zig-zag path. They were getting close to the central greenhouse room, where Cactus Man was keeping Gary Goldstein and the other lawyers. Flytrap would have to do something about it soon, or his brother was going to be violently pissed.

Flytrap crept to the center of the greenhouse path, and stood directly in front of them, then he shed his camouflage.

"Why if it isn't the famous *Toenail Girl*, and The Ultra Lame Mega Losers," Flytrap quipped with an unnaturally wide grin, "I'm afraid I can't let you pass. Go back *now*."

"Let us pass...or you'll be *sorry*," Hawkette warned.

Flytrap laughed a deep and menacing laugh. Then, said:

"Oh no, Toenail Girl's going to beat me up with her terrible toenail powers! Guess I better back down."

Ghost Gal vanished and reappeared, strangling Flytrap's neck with her white-stocking-clad thighs. His face turned blue and he gasped for air, attempting the knock her off as she clawed at his eyes and grabbed fistfuls of his fire engine red hair. She bent down close to his ear and whispered: "Don't you disrespect her. *Ever*."

Flytrap ripped Ghost Gal off of his neck. Then, he threw her against the wall of the greenhouse. Her skull hit the glass and it cracked into a jagged spider web around the point of impact. Hawkette and Death Laser charged at Flytrap. Hawkette jumped into the air and aimed at their enemy's exposed throat with her sharp talons. Death Laser's eyes glowed red, and his fingerless-glove-clad hands were balled into fists.

Flytrap grinned an uncanny grin that was somehow too wide for his face. Then, he opened his mouth, revealing two sets of very large and sharp teeth that were not unlike the prongs on the lips of a Venus Flytrap. A large, long tongue, which resembled a green flower pistil, emerged from his throat and knocked Hawkette out of the air, causing her to crash. As she was falling, her sharp foot talons sliced the bell of a giant pitcher plant and a torrent of acid spilled out into the surrounding soil. She screamed as the foul substance splashed on her, burning holes in her boots and stockings, and searing her skin. Her mask was pulled free from her face as Flytrap's sticky tongue withdrew back into his mouth, and the pink pleather costume piece was pulled in with it.

Flytrap swallowed the mask whole and then spit a ball of acid in Death Laser's direction. Death Laser ducked and aimed a pair of crimson eye lasers at Flytrap's face. Flytrap dodged behind another giant pitcher plant to avoid the blow. The lasers hit the pitcher plant, causing it to explode. The acid contained within its bell sprayed him but it seemed that the genetically altered man was immune to its effects. His mask and tight shirt were melted off of his unharmed skin. The corroded fabric slid off of his body in rivulets of green liquid.

Hawkette staggered to her feet, leapt into the air and flew at Flytrap again. This time, she swung her sharp foot and sliced his bare chest, managing a brutal hit. The talons cut deep red slashes in his skin and he cried out in pain, instinctively shielding his gushing wounds. Flytrap swung around and aimed a punch at Hawkette. But he staggered awkwardly, clearly weakened by his seeping injury. She kicked out his legs from under him and he fell in the dirt, face first.

Lilly vanished from the pile of broken glass, near the greenhouse wall, where she had fallen, and reappeared standing on Flytrap's back. She quickly knelt and secured his arms and legs with two pairs of metal cuffs, which she crossed together in order to hogtie him. She disappeared again, and then, reappeared standing next to Hawkette.

"When we're done here, we can bring him back to the police," she whispered meekly.

"Looks like you girls don't need *me*," Death Laser remarked, sounding impressed.

"Of course we need you, Death Laser. You're a very important member of this team," Viola said. She walked up to

Flytrap who was still hogtied on the ground. He rolled onto his side and stared up at her with imploring green eyes. She knelt beside him and he recoiled fearfully.

"P-please...don't kill me...I...I want to live..." he moaned. Blood from his injury was seeping into the surrounding soil, staining it red.

"Shh...it's ok," Hawkette said quietly, and then, she ripped off her yellow cape and pressed it against his open wound to staunch the flow of the blood.

Then, she looked up at Death Laser and Ghost Gal, and shouted:

"You two go ahead without me. I'll stay here and tend to his wounds."

Death Laser and Ghost Gal nodded silently in agreement. Then, Ghost Gal vanished and Death Laser continued forward, seemingly alone.

Chapter 8:
The Sexy Rad Super Pals vs. Greenhouse Mob

Harriet, Benjamin, and Finsveld walked down the west corridor. They were silent for a while as they walked past rows of poisonous and deadly plants. Genetically altered strains of poison sumac, and poison oak, with leaves the size of umbrellas, snaked up the walls in massive vines. Some of them had bright purple spots or red veins. A few sprouted large and colorful flowers from their serrated foliage.

"These plants are deadly, you know," Benjamin commented to break the silence. "The ones with the purple spots are so deadly that if you brush up against one, you could absorb the toxins through your skin and go into cardiac arrest."

"Hmmm….Finsveld just remembered that he has something better to do," Finsveld said and then he turned to leave. Harriet watched as he carefully inched his way past a bushel of green foliage that had grown out of its row and spread out onto the path. Then, he walked through the entrance of the greenhouse and disappeared from sight.

"Well…he was about as useful as he usually is," Harriet said sarcastically.

"I still rather have him for company than *you*," Benjamin replied nastily.

"Are we still doing this?" Harriet said as she continued to walk.

"Doing what?"

"All of this needless hostility," Harriet said.

"Don't talk to me about needless hostility, Justice Bitch. You're the queen of that," Benjamin said.

"Whatever, asshole. I was willing to try and get along with you this time but I guess, forget it. You're clearly too much of a massive dick," Harriet grumbled.

"Well, it takes one to know one," Benjamin said.

Harriet could sense a very potent corruption in

Benjamin's aura that she had scarcely experienced anywhere else. It told her very plainly that during his career as a villain, he must have killed many, many people and in an extraordinarily brutal fashion.

"Don't think that I'm not still watching you," Harriet said, "Because your aura's telling me that under all of your 'I'm reformed' bullshit, you're secretly a lot like your dad, you know, the Nazi cannibal."

"You couldn't be more wrong, Harriet," Benjamin said with an odd expression that was something between a grimace and superior smirk, "And if you compare me to that piece of shit again…my hand might tragically slip and shove your head into that bushel of poison sumac over there."

"Ha! I'd like to see you try," Harriet retorted indignantly, slightly surprised by Benjamin's boldness. Usually, he only expressed his dislike for her when no one was present, and in subtle, passive-aggressive ways. "I could crush you like a bug under the heel of my boot, little man."

"That may very well be true," Benjamin conceded as he ducked to avoid brushing a low hanging branch with the top of his head, "But you're still a completely disgusting, repulsive, little, evil bitch, and no amount of violence on your part is ever going to change that," Benjamin stated bluntly.

"Whatever, asshole. I'm just here to save my friend, so you can keep your shitty comments to yourself for a change, alright? I'm not going to let any of your bullshit jeopardize this mission," Harriet said.

"Oh, please. Don't give me any of that shit. You're a two face Harriet," Benjamin accused confidently, "You pretend to be nice and moral and to care about justice but I know your type. What you really care about is getting your sick kicks. You're a sadist. I can see it in your eyes."

"Well, it takes one to know one."

"Don't think that I haven't noticed how your new 'butler' cowers when you throw a tantrum. Don't think that I haven't noticed the bruises on his arms," Benjamin said, "I don't need aura bullshit to see straight through *you*."

"Well for your information, Spencer *likes* to be smacked around a little bit. He's a bit of a freak actually, not that I should have to justify my relationships or how I live my life to *you*," Harriet growled.

"And it doesn't bother you at all that you're taking advantage of a mentally ill person?" Benjamin said.

"Oh, please. Spencer is *not* mentally ill," Harriet said, "That is such a vanilla way of looking at it. And you're probably a hypocrite anyway. What about you and *your* girlfriend, Ghost Gal? You know, the girl who won't look people in the eye or raise her voice above a whisper? I've got a feeling that what you've got going on with her is a little bit..."

"A little bit *what*?"

"You're not the only one who has suspicions you know," Harriet said.

Before this point, Benjamin had spoken in measured tones, but the last comment seemed to set him off, because his voice rose an octave with indignant dismay: "Don't talk about her like that. You don't know *anything* about her."

"Ghost Gal is a battered woman if ever I saw one," Harriet theorized confidently.

Benjamin settled back down into his previously calm demeanor and replied in a snarky but measured tone: "Oh, Harriet...if only you knew how *wrong* you are."

The two glared at each other for a moment. Gary's time was running out. Harriet knew that she didn't have time to worry about what Benjamin might be secretly plotting. She pushed all paranoid thought from her mind and tried to ignore the meddlesome reek of his corrupted aura as she continued forward.

It was then that Poison Oak decided to make himself known. Harriet recoiled as he appeared before her without warning. His aura must have been masked from her by the overwhelming contamination cloud that was Benjamin's alarmingly corrupted aura.

"I am Poison Oak!" the tall, masked man in green announced, "Turn back now, or you'll be forced to fight me!"

Harriet's immediate instinct was to grab Poison Oak by his stupid red hair, rip his head off, and fling it across the room, thus sparing herself the tedium of having to fight him. It was certainly in her power to do so, however, she suppressed this urge. After all, she had promised Viola that she would not use deadly force during these missions. Also, as much as she hated to admit it, a small part of her sort of cared about what Benjamin thought a little bit. Brutalizing Poison Oak would definitely enforce all of the insulting things that he believed about her. And as much as she did not like or understand the desire, she kind of wanted to prove that Benjamin was wrong about her.

"We don't want to hurt you," Harriet snarled, through gritted teeth. This was definitely a lie. She was currently battling a powerful desire to hurt him, which consumed most of her conscious effort, "So give up now, or we won't have a *choice*."

Poison Oak laughed a deep, menacing laugh.

"Oh no, I'm so scared," he mocked with a sinister smirk, "Little, tiny, belly shirt girl's going to beat me up!"

"Uh...what the fuck did you just call me?" Harriet fumed.

"You heard me."

Harriet aimed a punch at Poison Oak and he ducked. Poison Oak removed his green gloves and discarded them on the floor. Harriet came back at him again and he quickly sidestepped the blow. In a fit of adrenaline, Harriet reached out to grab Poison Oak and restrain him; possibly handcuff him to a vine and surpass him as an obstacle. However as her hand closed around his wrist she felt a stinging sensation in the palm of her hand that shot straight through her glove, and seared her flesh like a ball of fire or a thousand angry bees. She yelled and recoiled, backing away from Poison Oak and withdrawing her limbs protectively. The villain grinned.

"What kind of a man are you, I wonder? That you would let this tiny little woman battle me alone?" Poison Oak goaded Benjamin, who had been watching the encounter between the two with indifference, perhaps rooting for Harriet to lose. "You must be scared of me! How pathetic! Do you always let little girls fight your battles?"

Benjamin took the bait immediately.

"You big-mouth piece of shit…you're going to regret saying that to *me*," Benjamin said in a dangerous, but measured tone. His eyes glowed green and a few dozen vines tore themselves from the walls of the greenhouse, springing to life. They grew ugly faces and hissed as they snaked down the greenhouse path, toward Poison Oak. Now Poison Oak was battling the corrosive vines. They twisted around his ankles and he kicked and tore at them with his hands, never flinching once, as his powers made him immune to the effects of their toxins.

Without looking back, Harriet ran ahead toward the main greenhouse building. Poison Oak and Benjamin could kill each other for all she cared. As long as they were preoccupied with fighting each other they were no longer an obstacle to her.

Harriet heard a shrill, male scream. Followed by deep, menacing laughter.

"*Gary!*" she cried, and then, she darted forward into the main greenhouse building, her own heartbeat pounding in her ears.

Chapter 9:
Needles and Thorns

As Harriet entered the main greenhouse building, she could see towering cactuses in an impressive array of shapes and colors. This massive and menacing terrarium of desert shrubbery was surely an impressive attraction for weekend sightseers under happier circumstances.

Harriet quickly and cautiously walked the winding path, through walls of cacti as tall as buildings. She spotted a large, round cactus with an impressive pink bloom sprouting from the top of it. This circular plant was about the size of a van, and its sword-like needles were dripping with what looked like human blood. Harriet walked faster, very careful not to brush up against the genetically altered plants. She could hear deep, menacing laughter in the distance.

"Harriet!" a familiar voice called.

Harriet turned her head in the direction of the sound and spotted Spencer, as he approached the place where two winding paths converged. Lilly was not far behind him.

"Harriet, they're plant men," Spencer told her, "I think Greenhouse Mob is all plant men."

"Yeah, it does seem that way," Harriet concluded.

"It looks like we were too late," Lilly whispered, she pointed at a tall cactus, where an old woman in a mauve suit was impaled in multiple places through her arms and torso, with long spikes. The color had drained from her contorted face and she hung limp, like an inanimate wax doll, the ghoulish loll of her shredded tongue and blood-stained lips was indicative of some ghastly oral torture.

"Shit. She's dead," Harriet observed, picking up her pace a bit. "I guess we better get moving."

Spencer nodded in silent agreement. Lilly vanished wordlessly.

The team darted past massive and spike-covered desert plants. A bald man in a grey suit lay dead, on a squat circle of green cactus spikes. One of the spikes protruded from the center of his shiny forehead grotesquely. His grisly, blood-soaked mouth was packed wide with a generous bundle of thorny rose stems. The dead petals of the wilting flowers littered his mangled remains.

Harriet repressed a shutter as she strolled past this massacred lawyer, and tried very hard not to imagine Gary in the same state. Her imagination betrayed her, however, as she was pestered by the image of her former lover having thorny rose stems shoved into his open mouth by a cackling mad man. Her stock memories of slasher horror flicks were heavily at play in this imagery.

Another male scream punctuated Harriet's grim fantasy. She sprinted forward toward the sound of the noise, past a massive wall of thorns and needles. Here, another red-headed man in green spandex stood, waiting for her. He looked identical to the first villain she had confronted, tall and young, with shockingly green eyes. This startling similarity was either proof that the first guy could teleport, or evidence that her initial premonition about the existence of red-headed triplets in this greenhouse had been correct.

The villain was standing in front of two empty chairs, laughing in a menacing way, and inviting her to admire his handiwork with a wide, sweeping gesture. The two empty chairs had likely once contained the pair of dead lawyers who now hung from the shrubbery by jagged spikes. What remained of the ropes that had once bound their wrists and ankles to the arms and legs of the chair, made that very clear.

Harriet heard the scream again. She craned her head up in the direction of the noise and spotted Gary bound to a third chair, which hung from the high ceiling by thick, thorny vines. His forehead was bloody and he looked a combination of terrified for his life and groggy from head trauma. The vines swayed precariously. In places, they looked stretched and ready to snap. Gary yelled again as one of the vines frayed and he lurched an inch or two downward. Surely a fall from that height would have been enough to kill him. However, a villain's fondness for overkill paired with his pathological desire to stick to a theme, seemed to have spurned Harriet's opponent to place a large potted cactus under the spot where Gary was projected to fall, as well as a ring of acid-filled, man-eating pitcher plants interspersed with bushels of poison sumac.

"Foolish superhumans! Your heroics are wasted on these rich assholes!" the villain pronounced, jumping down from the high ledge where he stood, surrounded by sandy desert soil and massive thorny plants. He walked over to Harriet, holding out a single, red, thorny rose as though it were a piece offering or an expression of courtship.

"Our world is dying! Climate change is melting the polar ice caps! Our rainforests are being harvested into extinction in order to be put into the cheap palm oil in packaged foods! Justice Bitch, if you think about this rationally, I think you'll find…that there are more worthy causes in this world," he said, offering Harriet the rose, "Forget this Ross Foundation schmuck. Join me. My name is *Cactus Man*."

"Let him down now, or you'll be sorry," Harriet fumed, ripping the rose violently from Cactus Man's hand and then throwing it across the room. He flinched as the thorns from its stem sliced his palm.

"Not every life is worth saving," Cactus man replied with a snarl, wiping the blood from his injured palm off on the front of his green shirt, "These lawyers…this man who's about to die…the world will be better for his absence. Intervening in his death would be nothing short of a tragedy."

"Don't say that about him. You don't even know him!"

"Oh…I see how it is," Cactus Man replied with a knowing smirk. He seemed to have sensed, based upon

Harriet's reaction, that her connection to his hostage was of a more intimate nature.

Cactus Man took a step closer to Harriet, staring threateningly into her eyes. There was something amorous about the jilt of his brows. He licked his lips and balled his hands into fists, then, several dozen huge cactus spikes sprouted from his hands, so that they resembled a pair of threatening maces.

Spencer quickly stepped between Cactus man and Harriet, then, shoved Cactus Man backward: "If you want to fucking touch her, you'll have to kill me first!"

Whatever, Count Fagula, consider yourself fucking dead!" Cactus Man shouted back, swinging his spiky fist at Spencer's face.

Spencer ducked, narrowly avoiding having his face impaled. Then, charged at Cactus Man in a rage, with his eyes lit crimson and his fists raised. Harriet backed up a bit and bit her lip as she watched the two men scuffle, kicking and punching each other with reckless abandon. Spencer shot a few dozen laser blasts from his eyes and Cactus Man dodged them awkwardly, spraying a torrent of needles from the palms of his hands in retaliation.

Spencer punched Cactus Man in the jaw and drew back a brutalized hand covered in cactus needles, but he didn't flinch or withdraw. Instead, he grinned in a demented way and punch Cactus Man again, and again, and again, ignoring the needles completely. Cactus Man head-butted him in the chest, and then, swung at his face and neck wildly, clearly frustrated and exhausted by Spencer's unusually high pain tolerance. Now, lasers and cactus needles were flying everywhere. Instinctively, Harriet averted her eyes to avoid being blinded.

Harriet heard Gary scream again. She glanced up and saw that while she had been bantering with her opponent, the vines had loosened slightly and the chair had dropped a good 4 or 5 inches.

"Harriet!" Gary screamed, sounding both mortally terrified and righteously indignant, "Harriet, stop fucking around and help me!"

Harriet thought for a moment. She couldn't fly, so getting Gary off of the ceiling would be a difficult if not impossible task.

"Lilly!" Harriet shouted, as she realized that she would have no hope of rescuing Gary without the use of Lilly's power.

Lilly appeared in front of Harriet like a genie.

"Yes," she whispered meekly.

"Can you teleport up there and untie him?" Harriet asked urgently.

"Yes, but then he will fall to his death even faster," whispered Lilly, "It's quite the conundrum."

"Why!" Cactus man shouted in frustration, driving his spiky fist into Spencer's already needle-saturated chest, "Won't!" he punched him again in the same spot, "You!" he punched him again, this time in the face and as hard as he had ever hit anything, *Go down!*"

"Well, shit, Lilly, we have to try something!" Harriet panicked.

"Yelling at me...will get you nowhere," Lilly whispered.

Spencer grabbed Cactus Man by one of his arms to avoid being struck again, then, wrestled him to the ground, twisting his arm painfully behind his back.

"Agh! *Ow!* Stop it! Get off me!" Cactus Man yelled indignantly, and Spencer responded by twisting his arm more aggressively. *"Oww!"*

"It might be beneficial to stop staring at the men and actually try to think of a plan now," Lilly suggested to Harriet passively.

"Uh, right, ok," Harriet said quickly, flushing slightly as she tore her eyes away from Cactus man who was still struggling to free himself from Spencer's grip on the floor.

"*Ow!* Let me go!"

"Not until you say you're a dumb asshole!"

"*No!* Fuck you!"

"So...um...maybe...hmm...." Harriet thought out loud as she tried to block out the alluring sounds of men screaming and hitting each other, "Got a big trampoline on hand?"

"That's Finsveld's department. He's the one who can teleport objects," Lilly whispered in reply.

"Um...so could you maybe just teleport up there and bring him down?"

"No, I don't think I could lift him," Lilly whispered in reply.

"Oh, come on, you'd only have to lift him for, like, a few seconds, couldn't you *try*?" Harriet goaded.

"No, he's much too heavy," Lilly whispered.

"Oh, come on, Gary's not *that* heavy," Harriet argued.

"Harriet, he's *super* heavy. Just look at that big fat *ass*," Lilly whispered so quietly that Harriet could barely even hear her. It seemed that she got even quieter when she was angry.

"Why are you so useless? Just do it!" Harriet growled.

"Here's a thought. You've got super strength, right? Maybe....you could pull one of those super tall cactuses out of the ground...and let him fall on that. It might cushion the impact...give him less distance to fall from," Lilly suggested quietly.

"But that'll hurt him."

"You want him to live...don't you?"

"There has to be a better way," Harriet said and suddenly she got an idea.

Harriet walked over to where Spencer and Cactus Man were struggling on the floor. Cactus Man yelled swear words and violently attempted to throw Spencer off of him. With some considerable effort, Spencer managed to grab Cactus Man's other arm and pin that one behind his back as well. He grunted with exhaustion, and then, secured Cactus Man's hands behind his back with a pair of handcuffs.

"You, ginger boy!" Harriet shouted, addressing Cactus Man as Spencer secured the villain's ankles with a second pair of cuffs. *"How'd you get him up there?"*

"Wouldn't you like to know?" Cactus Man spat hatefully, glaring at Harriet from the floor.

Harriet stomped over to where Cactus Man lay and put her foot down on his throat. He choked and his green eyes bugged out of his head as he thrashed and gasped for air. Harriet lifted her foot again.

"He's already cuffed, Harriet. Maybe you should dial it back a notch?" Spencer interjected meekly. He was presenting himself as the voice of reason, speaking in defense of the other man and arguing for mercy, but Harriet knew better. She could see right through Spencer's act.

"Oh, don't tell me you're *jealous*," Harriet scoffed, rolling her eyes. She directed her attention back toward Cactus Man, repeating the shouted inquisition: *"How'd you get him up there?"*

"I....I-I...I...." Cactus Man gasped fearfully.

"I-I-I-I-I," Harriet mocked cruelly, "Tell me or I'm gong to break all of the fingers in both of your hands."

"Ha! Yeah right! I'll never tell you how to get him down. You can send me to jail, but Gary Goldstein will still die tonight! And there's not a thing you can do about it."

Harriet grabbed one of Cactus Man's pinkies and casually snapped it in half. Cactus needles sprouted from it reflexively but they failed to penetrate her bulletproof skin. Cactus Man screamed in pain and involuntary tears poured out over his mask and down his face.

"Y...your crazy!" Cactus Man shouted between involuntary sobs, "...An..and *evil!*"

"Tell me how to get him down or I'm breaking the rest of them," Harriet replied bluntly.

"Ha! I'll let him die first!"

"If he dies, I'll break them all for fun," Harriet replied with an unnerving and sinister smirk.

"Ok, ok....Jesus Christ, just don't hurt me anymore, ok?" Cactus Man panted fearfully, eyeing Harriet like she was a demon from hell, who had just emerged from a flaming hole in the ground, "We used like...one of those really tall ladders to get him up there...it's in the storage shed, straight back and to the left of this room. The key to the shed's in....its in my back pocket..."

"Spencer, go get the really long ladder and bring it back here so that we can get Gary off of the ceiling," Harriet ordered briskly.

Spencer nodded silently and then obeyed, retrieving the key from Cactus Man's back pocket, and then, exiting the room.

"Y...you can have all of the names and secret identities of the w-wanted criminals I've worked with if you...if you go easy on my brothers...just promise you won't h-hurt them like this, p-please..." Cactus Man sniffled between fits of pain-wracked sobbing.

"I don't negotiate with terrorists," Harriet dismissed bluntly.

Spencer returned with the really long ladder.

"What a delightfully mundane solution," Lilly whispered and then she quietly vanished from sight.

She reappeared again at the top of the ladder just as Spencer finished setting it up. Then, she cut Gary free of his vine bindings and swiftly vanished again. Gary stumbled and almost fell to his death, hastily steadying himself on the top of the ladder and then slowly, climbing down.

The journey back to the police station was awkward and cramped. The Sexy Rad Super Pals, Gary, and Greenhouse Mob rode in silence for a while, as neon lights and thick city traffic rolled by. To Harriet, Viola's van felt like a crowded clown car filled with a menagerie of random and wacky people.

She looked to her right and saw Gary, who looked embarrassed and thoroughly shaken. His face was flushed crimson and he stared down at his lap in a timid way that reminded Harriet forcibly of the little boy she had once known.

She wanted to reach out and touch him, put her hand in his soft auburn hair and tell him that this wasn't his fault. But on a certain level, she understood that this just wasn't true, at least not entirely. Despite being a shareholder, and the descendant of its founder, Harriet had a vague and very tenuous grasp on what The Ross Foundation actually did. She was beginning to think that maybe that secrecy was by design, as the company seemed to be engaged in some morally ambiguous activities.

But then again, how could she blame Gary for being involved in a morally ambiguous company when she herself was intrinsically tied to it? How could she blame him for selling his soul, when (going by that metaphor) she was essentially the devil? She watched Gary for a while and wondered about him. He wrung his hands together nervously and fidgeted in his seat. When had the pressures of being a grown-up robbed him of his innocence? Was there anything of the boy she remembered left in him? She did not touch Gary, even though she wanted to. She just stared at him for a moment in silence and then looked away awkwardly.

Then, she looked to her left and saw Spencer, who was still covered in little cactus spikes. His face and neck were still very bruised from the brawl with the villain but he didn't show the pain clearly on his face. He just stared out the window with a very practiced-looking neutral expression, and casually pulled the little spines out of his hands one at a time. When the spines were out of his hands, he moved up to his forearms, flinching slightly as he removed each spine.

Harriet grabbed one of the spines from the arm that was closest to her and gave it an experimental little tug:

"May I?" she inquired sweetly, smiling tiredly for a moment in his direction.

"Please."

Harriet yanked the spike out of Spencer's arm and he cringed. She grabbed another spine and repeated the action. Silently Harriet resisted the urge to berate Spencer for not letting *her* fight Cactus Man. After all, she *was* bulletproof. Those little spikes couldn't have damaged *her*. Instead, she asked him quietly:

"Does it hurt?"

"Ouch...owie...it hurts so much...I wanna' cuddle..." Spencer moaned.

Harriet leaned into him and put an arm around his prickly shoulders. He grinned and chuckled, like he'd just tricked her into falling for a hilarious prank.

"Heheheh...just kidding, pain doesn't bother me like at all," he told her.

Gary groaned and muttered to himself. Harriet thought she heard the word "moron" mixed in there somewhere.

"I'm sorry, what was that?" Harriet inquired for clarification.

"Uh...nothing...never mind," Gary said quickly and then averted his eyes from her.

Spencer leaned in close and whispered in Harriet's ear: "Tonight...I want you to hurt me, like you hurt Cactus Man."

"I'm not breaking your bones, Spencer. That's where I draw the line."

"Seeing you kick ass tonight...holy shit, Harriet...you're so beautiful...when you have blood on your hands...and you get that look in your eye, like you're going to kill...my God...I was hearing electric guitars in my head the entire time," Spencer whispered in Harriet's ear, "Please...hurt me tonight...and don't hold back. I want to see how much I can take...hurt me until I can't take it anymore...hurt me until I want to die...until I cry and beg...and have no dignity left..."

A startling thought occurred to Harriet.

Huh...Maybe Spencer really is mentally ill, she thought.

Benjamin's snarky comment about what he perceived as Spencer's mental instability resurfaced in her mind, and for a moment she was lulled into humoring the notion as a potential reality. Maybe Benjamin was right. Maybe it was harmful to indulge Spencer in all of his masochistic ridiculousness. Maybe what he really needed was, like, a psychiatrist and some pills or something. She shook her head and dismissed the thought as absurd. *Spencer's fine*, she told herself. *And if he's not fine, then that's not your fucking problem.*

Viola's van pulled into the police station. The triplets were escorted out of the car by cops. One of them (Harriet couldn't tell which one) screamed and kicked as he was being escorted into the building, so that one of the officers had to tase him to prevent his attempted escape.

"Aw man, I can't believe I'm going back to prison again," one of the triplets complained, "Terry, you promised this wouldn't happen!"

Paperwork was filled out. The journey back to the van was delayed slightly by Viola, who stopped to pose for a photo with two nice-looking younger cops who had asked for her autograph.

"I feel sorry for those triplets," Gary said as Harriet returned to the van.

"Don't," Harriet replied grimly, "They're terrorists. They get what they deserve."

"Did you know that their father was the CEO of Greenhouse Incorporated? Ten years ago, he committed suicide because the Ross Foundation funded a super PAC to support the candidate who would tax their company into bankruptcy," Gary said.

"A pretty tenuous connection if you ask me. And besides, that didn't give them the right to murder your friends," Harriet said.

"They weren't my friends, they were my coworkers. Believe me, there's a big difference," Gary corrected with a shrug, "Though, I guess, you've got a pretty good point. But still though, even though they tried to murder me, I can't help but feel a little bit bad for them...and as weird as it sounds, I still wish them the best."

"Your trophy's in the mail," Harriet grumbled.

"Psh. Man, this guy's a dip, am I right?" Spencer interjected unceremoniously.

"Shut up, Spencer," Harriet growled elbowing Spencer in his spine-covered ribs so that he whimpered and lurched forward involuntarily. "The only one who's allowed to make fun of him is *me*, ok?"

Chapter 10:
Not Ok

Harriet and Spencer returned to the manor that evening, very disheveled. The manor staff eyed them suspiciously as they entered the premises. So much so that Harriet was actually prompted to look down at her clothes and see if she'd forgotten to change out of her costume. She hadn't though. She was dressed in the white button-down blouse and the ankle-length black skirt, just as she had been when she left. Likewise, Spencer was still dressed in his black and white butler's tuxedo.

It must have been the bruises on Spencer's face and the drowsy, pained way that he lurched forward. An older maid with short grey hair tutted and shook her head quietly as they walked past her. Probably the old woman assumed that Harriet was the one who'd hit him.

They think that I'm a bad person, Harriet thought as she walked up one of the winding staircases to her bedroom. *I may be a mean bitch but somebody's got to be sometimes. And goddamn that doesn't make me a bad person. I'm not a bad person.*

Harriet glanced over at Spencer, who grinned at her, showing the blood and cactus needles in his teeth.

...Am I? Harriet couldn't help but question herself silently.

Harriet retreated to her room. Spencer followed with his head bowed. The large and elaborately engraved onyx door clicked shut behind them. Then, Harriet threw the latch on the lock just to be sure that no meddlesome manor staff would barge in and witness her inappropriate relationship with the butler.

Harriet sat down on the bed and removed her shoes. Then, reached behind her back and unlatched the clasp on her braw before removing it from under her shirt and flinging it across the room. Spencer watched her do this a little more attentively than was probably dignified, looking thoroughly randy as he did so.

"My cruel mistress," he addressed her with a bow, and he continued poetically, "Your thoughtless brutality is truly a thing of beauty. What bliss it must be to fall victim to your unbridled rage; to fear for your life and come so close to death that you can taste it...what a rush that must be..."

"Yeah, yeah, save it for your guitar," Harriet groaned dismissively.

"I want you to hurt me like you hurt Cactus Man tonight," Spencer said again.

Harriet looked him over skeptically. He was still bruised from the confrontation at the Greenhouse, and a lot of little cactus spikes were still sticking out through his clothes, all over his body.

"You can't be serious," Harriet said with disbelief.

"I'm a bad man, Harriet. And I've done really bad things," Spencer said, sounding far more serious than was typical of him, "I deserve to be punished."

"Jesus Christ, Spencer, haven't you been punished enough? I want to go to bed," Harriet moaned.

"Oh, come on. I can take it. What'd you think? You think I can't take it?"

"What I think....is that you're *already hurt* but that you don't want me to know," Harriet said. She got off of the bed and walked over to him angrily. He flinched as though expecting her to strike him. "Do you really want me to pound those cactus needles *further* into your ass? What's your problem, anyway!"

"Have I displeased you, Mistress?"

"Come over here!"

Spencer obeyed and followed Harriet to the bed.

"Lay down!" Harriet ordered aggressively.

Spencer obeyed. Harriet sat down at the foot of the bed and started yanking cactus needles out of Spencer's back.

"You're being nice," Spencer mumbled into the pillow, "I don't want you to be nice."

"Shut up, dumb-ass. I don't care what you want," Harriet said, stroking the back of his head gently. He relaxed slightly and exhaled, probably enjoying the attention despite his initial protests.

"I don't deserve your pity," he said.

"Too bad."

The room was quiet for a moment as she touched the back of Spencer's head with lust-inebriated tenderness.

"Take your shirt off, so that I can pull the needles out of you," Harriet said quietly. Her voice was barely audible above the quiet ticking of a nearby grandfather clock.

"If you wanted me to take my shirt off, all you had to do was ask," Spencer responded flippantly.

"Just do it."

Spencer sat up, removed his black jacket, undid his bowtie, and unbuttoned his white shirt. There were a lot of cactus needles concentrated near his chest and stomach where he had taken the most hits.

Harriet was silent as she plucked the needles from Spencer's pronounced abdominal muscles. In the absence of words, all of those little noises that usually go unnoticed trickled to the foreground. The clock ticked. Harriet could hear her own heartbeat in her chest, and she could hear Spencer's labored breathing; the nearly imperceptible hitch in his throat as each needle was swiftly removed from his body. She felt heat rush to her face, as she noted Spencer's pierced nipples and the flaming skull tattoo on his bicep. In her mind, these were the telltale markings of poor white trash. If her father were alive, he would certainly have disapproved.

The growing pile of bloody cactus needles on the bed left little red stains on the black satin sheets. The prolonged silence prompted Spencer to speak:

"You're not as bad as people think you are, are you?"

"People think I'm bad?" Harriet replied, sounding slightly affronted, though, in truth, the news didn't surprise her much.

"Uh…"

"I can't have my butler wandering around, looking like a beat-up porcupine. People might start to ask questions," Harriet explained her behavior curtly.

"Heh heh heh…guess that makes sense," Spencer said quietly. A slight grin twisted the corners of his thin mouth, "So uh…what's up with you and that Gary guy, anyway? You seemed a little bit…*too* fired up over saving his life…I mean, he's just some jerk who tells lies on the TV."

"Yeah, well, I knew him before he was a jerk. He was an innocent boy once. I guess I'm having some trouble letting go of that," Harriet said.

"Hey, I was an innocent boy once too, you know," Spencer said.

"Somehow I have trouble imagining that," Harriet said.

"No, for real. Like, in elementary school, I was a theater kid. I played Seymour Krelborn in our school's production of Little Shop of Horrors," Spencer said.

"Like, with the sweater vest and big glasses and everything? Jesus, what a nerd," Harriet said.

"Heh…yeah. And I was in the marching band my freshman year of high school, which is like the most un-cool thing ever. Not that I'm equating un-coolness with innocence, I was well past innocent by that point," Spencer said.

"Was all of that before you put on your prince of darkness persona?" Harriet asked a little sarcastically, "What's your point anyway?"

"I guess my point is that innocent boys grow up to be giant pieces of shit," Spencer said, "You should watch out for that, Harriet"

"Noted," Harriet replied bluntly.

They were quiet again for a time. Harriet sat behind Spencer on the bed and started pulling cactus needles out of his shoulder blades.

"…I feel like I barely know you," Harriet said quietly, after she had accumulated another pile of bloodied cactus spines. "Like you could be making all of this stuff up and I would never know it."

"But you'd be able to sense it in my aura, if I was lying, wouldn't you?" Spencer asked.

"I don't know. Maybe," Harriet said, "I've been fooled before."

"If I was going to lie, I'd make up something way cooler, like, I was a crime-solving super genius who invented the cure to cancer and got in the yearbook for having the biggest wiener," said Spencer.

"Yeah, but I wouldn't believe that," said Harriet.

"Will you tell me something about you? I want to know something about you," Spencer asked.

"You don't need to know anything about me," Harriet shot him down bluntly.

"Oh, come on."

"My father was a philandering, pansexual adulterer," Harriet offered briskly.

"Everybody knows that. Tell me something that nobody knows."

Against her better judgment, Harriet found herself recounting a memory from her childhood, something she did not often reflect upon or talk about. She did not know why she did this. She had not intended to share something so personal, but there was something about the way he was looking at her; that expectant little grin. It made her forget herself:

"My father used to host these…*sex parties* in the manor. My mother didn't know about them. He always used to have them when she was on one of her extended outings. She'd take the private jet to France or Italy, usually for the weekend, sometimes longer, and then he'd invite a bunch of celebrities and prominent people over to fool around, the maids and the service staff sometimes got mixed in with it too. I know because sometimes I'd hear them whispering about it to each other when they were walking around, cleaning…and I would hear them talk about...you know...the drugs and the weird sex, and things my father said to them. And there was this one maid, a really blond one, who I heard swear to her friend that she thought she was in love with my father. Not surprisingly, that maid was fired shortly after that. But, you know, I didn't really understand what was going on when I was a little kid, I'd just see all of these people come to the manor and go into a room, and then, I'd hear them smashing around in there...and the weird things that they were saying, and I just...I didn't understand. But as I got a little bit older, I sort of gradually figured it out. It was kind of annoying...but it didn't bother me that much really. I kind of learned to ignore it, but my mother...she was starting to get suspicious... and that led to a lot of problems between my parents. My mother wanted a monogamous relationship, but my father didn't believe in monogamy. Well, at least not when he was young. I think he must have calmed down a lot after he met Reynolds...But anyway, when I was about ten years old. My mother came home from one of her trips early and discovered one of my father's orgies. There was no shouting after that, I don't think. She didn't speak another word to him. She just packed up all of her stuff that night and she left forever."

"Wow, so the rumors about him are true. He really got busy..."

"Take off your pants so that I can get the spikes out of your legs and ass," Harriet interrupted, mostly to change the subject.

"You know, if you wanted me to take my pants off, all you had to do was ask," Spencer said with a slight grin.

"I *did* ask. Which makes that *not funny*," said Harriet with a humorless scowl.

Spencer stood up and stripped off his slacks.

"Well have at it, darlin'. I'm not shy," he said.

Harriet started yanking at the sparse scattering of cactus spines in Spencer's thighs. He stood there and let her do it, quiet at first. Even in the silence, Harriet felt herself feeling things that she should not have been feeling about him. Stupid things. Inadvisable things. Her reluctant fondness must have been palpable because he grinned and chuckled under his breath. *He must have figured it out that I have feelings for him beyond just shallow, sadistic lust*, Harriet thought with some distress. *Shit. Shit. Shit. I can't trust him. He's just playing me. Probably he's only pretending to like me because he's got designs on my fortune. That's why he's only good as a punching bag and not as a companion. I have to stop this. Stop this, Harriet, you stupid asshole. Stop feeling things.*

It occurred to Harriet that Spencer had been talking while she had been distracted by her frantic internal monologue. By the time she had come back down to reality, he was in midsentence:

"...because I knew this girl in high school, her name was Janice Laxley, and she was a freshman at the time. Anyway, Devin liked her...but she liked me. And, of course, that drove him *nuts*."

"I can imagine," Harriet interjected. Spencer's current nemesis, Devin Forress (now known as Freeze Out), was a mean, rich, handsome, blonde, entitled, Adonis who was very used to getting whatever he wanted. The mere idea that any girl might prefer Spencer to him must have sent Devin spiraling into a hilarious, self-absorbed rage.

"Yeah, I mean, at the time, I was kind of like, yeah, whatever dude, you can have her. I mean Janice and me were friends and I guess she was pretty, but she was way too *nice* for me, you know, and I never thought about her that way. But yeah, that didn't matter at all because she didn't like Devin, she liked me. I don't know why. Probably because me and Janice used to talk about books and nerd junk. But, you know, I still never thought about her that way...I mean...maybe I considered it once...for a moment or two...but she was too innocent, you know? I didn't deserve that kind of love."

"Are you trying to make me jealous?" Harriet

interjected with slight annoyance.

"Is it working?"

"No."

"Hehhehheh…." Spencer chuckled, stretching his arms wide, yawning, and then, cracking his bruised knuckles. He looked at her in a knowing way that she didn't much care for. It was a look that said plainly that he suspected she was full of shit.

"I don't know what you think you're laughing at, you massive ass," Harriet hissed coldly.

Much to Harriet's chagrin, Spencer's mischievous smirk did not flicker. By this point, she had managed to pluck his entire body clean of cactus needles. The needles lay in a bloody heap on her black satin sheets. Spencer's body was scratched and bloody in some places but these injuries did not seem to trouble him.

Spencer stood up and redressed himself.

"I apologize if I've angered you, mistress," Spencer said with polite formality, "I'll clean his mess up and prepare you a hot bath."

Chapter 11:
Meanwhile...At The League of Evil Doers' Secret Underwater Base

After having lost the battle for control of The Ross Manor, The Jay Walker and his minions had returned to their secret underwater base. Funded by Death Laser and The Ross Foundation, this large, disk-shaped, structure was vast and stylishly furnished; a mansion in its own right. It had a modern look with light-colored wood and simple, boxy, royal-blue-colored furniture. Tall, leafy, and oxygen-producing areca palms decorated each room. The outer wall of this airtight, underwater structure was made of thick glass, and through it swarms of mud-colored fish were visible. The occasional shark was among them.

Through a periscope, which, when fully extended, ran all the way up to the surface of the water, The Jay Walker watched The Ross Manor, frustrated and brooding, because the grand property, did not, at that moment, belong to him. Beneath the rubber Donald Trump mask that he wore to conceal his identity, The Jay Walker's expression contorted with bitter annoyance, as he pictured Justice Bitch and that "butler" basking in the luxury of that ridiculous palace. Jason readjusted the orange cone that he wore on his head (for theme-related purposes) as it was currently slipping down his greasy hair.

While this was happening, Devin, his frozen head cracked and bleeding from battle-related blunt force trauma, glared at The Jay Walker impotently. Devin was a twenty-something ex-rock star with ice blond hair and disarming good looks. Currently, he was dressed as his super villain alter ego, Freeze Out, in white and blue spandex, and a clear, ice-like plastic mask. The outfit might have looked comical on a less attractive man, but Devin was so obnoxiously sexy that he could pull off basically any ridiculous getup.

"I can't believe that stupid Justice Bitch slut keeps on

defeating this great evil team I've assembled!" The Jay Walker shouted in frustration as he continued to peer through the periscope.

"Whatever, Jason, you little asshole," Devin muttered under his breath, "If you hadn't put your stupid dumb-ass self in charge by enslaving me with your fuckin' mind control powers, I'd be in that mansion right now, standing over their dead bodies."

"What the did you just say to me, Freeze Out?" The Jay Walker growled dangerously as he turned on Devin. The Jay Walker's hand shot to the yellow notepad in his breast pocket, which was the tool that he used for mind control. Any order he wrote on it, once read by a victim, was promptly obeyed.

"You're super smart boss," Devin replied boredly and sarcastically, rolling his bright blue eyes.

For the first time in his life, Devin was being forced to play second fiddle. Under The Jay Walker, he was little more than a sidekick, a crony, a henchman to be used as a weapon for the purpose of accomplishing somebody else's goal. Devin's considerable pride would not allow for this indignity. He would not take orders from some pimple-faced kid with a parking cone on his head, not for long anyway.

Devin leaned back in one of the boxy, minimalist chairs, still glaring at The Jay Walker and silently plotting against him. He stuck a cigarette in his mouth. It froze. He withdrew a silver, skull-shaped lighter from his pocket and instinctively attempted to light it, but, as always, it refused to light. Devin let the fire linger near his lips for a moment, easing the frosty sting, which was constantly assaulting his face, and as he did this, he continued to glare at The Jay Walker, who was not looking at Devin and did not really consider him a threat.

"Alright, new plan!" The Jay Walker spat hatefully as he watched a tuxedo-clad Spencer, enter The Ross Manor with a paper bag filled with pastries from The Corner Store. The other villains that The Jay Walker had recruited, who were all present in the room, and mulling about, turned toward him expectantly. "We wait for them to leave and then lock them out," The Jay Walker announced bluntly.

"Ah, there is a beauty in the simplicity of it," Miz Mayhem, (a beautiful woman with long, blond hair who wore an 18th-century gown and a feathered Marti Gras mask) gushed, twirling so that her long skirts billowed around her. "Simply divine!"

"What did you do with the henchmen and the manor staff, anyway?" Trauma (an evil psychiatrist who wore a purple suit and an ink-blot-shaped mask) inquired for the benefit of the others in the room. Because of his mind reading ability, he knew the answer already. He could read it on the tip of The Jay Walker's tongue.

"They all work for me now. I wrote some detailed instructions for them on The Ross Foundation company bulletin board. And once Justice Bitch has fallen for my clever diversion, I'll have them change all of the locks. The Bitch hasn't won. She can't win. A person with powers like mine is destined to rule the entire world, and I'm going to make sure that person is me," The Jay Walker said with both frustration and smugness.

Chapter 12:
A Hostile Takeover

As the week progressed, Harriet withdrew into herself. She waited for Reynolds to call and reclaim his property, but he never did. The suspicious absence of the old butler disturbed her slightly, but perhaps she was worried about nothing. Perhaps his long hiatus was a form of grieving. The relatively recent death of Harriet's father must have been taking its toll on him.

Still, Harriet could not help but feel betrayed. She spent her days watching television, and having her meals delivered to her locked room. Spencer's knack for weaseling his way closer to her was a hazard, and so, Harriet made a point to start distancing herself from him more. She started giving him labor-intensive jobs that would keep him busy, and spent considerably less time interacting with him, cutting out inappropriate activities entirely, so that their relationship became that of the typical boss and employee.

While Harriet was riding her father's golf cart through the manor grounds, past elaborate topiaries and fields of professionally maintained perennial flowers, she felt morose. She thought about the battle with Greenhouse Mob, and the incredible rush that she had gotten when she'd broken Cactus man's finger. She kept thinking about that look in his eyes, that fear, that desperation, all of his well-practiced bravado and showmanship had been stripped away, like the mask of a costume. What was underneath was different, primal, unfiltered. He had been like a cornered animal, and she, like a ravenous predator closing in for the kill.

Harriet tried not to think about these things. She was a good person, damn it, and good people didn't get all hot and bothered when they thought about violence. Good people hated violence, and only used it as a last resort, when the results would benefit the greater good. Still, she could not help but think about that moment when he was most desperate; when his performance had been stripped away, again and again and again and again. Sure he was a murderer, but did that make these thoughts she was having normal or ok? Harriet had always seen herself as a hero, but when it came right down to it, heroism wasn't her motivating drive. Harriet's motivating drive was something darker; more selfish.

Harriet drove the golf cart under arches covered in ivy, grapes, and variously colored roses, past a decorative maze of hedges and some white marble benches. Suddenly, the temperature dropped dramatically and she felt an unseasonable cold that burned her sun-kissed skin with its cruel intensity. Now, she could see her breath come out in white clouds. A few fluffy white snowflakes began to drift from the sky.

Then, Harriet spotted the source of this unearthly climate phenomenon. Through the gently falling snow, she could see a man in a white coat, sitting on one of the white marble benches, beside a decorative fountain that had frozen solid. His hair was blond and perfectly tousled. His expression was indifferent and cold and he was sucking on what looked like an unlit cigarette. Harriet stopped the golf cart and called out to him:

"What the hell do you think you're doing here, Devin!"

"You can untwist those panties, sweetheart. I'm not here to fight," Devin replied coolly.

"How did you get past my guards?" Harriet yelled to him.

"I'll never tell."

Harriet got out of the golf cart and walked over to him, looking him over with incredulity. Devin was all laid back California charm and much too cool to appear in any way uncomfortable with her intimidating glower. As she approached, he just kind of looked at her like she was part of the mildly interesting scenery, a rose-covered arch or a dollar-bill-shaped piece of topiary. Then, he shrugged at her as if to say: *Meh, well that's something, isn't it? Don't see that every day.*

"Why are you here?" Harriet asked again.

"I'm here because Jason's a little asshole," Devin replied coolly.

"I'm sorry you'll have to be more specific."

"So, like, as you know, The Jay Walker has mind control powers or whatever, and he's using them to make me work for him. It's how he controls all of his henchmen, he tricks them into reading something and then they have to do whatever he says, it's like a compulsion," Devin said.

"So, you're here on his orders, huh?" Harriet said.

"No, actually, he never specifically told me *not* to come here, so I'm exploiting a loophole. The Jay Walker thinks he's hot shit because he's got mind control powers, but without that, he's just a little asshole."

"Is this going somewhere?" Harriet asked.

"I'll make this simple for you: Jason's a dumbass, moron, garbage person, who doesn't know what he's doing and makes us all look like idiots. He's a shitty boss. He makes my life miserable. And I'd like you to kill him for me," Devin said.

"What?"

"Well, *I* can't kill him. He's already ordered me not to. And you're about to have the perfect opportunity. So, like, The Jay Walker hates you, since that one time that you fucked him up," said Devin, "And so, like, he's been talking about how he wants to fuck with you by taking over your house for his evil headquarters and shit."

"And *shit*?"

"And all of the shit, Harriet. Every last turd of it. Fuck."

"Sorry, I just wanted to make sure that you didn't mean that literally," said Harriet. With the kind of supernatural powers that were popping up around this city, she couldn't be too careful. She couldn't risk confusing Devin's inability to finish a sentence without cursing, with an actual warning about a literal shit-related threat.

"I think you know that I didn't mean it literally," said Devin. He pulled the thing that he had been sucking on out of his mouth and Harriet saw that it was not a cigarette, but a lollypop. Perhaps Devin had finally given up on getting his cigarettes to light again. "So, yeah, like, anyway, that little asshole's planning to lay seize to your property, probably tomorrow around noon. Just thought I'd warn you. Be prepared."

"So, all of a sudden you want to help me?" Harriet interjected skeptically, "The last time I met you, you tried to kill me. *And* you tried to kill my butler. So why the hell should I trust anything you say?"

"Yeah, and that worked out really well for me...with that little asshole, Jay Walker, pulling the strings...it's a miracle I can walk a straight line, really," Devin said, "No you and that fuckin' dickhead, Spanky Fuckerson can go along doing...*whatever it is that you do*. Makes me fuckin' shutter to think about it...but, yeah, I no longer give a shit about whether he lives or dies. Jason is my priority now. He has to die so that I can be free. So, how's about this, little miss bitch? If you manage to kill him for me tomorrow, I'll forget about killing you."

"Gee thanks."

"And as an added bonus, I'll forget about killing Spanky," said Devin.

"You're a very generous man," Harriet replied sarcastically, "...And for curiosity's sake, would it kill you to call him Spencer just *once*?"

"Yes. My fuckin' heart would explode. So how's about it? Huh? Can you promise me you'll cut that little fucker, Jay Walker, down tomorrow? I don't care if you put him down clean. Make him suffer first. Indulge that sick little slasher fetish of yours, I don't care," said Devin.

"Get off of my property before I call security," Harriet replied coldly. She did not know if he could sense the forced calm in her voice; the rage building under the charade of her coy banter. His last comment, about the "slasher fetish" really dug at her psyche in a way that she did not want to let on. Was it really that obvious to Devin, just by watching Harriet in battle, that violence was like a drug to her? Could he have read it in her eyes when they fought?

"You know," said Devin, "You should be more polite to me. I'm trying to help you."

"Oh look at that, my hand is dialing security," Harriet said, punching a few number keys in the dashboard of her father's golf cart.

"Ok, ok, fine. I'm leaving," Devin said, "Just be ready for them tomorrow."

"I will be," Harriet said, and then she finished dialing security.

A few guards emerged from an exterior building on the grounds and walked up to Devin, who shrugged and grunted in derision as he allowed himself to be escorted out. The heat of the sun returned gradually as he grew further away. The snow stopped falling, and the nearby decorative fountain unfroze.

Harriet started the golf cart again. As she was riding past a maze of topiary, and under a few dozen arches of climbing roses, she considered Devin's warning. Could she really trust anything that Devin had to say? Was his warning legitimate, or just some ruse to justify him trespassing on the manor grounds. Either way, Harriet did not have the energy nor the patience to battle The Jay Walker and his "League of Evildoers" yet again. She had too many things to think about and figure out, too many feelings to suppress, and too much mediocre TV to bore herself with.

Should I prepare for an invasion? Harriet wondered to herself, *How would I even go about doing that? It's not like I can warn my staff. I'm not about to go telling them all that I'm Justice Bitch.*

Harriet rolled past a few rows of dollar-bill shaped

topiary bushes, and a statue covered in black plastic trash bags and duct tape. It stood out awkwardly amid the lavish extravagance of the well-maintained grounds. Harriet got out of the golf cart and walked over to it. The ugly thing was in a prominent place, at the center of a cul-de-sac, in front of the manor's, tall, arched entrance. Harriet recalled the statue of her father that had once stood in this spot. During Spencer's career as a villain, he had knocked down the statue and replaced it with one of himself dressed as Death Laser. It was still there, concealed under the plastic bags. Harriet had yet to demolish it.

"Why is this stupid thing still here?" Harriet muttered to herself. Though of course, she knew the answer. It wasn't like she couldn't afford to knock it down and rebuild it the way it was, she just had not bothered to call anybody about it.

It's still there...because you like *him,* a stupid little voice, that Harriet did not much care for, teased. Harriet answered herself a little defensively: *Yea, well, so what. Maybe I do like him, but, like...not on an interpersonal level...He's just really hot and can play the guitar.*

You idiot, he's such an ass, The little voice in Harriet's head muttered back. *You should knock it down before you give him the wrong idea...I mean...come on...no...he's not that bad...he's actually kind of sweet...I guess...sort of...in a socially-retarded man-child way...or maybe not. Maybe I'm just fooling myself. Stop it, Harriet. Don't forget what he's capable of, the fucking chaos he caused, the people that had to die for all of his childish bullshit. All so that he could get exactly what he wanted and exactly what he got, attention from you. The fact is, that after all of your struggles, your arch nemesis was the one who arose victorious.*

"Ok, now you're making me angry," Harriet muttered to herself as she returned the golf cart to one of the outside garages on the grounds and parked it, "He didn't win. I won. He's my slave, now."

Yeah, but is he really your slave, Harriet? ...Or are you his *slave? Face it Harriet, he knows exactly how to manipulate you. And he's probably plotting something. Be smart. Ditch him now before you're sorry.*

With some effort, Harriet dismissed these thoughts and pushed them to the back of her mind. Breaking it off with Spencer was a little like throwing a half-eaten bag of potato chips in the trash; in that it was probably a good idea for her health, but also, she didn't fucking want to. No, self-restraint was not her forte. She was going to sit back and eat that entire bag of metaphorical potato chips, all twelve servings of it. Consequences be damned.

Chapter 13:
The Vaguely Off-topic Adventures of Super Annoyo and Mr. Exposition

"Using his awesome powers of *super annoyingness*, Super Annoyo, the arch fiend of irritation; the crown prince of *pissing people off*, managed to escape from Propopolous City High-Security Super Prison! Having annoyed the guards into submission, Super Annoyo sought out the assistance of your omniscient narrator, yours truly, in his pursuit of vengeance against The Justice Bitch—stuck-up anti-hero and soon-to-be villainess extraordinaire!" A man with a megaphone exclaimed. This was Mr. Exposition, a villain with the power to spout plot-related exposition. After his exposure to the radiation, this man had attained a deep, clear intonation, which lent itself to voiceover work. He had also acquired an eerily accurate innate knowledge about facts relating to surrounding people and events, and a Tourrette's-syndrome-like compulsion to announce them.

"Yes, yesss, oh yes, yes, yes, Mr. Exposition. Misss-ter Ex-po-si-tionnn…Your irritating tendency to re-state the obvious plays very well with my theme of super annoyingness!" Super Annoyo gushed, "This alliance of ours, in pursuit of vengeance against The Justice Bitch, will surely be beneficial to us both!"

Super Annoyo wore tight purple spandex, a mask, and an exuberantly pronounced codpiece. Currently, he was driving a stolen car with New Jersey plates. His new sidekick, Mr. Exposition, sat in the passenger seat with his megaphone. Mr. Exposition wore black and white spandex and a striped utility belt on which to hang his megaphone and megaphone-related accessories. Super Annoyo started clicking his tongue repeatedly against the roof of his mouth.

"Due to his psychotic compulsion to stick to a theme at all times, Super Annoyo broke into a spasm of what he judged to be, very irritating little clicks and noises. Due to his super resiliency attribute, however, the great and powerful *Mr. Exposition*, was not affected!" Mr. Exposition announced through his megaphone.

"Not affected, huh? I'll show you not affected!" Super Annoyo muttered in annoyance, and then he increased the volume and frequency of his irritating noises.

"In an attempt to prove his superior power, Super Annoyo increased the volume and frequency of the super annoying noises designed to incapacitate his enemies in battle. However, this childish ploy did nothing to harm the marvelous and well-hung *Mr. Exposition*, whose true power is far greater than anyone dare suspect! In a typically annoying fashion, Super Annoyo also neglected to mention to his new sidekick—what his plan for vengeance *truly was!*" Mr. Exposition spouted.

"Hahah ha ha har har! And I shall never tell you! You will be confused to the end!" Super Annoyo boasted.

"Unaware of Mr. Exposition's general omniscience attribute, Super Annoyo boasted that he would not reveal his plan for vengeance against The Justice Bitch. However, Mr. Exposition was well aware of the plan already!" Mr. Exposition spouted.

"Oh, you are, open bar? Well, I'm still the boss, apple sauce," Super Annoyo said.

"Using his eye-twitch-educing *rhyming dad humor*. Super Annoyo responded to Mr. Exposition's intelligent and very well worded comment. However, the handsome and very good-looking *Mr. Exposition*, was still not swayed. He knew already that Super Annoyo's plan was to find The Justice Bitch and steal her very expensive *red hat*."

"Shh...put the megaphone down! I see her!" Super Annoyo exclaimed as he pointed into the distance. Harriet was walking down the sidewalk. She was wearing a big, wide-brimmed, red sunhat, and accompanied by a young butler in a black tuxedo. The butler was carrying a couple dozen shopping bags, covered in designer brand logos.

Seeing that their target was in range, Mr. Exposition dropped his voice to a whisper.

"As Super Annoyo and Mr. Exposition were cruising through the Propropolous city shopping district, they spotted, *Justice Bitch* – the burly, busty billionaire-ess; the boisterous broad with the big bucks! She was accompanied by her trusty sidekick, and former arch nemesis, *Spencer Tuckerson*. Who is, in the author's estimation, the perfect amalgamation of virgin and whore."

Super Annoyo slowed the car down to a crawl and slowly rolled down his window.

"Uh...Harriet?" Spencer murmured as he noticed Super Annoyo driving slowly closer to them.

"Silence butler," Harriet interrupted him coldly, "Your function is not conversation. Your function is to carry my shit. The professional shit-carrier speaks when spoken to, got that?"

"Yes, ma'am."

Super Annoyo reached his hand out of the car and snatched the red sun hat off of Harriet's head. She yelled indignantly and turned around.

"Hahahahaha! *LOSER!*" Super Annoyo, shouted out of the car window, placing the lady's hat on his own head. "You'll rue the day you foiled my plans, *Justice Bitch!*"

Super Annoyo flipped Harriet the double bird and then sped away, cackling madly as he did so.

"Spencer, *Spencer!* Get the limo!" Harriet demanded indignantly, slapping Spencer on the arm so that he had a spasm and accidentally dropped all of the bags, "That dastardly fiend just stole my big, stupid, red hat! I'm going to crush his skull like an eggshell in the palm of my hand!"

"Uh...*Harriet*, you're super rich...Couldn't you just buy another one?" Spencer murmured timidly, as he saw the vein throbbing in Harriet's forehead and the psychotic rage burning in her eyes.

"God damn it. It's the principal of the thing!" Harriet

shouted in reply.

"And with those words, the harlot with the horrendously horrible personality; the dame of *damn did she really just do that?* — rushed to her limousine," Mr. Exposition said, "Meanwhile, Super Annoyo and his dashing sidekick, Mr. Exposition, were stopped at a red traffic light."

"Would you *stop* narrating? You're doing my shtick better than I do it! It's making me look bad!" Super Annoyo complained.

Harriet's limousine pulled out of its parallel parking space and shot forward. Super Annoyo sped up and ran the red traffic light, racing into the distance. Harriet's limo sped up to catch him.

Mr. Exposition continued his narration as though he had not been interrupted, picking up his megaphone once more:

"Now, in the passenger seat of her father's old limousine, Harriet screamed at her butler to accelerate and run Super Annoyo's vehicle off of the road. Any reasonable person would decline to obey this order, but Spencer, who liked his women caustic and unreasonable, obeyed without hesitation!"

The limousine accelerated and nearly ran Super Annoyo's car off the road. Super Annoyo accelerated to avoid the crash. A few dozen cars swerved out of the way to avoid being hit.

"Let's make them chase us around in circles for a few hours, see if we can tire the bitch out!" Super Annoyo cackled, taking out a fire hydrant, as he cut a corner, and sending a pack of pedestrians fleeing for their lives.

Meanwhile, in the other car, Harriet said:

"This shit is so beneath me. Spencer, *kill them.*"

A wicked grin twisted Spencer's face and he slammed his foot down on the gas, cackling wildly:

"Heh heh heh-heh-heh hehehehehheh! *Whoo!* I'd kill and die for you, baby! *Kill* and *die!*"

Spencer cut a tight corner and took out a traffic sign that cracked the windshield of the limo.

"Watch where you're going *idiot!*" Harriet yelled.

Spencer did not respond. There was a crazy look in his eye and his teeth were bared. He looked like a deranged psycho; an adrenaline-crazed predator closing in for the kill.

"They're slowing down, they're slowing down! *Get them!*" Harriet yelled.

"Meanwhile, in the other car!" Mr. Exposition spouted, "Super Annoyo and his cunning sidekick, Mr. Exposition were still in possession of Harriet's stupid big hat! The two shared a maniacal laugh at her expense! *Hahahahaha!*"

Mr. Exposition and Super Annoyo cackled loudly together.

"The chase would continue for hours and hours and hours and hours. And hours and hours. And hours. Harriet and Spencer would chase Super Annoyo and Mr. Exposition, into the country, get run off the road, and subsequently,

become lost in a cornfield. It would take them a long, long, long, *long* time, to find their way back to Propropolous City. And by that time, Harriet would be thoroughly exhausted and pissed-off. Upon her return, the blood-thirsty babe, would discover that Devin's warning about the hostile takeover of The Ross Manor should *not* have been ignored, that she had fallen for a diversion, and that The Ross Manor is now *under new management.* What's next for our cringe-worthy anti-hero? How will she defeat The League of Evildoers and reclaim The Ross Manor once and for all? Find out next time on the exciting adventures of *Justice Bitch!*...Same bitch time! *Same bitch channel!*"

Chapter 14:
Goddess of War and Sex

Harriet's black Jaguar pulled up in front of the gates at The Ross Manor. Harriet rolled down the window and pushed the button on the intercom. A nasally voice greeted her from the other end of the intercom system: "Welcome to Castle Jay, formerly The Ross Manor. How may I help you?"

"Uh, yeah, this is Harriet Ross. I'm going to be staying here until Reynolds Sanderland turns up to take the place off my hands," Harriet said.

"Oh, no, I can't let you in, I'm afraid," the voice replied dutifully. "You see the manor is under new management. The Jay Walker snuck in and changed all of the locks while you were gone tonight. Then, he had his psychic guy put one'a those impenetrable force fields around the place. No one can get in or out anymore without The Jay Walker's express permission. "

"Oh, goddamn it," Harriet swore.

She made a K-turn and backed her car out of the long cobblestone path, leading up to the front gate. As she turned around and started driving away from the manor, she said to Spencer with a groan: "I'm too tired to deal with this shit. It looks like we're getting a hotel tonight."

Spencer stretched and yawned, smiling slightly as he watched the city skyline roll by through the passenger side window.

"That's ok with me," he said.

"Oh, yeah, because with me, it really fucking sucks."

"Nah. I used to sleep in my car every night," Spencer said, "And it wasn't a really nice car like this either. The seats were all ripped and deflated."

"Jesus, I forgot that you used to be homeless. The holiday Inn's probably heaven to you."

"Ah, well, I'm not picky. Being super rich was fun for a while but it got old pretty fast. And it was never about the money, anyway. I'll be happy to live in a box by the side of the road as long as I'm with you, baby."

Harriet turned the corner, driving past lit office building windows and shuffling pedestrians.

"Yeah, somehow, I find that doubtful," Harriet said.

"I swear. It's true."

"...There's a couple of trench coats that I keep in the back seat, for when Finsveld flakes on the Sexy Words Long Name Squad, like he always does...and I don't get my clothes back," Harriet said.

"He's probably selling them...or *sniffing* them," Spencer postulated matter-of-factly.

"Yeah, probably. Anyway, grab one of those trench coats and put them on. Then hand the other one to me. I don't need people seeing us get out of this car, in full costume," Harriet said.

Spencer grabbed a couple of black trench coats off of the back seat, put one on, and then, handed the other one to Harriet, taking off his mask as he did so. As the car rolled to a stop at a red light, Harriet did the same, covering her costume with the trench coat, and then, removing her mask and putting it into the pocket of the coat.

Harriet pulled into the parking lot of a roadside motel, the rage building inside of her as she thought of The Jay Walker passed out in her childhood bedroom, asleep, with some awful, rubber politician mask clutched in his hand. Then, she imagined Finsveld passed out on a mountain of discarded clothes, asleep, with a pair of her underpants draped over his snoring face. Her eye started to twitch, and for a moment, her formal level of debilitating blood lust made a resurgence. It was the same blood lust that had stopped her from eating, showering, and sleeping, after her initial exposure to the radiation, and it pulsed inside of her, now, paralyzing her with its intense and undeniable power. She gripped the wheel of the Jaguar with too much force and the plastic made a dry pop as it cracked in her grip, sending ugly fissures up and down the wheel.

"Fuck," Harriet swore, releasing the wheel and surveying the damage.

"Are you mad?" Spencer asked her, leaning close, a nervous blush tinted his pale cheeks and he swallowed apprehensively.

"*Yes*."

"Take it out on me," Spencer invited, softly, timidly, his blush deepening. She looked into his eyes and he looked back pleadingly, silently begging her to satisfy his perverse desire. "You can do anything you want to me. I'm tough. I can take it."

Harriet leaned close and kissed him on the lips, inhaling slowly, breathing in his scent.

"Ok," she said. "But only because you're such a pathetic little man whore," Harriet replied.

She drew her lips away from him and opened her eyes slowly, surveying his attractive, youthful face for a moment; the sharp nose, pointed chin, and dark, arched eyebrows; the smooth, pale skin that glowed with the health of residual adolescence; the thin lips, and large dark brown eyes. Spencer was handsome, in a way that Harriet's previous boyfriend, Gary, could never have been; passionate, spontaneous and alive. The soul-crushing responsibilities of adult life had yet to catch up with Spencer, and he maintained a certain purity; a whimsical naivety, which inspired in him an endearing and yet-to-be-dashed belief in true love.

Spencer stared back at her for a moment, grinning. There was something lost in his eyes, that thing being logic and lucidity; a reasonable grounding in reality. At that moment, in the presence of his goddess, it seemed, what sense he possessed had been tranquilized. It lay drooling and immobile in some quiet, buried place, far, far away from that black Jaguar. He leaned toward Harriet and kissed her again, for what might have been the hundredth time that night, wrapping his arms around her, nuzzling her neck with his chin. He moved with the senseless veracity of a feral animal compelled to breed.

Slowly, nervously, experimentally, Spencer's fingers slinked underneath of the trench coat, walked up Harriet's leather bodice to her breasts and, for a moment, caressed them tenderly, before moving to unclasp the first button. It was then that Harriet pushed him off of her. He staggered backward over the car's clutch, his shoulder's hitting the passenger's side door.

"Not yet," Harriet growled with annoyance, straightening her leather bodice so that it covered more of her breasts. "If you want to fuck me, you'll have to earn it."

"I..." Spencer stuttered in reply, still in shock from this sudden rebuke. He ran a hand through his dark hair nervously, slouched and bit his lower lip. Then, he lowered his eyes in a gesture of repentance, "...I'm sorry, Harriet."

"Well, you should be, you jerk," Harriet said, crossing her arms defensively.

"...I don't know why I...I was being stupid, I guess," Spencer apologized, shaking his head. She loosened her tense posture, and he took her hand in his, kissing it on the knuckle, "Make me worthy of you, my cruel princess."

"You've still got a lot of repenting to do, butler."

Like an awkward, flustered man, eager to impress a potential future boss in a job interview, Spencer replied: "I welcome the opportunity to prove my devotion to you...through my service."

He kissed her hand on the knuckle again. She withdrew it with a scowl. Then, without a word, exited the car and started walking toward the hotel.

"Harriet..." she heard Spencer call out behind her.

"Shut up."

Harriet walked through a revolving door into the hotel lobby. An old man in a red uniform, behind the front counter, stood up as she entered.

"There's no room at the inn," the old man informed her

in a cracked, withered voice. She walked past a rack of brochures, and exhaled tiredly, resting her hands on the counter of the desk.

"Are you sure?" she inquired of him, tiredly, huffily. There was a crazy, desperate look in her bloodshot eyes. She *did not* feel like looking for another hotel.

"Yes," the old man replied, but she could sense that he was hiding something from her.

"Because I'll take any room. I'm not picky," Harriet said.

She could sense Spencer, standing a few feet behind her, messing with the rack of brochures; opening them; closing them; picking them up off of the shelf; putting them back in the wrong places.

"Well...since you put it that way, there is one room that we always keep vacant, room 66...but I don't recommend that you stay there. That's where ah...the manager doesn't like me to mention this..."

"What?"

"Some people say that a poltergeist lives there. The last guy who stayed in that room...about a month ago, he said that in the middle of the night, the walls started bleeding and that his kid's dolls and teddy bears started moving around, crawling up the walls, and cackling. Real crazy stuff, and you would have thought he was crazy too, except that there were three or four people who stayed in the room before him, and they all had pretty similar stories. This one lady, ran out of the room in the middle of the night; claimed that the television in the room kept turning itself on and whispering her threatening messages while she was trying to sleep. The manager was pretty skeptical fora while, but then, he was up there, talking to the cleaning lady, while she changed the sheets...and...he says a hand reached out from under the bed and grabbed his ankle. Then, the lights went out and the TV came on, and it was just a man in a mask laughing and laughing...then the walls started bleeding and bleeding. He and the maid ran right out of there...and he hasn't rented the room out since. It's still all bloody anyway, miss, believe me. You don't want to stay there."

"Don't tell me what I do and don't want to do. I'm tired as fuck. Where's the key?" Harriet murmured groggily.

Spencer (who seemed to have found the old man's ghost story more interesting than the brochures) had wandered over to the counter, and was now leaning tiredly against it.

"I'm sorry, miss. I can't rent anybody the room. The manager strictly forbid me."

"Oh, this is bullshit. I don't even believe in ghosts. Just rent me the room," Harriet muttered.

"I can't, miss. The manager strictly forbid me."

"What about if I bribed you?"

"I'm very sorry, Miss. There's a Holiday Inn on..."

"Oh fuck you and fuck the Holiday Inn. Just rent me the room," Harriet swore in frustration.

"Believe me, I'm tempted," the old man replied with a snarl. "But no."

Harriet turned from the counter and stormed out of the lobby. Spencer turned toward the old man before following her, shrugged and said: "Yeah, don't let her get to you, she's pretty tired. Thank's anyway, though."

"No problem, kid.

Spencer exited the lobby. Outside, Harriet, was propped up against one of the white pillars outside of the hotel entrance.

"New plan," she said, the moment she saw him emerge. "You phase through the wall of room 66, unlock the door and let me in."

Spencer grinned and chuckled, nervously scratching the back of his head: "Wow ...that's...you really want to stay there, after what that guy said?"

"I'll just leave the money that I owe him for the room on the desk in the morning and then hightail it out of there.

They'll never know we were here," Harriet said.

"But what about the poltergeist?" Spencer asked.

"Poltergeist, shmoltergeist. That's all a bunch of nonsense, anyway. Do you actually believe in that crap? Like, where the people walk around in an empty house with an infrared camera, and then shake the camera a lot and start freaking out, then call that proof of a ghost? You don't think any of that is at all stupid?"

Harriet started walking right past a row of numbered doors, which started at 08, and crept upward to 09, 10, 11, and 12, as she moved. Spencer walked next to her, slouching slightly and putting his hands in his pockets.

"I don't know. I guess anything's possible," Spencer said, "But you know what, you're probably right. I'm sure it's all just some hilarious misunderstanding, or just a made-up story that they invented to attract customers."

"Exactly," Harriet said, tapping her forehead with one finger. "*Now*, you're making sense."

"I like to do that sometimes."

Together, dressed in black trench coats and without a scrap of luggage, Harriet and Spencer stopped in front of the room marked 66. The pair of flat golden sixes and the door they were nailed to appeared harmless; non-threatening; no different than the door marked 65 directly to the left of it.

"Ok, go inside," Harriet said.

Spencer took his hands out of his pockets, stretched and yawned. Then, inhaled deeply and stepped through the door, his head passing through the golden 66 above the door as though it were made of mist. He disappeared inside. A few seconds passed. The door's lock clicked open and then the door swung forward. Now, Spencer stood under the door frame, with large, apprehensive eyes; his posture rigid; his hands trembling slightly as he wrung them together nervously.

"Harriet, I think we should leave," he said with some uncharacteristic urgency.

"Don't tell me you're scared," Harriet scoffed with annoyance, rolling her eyes.

"I'm not scared," Spencer replied a little defensively, "It's just...uh....why don't you come in and see for yourself..." He turned and strode back into the room.

Harriet stepped into the room, removed her trench coat, and then, discarded it on a cleaned and pressed double bed with floral patterned sheets. As she did so, the door slammed shut and locked itself behind her. She glanced around the room, observing the stark white walls. The room was streaked and stained with a dried brownish-burgundy substance that might have once been streams of blood, pouring from the upper edges of the walls where they joined at the ceiling. The furniture, it seemed, had been replaced after the alleged blood incident, because it was clean and new. But the edges of the grey carpeting were stained a deep crimson, and made a gooey squelching noise as Harriet sloshed through them. The paintings of fruit and flowers on the walls, it seemed, had been turned upside down. The words "GET OUT" were scrawled over all of them, and it appeared as though those words had been written with a shaky, blood-covered finger.

"Well," Harriet said with a shrug, kicking off her shoes. "At least there's a TV."

She pointed to the small flat screen, which was positioned atop a dark-stained cabinet across from the bed.

"Uh...yeah..." Spencer said.

Harriet walked into the bathroom. The walls in there were also streaked with brownish crimson.

"Of for fuck's sake they couldn't clean this room better?" Harriet muttered. Though the walls were stained, the toilet, bathtub, and sink, were shiny white porcelain, scrubbed immaculate. There were a lot of little hotel soaps, and tiny, cylindrical, shampoos and conditioners, around the sink and the bathtub. The silver rack on the wall was stocked with a lot of clean, white towels. Harriet showered and used the toilet, then, exited the bathroom, and walked over to the bed, where Spencer was sitting, watching the news. He put the television on mute for a second and said:

"Do you hear that?"

A faint malicious-sounding cackle could be heard in the distance, followed by a scratching noise that might have been fingernails trying to claw through wood.

"I'm sure it's just the TV from another room," Harriet said.

She shut out the lights, and then, crawled into the bed and covered herself with the blanket, shutting her eyes, and falling asleep almost instantly. The evil cackling and scratching noises were as good as a lullaby to her. They were at best, intermittent, faint, only occasionally, loud enough to be annoying. Spencer lay awake for a while, his eyes wide, apprehensive, as they darted around, searching for the source of the faint, intermittent noise in the dark. He put an arm around Harriet as she slept, playing with a strand of her long, dark hair, as he stared at the blood-stained ceiling, with bloodshot eyes. His eyelids sank slowly, and he fell into a shallow, uneasy sleep.

Chapter 15:
Unwelcome Guests

A couple of hours later, a shrill, scream woke Harriet from her deep sleep. Spencer jerked awake, exhaling with anxiety. The scream stopped for a moment and then started again. This time it went on for a long time, stopped, and then started again.

"Oh my fucking Christ, are you serious? Are you fucking serious? How in the name of *fuck* am I supposed to sleep with all of this noise!" Harriet shouted to be heard above the ear-shredding din of the high-pitched, ceaseless screaming as she sat bolt upright and tossed the blankets off. It sounded like angry screaming, not fearful or distressed screaming. It was the scream of someone so utterly pissed that they could not find the words to express just how pissed they were, and it was so loud that it might have been coming from inside of the room.

"I think it might be coming from inside of the closet," Spencer whispered.

"Yeah, it does sound like that, doesn't it?"

Harriet stood up and walked over to the closet, across from the door to the bathroom.

"Harriet...maybe that's not a good idea...," Spencer murmured groggily. She ignored him and kept walking.

The sound grew louder as she approached the wooden sliding doors in the wall. The noise stopped suddenly. Harriet hesitated for a moment. Then, she flung the door open. She flicked the light on in the closet and looked inside. There was nothing there, except for an open suitcase filled with women's clothing. Perhaps this was the property of some previous inhabitant who had fled, and abandoned her luggage.

Harriet turned back toward Spencer and shrugged.

"Huh. Must be coming from the room next door," she said.

"Yeah, must be," Spencer conceded with a sigh. "I just wish that the screaming would stop. I'm kind of...really tired."

"Well...she has to shut up eventually..." Harriet said, though she sounded less hopeful about this prospect than she had intended. "Maybe we should...I don't know, give up on trying to sleep in this room..."

Spencer grinned, and said in a mocking tone: "Don't tell me, *you're scared.*"

"Shut up. No I'm not."

"I think you are," Spencer teased with a grin.

"No, actually. No, I'm fucking not," said Harriet, The screaming kept going for a long time. Stopped for a moment and then started again, "It's just that I stopped here to sleep, and I'm not about to sleep with that fucking noise going on for hours on end. Let's get out of here."

"Heheheh...heh...you're scared. I knew it."

"Shut up."

The television flicked on. A white, blurry, hooded figure appeared in a buzz of static, opened its gash of a mouth, and let out another ear-shattering scream. Then, all at once, every light in the room flicked back on. Harriet was blinded for a moment. She blinked a few times. The stark white, burgundy-stained walls came into focus. She glanced over at Spencer, who stood a few inches away from her; mask-less and disheveled; his muscles tense; his eyes glowing crimson. The TV flickered a few times and then turned to static. Blood began to drip from the ceiling in slow, oozing rivulets, covering the walls in thick, gory stripes, and gathering in pools along the edge of the carpet.

"Tick tock, motherfuckers..." a deep distorted voice bellowed. It seemed to be coming from the very walls of the room; from the floors and from the ceiling, "You have thirty seconds to get the fuck out of my realm...or before you know it, you'll both be in pieces under the floorboards."

Spencer nudged Harriet's shoulder, mouthed the words, "let's go", then, turned toward the door, and started speed walking in that direction, Harriet put a hand out and grabbed him by the back of his shirt collar, pulling him backward.

"Who the fuck are you!" Harriet yelled, in response to the deep, disembodied voice.

"I am the darkness! The emptiness! The very embodiment of every evil that you feel in your heart but cannot name! And this room, my sanctuary, is a portal to the very gates of hell!" the voice boomed threateningly, there was something gargled about it, as though it were being transmitted through some reality-bending filter.

"Harriet..." Spencer murmured as the floor shook beneath their feet and blood oozed from the ceiling, like water down the clear, glass pane of a decorative office fountain.

"So, you're The Poltergeist that that guy was talking about, huh? Well, fuck you, Poltergeist. I don't *believe* in demons! What I *do* believe in are superhumans who pose as demons so that they can squat in a damn hotel room for free!" Harriet shouted.

"Oh...huh. Heheh...heh...I guess that does make more sense," Spencer chuckled.

All of the lights in the room went out all at once. Five or six, bald, naked baby dolls, with red magic marker scribbled over their eyes emerged from the closet and hobbled over to where Harriet and Spencer stood. Spencer inhaled slowly, willing the subtle tremor that had crept over his body into submission, and then, to prove to his lady love that he was not afraid, knelt down and picked up one of the dolls. It thrashed and made demonic gargling sounds in his hand. He gripped it tightly to stop it from escaping, beaming at it with morbid delight. The other dolls just stood there and stared. Spencer held the thrashing, apparently, harmless doll up for Harriet to see and chuckled: "This thing is metal as fuck."

"Do you hear that, Poltergeist?" Harriet shouted for the demon's benefit. "Your tricks are dumb! Now shut up and let me sleep!"

"Never!" the demonic voice boomed and then it began to scream shrilly, apparently, for the express purpose of keeping her awake.

Harriet shrieked to be heard above the din of the screaming demon:

"Fine, *fine*! Two can play at this game! Apparently, you don't know how this works, *I* stay in the room and *you* run out screaming!"

Harriet turned toward Spencer and bellowed urgently:

"Spencer take all of your clothes off!"

"Huh? *What?*" Spencer replied faltering, a grin spread over his face and his cheeks flushed. He chuckled nervously and unzipped the front of his pants.

"If this poltergeist isn't going to let me sleep, then I'll just have to find something else to do all night! The doll in Spencer's hand thrashed its limbs and cackled, and he dropped it back onto the floor, where it scurried off, back to the closet, like a glitchy, jerking spider on four legs. The other four dolls ran up the ceiling and started running against the walls, in circles around the room. The walls began bleeding again, dripping and gushing, coating the dolls in a shell of sloppy red gore as they ran.

"Hehheheh...hehheh...heh...Does this mean, we're going to do it?" Spencer inquired cautiously, the goofy, lust-drunk grin on his face overtook his previous expression of caution, and suddenly, he was completely oblivious to the fact that the room they were standing in was a screaming hell that may or may not have been the gate to an inescapable realm of horrors. He removed his pants and his underwear. The walls were bleeding. The dolls were running around in circles around them. The television and lights were flashing rapidly on and off. He pulled his shirt over his head and discarded it on the floor.

"No, we're not going to 'do it'," Harriet repeated a bit crossly. "I told you already, you haven't earned that yet. Do you really think that the prize for burning a massive pile of my money and sending a priceless piece of art to the bottom of the ocean is sex with me? No. Instead, you're getting another punishment."

"Yes ma'am, I hear and obey," Spencer replied, attempting to disguise the fact that beneath his jittery, suppliant facade, he was nearly drooling.

Harriet grabbed the wrist and ankle cuffs out of the pocket of her discarded jacket, spun Spencer around and secured his wrists behind his back. Then, pushed him face-first onto the bed. The fifth naked baby doll, the one that had retreated to the closet, crept back out, and slowly, jerkily, climbed to the top of the bedside table, where it propped itself against the lamp and sat there creepily, staring at them, its puppet hinge of a jaw falling slowly open.

"You've been a really naughty boy, Death Laser," Harriet teased.

"Punish me, Justice Bitch," Spencer murmured his voice muffled slightly by the bed underneath of him. "I deserve it."

Harriet's eyes darted around the room, searching for some kind of an implement, not something to make the punishment hurt more, but rather, something to defuse her supernatural strength and reduce the risk of accidentally causing permanent damage. There wasn't much in the room, other than the TV, a couple of lamps on the bedside tables, a digital clock, and furniture. *And*, of course...the dolls with the scribbled out eyes. Four of them were still running around the walls of the room. The fifth was still sitting on the bedside table, staring at them.

"Like voyeurism, doll?" Harriet whispered with a sinister grin, bordering on psychotic. She reached out and quickly grabbed the doll by one of its chubby, hollow plastic legs. It thrashed in her hand and spit out a string of demonic gargling noises in protest. "Well, today's your lucky day."

Harriet lifted the thrashing doll into the air and swung it downward in a violent arch, with much too munch indignant delight, striking Spencer across the chops with it.

"*Ow!*" Spencer yelped with surprise, as his body jerked in response to the pain. The fear of what grisly death the demonic entity in the room, might have been plotting for them, competed fiercely with the fear that Harriet might figure out that he was afraid. They were two fears at odds, and, until this point, they had mostly canceled each other out, but now, as Harriet prepared to strike him a second time with the poltergeist's protesting possessed doll, he could feel the fear start to swallow him up, witling away his bravado and his certainty. He was now painfully aware of his nudity, of his vulnerability, of the cold air against prickling skin. "Wait!" he shouted fearfully before Harriet could strike him with the doll a second time. "What's the safe word?"

"Safe words are dumb," Harriet said.

"Oh, come on, Harriet."

"How about 'stop', or alternatively, 'I forgot the safe word'," Harriet said with a roll of her eyes. "I'll also accept 'please stop', 'for the love of God, please stop', 'ow, I need a hospital', and 'I am in excruciating pain because you just broke my tailbone.'"

"Maybe you don't get what the purpose of a safe word is," Spencer replied in a slight tone of exhausted annoyance, "If you have to constantly wonder if anything I say is asking you to stop..."

"Fine," Harriet replied shortly, swinging the thrashing possessed doll as she threw her hands up in supplication, "From now on, the safe word is 'safe words are dumb', do you think you can remember that?"

"Yeah, I'll manage."

"Ok then, without any further bullshit, let's begin."

"Get out! Get out! Get out! *Get out!*" the deep, disembodied voice bellowed. But its intonation was different now; indignant; frustrated.

Harriet swung the flailing doll and slapped Spencer hard on the ass with it. Spencer yelped and balled his hands into fists as a purple bruise blossomed across his already reddened backside. The lights in the room flickered on and off, the dolls opened their mouths and started singing: "La la. Laaa....La. La. *Laaaaa*," over and over again in shrill off-key little voices. Harriet ignored all of this. With psychotic abandon, she whaled on her new "butler" sending the doll which she gripped in her hand flying through the air again and again and again. This seemed to enrage the poltergeist, which, if Harriet was being honest with herself, was only enhancing her pleasure.

"Get out! Get out! Get out! *Get out!* Stop that! Stop that immediately!" the poltergeist shrieked, its deep bellow scratchy and distorted, yet still, distinctly flustered.

Harriet swung the doll viciously, and this time its ceramic head shattered into a thousand jagged pieces against Spencer's reddened ass. He yelled out and arched his back.

"S...safe words are dumb...," he murmured timidly, shutting his eyes tightly, and swallowing hard. Then he added in a small voice: "Harriet...I want to leave."

"Did you see that, Poltergeist?" Harriet yelled, staring at the ceiling as though there were someone standing there, "I broke your stupid doll!"

"Get out! Get out! Geeeet ouuut!" the poltergeist yelled, now no longer attempting to mask its indignation. If you freaks aren't out of my room by sunrise, I swear, you're going to be *dead*! Dead! DEAD! Do you understand DEAD, *bitch*?"

"Oh what's that you're going to kill me?" Harriet yelled at the ceiling.

The dolls responded this time in creepy, high-pitch, sing-song voices: "La, laaa-la la *laaaa*.... You killed our sister. Now the walls will run red with your blood."

"Yeah, bullshit! Because if you kill me the precious room you've been squatting in will be swarming with cops and you don't want that at all, do you?" Harriet yelled.

"Do you really want to risk it, Harriet?" Spencer interjected hesitantly.

"You know, it's funny, I don't remember asking for

your opinion, butler," Harriet muttered and with a delighted smirk, she added: "It's kind of funny how you're scared of all of these dumb tricks."

"Not everyone is indestructible like you, Harriet," Spencer said with some anger. "And I'm not scared, by the way."

"Oh, you're not?" Harriet teased.

"No way," Spencer replied, rolling onto his back and phasing through the pair of handcuffs. "Forget staying the night, I could live in this room and it still wouldn't be scary. Because that's how dumb it is."

"It is really dumb, isn't it?" Harriet agreed.

"The dumbest," Spencer confirmed, "I've seen children's shows that were scarier."

Harriet reached out and tugged at one of his nipple piercings with a curious grin. The corners of his mouth curled slightly at the pain. She reached out and tugged at the other piercing, careful to avoid ripping the piercing from his body with accidental obsessive force. She crawled on top of him and he laid back down. Her face was now parallel from his, and her eyes were filled with a frightening, sadistic intensity. A blush crept over his pale cheeks and he grinned, asking again with some hopefulness: "Are we going to *do it* now?"

Harriet slapped the side of Spencer's face playfully. Though not intended to be a harsh blow, her supernaturally powerful palm pinkened his right cheek for a moment.

"I told you, not yet," she whispered in his ear.

The poltergeist's yelling had died down to silence. The walls had stopped bleeding and the remaining dolls lay immobile, in a heap, on the floor.

He kissed her, closing his eyes and using a liberal length of his tongue to feel out the corners of her mouth.

"I'm sorry I asked again," he said tiredly, closing his eyes slowly and wrapping his arms around her, "It's just that you're *so* beautiful."

"Yeah, *yeah*...I've heard it all before," Harriet said with a yawn, closing her eyes.

Chapter 16:
Shattered Sister

In the morning, Harriet opened her eyes slowly, and stared up at the blood-splattered ceiling. Slowly, she became aware that she was lying on a bed littered with ceramic doll shards. A naked and snoring Spencer had his arm around her and his face buried between her breasts. She could feel the warmth of his breath against her skin as he exhaled periodically, and the hard muscles in his arms against her bare midriff. The horizontal bars of light, which poured through the drawn window shades on either side of the hotel room's door, illuminated the bloody walls and Spencer's huddled, sleeping form, pressed against her like gum stuck to the underside of a table. As Harriet observed the sight with disbelief, she began experiencing a bizarre shame, not unlike that of someone waking up with a hangover after a night of wild partying.

"Spencer...are you awake?" Harriet whispered, tapping one of his arms tentatively.

"...Well...I am now..." Spencer replied groggily, lifting his face from her chest and crawling up toward her face, kissing her lightly on the lips. "Good morning, princess."

"I think we're going to have to check out soon," Harriet said.

"Heheheh...we broke in, remember? Nobody knows we're here. We can stay as long as we want," Spencer said with a weak grin. Then he nuzzled his face against her neck, shut his eyes, and started snoring again.

Harriet shut her eyes, the sound of Spencer's snoring and of birds chirping outside of the hotel window filled her ears.

She opened her eyes again. Hours must have passed because the light pouring through the drawn shades of the windows was much brighter, and Spencer had dressed himself. He stood at the opposite end of the room, in front of a small microwave, set on top of a low table, next to an unplugged hotplate. He watched the microwave as it buzzed and the platform inside rotated. The microwave beeped and he opened it, extracting a couple of burritos in paper pouches. Then he turned around, holding two burritos, one in each hand.

"...Oh, you're awake," he said, staring at Harriet and scratching the back of his disheveled head with one hand. "I got these out of the vending machine outside. Now, I *technically* stole them, but I didn't really have a choice. I think Finsveld still has my wallet. And they were only, like...five dollars anyway."

"Wait?" Harriet said, sitting up quickly, "Finsveld took your wallet?"

"Yeah, when he did that clothing change thing that he does," Spencer said.

"He didn't leave it...he usually leaves it. Just like he usually leaves...*my purse*..." Harriet murmured. Her eyes shot open as something that should have been fairly obvious from the beginning occurred to her and in a tone of panic she exclaimed: "Shit, my purse! Finsveld's been taking my purse and then sneaking away early to go riffle through it, hasn't he? He must have been doing it to all of us this whole time!"

"So what was in there?"

"Oh I don't know, just my credit cards and my social security card."

"Uh...I don't think you're supposed to carry that."

"But maybe I'm just being paranoid, maybe he hasn't done anything with it," Harriet breathed with uncertainty, standing up and pacing the room once.

"There's only one way to be sure. Check your credit card balance and your bank account balance."

"I can't!" Harriet exclaimed, "...Finsveld has my cellphone..."

Spencer handed Harriet one of the burritos. And then unwrapped the second one and shoved it in his mouth, chewing slowly. He swallowed and said: "There's, I think...computers in the public library where I used to hang out when I was homeless. Why don't you check it there?"

"Ok...ok....I guess I can do that. It's probably nothing. I'm probably worried about nothing, right?"

"I don't know," Spencer said, shrugging, "But I'm sure it's fine...don't even worry about it."

Harriet grabbed Spencer by the shoulders and shook him: "How the hell am I supposed to not worry about it?"

"Your friend, whatserface, trusts him, doesn't she?" Spencer said, taking another bite out of the burrito.

"Yeah, I guess so..."

"And he's always given your stuff back before, right?"

"Yeah, I guess he has..."

"So, what are you all tensed up about, huh?" Spencer said, taking another bite of the burrito. "Don't stress, princess."

"I'm not going to be able to rest until I know for sure," Harriet said, brandishing the burrito as though to ward off a phantom attacker.

"Are you going to eat that?" Spencer asked, eyeing the remaining burrito lustfully, as he finished the burrito he was holding and discarded the wrapper on the hotel floor.

"*Yes.*"

"Aw, man..."

Harriet unwrapped the burrito and took a bite out of it. She swallowed and then said: "Ok, I'm out of here. I've got to go check my credit score."

"You sound like that TV commercial I've seen five hundred times..." Spencer said, following her as she exited the hotel room.

The sound of the door snapping shut and locking itself behind her seemed a world away, as Harriet stepped out into the parking lot and spotted her black Jaguar parked outside of the hotel room. All of the windows were smashed, and every inch of it was covered in a deep, violent keying, which disrupted its once smooth black surface with chaotic curved lines. Harriet walked in a circle around the vehicle, with clenched, shaking fists, observing that the word "SCUMBAG" had been written across both sides of the car in dripping, red paint.

"Oh man," Spencer murmured, running his hands nervously through his hair. "Somebody trashed your car."

"How did you not notice this?" Harriet fumed, "Did *you* do this? Because fuck you if you did this! This isn't cute!"

"I didn't do this, I swear," Spencer defended himself quickly, "I left through the back wall this morning so that no one would see me coming out of the door and tell us to get lost. I mean, I did hear some banging and smashing noises when I was in the shower...but I didn't think....you know, I thought it was just the poltergeist in the room again."

Harriet noticed a note sticking up out of the broken windshield, pinned beneath what remained of a twisted windshield wiper. She removed the note and shook off a few shards of glass, then, unfolded it. Inside was a short message written in what appeared to be blood: *"You killed our sister. Now the walls will run red with your blood. Enjoy your new car while you can, scumbag bitch. We will come for you in the night, maybe not today, maybe not tomorrow, but soon. — The Poltergeist"*

Harriet handed the note to Spencer and he read it quickly before slowly lowering the paper and muttering: "Shit."

Chapter 17:
Scumbag

The black Jaguar rolled past tall buildings and swarms of people shuffling down the broad sidewalks. Occasionally someone would stop to stare at the vandalized vehicle, and mouth the word "scumbag" as they read the bright red letters painted over the doors with curiosity. Harriet was quiet for a while, as she brooded about the potential theft of her credit cards and the recent damage to her very expensive car. Not daring to touch the radio dial, Spencer whistled a nervous tune.

"Hey, Spencer?"

"Yeah?"

"When you stole the Ross Foundation, did you ever um...this sounds stupid to say...find out what the foundation *actually does*?"

"What? How the hell am I supposed to know? Your father's board of trustees never let me near it. They just handed me the money from whatever they were doing and then told me to back off."

"Yeah...it was always like that," said Harriet, "Very secretive, you know. My father never had a clue what the foundation did either. But I think his father knew, and probably also...*Reynolds*...I think he knew."

"Makes you kind of wonder what they're hiding," Spencer said.

"Yeah....though I'm sure it's not interesting at all," Harriet said.

"What makes you so sure of that?"

The black Jaguar rolled past Victorian style, ocean-side homes built on a steep rocky ledge overlooking the water. Harriet glanced down at the dashboard, now splattered with red paint, which obscured the digital clock above the CD player. Then, she glanced over at Spencer, who was driving, his expression slightly worried. He was wearing the black trench coat over his costume, and his disheveled hair was still slightly wet from the shower.

"The truth is your dad's board of trustees didn't really tell me much about the company, how it's run or even what it does really. That might have been because I was an invader...but I got the feeling that they didn't care much about who was officially 'the head.' It's almost as though whatever they were really doing...was something they shouldn't have been doing. You know, like something they were trying to hide."

"I used to get that feeling too. My dad was never worried about it though. He was always the happy-go-lucky type. Ready to take the money and let someone else worry about how it got there. Maybe he really did know but just never told me, maybe he thought I wasn't ready to know, or maybe my grandfather just never told him because he thought my father was too irresponsible to handle it. Either way, I sure as hell don't know, and now that I don't own it, I'll probably never know," Harriet said.

"Because your father left it to Reynolds, right?"

"Yeah."

The black Jaguar parallel parked in front of a string of storefronts in the shopping district.

"Uh. This parking spot is so far away. Is this really the best you could do, butler?" Harriet complained.

"Ah man, I don't know, I really don't want to circle a block looking for another space. Do you want to check your accounts or what?"

"Fine. At least no one in the building will see me getting out of this car."

Chapter 18:
Of Identity Theft and of Betrayal

In the public library, Harriet stared at the computer screen in front of her, as the credit website that she had typed into the address bar loaded slowly. If computers were people, this computer would have been a senile elderly man with a walker, struggling to hobble along. It was old and slow and Harriet was unaccustomed to the machine's clunky, inconvenient obsoleteness.

"So do these computers ever load or what?" Harriet said, motioning to indicate the row of old, square computers, in the public library, where she sat.

"Uh, yeah, but it takes a while..." Spencer replied. He was standing behind her, moving the mouse on the computer around and clicking it randomly, as if that would help.

After two long minutes, the page loaded and, with a cringe, Harriet clicked on the button to go to the next page. Slowly, the page loaded, until, finally, it had loaded enough for Harriet to scroll down and read the information on it. She stared at the screen for a moment, and then, muttered with disbelief. "My credit card balance...is *200*."

"Is that bad?"

"Yes, Spencer. That's *bad*."

"Well, what the hell do I know?" said Spencer with a clueless shrug. "I don't even have any credit, I don't think. What's a credit?"

Yeah, 200 is *really* bad. And it probably means that Finsveld has been going through my purse and that he probably, definitely, has been using my credit cards."

"Oh...ok, I get it."

"And if he's been using my credit cards, he's probably been using my bank cards too," Harriet finished, sounding both mortified and emotionally exhausted.

A slow, *slow* check of her bank balance confirmed this suspicion. As she discovered that the 500,000 dollars she had inherited was missing. Only about 900 remained in the account, and most of the 900 was probably owing to her recent cashed paycheck from the art museum.

"I can't believe this is happening," Harriet muttered, slamming her head down in the keyboard in frustration. The plastic cracked under the force of the blow, and the keyboard splintered into four or five jagged, wedge-shaped fragments.

"What are you going to do?" Spencer asked.

"I don't know."

"Shouldn't you try and get your money and stuff back from him?"

"Yeah..." Harriet said with a sigh, "But the money's already spent. What the hell am I going to do about it, ask Reynolds for money? After the way he ditched me after my dad's funeral, forget it. I'm not about to ask him for anything."

"But what about, like, your clothes and the stuff in your room that was yours, don't you have a right to any of that?" Spencer said.

"Yeah, but The Jay Walker's been in there...doing who knows what with it," Harriet muttered, "And I haven't decided who should be dealt with first. The Jay Walker or Finsveld..."

Harriet attempted to contemplate this decision, and found that the animal rage building inside of her was impeding her ability to think clearly. The capacity to decide what she should do next, it seemed, had fled from her out of fear of retribution. Overcome with emotion, Harriet stood up and walked away from the row of computers, blinking back angry tears.

"Are you ok?" Spencer asked.

"Yes. Shut up."

"Are you sure?"

"I thought I told you to shut up."

"You know...you don't have to decide who you should fight first. I can sneak into The Ross Manor and steal back some of your stuff for you while you confront Finsveld."

Harriet chuckled to herself.

"Do the lengths you'll go to get laid know no bounds?" she sighed.

"None at all," Spencer confirmed proudly. He wrapped his arms around her, slouched slightly and kissed the top of her head.

Chapter 19:
The Face of Fear

The Jay Walker sat in the center of The Ross Manor's large eating hall, on a large, plush, green chair that was not unlike a thrown. He discarded his rubber Donald Trump mask, revealing the scrawny, pockmarked face underneath. He laid the mask down on the arm of the chair, stretching and yawning boredly as he spotted his henchman, Crunchy Toast Muncher, (a man with the ability to turn people into bread) entering the room. The man still wore his skin-tight, bread-textured, spandex suit and loaf-shaped mascot head but he had abandoned the creepy, slow, and silent way of moving that characterized his performance in battle. The Jay Walker noticed that he was holding a black plastic trash bag.

As Crunchy Toast Muncher approached, he kneeled and removed the loaf-shaped mascot head, revealing his true face, that of the artist, Vigo VonCrucible.

"Vigo," The Jay Walker greeted him without enthusiasm. "This better be about my meal."

"It is not," VonCrucible replied in a thick German accent, "Though you will eat from the flesh of those who remain loyal to your predecessor, tonight, as requested. Gordeau is searching the minds of your henchman for treachery as we speak. So I think that you will be very satisfied by the bread tonight. It is more delicious, you will find, when taken with purpose."

"Right, right, and all that creepy shit. I'm the baddest motherfucker up in this place. Up in here, chillin' in my stolen mansion, eating people. Like a boss."

"I've come here with a purpose, Jason," VonCrucible said, still kneeling. He held the black plastic garbage bag up for Jason to see. "I could not help but notice your costume. Why do you wear the faces of history's most divisive American presidents?"

110

"Because they're heinous motherfuckers. When they walk down the street, normals get the fuck out of the way," Jason explained as though this reasoning ought to have been obvious.

"Because they take everything...whatever they can without thinking twice about it? Because they inspire dee fear in people?" VonCrucible inferred.

"Yes."

"Jason, I think you should know that I am not only a painter. I also dabble in taxidermy. With my skill set," VonCrucible opened the plastic bag and stuck his hand into it withdrawing a mask, "Well...I think my work speaks for itself. Go ahead, take it. It's my gift to you."

Jason took the mask out of VonCrucible's hand with bored indifference, observing its waxy stiffness with his fingers. The sparse, greasy, hair on its scalp appeared to be real human hair and the skin on its face appeared to be real, dried and cured human skin. Jason turned the mask a couple of times in his hands, attempting to determine the identity of the taxidermy head's previous owner. It took Jason a moment to recognize its face as belonging to one of the guys from the Super Powered Ex-Con support group. The large, fat man who had talked about stealing cookies from girl scouts, this was his face, uncannily stretched and distorted, yet still startlingly recognizable. It was really expertly preserved.

"There are better ways to inspire fear than with a plastic mask," VonCrucible said. "A true warrior, a true demon, the true master of this world, he should wear a mask of human skin. Wear the faces of those you slay as your helm in battle, and your enemies will bow before you."

"It's true what they say about you, VonCrucible," Jason said, "You really are a creepy as fuck. How did you make this? Did you decapitate him before you turned his body into bread or something?"

"Precisely," VonCrucible confirmed and then his intense green eyes locked on Jason and he inquired: "Do you like it?"

Jason stared at the mask for a moment and then smirked.

"Yes," he replied, putting the taxidermy mask over his own head like a second skin. He looked like a tortured demon from hell wearing it; frightening and uncanny beneath waxy, expressionless lips, and large, floppy eye-holes.

"It is a natural evolution for you, boss. From plastic to skin. I can make many masks like this for you, you understand. With my skill, you may wear the skin of a child to kill his mother, and the skin of a mother to kill her sister, and the skin of the sister to kill her lover. All will fear you as the superior being, and the ruler of this entire world."

"And what about you?" Jason inquired with some suspicion. He was smart enough to know that a man with as much talent, intellect, and madness as VonCrucible would likely not remain subservient to him for long.

"I am a Darwinist," VonCrucible replied.

"You mean a Nazi."

"Call it what you will, I acknowledge that superhumans with mind control are destined to conquer this world; that they have this capacity to bend the will of others because they were chosen to rule by God. Therefore, it would be my honor to serve as your right-hand man. As a Christian, this is my sacred duty. Unlike the others, Jason, I serve you willingly...*and*...I will make you many masks like this one, as many as you require."

Hearing this, The Jay Walker laughed wildly. He suspected that VonCrucible's pledge of loyalty was something less than trustworthy, yet, at this moment he could not bring himself to fear such a ridiculous man. VonCrucible put the loaf-shaped mascot head back on and rose slowly, spinning and jumping a few times around Jason's chair, before he skipped to the exit of the room. He made strange nonsense noises as he did this, oddly magnified and distorted by the hallow cavity of his bread-shaped mascot head.

"Vigo!" The Jay Walker called just as VonCrucible was about to leave the room.

VonCrucible spun to face The Jay Walker, bowing low, and miming the removal of an invisible top hat.

"I've decided I'm going to kill The Justice Bitch, wearing a mask made out of Death Laser's face. So, if you see him snooping around in here, be sure to cut off his head and save it, before you eat him."

"If it be thy will, oh superior being," VonCrucible replied, and then, he turned again and skipped out of the room.

Chapter 20:
The Confrontation at Castle Jay

Harriet drove to The Ross Manor. The black Jaguar rolled to a stop outside of the tall, black gates, which marked the entrance of the property. She parked, and then, turned to Spencer, who was sitting in the passenger seat of the car, wearing black jeans and a black T-shirt recently purchased from a local Walmart. He grabbed an empty black backpack from the spray-painted floor of the ruined car, and quickly put it on.

"Ok, so I guess I get some of your stuff, while you go and confront Finsveld, then we'll meet, let's say at the Convenience Mart on the corner of 3rd and Jackson, at let's say...4 p.m.," Spencer said.

"Right. 3rd and Jackson. 4 p.m.," Harriet repeated. She leaned over the gear shift and kissed him on the mouth quickly, "See you then."

Spencer phased through the passenger's side door. Harriet turned the car and drove away from the manor. Spencer darted up to the fence, stealthily passing through it, as he leaned against it with one arm, waving goodbye to her with a grin and a wink.

...

Crunchy Toast Muncher straightened the bread-shaped mascot head, which obscured his face, strolling with purpose through the long hallways of The Ross Manor. He stopped abruptly as he spotted Trauma, sitting in the library, reclined in one of the plush green sofas and reading a thick book entitled: *Chasing Freud*.

Trauma must have sensed that Crunchy Toast Muncher intended to speak to him, because he lifted his head from the book, marked the page and set it down by his side.

"Please," Trauma invited warmly, gesturing toward Crunchy Toast Muncher who stood in the hallway, staring creepily at him through the entrance to the library, "Come inside."

Crunchy Toast Muncher entered the room, and strode up to Trauma. He remained standing before the sofa where Trauma sat. He did not remove the mascot head. He did not have to. Trauma could read his intentions well enough without ever glancing at the look on his face.

"I'd like you to help me kill Death Laser. He is fast. You will slow him down for me," Crunchy Toast Muncher said.

"So that you can gain the trust of The Jay Walker?" Trauma said with a tone of inquiry, though, in truth, this was really more of a statement than a question. Trauma knew that was the reason.

"Yes," Crunchy Toast Muncher confirmed, though the confirmation was not necessary.

"Because you believe that The Jay Walker is one of the only superhumans alive with the power to free your son, Benjamin VonCrucible," Trauma said.

"Yes," Crunchy Toast Muncher said, "I need him to like me so that he will agree to do me a favor. The best way to do this, I think, is to kill Death Laser and make a mask out of his head, dat The Jay Walker can wear when he kills The Bitch. If I do this...."

"He will owe you, and he will help you free your son," Trauma finished, predicting the sentence's end with accuracy down to the syntax.

"Yes," Crunchy Toast Muncher confirmed, though no confirmation was necessary.

"What makes you think that your son needs rescuing? I'm panning over your memories of him right now and none of his behavior seems very suspicious to me," Trauma said.

"Dat is because you do not know my son," Crunchy Toast Muncher said, "He has stopped calling me. He has stopped visiting me. The last time I saw him...I spoke to him in German and he did nothing but look at me like he did not understand."

"Perhaps Benjamin was just ignoring you. Young people do that from time to time, you know," Trauma said with a patronizing little grin.

This assertion enraged Crunchy Toast Muncher and in a quick confrontational tone, he exclaimed: "Don't fuck with me, Trauma. I see the truth clearly. I see through your Pollyanna facade. You speak in nonsense and riddles. You try to make me doubt my sanity like every shrink dat has ever been shoved down my throat! But you cannot fool me! You will never fool me with your patronizing lies! Your *lies*! Which taste like vomit and burning tires, and the bloated corpses of liberal science majors, which must latch on to the bull's anus and then suck with all of their might to survive! I am not nor have I ever been insane! My son, he must be freed. The J-Walker is the only superhuman I have met who can do it. Will you help me kill Death Laser and win his favor?"

"I....*hmm*....honestly, Vigo, there doesn't seem to be very much in it for me," Trauma replied, "And in my professional opinion, you do sound a bit insane, actually," Trauma picked his book back up, leaned back, crossed his legs and resumed reading: "Yup...I have to call them as I see them."

"You know nothing and you are nothing. Benjamin must be free," Crunchy Toast Muncher said, slapping the book out of Trauma's hands in a vain attempt to rile some emotion.

"Maybe he doesn't want to be free," Trauma replied in a tone of infuriatingly indifferent professionalism, "Did you ever think about that?"

"Don't talk down to me, shrink. He's being held captive by *that woman*."

"Yes, but that's the thing...*is he*?"

"I know that he must be a captive. That is the only explanation."

"But *is* it the only explanation?" Trauma challenged again, "Love is strange, after all."

"Forgive me if I'm not about to take advice about love

from a man who murdered his wife," Crunchy Toast Muncher muttered with frustration, "Will you help me kill Death Laser or won't you?"

"No," Trauma replied simply, retrieving his book from the floor and flipping back to the marked page, "When the boss tells me to kill him, I'll kill him. But I *do not* take orders from you. You have a nice day, now."

"Nice day? *Nice day?* You insufferable piece of shit! My son has been imprisoned and you will not lift a finger to help me?" Crunchy Toast Muncher yelled. "When this is all over, I will be wearing your skin like the ugliest poncho!"

"Right, of course," Trauma said, "What can I say, I'm a villain. I don't do favors out of the goodness of my heart. You of all people should appreciate that."

Cursing in German, Crunchy Toast Muncher turned and stomped out of the room. Just as he was about to exit, however, Trauma called to him in a friendly tone of voice: "Vigo!"

Crunchy Toast Muncher turned to face the shrink once more.

"Finding Death Laser will be a lot easier than you think. I can sense his brain waves buzzing around in Harriet's old bedroom right now. So you better hurry, if you want to catch him."

"Thanks for dee tip, you insufferable *quack*." Crunchy Toast Muncher replied somberly and then he sprinted away, with purpose and determination.

Trauma, now alone in the library, resumed reading his book.

...

Spencer phased through a wall and into Harriet's bedroom, where a lot of her personal effects remained. Though the furniture had been changed and the walls had been painted black, Harriet's belongings were still here, in boxes piled inside of the walk-in closet, which remained untouched. Spencer knew this because he had put them there himself.

In hindsight it might have been wasteful, renovating the entire place, but his mentality at the time had been that of a man with nothing who had suddenly slipped into a life of absurd extravagance; a surreal world where he might realistically attain *anything* that he desired. His objective at the time had been to spend as much money as humanly possible. He had become overwhelmed by the thrill of wasting millions upon absurd luxuries; the rush that came with the realization that he could spend and spend *and spend* without consequence; without ever having to worry about running out, or even, running low.

The wastefulness of it all hit Spencer like a guilty brick to his face as he observed the extravagant room.

Look at all of this shit, he thought, observing the intricate woodwork and stained glass; the checkered black and red marble floors. *I don't need all of this shit. Some people have next to nothing. Some people live on the street. Some people work their lives away to spend their nights in a shitty room, with hardly enough food to feed their kids with. None of those people are less deserving than me.*

With that thought, Spencer phased through the wall into the walk-in closet and flicked on the light. The boxes containing Harriet's belongings were still there. He had spent enough time alone in this room, snooping through them, to know their contents well, and already had some idea of what he would take to Harriet. He took some of Harriet's clothes first; skirts, pants, blouses, socks, and underwear. These were chosen hastily and nearly at random. He shoved them in the backpack and then turned his attention to the boxes. She had not given him any instructions about what to take, or any stories about what objects were most valuable to her, perhaps out of a fear of being viewed as vulnerable; perhaps out of a genuine indifference. Spencer opened one of the boxes and found some photographs of Harriet with people that he assumed must have been friends and family members: An old butler, an attractive older woman with short grey hair and a tight-lipped scowl, a beautiful blond model wearing an extravagant diamond necklace, and a timid looking little boy with large glasses. Spencer grabbed a pile of photos with this one at the top and stuck it in the bag. He selected also, a music box with a twirling ballerina on it, a tube of red lipstick, a yearbook, featuring pictures from a posh boarding school filled with the teenaged children of rich people, a pair of large, diamond earrings, and a small, white teddy bear with cute stubby limbs and a pink bowtie. He was not sure if any of this stuff had any sentimental value to Harriet, but he was hoping that all of it did and that his guesses about what she would want returned to her most were accurate. In his mind's eye he pictured her cradling the teddy bear close to her breasts, beaming at him with love in her eyes, praising him in her silky, sensuous voice:

"You're such a good butler."

"Are we going to do it now?" Spencer imagined himself reply stupidly.

"*Yes*. Take that dick out."

Before he shoved the bear in the backpack, Spencer held it up and grinned at it.

"You're my ticket to getting my dick sucked, Mr. Bear," he said to it.

In a high-pitched, funny-sounding voice he replied to himself as the bear: "Why it's my pleasure, Mr. Death Laser! Yup! Mr. Bear likes to help!"

Spencer narrowed his eyes.

"You keep your paws off of her Mr. Bear, I saw her first," Spencer said to the bear with some suspicion and then he shoved the bear in the backpack and zipped it closed. Spencer put the now heavy and full backpack back on and phased through the wall of the closet, back into Harriet's bedroom. Now the air was cold, so cold that it burned his skin. He hugged himself and shivered.

119

"There you are, you fuckin' dickhead," a familiar voice muttered in a tone of cool indifference bordering on contempt.

Spencer turned his head in the direction of the voice and saw Devin, standing at the opposite end of the large room, leaning against the wall with a frozen cigarette in his mouth. Devin exhaled a fog of cold breath as he stepped forward, tossing the cigarette to the ground. The sound of it shattering to pieces pierced the quiet room and echoed off of the walls.

"Did Justice Bitch send you in here to die, just so that she could get some of her shit back?" Devin taunted with a slight smirk, "Is that how disposable you are to her?"

"Shut up, Devin," Spencer grumbled, walking right through the other man and toward the wall leading to the next room.

"Because you are going to die here, Fuckerson. Make no mistake about that," Devin muttered. Before Spencer could reach the wall at the other end of the room, Devin shot a barrage of knife-sharp icicles at Spencer's head and he ducked to avoid having his skull skewered.

Spencer darted toward the wall again but then Devin shot steams of snow out of his palms, which formed a thick wall and then froze into solid ice. Spencer held his breath and phased through the wall. But then found himself confronted by another wall and then another. Soon, Spencer was hyperventilating, unable to catch his breath and unable to phase through the wall that he had his back up against, as Devin approached, smirking and wielding a massive icicle like a club.

"You always have to hold your breath when you phase through shit, don't you? And I bet you thought I wouldn't notice," Devin boasted with a superior smirk.

Spencer ducked and darted around Devin and away from the wall as Devin swung his icicle club, nearly clocking him in the head again. Spencer shot a pair of lasers out of his eyes, hitting Devin in the chest with them. They burned a pair of holes in his shirt but failed to singe the skin.

"You that you're such a great singer," Devin scoffed as he ran at Spencer, swinging his icicle club wildly, attempting to strike the other man in the face with it. Spencer yelled and ducked away, still hyperventilating, "But I see you for what you really are, you fuckin' dickhead, little piece-of-shit wannabe."

"Hey....fuck you, Devin. Everyone knows that *auto-tune* could do your job," Spencer gasped between fits of hyperventilating, and his glowing crimson eyes locked on Devin's ice blue ones.

Devin yelled and ran at him, raising his club high, prepared to strike the other man over the head with it, but this time, instead of attempting an escape, Spencer stared Devin straight in the eyes, shooting a pair of lasers as he did so. One of the lasers hit Devin's right eye. The other grazed his pallid, frozen face, melting into a harmless cloud of steam. Devin screamed as blood squirted from the eyehole of his clear mask. He dropped the club and collapsed onto the floor, clutching the gushing wound and yelling: "Fuck! Fuck! *Fuuuck!*" as he curled into the fetal position, rolling around on the icy floor.

Spencer stepped over his thrashing body, opened the room's door, and stepped through it. Eyes lit and breathing hard he darted away from Harriet's bedroom. The weight of the full backpack he carried was restrictive and it slowed his movement but he was determined not to drop it. Instead, he slowed to a craw, gasping for air, struggling to catch his breath.

From the corner of his eye, Spencer saw the gleam of something metal. He turned around quickly and ducked just as Crunchy Toast Muncher (who had been creeping slowly behind him, dragging a heavy ax) swung the weapon at Spencer's neck with the intention of decapitating him.

Spencer screamed and then started running as fast as he could in the opposite direction. Crunchy Toast Muncher swung the ax over his shoulder and bounded after him, cackling madly, knocking over vases and toppling furniture. Spencer darted away. He could hear the sound of Crunchy Toast Muncher's light footfalls pattering behind him. In an instant, he could feel the man's breath on the back of his neck and hear the metallic swish of the ax being thrust at him again. He ducked, narrowly avoiding decapitation as the edge of Crunchy Toast Muncher's ax swung past him and hit an onyx pillar with a loud *clank*. Spencer held his breath and phased through the wall. In that moment, it did not occur to him that he was still on the third floor.

As he darted through the wall, he imagined his feet hit the marble floor. Instead, they hit nothing, treading air stupidly as he screamed and his body plummeted straight down.

Chapter 21:
The Finsveld Adventure

After dropping Spencer off at The Ross Manor, Harriet drove back down the hill and into the city. She dialed Viola's number on the car phone. Though the number keys on her dashboard had been scratched and gouged by The Poltergeist's spiteful rampage, it seemed, they were still functional.

"Hey, girl," Viola's voice greeted her from the car's speaker.

"Hey, Viola," Harriet replied, "Did Finsveld ever bring my purse back? Maybe he left it at your apartment or something?"

"No, I haven't seen him for a while," Viola said.

"Are you sure because um..."

"What?"

Harriet debated with herself about whether or not to tell Viola that she suspected Finsveld of identity theft.

"Did Finsveld ever...steal anything out of your purse, after he poofed it off of you?" Harriet inquired innocently, deciding that it was better not to let Viola know just yet that she suspected Finsveld of treachery.

"No way. Finsveld's a great guy. You know, the other day he bought me the cutest mug. It says 'World's Best Super BFF'. You should have seen him. It was adorable. Yea, Finsveld'd never take advantage of my trust like that," Viola replied a little defensively. There was something dangerous in her voice, something willfully ignorant: a certainty in the goodness of others, which refused to be questioned. Harriet knew better than to pull on that thread.

"Uh...of course," Harriet conceded with a sigh, "So if I wanted to uh...visit him, and ask him for my stuff back...where would his apartment be?"

Viola gave Harriet Finsveld's apartment number. Harriet thanked her for the number and then hung up the phone. She drove until she reached an apartment complex near the edge of the city. It was stout, yellow, and dingy-looking with rickety-looking balconies sticking out from the sides of its many apartments.

Harriet parked her car and entered the apartment complex, walking up to the room number that Viola had indicated on the phone. She considered ripping the door off of its hinges but then, reconsidered. Instead, she knocked.

The door creaked open. Finsveld was standing behind it, his morbidly obese contours filling the space between the wooden door frame in an intimidating way. He was a very tall man. Harriet had not noticed that about him before. He towered over her. If she had not possessed super strength, she might have feared his physical power.

"Do you have my purse?" Harriet asked suspiciously, her eyes narrowing into slits.

Finsveld belched indifferently and replied: "*Yes, Finsveld has your purse.*"

"Can I have it back?"

"*Bitch, if you can find it, you can have it...says Finsveld,*" Finsveld said.

He stepped back and motioned into the apartment. Harriet entered with apprehension, noticing the mustard stains on Finsveld's stretched-to-capacity white T-shirt, and the stench of his unwashed folds.

The apartment emitted a similar foul odor. A narrow path littered with empty soda cans and pizza boxes snaked between piles of clothing nearly tall enough to touch the ceiling. Harriet glanced around the room in amazement, at first, scanning the piles of debris, searching for her purse in the mess. This was very frustrating, however. And she quickly gave up on the endeavor.

"Uh, Finsveld...I had some money in that purse..." Harriet said with annoyance.

"*Yes, Finsveld knows. Finsveld spent the money,*" Finsveld explained, pointing at a large flat screen T.V. and the massive speakers of a high-end stereo system, which sat at the center of a clearing amid a scattering of candy bar wrappers, "Finsveld also bought a lot of stuff at the famous movie prop auction with your credit cards. Finsveld knows the stuff's in here somewhere and will find it....eventually."

"*What?*" Harriet hissed dangerously. Though she already suspected that this was the truth.

"Finsveld thinks it's funny that there's nothing you can do about it. You can beat Finsveld up, but then you'll just be sued for assault. And you can't prove Finsveld did anything. Finsveld can just poof the stuff he bought to another location and you have no proof....hmm.....*Finsveld*."

"I...I just can't deal with this right now..." Harriet muttered with disbelief, shaking her head, attempting to control her mounting blood lust. She could feel the anger welling up in her violent, chemically-altered brain. There was a mad voice yelling inside of her head: "Kill him! *Kill* him! He's a fat, disgusting rat, who shits where he eats and sleeps where he shits! *No one* will miss him! No one! No one! *No one!* Do the world a favor and *snap his neck!*"

Harriet was snapped out of her violent musing as she became aware of the fact that her bra had vanished. Finsveld was now holding it in his piggy hands, eyeing the cup size, attempting to try it on, by experimentally stretching it around his massive frame.

Harriet wrenched the bra out of his hands angrily.

"Give that back!" she yelled indignantly, suddenly aware that under her leather pants; she was no longer wearing underwear.

Finsveld winked and then said: "Finsveld is wearing lady's underwear."

"Agh!" Harriet exclaimed with revulsion, as the image of her underpants, bursting at the seams, stretched to capacity against Finsveld's planet of an ass, forced its way into her mind.

Before he could snatch away any more of her clothing,

she turned and ran from the apartment, screaming: "You won't get away with this, Finsveld!"

Finsveld belched and replied indifferently: "Finsveld already has, bitch."

Chapter 22:
Sobriety

Spencer screamed as he fell straight down. The lawn outside the manor was growing closer by the second, and in a mad attempt to save himself from being crushed by the impact of the fall, he flailed his arms, searching for something to grab onto. While he was doing this, the fingers on one of his hands phased through the stone face of the manor, hooking into the wall. He grabbed on with his other hand, quickly, and then, phased the tips of both of his feet into the wall, steadying himself against it. He breathed a sigh of relief, and then, began climbing down the side of the building as though it were a rock climbing wall, phasing his hands and feet through the solid surface and then re-solidifying them, creating tiny nooks in the stone. As he did this, the wall pressed against his digits harshly, scraping the skin and pushing on the muscles and bone with intense force. Spencer held his breath, knowing that if his limbs went fully solid while they were in the wall, he might lose them.

Spencer moved very quickly toward the ground, dislodged his bloody fingers and toes from the wall, and then, darted away. He ran down the hill, past hedges of white roses and topiary bushes shaped like hundred dollar bills. The weight of the full backpack slapped against him as he ran, chafing his shoulders with its broad straps. Spencer reached the gate to the manor's grounds and phased through it, slowing to a crawl as he ran toward the city.

He limped to the Convenience Mart at the corner of 3rd and Jackson, his half-eaten shoes and raw toes, trailing smears of blood.

"What time is it?" he gasped as he burst through the door, of the Convenience Mart, very grateful that he was not, at that moment, dressed as Death Laser and that the people there were likely to regard him as a regular customer.

"It's two p.m.," the chubby, pockmarked girl behind the

counter informed him.

Spencer collapsed against a wall, stroking his bloody fingers and hyperventilating

"We uh...we don't have bandages here if that's what you're looking for," the girl told him.

"I'm not looking for bandages," Spencer informed her tiredly,"...I'm...I'm...looking for ....this sexy lady in a tight leather outfit...she'll be here around 4..."

"Um...," the girl behind the counter murmured with confused incredulity.

"Yea....I'm just gonna' hang out in the men's room for a couple of hours..." Spencer said tiredly, and then he staggered off to the men's room to do just that.

Harriet arrived at the Convenience Mart around 5 p.m. This was because she had spent the day, first, confronting Finsveld, second, running to the bank to change her account information (and withdraw the 900 dollars that she had left to her name before Finsveld could take it), and third, drinking alone in an empty bar while she moaned to the elderly bartender that her life was shitty. After a point, however, she had to concede that her super resiliency attribute made her impervious to drunkenness.

"...Fuck, I forgot about...*Spencer*," Harriet said to the bartender after a while. She had changed out of her superhuman costume before entering the bar so that she would be regarded as a regular customer. Throughout her life, Harriet's father had always had the good grace to keep the paparazzi far away from her, so she could expect virtually no one to recognize her as a person who had once been extraordinarily rich. Despite the occasional insignificant media coverage, she was not, as her father had once been regarded, a celebrity.

"Who?" the bartender inquired, cleaning a glass with a damp towel.

"This lunatic I know with a super cute butt," Harriet said with a shrug. "I was supposed to meet him in a place...but then I forgot."

"Oh..." the bartender replied passively, assuming that Harriet was drunk, which she was not. She simply did not care enough about the elderly bartender to filter what she said in his presence.

Harriet paid the bartender and then left. She drove to the Convenience Mart in her "scumbag" mobile, parked and then, walked inside.

She spotted Spencer, leaning against a wall of soft drinks, cradling a couple of bloody hands wrapped in toilet paper from the men's room. The second he spotted her, his sullen expression melted into a goofy, lust-drunk grin.

"Harriet!" he greeted her with an undignified degree of delight.

"Hey, Spencer," Harriet replied tiredly, "I guess you don't have anything better to do than follow me around all day, huh?"

"I definitely don't," Spencer confirmed happily, wrapping his arms around her, kissing her neck and nuzzling his face against her hair.

"What the hell happened to your hands?" Harriet remarked as she noticed Spencer's bloody, toilet-paper-wrapped fingers. She touched them with her hands, carefully peeling some of the soggy toilet paper off of them.

"Ow." Spencer winced, flinching as the toilet paper was peeled from his hands in bloody clumps, and then he explained in a tone of nonchalance bordering on bragging: "This is nothing. Pain doesn't even bother me," he smirked and added: "Wait 'till you see what I got for you."

Chapter 23:
The Slaughter

Harriet drove the "scumbag" mobile past tall buildings and crowds of pedestrians. Fora while she drove without a destination, silently pondering what she should do or where she should turn now that she had virtually no money saved to fall back on.

Harriet glanced at Spencer, who was sitting in the passenger seat, a thin layer of translucent toilet paper clung to his bloody fingers grotesquely.

"Are you ok?" Harriet asked him.

Spencer glanced back at her and grinned, far too delighted that she had bothered to ask.

"Are you?" he replied flippantly.

"I asked you first."

"I'm fine," Spencer informed her, "I'm great, actually. Because, right now, I'm with you, baby."

"Excuse me while I pull over and throw up," Harriet groaned.

"Heheh..heh..."

"Finsveld stole my credit cards, and basically everything that I have left," Harriet informed Spencer, "He told me, to my face, that he did it. And that if I try to tell anybody he'll just hide the stuff that he stole and deny it."

"There must be some way you can prove it," Spencer said.

"I don't know..." Harriet exhaled with exhaustion, "I'll have to call my lawyer and see what he has to say about it. Maybe there's something I can do."

Harriet drove to Viola's apartment. She did not know where else to go, and she had never known Viola to refuse a stranger a room, let alone a friend that she had known since high school.

She dialed Viola's number on the car phone again.

"Hello?" Viola's voice said over the car's speaker.

"Yeah, hey, Viola," Harriet said, "I need a place to stay. I have...not that much money left, so I probably shouldn't waste it staying in a hotel every night until I get this all figured out, and probably I shouldn't be breaking in to hotel rooms so..."

"Hey, no problem Harriet," Viola said cheerfully, "I haven't even found a new roommate yet. There's lots of room."

"Thanks, Viola, I really appreciate it. And, I mean, I still have my job so I can pay rent and stuff. Oh, and can my butler stay too?" Harriet asked.

"Sure, no problem. I always wanted a butler for my apartment. It'll be like living in a wacky sitcom," Viola said.

"Thanks, Viola. I appreciate it," Harriet said.

...

Harriet spent the afternoon on the couch, in Viola's living room, pulling the toilet paper off of Spencer's fingers and toes, while the news played on the TV, in the background. The paper clung to his scraped skin in a sheer, difficult-to-remove layer. He winced as she rubbed it off, and then, started roughly spreading Neosporin over the raw portion of his hands.

The buzz of the news lady on the television and Viola in the kitchen, chatting on the phone with Benjamin, melted together into a sea of indistinguishable background noise, which seemed a world away. Harriet's hands moved over Spencer's as she wrapped his fingers tightly in gauze, thinking about Finsveld's revolting apartment; and about the rotting, vulgar smell that emanated from his stolen clothing hoard. The memory of it made Harriet shutter, and again, she wished that Finsveld were dead; that she could somehow kill him and get away with it.

Harriet finished wrapping Spencer's hands. He opened and closed his hands experimentally, testing the strength of her binding. Then, reached out and traced the edge of the circular scar on her shoulder with the tip of his bandaged finger. It was a mark left from the injury that he had inflicted with his laser during their fight at The Ross Manor, back when he was still a villain.

"I'm sorry," he said quietly, touching the circular scar with bandaged hands.

"You better fucking be. Now let me see your feet," Harriet said.

Spencer obeyed, laying back on the couch and putting his bloody feet in Harriet's lap. She removed his ruined shoes and half-eaten socks, then, started picking the toilet paper off of his scraped toes. While she was doing this, Harriet silently pondered whether or not she should tell Viola what Finsveld was up to. On the one hand, Viola was likely to defend Finsveld and disregard anything negative that Harriet had to say about him as pure conjecture. On the other hand, Finsveld might have been stealing from Viola too, and Viola had a right to know. Harriet owed her that much at least.

Viola put down the chorded phone and walked into the living room. Harriet turned her head in Viola's direction, and with Spencer's bloody foot still cradled in her hands, inquired: "Hey, Viola...Did Finsveld ever uh...take anything out of your purse?"

"I told you Harriet. Never," Viola replied.

"Well um...I went to see him today, and he told me....that he's taken everything in my purse and that he's not giving it back."

"I don't think he was being serious, Harriet. He has a strange sense of humor," Viola replied.

"Viola, five hundred thousand dollars disappeared from my bank account and my credit cards are maxed out too," Harriet stated plainly.

Harriet had already told Viola about everything that had happened that day, as well as most of the things that had happened the day before; about The Poltergeist and about The

Jay Walker taking over The Ross Manor. However, she had omitted any mention of her meeting with Finsveld, having predicted that Viola's response to hearing her buddy accused of identity theft would be less than friendly.

"So what are you saying?" Viola muttered with annoyance.

"I'm saying that Finsveld stole my credit cards, and bank cards, and all of the information in my purse, and, also, he's probably been stealing from you and the other members of the team this whole time too. You need to stop trusting him with your wallet," Harriet said.

"How the hell do you know that *Finsveld* took it?" Viola retorted angrily and with uncharacteristic venom. "Maybe The Poltergeist took it. Maybe your scummy, homeless, ex-villain boyfriend took it."

Harriet synched the bandage a little too harshly around Spencer's bloodied toes and he winced, gritting his teeth.

"I know because Finsveld *told me* he took it. That's how I know," Harriet interjected angrily, interrupting Viola's hateful rant with annoyance.

"Well, I bet if I call him right now, he'll tell me that he was just kidding when he said that," Viola argued, "He's not really good at talking to people. You probably just misinterpreted what he said."

"I didn't misinterpret what he said," said Harriet, "He stole my wallet, he's a fat, disgusting, rat and he stole my wallet and..." The dangerous look on Viola's face made Harriet give up on her argument mid-sentence. "And you're probably right...I'm sure it's all just a big misunderstanding. Forget I said anything about it."

"I'll talk to him for you, Harriet," said Viola, "And see what's going on."

"Yeah, ok."

An hour or so passed. Harriet finished wrapping Spencer's injured feet. He snuggled up to her on the couch, kissing her neck and playing with a strand of her dark hair.

Viola sat down in a floral print chair adjacent to the couch where Harriet and Spencer sat, and opened a small bag of pretzels, which she ate one at a time while she watched the TV.

"Want to see what I got for you?" Spencer whispered in Harriet's ear.

"If it's your dick, you can keep it," Harriet said as she watched a square-jawed newsman interview survivors of the recent building collapse. Allegedly, collateral damage caused by a metal bending superhuman's bitter custody dispute against his ex-wife, "I told you, you haven't earned that yet."

"No, I mean, the stuff that I got out of The Ross Manor," Spencer said, indicating the black backpack, which sat on the glass coffee table, between the couch and the TV."

"Oh. Right. Thank you," Harriet said, having, for a moment, forgotten about the backpack. She picked it up off of the table and unzipped it, retrieving a high school yearbook, a music box with a ballerina on it, and a white teddy bear.

"Do you like it?" Spencer asked her expectantly as she watched her pick through the items in the bag and survey them with a silent, ambiguous stare.

"Good job, I guess," Harriet replied with a sigh. None of the items that Spencer had thought to steal back were what Harriet would have chosen for herself, "Though I was hoping never to see this again. I didn't even know I still had it," Harriet said, picking up the pink ballerina music box.

She handed the music box to Viola, who surveyed it with delight. Harriet stopped her before she could twist the metal pin and make the music play, by snatching the thing out of her hands.

"Don't make it play, please," Harriet said, "My mother gave me this when I was a little girl, right before she left my father and fucked off to New York to be with her 20 something, male model boy toy. I haven't seen her since and she only calls, like, once every five years. She didn't even come to my father's funeral, or even show up to claim the stupid necklace he left her."

"I'm sorry, Harriet," Spencer apologized a little disappointedly.

"It's ok, Spencer," Harriet replied, "You didn't know."

Harriet handed the music box back to Viola and said: "If you like that you can have it. I don't really want it anymore."

"Thanks, Harriet, I'll hold onto it in case you ever want it back," Viola replied.

"Then expect to be buried with it. I'm never going to ask for it back," Harriet informed her bluntly, crossing her arms.

"Well, thanks for the present, anyway," Viola said.

"You're welcome."

"Well *um*..." Spencer interjected awkwardly, and with a tone of forced optimism he added, "At least you still have Mr. Bear."

Harriet briefly considered informing Spencer that the bear had been a gift from her ex-boyfriend, Gary, and that, like the music box, looking at it only made her depressed and angry, but she thought better of it. After all, he had hurt himself retrieving it for her. To spare his feelings, she picked the bear up and gave it a forced, pity hug. This seemed to please him, because he smiled at her like she was some kind of an adorable, large-eyed, puppy with a new squeaky toy in its mouth.

"I'll treasure it always," Harriet lied, putting the bear down. Spencer grinned at her, leaning his body into hers, stretching his arms and then draping one around her shoulder.

"Your welcome, baby," he said.

"But don't think this means you can stay here for free," Harriet said, "Because if you think I'm paying your rent for you, you're insane. Tomorrow, you better start looking for a job."

"If my dark princess commands it," Spencer whispered

in Harriet's ear, nibbling playfully at its edge.

"She does," Harriet muttered bluntly, staring at the television screen with gruff indifference. The square-jawed newsman finished his piece and the camera cut to the blond news lady, standing in front of a familiar row of apartments, now swarming with police.

"This just in," the news lady announced, "A 24-year-old autistic man was found murdered in his Propropolous apartment this evening. He was discovered by a neighbor, merely hours ago. Witnesses claim that the body was discovered shortly after Justice Bitch was spotted exiting the premises, visibly enraged."

A photograph of the victim flashed on the screen. It took Harriet a few moments longer than it should have to recognize the face in the photograph as belonging to Finsveld. Viola gasped and covered her mouth, her eyes welling with tears.

"This senseless tragedy has left a community enraged and terrified, but more than anything it's the unusual brutality of this crime that has reawakened a political argument surrounding superhuman population control and settlement regulation," the female newscaster said, "Superhumans using their powers to murder their enemies in terrifying and unusual ways is certainly nothing new but it's the prime suspect in this murder investigation that has got the people talking. Proproplous city's own Justice Bitch, who first rose to fame in the aftermath of the Super Annoyo mass mind control incident, is the primary suspect in this case, as security camera footage has confirmed that she was in the slain man's apartment just hours before the body was discovered."

A clip of the surveillance video from the hallway of Finsveld's apartment building played on the screen. The clip showed Harriet fleeing from Finsveld's apartment, with an expression that was all at once disgusted, terrified, and enraged. One might have easily assumed that she had just murdered him in a fit of passion.

136

Harriet pushed Spencer off of her and stood up, staring down Viola with a look of urgency: "I swear, I didn't kill him."

Viola put a finger over her mouth and murmured: "Shh!"

A stocky policeman was now disclosing details about the brutal and shocking crime scene: "It's a blood bath in there, Susan, and I've seen a lot of strange things too...but never anything like this. The sheer evil of this is just...it's surreal. There's this young guy in there, cut into pieces, with his guts torn open and ripped out. I mean...it looks like he was put in a blender from the shoulders down, and the walls are just covered in his blood. On top of that, somebody crammed a headless doll down his throat. As I said, just surreal. My thoughts and prayers go out to the family, of course."

"The headless doll!" Harriet remarked, remembering the ceramic doll that she had smashed the head off of in the Poltergeist's hotel room, "It was The Poltergeist! The Poltergeist must have killed him!"

Viola stared at the television with a faraway look on her face, still registering this startling rush of surreal information.

"You do believe me, don't you, Viola?" Harriet said.

"Yea, of course I do," Viola replied. She wanted to believe that Harriet was not the killer, she had some doubts, but she disregarded them, dismissed them, and pushed them down, "No I don't believe that you would do something like this...It must have been The Poltergeist."

"You don't think it'll come for us next, do you?" Spencer murmured, his eyes reflecting the glow of the lit television screen.

"Don't you see..." Harriet muttered, "It already has."

"Only an evil, *dominant* woman could have done this," a bystander growled hatefully from the television set. He was an older man with thinning, grey hair, and a harsh, rough voice, "Enough of this PC, liberal bullshit. They need to line up *Justice Bitch* and *everyone like her* and shoot them all *in the head* before they overrun the planet!"

"Turn it off, Viola," Harriet muttered, putting her face in her hands.

Now the female newscaster stood in front of Finsveld's apartment building, speaking with repetitive intensity about the known details of the incident. A crowd had gathered behind her, holding picket signs and chanting: "Justice for Martin Finsveld!"

"Viola, turn it off," Harriet said again.

"Ok, ok," Viola said and she hit the off button on the remote, at long last, silencing the television. The room went dark as the glow of its rectangular screen was extinguished.

Harriet exhaled slowly, glancing back at Viola and Spencer.

"I didn't kill him, you know," she said again.

"It's ok, Harriet. We believe you," Viola said, though she did not sound sure.

"...Yeah..." Spencer said, looking nervous and worried, "I mean, you said it yourself, it had to have been The Poltergeist. And The Poltergeist is probably just some superhuman's alter ego, right? So if we find out who The Poltergeist is...."

"...Then we find Finsveld's killer," Viola confirmed intensely.

Harriet heard her phone ring. She grabbed it quickly off of the glass table by the couch and answered it quickly.

"Hello?"

"Harriet, *It's Gary*. Are you watching the news?"

"Yeah, I saw it," Harriet confirmed.

"After everything I did to keep you from being unmasked in court, this is what you do, *murder a guy*? This shit is just....I can't handle this shit, Harriet!"

"Well, he was a thieving piece of shit anyway, and also *I didn't kill him*!" Harriet shouted back.

"Really, you *didn't* murder him? Is that why you left his apartment, five minutes before they found his mangled body, looking like a deranged psychopath? What the hell's wrong with you, anyway?"

"Oh fuck you, Gary, are you my defense attorney or aren't you?"

Gary sighed and conceded: "Yeah...I guess I am."

"You should know that Finsveld was a thief and that his apartment was filled from the floor to the ceiling with crap that he'd stolen from what was probably like, a thousand different people. Finsveld had a lot of enemies, ok? Not just me," Harriet said.

"Harriet, the apartment was empty," Gary said.

"What?"

"The police found his body in a completely empty apartment. No furniture. No nothing. Don't you see, Harriet. He couldn't have stolen anything. Because he didn't *have* anything."

"You've got to me kidding me..." Harriet muttered, "The Poltergeist must have cleared the apartment somehow...or maybe...Finsveld poofed it away himself before someone came for him? Yeah, that sounds more likely..."

"Harriet, what on earth are you talking about?"

"Just...I don't know....it's complicated," Harriet said. Then, she proceeded to tell Gary about her encounter with The Poltergeist the previous night. Due to her history as Gary's on-again-off-again girlfriend, and the sexual nature of her new allegiance with Spencer, Harriet omitted Spencer's involvement in the event, except to conclude her story with an: "Oh, yeah, and also Spencer was there."

"Spencer?" Gary replied incredulously. "Who's that?"

"My new butler," Harriet replied.

"Huh...and you're sure he didn't have anything to do with it?"

"What, *Spencer*, no way," Harriet said a little defensively.

"Well...you know what they say about butlers and doing crimes," Gary said only half jokingly, "Not that there's any evidence there to suggest that *a man* killed him. Just your fingerprints on the doll that they found shoved down Martin's throat."

"That's...I....I picked up the doll, when I was in The Poltergeist's hotel room," Harriet said.

"What? Why the hell did you do *that*?"

Harriet glanced at Spencer for a moment and then replied: "*Um*...for *fun* I guess?"

"Unless some different evidence comes out of the investigation, I don't even know how I'm supposed to argue that you *didn't* murder him. Any argument other than you murdered him just sounds insane right now," Gary sighed with exasperation.

"Yeah, that inspires real confidence coming from my *defense attorney*," Harriet muttered.

"Oh God, Harriet...I don't know, maybe I'll figure something out. Maybe this poltergeist person will become a person of interest...or maybe this new butler person that you just told me about."

Hearing Gary's voice say this over the phone, Spencer straightened up.

"...You can say that I did it. I'll go to jail for her. I'll take the fall," Spencer blurted out, jumping off of the couch and wrapping his arms around Harriet's shoulder's, resting his chin on the top of her head.

"Is that your *butler*?" Gary's voice murmured incredulously from over the phone. "He sounds really young."

"How young my butler is, is none of your damn business, Gary," Harriet replied bluntly.

"Also, I can't argue that he did the crime unless there's some kind of evidence to support it, and there isn't any right now," Gary said.

"So, then, plant some evidence," Spencer insisted urgently.

"Uh....*yeah*, I don't do that," Gary replied with irritation, barely stopping himself from tacking the word "moron" onto the end of the sentence, "Listen, Harriet, I've got another call coming in. You stop by my office. They're probably going to arrest you as soon as you walk outside of where ever you're staying. When they do, call me, and I'll pay the bail. After that, we should meet Tuesday, around 4 p.m. That's my next opening. And bring that suspicious sounding butler, I'd like to talk to him too."

"Thanks, Gary. I don't know what I'd do without you. See you then."

"Bye, Harriet."

Harriet hung up the phone and put it down on the glass table next to the couch.

"So that was Gary...." Harriet said. She picked up the stuffed bear and stared at it pensively, walking across the room as she did so.

"Yeah, we heard," Viola said.

Harriet exhaled, and turned the bear a few times in her hands as she contemplated: "Well....maybe I don't have anything to worry about...Gary's a really good lawyer."

Chapter 24:
Meanwhile, At Castle Jay

Trauma, who could enter the mind of any human on planet Earth, and who did so randomly as he slept, spent the night thinking about Justice Bitch. The pain of the injury she had inflicted upon him during their last battle permeated his dreams in stabbing, throbbing waves. It disrupted his ability to concentrate on one person's consciousness for very long, and he found himself randomly drifting in and out. First, he was in Justice Bitch's mind, frolicking with a large, man-sized, white teddy bear, as she lay out on the grass, staring at the sun. Then, he was back in his room at The Ross Manor, lying in bed, sweating, with his eyes closed, pinned back down to reality by a shooting pain in his broken arm. Then, he was back in Justice Bitch's mind. She got in his face and screamed: "Get out of here! Go away! *Go away!*" Then, he was back in his room at The Ross Manor.

He rolled onto his back and put a pillow under his broken arm, between his chest and the cast and sling. He closed his eyes, randomly thinking of people that he associated with Justice Bitch. A pale, dark-haired boy stared at Trauma with glowing crimson eyes. He was sobbing and shaking and covered with blood.

"I did a bad thing!" he warbled in a shrill, pre-pubescent voice. "Don't you understand, Ronnie! Mom'll never love me again! She'll never forgive me!"

"Oh Christ, not more of this shit," Trauma muttered shaking his head.

"Shut up, Ronnie! Get out of my room, get out!"

Trauma opened his eyes, groaned, shifted his throbbing broken arm, and then closed his eyes again. A girl from The Sexy Rad Super Pals was on a stage singing karaoke to an audience comprised entirely of what appeared to be clones of the same, morbidly obese young man. "Viola, find The Poltergeist. Avenge our deaths," the audience chanted in unison. "Ooh yeah, and I'll find that Poltergeist! I will a-a-avenge your deaths!" the girl sang back to the audience. Trauma, who now sat in the front row of the audience, stood up and applauded. Of the dreams he had invaded that night, this was the dream that he liked best. Everything here was pink and glowed as though lit internally by fireflies. Yet, still, a twinge of shooting pain in his broken arm dragged him away, and his mental connection to the dream was forcibly broken.

Trauma groaned as he randomly remembered another member of Justice Bitch's superhuman team: Captain Lawsuit. Overcome as he was by pain and a growing tiredness, Trauma found himself sucked into this man's mind. Soon, he was in an office, surrounded by bookshelves. It was late, and shades over the window were drawn. The clock above the desk indicated that it was near midnight. Gary Goldstein (a personal injury lawyer and defense attorney that Trauma had often seen on television, advertising his family's firm) was hunched over the desk with his arms folded over his face.

Trauma nonchalantly walked over to the lawyer and tapped him on his wavy, auburn head. The man sat up, he was wearing large, crooked glasses and his eyes were streaming with tears.

"So, what's wrong with you?" Trauma inquired curiously.

"...I...I don't know what I'm going to do. Harriet thinks I'm a great lawyer....but the truth is that I'm not a great lawyer... my dad was a great lawyer. I'm a *terrible* lawyer!" Gary shouted. His hair was disheveled and his eyes were wild and red from crying, he looked as though he were on the edge of a mental collapse.

"Hey, I thought you were one of the best lawyers around? Aren't you one of the most renowned lawyers in the country?" Trauma said.

"No, you're thinking of my brother, Everett Goldstein. I'm *Gary* Goldstein....Harriet doesn't know it but...I'm not losing clients because of Super Annoyo's smear campaign, I'm losing clients because I lose more than half of my cases! I'm the *worst* Goldstein!"

"Ah, well, don't be so hard on yourself, kid. You can't win them all. This isn't a television show, after all." Trauma interjected politely.

"Shit, *shit*! This is too much! I don't know what I'm doing! Harriet's going to hang!" Gary shouted, grabbing at his wavy auburn hair with both hands, he looked like he was about to have a heart attack.

"You're not acting like yourself, Captian Lawsuit," Trauma mused indifferently, sitting down in the chair, across from where Gary sat, "You're normally so stoic."

"Yeah, so maybe being all calm and collected is just an act! Maybe *this* is who I am on the inside!" Gary shouted, staring at Trauma with bloodshot eyes. His boring red tie was askew.

Trauma grinned evilly. Maybe he could make this work to his advantage.

"Listen, Gary, I'm a therapist, and believe me when I tell you this, because, as a therapist, I can assure you that I know what I'm talking about," Trauma said.

"Ok..."Gary considered cautiously. "I'm listening."

"As a therapist, I have to say, that you are ultimately doomed to fail. You can't help her. You're going to just end up embarrassing yourself," Trauma informed him in a calm, friendly voice.

"Yeah...you're right..."

"I mean, look at you. You're a mess. I mean, I wouldn't want you as a lawyer. Really, when you think about it, it's no wonder that Harriet's always hanging out with that other guy."

"Get out of my head, man. I just want to sleep..."

"No, you need to hear this. You are going to fail. Your old friend, she's going to jail, probably forever," Trauma said.

"Right, so what do I do about it?" Gary muttered back.

"I can't tell you that, Gary. I'm just a therapist. What I can tell you, however, as a Psychiatrist, is that the way you're feeling isn't healthy. From what I can see it's most likely the result of a chemical imbalance in your brain that can be corrected with pills."

Gary straightened up in his chair a bit, swiped the disheveled auburn hair out of his face, adjusted his glasses, and straightened his tie: "So what you're saying is...this...this problem where I can't concentrate on anything because of how worried I am about screwing up...it can all be fix....*with pills*?"

"Having observed you for quite some time, I suspect that you're on the spectrum," Trauma said.

"What spectrum?"

"Doesn't matter. This condition of yours is preventing you from reaching your full potential. I'm your friend, Gary. Trust me. The pills will fix the problem. They'll let you concentrate on this case in a way that will guarantee you a win. You'll be free of your insecurities and your distractions, for the first time in your life, cured of your doubts and your weaknesses."

"Um....I don't know..." Gary murmured in reply. Though a simple and instant solution to the doubt and insecurity, which had plagued him his entire life, would have been liberating beyond imagination, the offer was a bit suspicious (even through the haze of Gary's sleep-induced subconscious vulnerability).

"You try the pills, and if they don't work, you just stop. No pressure. No risk. What have you got to lose?" Trauma postulated with a non-threatening finesse.

"Uh....yeah, thank you...but um....where do I get the pills?" Gary asked uncertainly.

"See my friend, Dr. Meredith, she'll hook you up with what you need."

"What...*who*? Don't bother trying to remember her name. You won't remember it by morning anyway. But that won't matter. I've already implanted the unconscious

---

suggestion. When you see her, you'll know her. So if you feel that you would like to try the medication, this choice will be available to you," Trauma said.

"Ugh..." Gary moaned collapsing back onto his desk and beginning to fall asleep in his dream.

Trauma stood up and cackled, just as a painful twinge shot through his broken arm, and he was forcefully reminded of his intense hatred for Justice Bitch. He cackled and cackled through the pain, imagining as his hated adversary, Justice Bitch, was sentenced to life in prison. Due to his powerful mind-reading abilities, Trauma was aware of the true killer's identity. He could read the thoughts of the killer; disturbing, sadistic dreams of ultimate mastery and horrific mutilation. They plagued him from time to time, attached themselves to his consciousness, like an ad for a horror movie that flashes on the screen momentarily as you are flipping between channels. He understood and respected this killer's motivations, through long hours of observation, learning to marvel at the maniac's exceptional power and intellect. He understood the killer's plan and was proud to increase the likelihood of its success by contributing to it in a way that only he could: By wrecking her already emotionally compromised lawyer with pills, Trauma would assure the downfall of Justice Bitch.

Chapter 25:
A Story about Love, Abandonment,
and Dr. Meredith's Magic Pills

The next day, Harriet received a call from Reynolds Sanderland. At first delighted to hear from her pseudo second father at this emotionally trying time, she picked up the phone, feeling the anxiety of her current predicament slip away, if only for one beautiful, hopeful moment. Reynolds would know what to say. Reynolds would know what to do. Her smile melted slowly, however, as Reynolds spoke. He was behaving so very differently from the way he had before her father's death, so distant; so formal; so removed.

"I'm sorry, but I don't think that I can meet with you for lunch, Harriet," his voice informed her strangely over the phone.

"Oh...well, how about another time, then?" Harriet inquired hopefully.

"I'm very sorry Harriet, but, unfortunately, I am extremely busy at the current time and had to reschedule. I will call you back at my earliest convenience," Reynolds parroted artificially.

"Reynolds wait—"

The call was disconnected. Harriet attempted to dial it again but no one picked up. Feeling a bizarre emptiness, Harriet was possessed by the rare inclination to call her mother. She dialed the number. Predictably, the answering machine picked up.

"Hello, You've reached the cell phone of Kathleen Love," Harriet's mother' informed her in a voice overflowing with perky, girlish elation, "If you can't reach me right now, it's probably because I'm too busy being *beautiful* and *amazing*! Leave a message and I'll be sure to give you a call back when I get a break from modeling with my delicious hubby and living my *fabulous* life! Ciao for now, beautiful!"

Harriet hung up the phone. She did not bother to leave

a message. There was not really a point. Harriet's mother's breaks from her "fabulous life" were usually few and far between.

Harriet put the phone down and walked into the living room. It was dark and empty. It was a Sunday, and the art museum, where Harriet worked as a curator, was closed, so Harriet had nowhere to be. Viola was at her family's costume shop, suiting up customers for the upcoming 4th of July parade. Spencer was out somewhere, supposedly looking for a job.

Harriet changed out of her pajamas and into some cheap clothes from the local Walmart: a plain white T-shirt and a pair of washed-out off-brand jeans. Then, she left the apartment, with no apparent goal in mind.

She was not, as Gary had indicated she would be, immediately arrested. After all, it was Justice Bitch, who had allegedly murdered Martin Finsveld, not Harriet Ross. Still, the media had its suspicions about her secret identity. The suspicious resemblance between Harriet Ross and Justice Bitch was simply too obvious to be overlooked. As Harriet was walking, a square-jawed reporter in a three-piece suit and a bowtie approached her, holding a microphone. He was flanked by an eager camera crew and a Channel 16 news van.

"Harriet Ross," the news reporter addressed her earnestly, "What do you have to say about the victim's parents' assertion that their son, Martin Finsveld, told them that you were Justice Bitch, before he was murdered by her?"

"No comment," Harriet muttered with irritation, walking past the newsman and through his circle of camera crew.

The newsman was persistent. He called behind her: "What do you have to say about the rumors that Death Laser and Justice Bitch have united as Propropolous City's newest villain power couple?"

"No comment." Harriet muttered back. The newsman and his cameras followed her but before he could ask her another question, she was running to the end of the block and ducking behind a dumpster in the alley to get away from him. She crouched down, and cautiously peered out to see if she had lost them.

"Huh...where'd she go?" the newsman murmured, glancing around, expecting to see her on the sidewalk or on the other side of the street, as he turned the blind corner with his trotting camera crew. A man holding a mic at the end of a long metal bar shrugged, and they all retreated to the news van. Harriet watched from her hiding place as the van drove away, and listened as the roar of the van's engine faded into the distance. She then emerged from behind the dumpster, brushing greasy candy wrappers and crushed cigarette butts off of her knees. They left brown stains on the powder blue denim of her off-brand jeans.

She resumed her walk; cautious and forlorn; constantly scanning the area for news trucks with paranoid eyes. She tried to remember the aura of the newsman so that she could recognize him if he tried to sneak up on her again, but it was unremarkable, a bit excited perhaps, but in this aura-confused sea of stressed-out pedestrians, it was hardly a stand-out quality.

Harriet walked for a while, content at that moment, to be alone in her own head.

...

Gary got out of bed, showered, dressed himself in a suit and tie, and then, exited his apartment building. Just as he stepped out of the front door, however, he bumped into a conservatively dressed woman with short, dark hair and large glasses. Upon impact, the woman fell backwards, awkwardly landing on her ankle, as her long, floral patterned skirt flew up around her legs.

"Ah—I'm so sorry, ma'am, let me help you up," Gary sputtered nervously. He grabbed the woman by her hand and helped her to her feet.

"Oh, that's quite ok," the woman said, "Accidents do happen, after all. However, I'm afraid my ankle's a bit twisted up. Would you help me to my office? It's not far from here. Just a few doors down."

"Uh, yeah, of course," Gary agreed.

"Excellent," the woman said.

She leaned on Gary, slinging one arm around his broad shoulders as she pointed to a navy blue door, at the end of the street.

"It's that way," she said.

Gary nodded and walked in the direction that the woman had pointed. She walked along with him, holding onto his shoulders for support. When they got to the short set of cement steps, beneath the blue awning, leading up to the door, the woman hobbled over to the steps, and, holding onto the railing, shakily ascended them. Before entering the building, she turned back toward Gary and said: "Thank you very much Mr..."

"Gary Goldstein," Gary said, completing the unfinished sentence politely for her. "And what's your name?"

The woman extended her hand for Gary to shake.

"I'm Dr. Meredith," she said.

Gary smiled and put his hand in hers, happily shaking it. There was something about this woman's melodic voice and elegant, professional demeanor, which put him at ease.

"Nice to meet you," he said.

"Please," Dr. Meredith said, "Come inside."

"Oh, no, I'm very sorry ma'am but I have to go to work," Gary said, a bit flustered by the bizarre offer.

"Please," the woman said again, opening the door to her office, "I insist."

"Um...ok..."

Dr. Meredith limped into the building, putting her yellow sweater on the coat hanger by the door as she entered. The room inside was painted a dark blue color and had dark-stained molding, as well as a couple of plush chairs and a large, old-fashioned-looking desk. There were watercolor paintings of fish on the walls, and Chinese luck plants lined the box windows.

"So what do you do here?" Gary inquired politely.

"Didn't you read the nameplate on the door? I'm a psychiatrist," Dr. Meredith informed him with a polite smile.

"A psychiatrist, huh?" Gary said, recalling the outlines of a deteriorating memory, perhaps he had heard of a psychiatrist named Dr. Meredith in a dream, "That's weird."

"What's weird about it?"

"Oh, nothing. Never mind," Gary said and he sat down in one of the plush chairs. "I just feel like I've heard of you somewhere before."

"Perhaps you've heard of my father. He's lent his name to a textbook or two," Dr. Meredith said.

"No, I'm not very familiar with your field, I'm afraid," Gary said, "I'm a lawyer."

"*A lawyer*," Dr. Meredith reflected enthusiastically. Then, she leaned close to him and smiled, "Tell me more about that."

...

Harriet walked past a newsstand. A multitude of photographs plastered repeatedly over a wall of tabloids caught her eye. She backtracked, and glanced at the newsstand again.

No. It can't be. I must be imagining it, she thought.

She walked over to the rack of tabloids and stared at it for a moment, at first, struggling to digest what she was looking at. Black and white, night-vision photographs of her making out with Spencer next to Viola's van were printed on the cover of every celebrity magazine. Though in the photographs they were both in costume, this was still more of her private life than Harriet wanted broadcasted for people's entertainment.

"How?" Harriet muttered to herself, picking one of the magazines off of the rack. This one pictured a particularly steamy photograph of Harriet grabbing a fist full of Spencer's ass with both hands while the couple were embraced, locking their lips together with aggressive abandon, "Who even took these pictures?"

Harriet glanced at the headline of the magazine, printed next to the picture in large, bold, pink font. It read: "Death Laser and Justice Bitch? Propropolous' newest villain power couple?!?!"

"Huh..." Harriet muttered, flipping through the magazine curiously. After a moment of contemplation, she shrugged and sighed: "*Well*...I guess I gotta buy it."

She walked over to the man who worked at the newsstand and paid for the magazine.

"Hey, haven't I seen you somewhere before?" the man asked in a conversational tone as he took Harriet's money.

"Nope," Harriet replied bluntly, and then, she turned and walked away with the magazine under her arm.

...

Gary spoke with Dr. Meredith for a long time that day, expressing his growing concerns about the case against Justice Bitch and his own insecurity concerning his youth and lack of experience as a lawyer.

"I've only been practicing for a few years...and the people that I'll be going up against...have done this a thousand times before. I've never even done a murder case before...I mean just personal injury suits. I've only started as a defense attorney recently and only because I'm the only lawyer that will work for her for free. I'm the only lawyer that my friend can afford right now."

"But you are a Harvard man, no?" Dr. Meredith challenged.

"What? How did you know that?" Gary murmured.

He did not recall telling Dr. Meredith where he went to school.

"Television," Dr. Meredith replied with a simple shrug. Still, her off-the-cuff familiarity with his background was a hair unnerving. Gary dismissed the creepy feeling her cold eyes gave him (as they stared with robotic detachment) as paranoia. The glare of reflected light, which illuminated the thick lenses of her large, non-threatening glasses, partially obscured a large portion of her face when her head was tilted in a certain way. So, to some degree, Gary associated the strange detachment in her demeanor to *that*: the frequent wall of glass which flashed between them, obstructing her gaze.

"Uh...right," Gary continued a bit unsurely. There was something surreal about Dr. Meredith's flashing lenses, something strangely hypnotic. She inclined her head toward him and smiled, silently inviting him to continue.

"Um..." Gary murmured, filling the uncomfortable silence with his uncertain voice, "Well...there's not much to say other than that. The client and I, we knew each other as children. We did date on and off again as adults but..."

Gary trailed off. To fill the silence, Dr. Meredith interjected: "I can see that you are working for this client because she means something to you personally. Am I correct in this assumption?"

"Um...yeah, I guess," Gary replied, "She's uh...well I don't know. She's nothing like me actually. Honestly, if I had met her yesterday, I don't think I'd like her very much...but when you've known someone for a long time, I suppose. No matter who it is, you're naturally bound to have some feelings for them."

"An intriguing perspective," Dr. Meredith commented, "So you feel that this person is special to you not because your personalities click, or because she's a particularly likable person, but because you've known each other for a long time?"

"Yea, essentially," Gary replied with a shrug.

"Fascinating," Dr. Meredith commented with a flicker

of enthusiasm.

"The truth is though, I don't like the guy she's seeing now. He's...I don't know. There's something about him that I just don't like," Gary said with some frustration.

"Tell me about it next week. Our hour is up," Dr. Meredith interjected with a smile, "Though, I could honestly speak to you for hours, Gary, and never grow tired of your fascinating tale, I do unfortunately have other clients, who should be arriving shortly. However, I look forward to our time next week."

"Yea," Gary agreed with a grin, "Me too."

"Before you leave, however, I should prescribe you something for your anxiety. Something to help you concentrate. The fact that you've made it so far without this medication is a testament to your incredible intellect. However, I feel that you would be far better off right now, if you had been medicated sooner," Dr. Meredith said. She did a little bit of typing on her computer. Then, informed him: "I've sent a prescription for Redevistraw to your preferred pharmacy. At first, there may be some side effects. But these will go away if you continue to take the drug. Its benefits, I assure you, vastly justify this small sacrifice."

"Uh...thank you," Gary replied. In truth, the promise that his crushing anxiety would be cured, along with the panic attacks, the loss of sleep, and the distressing, recurring fantasies of his inevitable failure, was a comforting one. At that moment, as he stood and shook the shrink's hand, Gary wholeheartedly believed that everything which he disliked about himself: his timidity, his lack of confidence, his feelings of inadequacy, could be cured by Dr. Meredith's magic pills.

Chapter 26:
We Hire High-Risk Superhumans

That day, Spencer returned to the shop with the sign in the window, which read: "We Hire High-risk Superhumans." Almost a year ago, Spencer had come here for an interview on the same day as EAR MUTILATOR's fateful meeting with Headless Records. This was the meeting, which, having occurred in Spencer's absence, would initiate both the band's rise to stardom and Spencer's spiral into a spiteful tirade of Justice-Bitch-obsessed villainy.

Before walking inside, Spencer stared at the sign for a moment, through the glass of the shop front, remembering his silent pledge never to return to this spot; to instead break all of the rules and take what he wanted by force, coercion, and trickery. He sighed, scratching the back of his head with one hand, as he remembered his promise to Harriet that he was "a good guy now." Then, opened the door of the shop and stepped inside.

The bell above the door jingled. The store inside looked like a deli, with a few plain tables and chairs set out by the glass shop front. A few soda and snack machines lined the right wall of this small, plain, interior room. The back and left walls were occupied by a white, L-shaped counter. An older black man wearing a white and red checkered apron stood behind the deli counter. Spencer recognized him as the man he had interviewed with the last time that he was in the shop, Mr. Cassidy.

"Hello," Spencer greeted him, with apprehension. He was not sure if this guy would be too keen on hiring him. After his initial interview, Spencer had never bothered to answer Mr. Cassidy's phone call and find out whether or not he'd gotten the job. Which he supposed, would have been fine if he had not gotten the job, but if he *had* gotten the job, the lack of a response could not have endeared him to Mr. Cassidy.

Mr. Cassidy looked up and glanced Spencer over with a look of recognition, then, acknowledged him: "Hey, you're that laser eyes kid, an't ya?"

"Uh...yeah...that's me."

"Whatever, happened to you, huh?" Mr. Cassidy asked curiously.

"Well...um....I found another job. But now, I uh....I lost that job and I'm having trouble finding another one," Spencer said slouching a bit.

Mr. Cassidy chuckled grimly and then said: "Yea, well, I imagine you are. California law makes hiring superhumans a damn liability for employers. If you blow this place up, I doubt my insurance would even pay for it."

"Oh...ok. Sorry I wasted your time," Spencer said a bit disappointedly. Then, he turned to leave.

"Wait, kid," Mr. Cassidy said, "I didn't put that sign in the window for nothing."

Spencer turned back around.

"My son was Carnage Kill. You know Carnage Kill, right?" Mr. Cassidy asked.

"Sure, wasn't he the villain that could blow up buildings just by thinking about it?" Spencer asked. He remembered the two months during which the news spoke of nothing but Carnage Kill's violent rampages, culminating in the destruction of a massive skyscraper.

"Yeah, after he was arrested in 1994 the government took him to a superhuman high-security resettlement facility in Area-51, haven't seen him since. But he was a good kid, you know, just troubled. It didn't help him that he couldn't find a job. That's why I hire high-risk superhumans," Mr. Cassidy said, "Somebody has to."

"Well...that's awful good of you, sir. I sure could use a job right now," Spencer replied humbly.

Mr. Cassidy smiled and said: "You're in luck kid, the girl who used to work here just got a job, powering a small frozen food company's freezers with her ice breath."

Spencer grinned and said: "Hey, cool. Good for her."

"So, I could use a new waiter. What do you say, kid? Want to be my waiter?"

"Yeah, of course," Spencer said with a grin and a sigh of relief. "Thank you so much, man. I've been walking around all day, thinking that I'd never get a job and I don't want to lose my girl, you know, so..."

"Hey, I get it, kid," Mr. Cassidy said, "Just show up on time and do what you're supposed to. You'll do fine. When do you want to start?"

"Today is good," Spencer replied, shaking Mr. Cassidy's hand.

"Then today it is."

...

Spencer returned to Viola's apartment that evening, after a day of waiting tables in Mr. Cassidy's restaurant. Because of his good looks and genial, laidback demeanor, Spencer got good tips and by the time the restaurant closed, he had acquired a thick stack of cash. Spencer threw off the checkered apron that was his work uniform. It landed on Viola's couch, a few inches away from where she sat.

"I hope you're not planning on leaving that there, butler," Viola said, changing the channel on the TV a few times, and then, turning toward him.

"Uh...no, of course not," Spencer said, scratching the back of his head, "Hey, where's Harriet?"

"I don't know. She wasn't here when I got back from the costume shop. She must have left to do something."

"Oh," Spencer murmured, a little disappointed. He turned in the direction of the TV. The news was on and the woman with the glossy Barbie-blond hair, was standing in front of a smoldering building, holding a microphone and describing a state of mass panic triggered by so many super-powered individuals wreaking havoc upon the city:

"When prisons cannot contain a society comprised entirely of living gods with insurmountable powers, some say, society will collapse and so will the government. That's why a string of laws devised to stop the spread of superhuman genetic traits is being brought before Congress. The Republican House majority is in favor of the bill. However, Democrats are presenting an opposition, citing parts of the bill which, in some instances, will require superhumans to undergo forced sterilization, and resettlement in removed, closely-monitored government outposts. Some argue that these previsions present troubling human rights infringements. Others argue that they are a necessary precaution, and the only practical way to protect the United States government from being overthrown by superhuman anarchist rebels."

The camera cut back to the studio where a news anchor with slicked-back hair and a square jaw announced in a deep voice: "In other news, the president has tweeted: 'Dems and Hillary support mega villains terrorizing this great country. SAD. We are working to deport all super LOSERS to Mexico.'"

"Ugh," Viola muttered. Then, she changed the channel to another news station. A bland, inoffensive car commercial that involved attractive people driving through beautiful landscapes was playing.

Viola turned toward Spencer, who was now leaning over the edge of the floral print chair near the door, staring at the television with unfocused eyes.

"So I saw you playing at the Hornet's Nest with EAR MUTILATOR," Viola said conversationally.

"Yeah, I remember. You were with Harriet when she came backstage right? Before the Super Annoyo thing happened?"

"Well…his viral video was objectively amazing," Viola said.

"It was, right?" Spencer agreed.

"I don't know if it's just the residual effects of the mind control telling me that. But it's kind of a shame that all of the copies of the video were destroyed," Viola said.

"Not necessarily, the government could have a copy of that video somewhere…and like, a team of people studying it and trying to figure out how to weaponize it or something," Spencer said.

"That's uh….a weirdly specific theory," Viola said.

Spencer shrugged: "I dunno. When you can walk through walls sometimes you hear stuff."

"You can walk through walls?"

"Harriet didn't tell you?"

"No," Viola said with a shrug.

"Well, don't tell anyone. It's kind of my secret power. Gives me a tactical advantage," Spencer said.

"Your secret's safe with me," said Viola, grinning.

There was silence for a moment and then Spencer said: "So uh…did Harriet tell you anything else about me?"

"Well if she did, I couldn't tell you. I don't disrespect the sanctity of girl talk, you know," Viola said.

"Yeah, I get that."

The door swung open and Harriet trudged inside.

"Where the hell have you been?" Viola asked.

"Out," Harriet grunted tiredly. She picked a leaf out of her disheveled hair and sighed, "I would have been back sooner but the channel 3 news truck started tailing me and then the channel 12 news truck. Apparently my resemblance to Justice Bitch is lost on no one. Gary says that the fact that I'm still denying that we're the same person protects me legally, though. So at least there's that. I'm going to deny until my last breath. Deny, deny, deny. And if they decide to unmask me, I'll just say that she's an evil clone or that aliens got in their brain and changed their memories or something. I'm denying forever. They can't prove *shit*."

"Yeah!" Spencer agreed doggedly and overenthusiastically.

He bounded over to her and threw his arms around her, locking his lips around hers as though he were afraid they might escape from him. She leaned into him, breathing in his scent.

"You better have gotten a job," she whispered in his ear, quietly. Her tone was both sensuous and threatening, and it made him recoil slightly, a frightened, amorous grin curling his thin lips.

"My goddess," he said, taking her hand in his and kissing it on the knuckle, "You will be pleased to know, that I have obeyed your orders promptly and to precise specification. It is my honor to serve you; to worship your deadly beauty; to be enslaved by it completely. This privilege, my princess, is indescribable bliss."

"Oh blah blah blah, get to the point, dork-face. Did you get a job or didn't you?" Harriet grumbled.

"Heheheheh...heh...yeah, I got it," Spencer said, tracing the lines of her pert lips with his pale index finger. As he did this, she glared at him with annoyance but this only made him grin amorously.

"I got a present for you," Harriet said and she handed Spencer the tabloid that she had purchased earlier that day, the one with them making out on the cover. "You should get a kick out of this."

Spencer took the magazine out of Harriet's hands and glanced at the cover for a moment, grinning as he read the headline.

"So it doesn't bother you at all that the media is billing you as a villain now?" Spencer inquired, flipping through the magazine to locate the article where he and Harriet were featured.

"It's annoying that us being seen together poisoned my reputation instead of improving yours...but I don't know, maybe after this whole murder case thing blows over people will get over themselves," Harriet said.

Viola got between them and grabbed the magazine out

of Spencer's hands.

"Gimme that! I wanna see," she exclaimed, quickly flipping to the featured article and scanning the page with her eyes.

"Oh man...." Viola said, flipping a page of the magazine. "This is trash, Harriet....whoever wrote this really hates you."

Viola handed the magazine back to Harriet. Harriet took the magazine and then stared at it for a moment.

"It's just stupid tabloid shit, anyway," Harriet said. She glanced down at the article and the incendiary phrases; *cold-blooded sociopath, psychotic murderer*, and *the skimpy outfit that launched a thousand villains*, jumped up at her from the page. "I'm sure nobody takes it seriously."

That night, Harriet retired to her room. She laid on the bed for a while, staring at the ceiling. Then, wandered over to the pile of items that Spencer had retrieved from The Ross Manor, still laying on the bedside table. She picked up the high school yearbook and flipped through it. Pictures of attractive, well-groomed students in black and navy blue uniforms littered the pages.

During her high school years, Harriet had attended Ross Academy, a posh boarding school for the children of wealthy aristocrats and entrepreneurs, founded by her great, great grandfather, Nathaniel Ross. Flipping through the pages of the yearbook, Harriet saw breathtaking botanical gardens, a grape vineyard, and an attractively laid out campus brimming with Victorian-style architecture. There was a picture of her and Viola on one of the club pages. In the picture, she and Viola stood grinning in front of a few paintings of fruit produced by Ross Academy students. Viola wore her hair relaxed and tied into an elaborate bun. Her button-down navy-blue sweater and pleated black skirt did little to distract from her overlarge shoes, which hid two sets of partially retracted talons.

Spencer entered the room through the adjacent

bathroom, in a pair of skull-print boxer shorts, his shaggy black hair still moist from the shower. Harriet put the yearbook down on the bedside table and turned toward him.

"You know I never really did thank you properly for getting this stuff for me," Harriet said.

"Heheheh..." Spencer chuckled, hitching up the elastic waistband of his slipping boxers. He walked to the edge of the bed where Harriet was sitting and knelt so that his face was level with her knees and said: "You don't owe me anything, Harriet. The pleasure of serving you is its own reward."

Harriet reached down and mussed Spencer's damp hair affectionately, questioning herself even as she did so. *This is stupid, Harriet,* she thought to herself. *It's stupid to let this low-class shmuck from Poor People Land weasel his way too close.*

Spencer stood up and walked over to a chair in the corner of the room, where his checkered apron from work was sprawled. Then, withdrew a stack of cash from the front pocket. He walked back over to her, and then, handed her the bills, which she took out of his outstretched hands with a look of incredulity.

"For you, my cruel goddess," he said.

"Uh...thanks."

Spencer grinned proudly and then explained: "They're the tips I got waiting on tables today."

"What, for me?"

"It's all for you, my princess," Spencer said. Then, he yawned and stretched before flopping down on the bed.

"Wait, what the hell do you think you're doing?" Harriet muttered.

"Uh...sleeping?"

"There's another guest bedroom, Spencer," Harriet groaned, "You can sleep *there.*"

"Aw, but *Harriet.* I wanna sleep with *you,*" Spencer whined.

"Butlers sleep in the servant's quarters," Harriet said,

shooting him a dangerous look. The expression failed to intimidate Spencer. He merely grinned back in a sedated, lust-drunk way.

"Aw, but *Harriet*," Spencer moaned, embracing her and burying his face between her breasts, "You're too mean...I wanna..."

"Complain about it again and you can sleep on the floor," Harriet growled, pinching the corner of his ear and dragging him off of her breasts by force.

"Ow, *ow!*" Spencer yelped. Harriet released him from her grip and he staggered backward, rubbing his pinkened ear.

"You can sleep in my bed when you've earned that privilege," Harriet said, content that this would put a healthy bit of distance between herself and her ex-nemesis. *This is right, Harriet,* She thought as he stood up and walked toward the exit of the room dejectedly. *It would be stupid to trust him. Absolutely stupid. For all you know, he might have been the one who trashed your car. For all you know, he might have been the one who murdered Finsveld and then framed you with the headless doll.* As he opened the door to leave, however, Harriet observed the contours of Spencer's pale, muscular, back and round, skull-clad bottom. A contradictory thought pestered Harriet with a sudden and voracious argumentative finesse: *But he's super cute and also what if he didn't do that stuff? What if I can trust him?*

Spencer turned back toward her and said: "Goodnight, Harriet. I remain contrite and look forward to serving you in the morning. Uh, hey, can I have a kiss?"

"Uh...sure," Harriet said with a sigh. She walked over to him and they embraced. His aura enveloped her, flashing, confused, and heated. The color rose in his cheeks as her lips brushed against his. She felt the coarse grain of his stubble; his furiously pumping heart against her chest. He leaned into her, resting his chin on the top of her head; clinging to her possessively.

Chapter 27:
Spencer Gets a Break

Time passed. Harriet spent many of her days talking to Gary about the murder case against her. He explained to her that under California law, superhumans could appear in court as their alter ego, and were only unmasked after being found guilty.

"Unlike Super Annoyo's personal injury suit, I'm afraid you will have to make an appearance in court. But as long as you always appear in full costume, no matter how obvious it is that Justice Bitch and Harriet Ross are actually the same person, they can't legally say that it's you. If they try to say that it's you, we can sue them," Gary explained, flipping through a large, thick book on his desk, "Yup, it's all right here...I'm pretty sure..."

Harriet picked up a bottle of pills that was sitting on Gary's desk next to a pile of thick law books.

"What's this?" she asked.

"It's something that Dr. Meredith prescribed. I don't know...it's supposed to make me less nervous or something. But I haven't decided if I want to take it yet. Psychiatric pills kind of freak me out."

As the days went by, the investigation into Finsveld's murder continued and the evidence against Harriet mounted. Gary became increasingly flustered each time a new piece of evidence was found.

"Now they're saying your fingerprints were all over the corpse! Oh god, *oh shit!* How am I supposed to argue that it wasn't you now? Was it aliens, Harriet? Do you have an *identical twin*?" Gary blurted out in frustration. He spent the next three hours pouring over records of every superhuman that the government had ever studied, and lists of every superpower to ever be observed. Convinced that somehow, somewhere, there must have been a superhuman with the ability to copy Harriet's fingerprints, Gary spent a long time, pacing the room, coming up with alternative explanations for the murder, that were, by his own estimation, ridiculous and implausible.

Harriet spent her nights in Viola's apartment. Viola was often absent, either working late at her parent's costume shop or out with her new boyfriend, a handsome podiatrist who had taken an interest in her unusually large shoes. The resulting empty apartment left Harriet with a multitude of opportunities to administer Spencer punishments for his past transgressions against her. Usually, this took the form of her dressing him like a butler and making him clean things, while she hovered over him, occasionally whacking his behind with a crop. Sometimes Spencer would insist that he had not polished the floors thoroughly enough, or that he had neglected to dust a shelf of Viola's bird-themed knickknacks and ask to be given a spanking. Then, Harriet would handcuff him to a chair or a bed or restrain him with ropes, yank the black slacks of his butler uniform down and whack his bare rump with a paddle, a wooden spoon, a hairbrush or a coat hanger until her arm got tired or he blurted out the safe word.

By the time September rolled around Spencer could have boasted without much exaggeration that he had been handcuffed to every piece of furniture in Viola's apartment. He had purchased himself a new guitar and spent many of his evenings, walking around the apartment in his underpants, playing songs on it.

Viola, who was becoming increasingly annoyed by Spencer and Harriet's continued presence in her home muttered with annoyance: "What kind of a butler stands around playing a guitar all day? Shouldn't he be cooking us meals or something?"

Harriet shrugged.

Viola stood up and crossed her arms, glaring at Spencer who was at that moment, dressed like a butler and playing an ambient rock instrumental on his guitar.

"At least Stuart could cook," Viola said, loud enough for Spencer to hear, "You're no kind of butler. Stuart was a better butler than *you*."

"That's true," Harriet agreed nonchalantly, remembering Stuart's filet mignon, lobster, and chocolate layer cake. There were certainly some benefits of being roommates with someone who aspired to be a professional chef that Harriet missed. "Spencer, you suck."

Spencer shrugged off Harriet's comment and kept playing. Secretly, however, this joking sentiment made him jealous and slightly paranoid that Harriet might lose interest in him. *Who is this Stuart character anyway?* Spencer thought, accidentally strumming a wrong note on his guitar. This awkward fumble made an ugly squealing twang that triggered Harriet and Viola to flinch reflexively. *And why is he a better butler than me? Because he can cook? So what? Old ladies can cook. And old ladies* suck, *if they can cook — then so can I.*

The next day, Spencer returned to the restaurant, where his boss, Mr. Cassidy, was stewing a pot of chicken gumbo on a boiler in the back kitchen.

"Hey, Mr. Cassidy," Spencer said, sticking his hands in the pockets of his checkered work apron and slouching.

"Hey, Spencer. How ya doin', kid?" Mr. Cassidy replied, adding a spoonful of red powder to the soup.

"I want to learn how to cook, you know, surprise my girl," Spencer said, "Will you teach me?"

"Sure kid, you want to work in the kitchen?" Mr. Cassidy said, "I'll show you how to make the soup. Your girl's gonna love it. Trust me. Girls love the soup."

Time passed. Harriet spent many of her days at the art museum, hosting guided tours, and exhibitions. Museum visitors, however, had developed an annoying habit of asking her if she was Justice Bitch. A question to which she always replied: "No." Often the visitors were not satisfied by that answer, and began asking her aggressive, accusatory follow-up questions like: "Did you murder Martin Finsveld?" and "Did you murder him because he was autistic? Do you hate autistic people? Are you an ablest bigot?"

Eventually complaints about the fact that Harriet worked there started irritating the Museum Director so much that Harriet was laid off. After that, Harriet spent many of her days sitting around Viola's apartment, watching TV programs about herself, and how evil she allegedly was, while drinking cases of Viola's beer. Due to Harriet's super resiliency attribute, this always failed to make her drunk.

Around the same time, Spencer started working in the kitchen at Cassidy's, where he learned to make different kinds of soups, sandwiches, and pies. The menu at the restaurant was a simple one and contained a limited number of rotating selections, to keep products fresh and service fast. Every morning, Spencer got to work early and helped Mr. Cassidy bake the pies and pastries that sat out on the L-shaped counter, under glass. Every evening, to prove that he was worthy of being Harriet's butler, and fully committed to playing the role convincingly, he came back to Viola's apartment and prepared a meal for his two roommates. Usually, this consisted of one of the simple entrees from the restaurant: salmon, steak, or potato dumplings, and a pie. The cherry pie was the most popular at Cassidy's restaurant, so he often made that one. He also acquired a habit of standing back as the girls ate, sometimes playing classical guitar in the background.

After losing her job at the art museum, Harriet became progressively more and more depressed. She drank a lot without hope of ever becoming drunk and sat on the couch, watching infomercials all night instead of sleeping. Plagued by elaborate nightmares about the murder trial ending in disaster, Harriet could not help but constantly anticipate a life in prison, and she withdrew into herself, mentally attempting to snap the bonds which tied her to other people, before they could be snapped by circumstances beyond her control.

Spencer responded to this behavior by making a show of presenting her with the majority of his minimum-wage income each week, bowing before her, kissing the knuckles of each of her hands, and saying something like: "A woman as pretty as you shouldn't work, anyway. She should be taken care of."

Time passed. Viola spent many of her evenings with The Sexy Rad Super Pals, tailing minor villains, who were known for littering, committing egregious parking violations, and/or being a general public nuisance. Harriet stopped attending Sexy Rad Super Pals meetings due to the harassment from strangers she always endured about her suspected connection to the gruesome and highly sensationalized Martin Finsveld murder case. Spencer stopped attending Sexy Rad Super Pals meetings the second that Harriet announced that she was no longer participating in them.

To replenish her quickly deflating team, Viola recruited two new superhumans: Fartnado and Magic Socks. In the basement of the costume shop, she introduced the two to Benjamin and Lilly.

"This is Fartnado," Viola said, pointing to a man in blue and white spandex. He wore a brown cape and a cowl, which covered his face and scalp completely.

Fartnado waved to Benjamin and Lilly who sat on the floor in different colored beanbag chairs, staring up at him with disinterested expressions that implied that they were not impressed.

"So what do you, like, kill people with the smell of your farts or something?" Benjamin postulated casually.

"No, they're just regular smelling farts. What's super about them is the wind speeds, they can reach over 300 kilometers. That's higher than a category 5 hurricane, in case you need the point of reference. You know, to appreciate just how impressive they are."

"And this is Magic Socks," Viola said, introducing a

regular looking guy with a cheap plastic Mardi Gras mask on. He was skinny, his hair was overlong, and he wore a pair of big glasses over the mask.

"Magic Socks, show them your socks," Viola instructed.

Magic Socks hitched up both of his pant legs, revealing a pair of long socks. The left sock was purple with white polka dots and the right sock was mustard yellow with black stripes. Magic Socks stood there in silence and did not say anything about the socks. He did not have to. The socks were, by everyone's estimation, impressive enough to justify this man's continued presence on the team.

Time passed. Having surmised a number of possible arguments that he could use in Harriet's defense, Gary paced his office, attempting to decide which of his arguments was the most plausible.

"You were cloned by an evil scientist and the clone did the murder?" Gary postulated, picking one of the fancy pens off of his desk and clicking it nervously.

"Eh...what else you got?" Harriet replied. She had Spencer with her that day and he stood next to the chair where she was sitting, with his hands folded and dressed like a butler. Gary had insisted that Spencer was a suspicious character and that it would be smart to question him about the events of Finsveld's murder.

"Aliens did it," Gary proposed experimentally.

"Yeah, I like that one," Spencer interjected sarcastically.

"Wasn't talking to you," Gary muttered, "Harriet?"

"He's right it's stupid," Harriet confirmed.

"Not as stupid as you think, Harriet. Juries *hate* aliens," Gary said.

"Are we talking space aliens or foreigner aliens?" Harriet asked.

"Space aliens," Gary said, very seriously, "You know green skin, giant heads. They ride around in flying saucers. Juries *hate* them."

"She said it was stupid. Can we move this along

already?" Spencer interjected.

"Again, I wasn't talking to you," Gary muttered angrily, glaring at Spencer.

Spencer glared back, and straightened his bowtie in a manner that was somehow threatening, before refolding his hands and regaining his previous acquiescent pose.

"You were being mind controlled?" Gary proposed.

"My super resiliency attribute makes me impervious to mind control, remember? Everybody knows that because of the Super Annoyo thing," Harriet replied dismissively.

"Right. A duplicate Harriet from an alternate reality emerged through a portal, ducked into this world just long enough to kill Finsveld, and then, was disintegrated by the resulting time paradox," Gary theorized.

"I don't know. Maybe?" Harriet replied. Spencer leaned close to her and whispered something in her ear, triggering the woman to unleash a snorting laugh. Gary glared over the desk at Spencer like he wanted to stab the other man through the neck with the pen that he was holding.

"A shape-shifter took your form?" Gary offered.

"That could be it. Is that all you've got?" Harriet inquired.

"That was all I could think of," Gary answered with a shrug, noticing with annoyance that Spencer seemed to have grown bored of the conversation. Spencer's hands wandered down to the edge of Gary's desk and started messing with the pens and highlighters in a clear glass pen holder, containing several subdivisions.

"Don't touch my pens. I have them organized," Gary snapped, sounding very tired and extremely annoyed. He massaged his aching forehead with both hands as Spencer defiantly continued to do what he was doing.

"Oh noo...I'm touching the pens..." Spencer muttered tauntingly, and then purposely moved some of the pens around in the glass holder.

"Spencer, don't touch Gary's pens," Harriet ordered

bluntly.

Spencer retreated, folding his hands again and regaining his servile pose: "Sorry, Ma'am. I promise that I will respect the sanctity of Gary's stupid pens."

"You better," Harriet said.

"Ok," Gary sighed tiredly, adjusting his glasses and smoothing back his wavy, auburn hair, "So, the hearing starts tomorrow. I recommend we practice what you're going to say when you're cross-examined."

"Alright," Harriet agreed.

"Are you or have you ever been Justice Bitch?" Gary asked.

"No," Harriet replied simply.

The questions went on like that for a while and Harriet answered them all calmly, having a simple and blunt response prepared for everyone. When she stumbled or drew a blank, she and Gary repeated the question and devised a better response for it.

That night, as Spencer was driving Harriet back to Viola's apartment, the streets were crowded with cars and the sidewalks were thick with pedestrians. Neon lights raced by. A flying saucer hovered in the distance.

"...Hey, can you not be an asshole to Gary. He's kind of doing me a big favor by representing me in this case, ok," Harriet said with a sigh.

"So what. I'm sure there are tons of lawyers that would like to make themselves a name by representing you in court," Spencer said, failing to mask the jealousy in his voice, "So what's so special about *this* guy?"

"That's uh...that's hard to explain. Gary and I...we have history."

"Yeah, I figured."

"Anyway, I don't much appreciate your disrespectful *tone*. It's not your place to ask me why my friends are who they are or about why I do anything *ever*. You're my butler. I tell you to do things and you shut up and obey me." Harriet said, "So be nice to Gary, ok? That's an order."

"All of this because I ridiculed his stupid, idiotic, retarded ideas and touched his dumb rich guy fancy pens," Spencer brooded, running a red light and then turning left onto 9th street.

"Spencer do you *want* to get smacked?" Harriet threatened angrily.

"*Yes.* But that's not the point."

"So, what *is* the point? Why'd you have to antagonize him by messing with the stuff on his desk? I told you he's doing me a favor."

"I couldn't help myself. He's such a stuck-up prick," Spencer said and then he continued to imitate Gary's voice poorly and insultingly: "Ooh, don't touch my pens with your dirty peasant fingers...I have them *organized*."

Harriet laughed.

"Well, how was I supposed to know that he'd *freak out* if I touched the pens on his desk?" Spencer said, still sounding cross.

"Well, he is kind of weird about things being organized. He's always been a little OCD, I think," Harriet said.

"Well, as long as we can both agree that he sucks and also that you like me better than him," Spencer said, running another red light, and swerving to avoid an oncoming truck that had meandered into his reckless path.

"Watch the fucking road, Spencer."

"Ugh...sorry."

"Can we stop this fighting about the pens bullshit? There's a real chance that I might go to jail for a very long time," Harriet groaned.

"Yeah, with that spazzed-out dumb-ass defending you, I'd say there is," Spencer said.

"Hey, I told you to be nice to Gary."

"What? He's not even here! I can't even talk about how much he sucks when he's not around?"

"No. Now be a good butler, and *obey me*," Harriet

ordered angrily. It irritated her greatly that Spencer seemed to have gotten over his initial fear of her and that her threats to slap him no longer made him blush or get flustered.

Spencer pulled into the parking garage outside of Viola's apartment.

"Right," he conceded with some reluctance, "Sorry, ma'am."

That night, around midnight, Harriet wandered into Spencer's room, in a bathrobe. She had crazy, bloodshot eyes, and disheveled hair that had bits of popcorn stuck in it. She hesitated for a moment, hovering creepily over his sleeping form. Then, jerked him awake and shoved him out of bed. He stumbled to his feet, confused and naked except for a pair of black boxer shorts with red elastic. She was creepily silent, as he followed her into the kitchen, asking her worried, confused questions about what she was going to do to him, which she ignored. She sat him in a kitchen chair and then tied his arms and legs to the chair with rope, before she roughly stuffed a ball gag into his mouth. Then, Harriet pulled Spencer's shorts down and grabbed his penis as though it were the on-off switch of a doomsday device and she only had a fraction of a second left to disarm it. Spencer moaned and jerked in her direction, his voice muffled by the gag.

Well, Harriet thought, as she drew her hands roughly up and down the shaft of Spencer's growing erection. *Since I might go to jail soon, this could be my last chance to ride that dick.*

Harriet flung her bathrobe open and Spencer grinned slightly despite the presence of the gag that was forcing his mouth open. This was the first time that she had allowed him to behold her full-frontal nudity. She slipped a condom on him and then climbed onto his lap; embracing him; lowering herself slowly onto his erect shaft. He bucked instinctively but the rope binding his arms and legs to the chair was tied so tightly that he could hardly move at all. Harriet did all of the moving, slow, careful, and deliberate. She teased him by sliding down and then up again, going still when his eyes

173

pleaded with her to keep moving. She could not have gone faster if she had wanted too, however, the danger of cracking his pelvis if she thrust too hard was ever present in her mind, even as she increased the speed of her careful bouncing, the weight of her powerful thighs left a deep, unintentional bruising around his waist as she wrapped them tightly around him. She steadied herself against his muscular chest with both hands, arching her back as a long moan of orgasmic pleasure escaped her lips. Then, there was a loud *crack* and the chair collapsed underneath of them.

Now, Spencer lay on the floor, staring up at Harriet as she straddled him. He phased through the gag and it rolled onto the floor. He gasped for air and pleaded: "...Please don't stop. It feels good."

Harriet leaned close and kissed him to shut him up. As she did this, the length of his member slid inside of her. Pinned underneath of her weight he bucked in her direction, phasing through the ropes that bound his arms, and slipping his hands underneath of her bathrobe. He cupped her breasts in his palms, gripping them and moving them around slightly. The sensation this act triggered was pleasurable, so Harriet allowed it to continue as he grinded against her. She bounced and her disheveled hair flopped around her shoulders, as with an enormous amount of effort and strength, he struggled beneath her supernatural weight.

"How the hell did you escape again?" Harriet whispered sensually.

"Guess I'm just slippery," Spencer replied, grinning. He panted with exhaustion and pushed her breasts in a circular motion. Then, moved his hands down her muscular stomach and toward her crotch, brushing the upper edge of her vagina with both of his index fingers. Harriet moaned and leaned into him. Spencer thrust forward and ejaculated with an undignified gasp.

Harriet returned to her room, collapsed onto the bed, and for the first time in a long time, slept well.

Chapter 28:
Justice Bitch V. The State of California

The next day, Harriet woke up with Spencer curled up next to her, hugging her stomach with one muscular arm. She lay on her back and stared at the white, metal, drop ceiling tiles, listening to him snore. The clock on the wall ticked slowly and Harriet realized with a spasm of panic, that the trial was set to start soon.

She pulled his arm off of her and stumbled toward the bathroom.

"Noooo..." he moaned groggily as she left the bed, "Come back..."

Harriet showered and then dressed in a conservative, knee-length skirt, and a white, button-down blouse. She brushed and dried her hair. She chose a set of sensible, flat dress shoes over heeled shoes, because if she cracked her heels while she was stomping around in the presence of the jury, it was sure to shed suspicion on her. Then, she put on a pair of large, dark-rimmed glasses that were nonprescription and merely for show. Gary had insisted that juries look upon suspects who wear glasses more favorably.

On the first day of the trial, Gary greeted Harriet outside of the courthouse.

"Don't worry, Harriet," Gary said and he added jokingly, "Remember juries hate aliens."

"Oh great, you're going with the aliens one?" Harriet muttered sarcastically.

Gary smiled and shook his head: "No, I have a better idea."

"Christ, I hope you do," Harriet said.

"There's one minority group that juries hate even more than aliens."

"Oh yeah? And what's that?"

"Superhumans."

That day, Gary's plan for Harriet's defense was made

clear. His opponent argued the more straight forward conclusion (that Harriet was the killer), and this was certainly a less challenging perspective to justify. Harriet's fingerprints were on the headless doll. The headless doll was shoved down the dead man's throat. Justice Bitch was seen on the security camera, outside of Finsveld's apartment, looking so angry that she might have just killed someone, mere *minutes* before the corpse was discovered.

The reason for Gary's comment about how juries hate superhumans became clear to Harriet quickly. During his rebuttal, Gary pointed out the fact that Martin Finsveld was a registered superhuman with the ability to transport and relocate items with his mind. The media frenzy that had followed Finsveld's murder had played heavily on the fact that Finsveld had been diagnosed in early life as mildly autistic. The fact that he had been a superhuman, however, was not well known.

In the days to come, the prosecutor played the surveillance tape of Justice Bitch exiting Finsveld's apartment and displayed gruesome crime scene photos, which made the jury gasp. Finsveld's seeping, shredded torso, and cold, terrified, bulging eyes made one of the older ladies on the jury sob and shut her eyes. The chilling murder weapon, a creepy, headless doll, splattered with Finsveld's blood, was displayed on a table while a forensic scientist explained in excruciatingly boring detail why Harriet certainly was the murderer and why it was simply *idiotic* to believe anything other than that.

Gary challenged this argument by disclosing Finsveld's criminal record. Finsveld had a history of using his superpower for pickpocketing and shoplifting that was well documented. Gary called a mall cop to the stand who could attest to this fact:

"Yeah, he used to creep around the mall, poofing brassieres off all the pretty girls," The mall cop told the jury, he was a fat, dumpy-looking guy with a scruffy beard and heavy New York accent, "A lot of times, a bunch a' TVs and big ticket items would disappear. Then, the next day, you'd see him in the parking lot trying to sell them out the back of his van...That's why he moved to California, I think, because people were starting to figure out what he was doing. He was banned from the mall after a while. I remember that."

"And also from two other malls in the area," Gary interjected informatively.

"Yeah, that sounds about right. Me and the guy who worked at the cheese cart, we used to joke that Finsveld must have moved to California 'cause he stole somthin' from somebody who wanted to kill him and they were after him. Man, I must have met a dozen people that wanted that kid dead. I wouldn't have been surprised if that's why he moved so far away. He wanted to put as much distance between himself and those people as possible...What can I say? I guess in the end one of those people must have traveled the distance to come find him. I can't say it surprised me much. Really, he had it coming."

"Objection. That's hearsay and conjecture. There's no evidence of that," the prosecutor accused loudly.

Days passed. The trial continued. Finsveld's grieving mother was brought to the stand, where she wept and described for the audience the emotional devastation she endured after having lost her 24-year-old son. She then implored the jury to convict, in the name of decency and to protect themselves and their families from the menace that was Justice Bitch.

When the grieving mother was finished speaking and returned to her seat, the prosecutor stood.

"I call Harriet Ross to the stand," the prosecutor proclaimed with confidence. Today the prosecutor wore a brown three-piece suit, and his grey hair was plastered back with a little too much gel.

Harriet walked up to the stand.

"Are you now or have you ever been Justice Bitch," the lawyer asked.

"No," Harriet replied simply.

"What is your opinion about this sadistic, cold-blooded killer who has the gall to call herself a hero?"

"I have no strong opinions about her one way or the other," Harriet replied without emotion. Gary had warned her that the prosecutor might try to goad her into confessing that she was Justice Bitch by getting her to argue against him and verbally defend herself.

"So you have no strong opinions about a person...who would do something...like *this*?" The prosecutor challenged, holding up an enlarged crime photo for the jury's consideration. The photo was of Finsveld's disembodied head and shoulders, laying on an autopsy table. Shredded organs and grotesque runners of mutilated flesh trailed out from the bottom of the pale, partial cadaver.

"Whoever did that was certainly a heinous person," Harriet responded, "But I have no strong feelings about Justice Bitch one way or the other because you haven't convinced me yet....beyond a reasonable doubt, that she did it. Finsveld had a lot of enemies."

"Oh really?" the prosecutor challenged, "Like *who*?"

"As my lawyer has said...." Harriet stumbled awkwardly, "He has said...he uh...he said...that you have to wait for him to tell you about that..."

Days passed. The trial continued. Gary called an old gypsy woman to the stand who told the jury that Finsveld had used his superpowers to steal her wallet and credit cards. The police report of the incident was presented as evidence.

"Objection!" the prosecutor interjected, "This incident is unrelated to the case. The victim's past criminal record should have no bearing on the decision of the jury."

As the trial continued, Harriet could not help but feel that Gary's argument was starting to fall apart. The fact that she had to constantly run to the bathroom to switch between her Harriet Ross and Justice Bitch personas was not helping either. The other lawyer seemed to notice that as he employed a strategy of calling Harriet Ross to the stand right before Justice Bitch, and then, Justice Bitch right before Harriet Ross. This made her lie about the two not being the same person apparent. Though he was not legally allowed to point out that the two were the same person, until after the accused was found guilty, the prosecutor understood that this tactic made Harriet appear deceitful and dishonest to the jury.

"I call Justice Bitch to the stand!" the prosecutor proclaimed.

Harriet, who was at that point, already at the stand, dressed in civilian clothes, turned to the judge and said quickly: "Your honor, I have to go to the bathroom."

"I'll allow it," the judge said with a frustrated groan. This was the third time that Harriet had asked to be excused that day and the fourth time that Justice Bitch had asked to be excused.

Harriet exited the courtroom, went into the bathroom, and changed into her Justice Bitch costume. Then, quickly returned to the courtroom and walked up to the stand.

"It is I, Justice Bitch," Harriet said, "I have returned from the bathroom."

"Oh joy," the judge groaned.

"Justice Bitch," the prosecutor questioned, "On the night of Finsveld's murder, why did you go to Finsveld's apartment?"

"He was an acquaintance from The Sexy Rad Super Pals, who used to use his powers to help us change into our costumes fast," Harriet explained.

"Bet you could have used that now," the prosecutor joked and the audience, delighted by his insightful witticism, broke into a spasm of laughter. The prosecutor grinned confidently, sensing that he currently held the jury in the palm of his hand. "And what happened during that visit, before you left?"

"Well...he used to poof us into our costumes before a patrol. And the night before, he'd done that, you know, and never bothered to give my clothes and purse back. So, the next day, I went to his apartment and asked him to give my clothes and purse back," Harriet said.

"Did he give your clothes and purse back?" the prosecutor asked.

"No," Harriet replied simply.

"And why not?"

"He'd said he'd lost them...in his clothing hoard," Harriet replied.

"And that made you angry?" the prosecutor goaded.

"Yes. But I didn't kill him. I just yelled at him...I think...and then I left," Harriet said.

Days passed. The trial continued. The conclusion of Super Annoyo's lawsuit came at an inconvenient time, while Gary was preoccupied with the murder case, and constantly pouring over information about Finsveld's past and about superhumans who might have had the ability to frame Harriet for murder. The courts ruled in favor of Super Annoyo and ordered Justice Bitch to pay 20 thousand dollars for his hospital bills and psychological damages. Rather than tell Harriet about this, Gary just paid Super Annoyo the 20 thousand dollars himself.

"Good news," he told Harriet before the trial one day, "The Super Annoyo lawsuit concluded."

"Really? How'd it go?" Harriet asked.

"I won," Gary lied.

"Oh my God. That's such a relief," Harriet sighed, "You really are a really good lawyer, aren't you?"

"Uh....yeah..." Gary lied, sounding slightly ashamed of himself.

That night, Gary returned to his apartment, and feeling disgusted by his own incompetence, grabbed the bottle of pills that Dr. Meredith had prescribed off of the kitchen counter. He unscrewed the lid with shaking hands, extracted a couple of pills from the bottle and quickly swallowed them, hoping that they would help him concentrate; hoping that they would alleviate some of the crushing panic that was constantly distracting him from the task at hand. This was the first time that he had taken the pills, and he did not feel their effect right away.

As the trial progressed, Green Lightning and Ghost Girl were called to the stand to talk about their known connection to both Finsveld and Justice Bitch. The security guard from Finsveld's apartment complex made an appearance also as the prosecutor called him to the stand to describe the shock and horror that he experienced the first time he saw the surveillance video. Gary grew more sedate and withdrawn with every passing day. He became sluggish, drowsy, and easily distracted. Until it got to the point where Harriet had to constantly shake him awake and remind him where he was.

The prosecutor, today dressed in a navy blue three-piece suit, stood before the court.

"I call Hawkette to the stand!" the prosecutor announced.

Viola walked up to the stand and adjusted the microphone to her height, clearing her throat.

"What do you have to say about the relationship between Martin Finsveld and Justice Bitch?"

"I believe they got along, you know," Viola replied, "They were never really close friends, but they worked together and there was never any kind of a conflict between them, as far as I'm aware. Though she did get mad when he held onto her purse that one time...."

Gary shut his eyes and surrendered to his fatigue. Harriet, who was sitting next to him, put her hand on his shoulder and shook him awake.

"What the hell are you doing?" Harriet whispered urgently.

"Um...I don't know," Gary droned back groggily.

"Stop falling asleep in court. You're making yourself look like a buffoon," Harriet whispered furiously.

"Right..." Gary murmured back detachedly.

181

"And if my lawyer's a buffoon. Then, that doesn't reflect well on me at all, does it?" Harriet whispered furiously.

"Ok," Gary confirmed without really being aware of what Harriet was saying. Halfway through her sentence, he had gotten distracted by a fly that was buzzing around the judge's head. It circled left, circled right, landed on the judge's gavel, and then, took off again. Gary could not help but follow it with his eyes as it buzzed down past Viola and into the audience, where it landed again on Finsveld's father's fat neck flap. Viola kept talking. Gary found it impossible to pay attention to her. The fly was too fascinating, with its bulging eyes and multitude of tiny black legs. He watched as Finsveld's father swatted the fly away and it whizzed into the air, landing on one of the fluorescent ceiling lamps overhead.

"I call Spencer Tuckerson to the stand!" the prosecutor announced with a confident smirk.

Spencer shuffled nervously up to the stand. He was wearing the only suit that he currently owned, the butler outfit with the black button-down vest and bowtie.

"Are you now or have you ever been Death Laser," the prosecutor asked him.

"Um...No," Spencer replied nervously, glancing at his feet and then back at the courtroom full of people. He glanced at Harriet, who stared back with cold brown eyes that growled silently: "Don't fuck this up."

"Uh...but, I mean, I did work with him," Spencer continued, nervously tugging at his bowtie with his index finger.

"You were the CEO of the Ross Foundation for a while, is that right?" the prosecutor asked.

"Yea, that's right."

"And during that time, did you meet Justice Bitch?"

"Uh...yes...I mean *no,*" Spencer corrected himself quickly.

Spencer continued to talk. Gary found it difficult to pay attention to what the other man was saying. There was a bird, sitting in a nest outside of one of the court room's tall windows. It flapped its wings and took off. The resulting bird-less branch was somehow just as fascinating.

"I mean...no wait that's not what I meant. I mean she's a real radical babe...just like...probably too cool to go for a guy like me. My boss though, Death Laser, he was really into her...and I mean, like, why wouldn't he be? Have you seen Justice Bitch? She's gorgeous and *so* cool."

"He's babbling," Harriet hissed angrily in Gary's ear, "You have to do something. Shut him up."

"Uh...what?" Gary murmured, only vaguely aware of what was going on and far too distracted by the fascinating branch outside the window to really pay attention to what she was saying.

"Yes, the rumor that Justice Bitch and Death Laser had a relationship of a sexual nature is a popular one in the tabloids," the prosecutor said, "As someone who worked closely with Death Laser, running The Ross Foundation and Headless Records, can you confirm for us whether or not this is true."

"Say you don't know," Harriet quietly muttered to herself, "Say you don't know, idiot."

"Uh..." Spencer hesitated, unsure of how he should answer, "...Yes?"

Taking this admission as further evidence of Justice Bitch's corrupted character, the audience gasped. Death Laser was a notorious villain. He and his henchman were responsible for billions of dollars worth of destruction to the city and multiple civilian deaths. Therefore, anyone who would willingly align themselves with him must have been just as depraved.

"But it's not what you think...I heard a rumor that he's reformed," Spencer finished lamely, attempting damage control without avail. The disgusted looks on the people in the courtroom told him plainly that they were not about to buy it.

"You see," the prosecutor said, "Justice Bitch is no hero. In fact, it is very possible that she is in league with villains!"

Gary stood up and intervened: "That's conjecture. And bears no connection to the Finsveld murder case! Whether or not the jury approves of Justice Bitch's personal life, should not affect their ruling."

That night, Spencer stepped into Harriet's room and bowed before her, wearing a penitent frown.

"I'm sorry I fucked up today," he said, "...I guess I just panicked and said more than I should have."

"Yeah, you think?" Harriet muttered angrily, "If I didn't know any better, I'd say you *wanted* them to convict me. Not that it matters, anyway. Everyone already suspected that shit because of paparazzi."

"Still, you should probably punish me," Spencer said.

"Honestly, Spencer, I'm too fucking exhausted right now," Harriet muttered collapsing onto the bed.

Spencer picked up her hand and kissed her knuckle.

"Please, my cruel princess, my goddess, my angel from hell," he said, "Punish me for disappointing you. Otherwise I'll feel terrible."

"Ugh...I don't know...." Harriet grumbled tiredly, "I guess drop and give me twenty pushups."

"I can do fifty," Spencer replied dutifully. Then he proceeded to drop to the floor and do fifty pushups, counting them as he went.

"One...two...three....four....." he counted. Harriet closed her eyes and listened to the sound of his voice as she lay there. She was too tired to do anything but lay awake and anticipate growing old in a maximum-security prison.

"Five...six...seven...eight....."

Harriet sat up and stared out the window at the city skyline. The sun was sinking low over the horizon and the sky was purple. Most of the curtains were drawn on the apartment building across the street and many of its small windows were lit so that they resembled glowing yellow squares.

"Twenty...twenty-one...twenty-two...."

Harriet glanced down at Spencer who was still on the floor doing rampant pushups. He had discarded his shirt and vest, which now lay in a crumpled pile at the corner of the room. His muscular arms and back glistened slightly from sweat. The skull tattoo on his right bicep stared at Harriet and Harriet stared back.

Should I tell Spencer I'll miss him, Harriet wondered. *No, I better not. It'll go to his head.*

"Thirty-five.....thirty-six.....thirty-seven....thirty-eight.....thirty-nine....forty...."

Harriet watched the man as he moved, committing the contours of his body to memory the best she could. She fully expected a guy as good-looking as him to move on fast after she was sentenced to a life in prison.

"Forty-eight...forty-nine," Spencer counted, between deep breaths as he continued to do pushups.

"Spencer?"

"Yeah?" Spencer said, doing the last pushup, and then, rolling onto his back and staring up at her from the floor.

"How old are you, anyway?" Harriet asked, though she had some idea. She had seen his age printed in magazines and knew that he was about five years younger than herself.

"Twenty," Spencer replied simply and then as a kind of joke he added: "And a half."

"You're still really young...and probably you're destined to go on to bigger and better things. Don't ruin your life waiting for me after I go to prison," Harriet said with a sigh.

"There's no way I'm going to let you go to prison," Spencer said a little too confidently and matter-of-factly for Harriet's taste. It was as though, perhaps, he had something nefarious planned for anyone who dared to put Harriet in prison. "But hey...I've got a present for you. I was going to wait for your birthday...but that'll be a couple of weeks after the trial ends...so um....just in case something goes wrong. I decided to get it early," Spencer grinned and he stood up, walking over to where she sat, at the edge of the bed, "Want to guess what it is?"

"Is it your dick?"

"Heheheheh.....Nope. But that's yours too if you want it."

"Jewelry? Is it Jewelry?" Harriet asked hopefully.

"Even better."

"Oh boy."

Spencer pointed to his left bicep and grinned. Harriet noticed a tattoo there that had not been there before, and her mouth fell open in a look of confused incredulity.

"When you own something, it helps to put your name on it," Spencer said indicating the new tattoo. It was a red heart containing the name "Harriet" in black cursive letters.

"Huh... Harriet murmured in disbelief, "That's uh...that's not a temporary tattoo is it?"

Spencer flexed his bicep and invited her to grab his arm.

"Touch it, babe. It's permanent," he bragged.

...

Days passed. The trial concluded and the jury began its deliberation. That day, Gary arrived in court with his jacket turned inside-out and his shirt on backwards, clearly intoxicated. He was slurring his words badly, and struggled to keep his dilated, glazed-over eyes open when he delivered the recap of his final argument, which even Harriet had to admit, sounded nowhere near as convincing as the argument against her.

After court was dismissed, Harriet pulled Gary aside on the steps outside of the courthouse and shouted: "Gary, *what the fuck*?"

"Huh....what?" Gary slurred in response as she shook

his shoulders with both hands, shooting him a psychotic, sadistic look, that really wasn't helping her look more innocent in front of the jury as they exited the building.

"You were supposed to protect me! Why are you acting all drugged up? Why is your fucking shirt on backwards?"

"Is it...*backwards*?" Gary slurred back, then he looked down at his own chest and touched his shirt, "Oh...where'd the buttons go...."

"I can't believe I thought that you were a really good lawyer. You're a horrible lawyer! You're the worst lawyer I've ever seen!" Harriet shouted, getting in Gary's face. He did not respond to the aggressive gesture, except to blink indifferently.

"I....I'm sorry Harriet...I'm....I'm on the spectrum..."

"What spectrum?" Harriet demanded, "What does that even mean?"

"How should I know? I'm on the spectrum," Gary replied with a shrug.

That night, Harriet lay awake in bed. Spencer crawled under the covers next to her, and draped an arm over her, holding her tightly against him. Feeling his breath against her neck, Harriet closed her eyes and pretended to be asleep.

"Are you ok?" he whispered quietly.

"Perfect," Harriet muttered back, annoyed that he had asked the question, "Go back to sleep."

"In my experience, people who are afraid to appear vulnerable are the most vulnerable people of all," Spencer said. It was not lost on Harriet that this statement was meant as commentary about her.

"Really, I'm fine," Harriet said with some frustration.

"Of course you are, indestructible, bulletproof Harriet Ross...you know, they say that the radiation doesn't change you...that it only amplifies what's already there...but I don't think that's entirely true. I think sometimes it makes you the opposite of what you were...like it can sense what you really wish you were and give it to you," Spencer said.

"That's ridiculous."

"No, I don't think it is. That's why I think it made you strong...because deep down you're really not strong. Strong is just what you wanted to be," Spencer said.

"You know, right now, you're being a really naughty butler," Harriet said annoyed by Spencer's comment.

"Does it bother you that I see through your bullshit?" Spencer inquired frankly.

"Yes," Harriet admitted.

"Heheheh...." Spencer chuckled.

"Stop giggling. It's not funny," Harriet muttered.

"Heheheh....It's funny because you're probably one of the most insecure people I know."

"I *am not*," Harriet defended herself lamely, and by doing so accidentally lending further credence to his point.

Spencer was quiet for a while as he lay next to her, stroking her hair. She turned away from him to hide her worried face as a wave of panic about the impending verdict washed over her.

"Hey, it's ok to feel....whatever way that you really feel. There's nobody here but me and my purpose is to serve you..." Spencer paused to sigh deeply and trace the edge of her ear with his fingertip. "That's why I'll let you hurt me if it'll make you feel good. I can take it and besides...I'm tired of being selfish. I want to live for someone else.....for you, my cruel princess. You might be made of the strongest diamond or the most delicate glass...but that doesn't matter at all, does it?....I am nothing and you are everything," Spencer whispered quietly, kissing the back of Harriet's head.

"You're not nothing, Spencer," Harriet said with some affection that she could not quite restrain.

"No, really I am. Those trashy tabloids say that your 'skimpy costume spawned a thousand villains' but even though that's probably not true....you did spawn at least one. Without Justice Bitch, there is no Death Laser."

The room was quiet for a moment. An owl outside the

window hooted softly.

"...I'm so afraid," Harriet admitted, leaning into him; giving in to her urge to feel safe in his arms.

"Don't be," said Spencer very seriously, running a hand affectionately through her dark hair, "I'm going to protect you"

Chapter 29:
The Verdict

On the final day of the jury's deliberation, Harriet felt as though her heart were being crushed flat beneath a large, heavy brick. Mad from stress-imposed sleep deprivation and her superpower-induced forced sobriety, she threw down her empty beer can in disgust.

Harriet's wild, greasy, black hair was sprinkled with neon orange snack food cheese dust and she wore her ugliest pajamas (a frumpy pink and white striped flannel set from the bargain bin at the flea market) as she crept into the bathroom where Spencer was showering. He was singing and his pitch-perfect baritone reverberated off of the moss green tiles, which enveloped the walls of the bathroom. The mirror above the sink was fogged over. Beads of precipitation clung to the tiles and brownish floral shower curtain.

Harriet stood there and listened to him sing for a while, staring at his silhouette through the shower curtain, with hungry, blood-shot eyes. His voice was soothing to her, not because of its disciplined melodic perfection but because she had learned to associate it with the slavish servitude of a man hell-bent on procuring for her, anything and everything that she demanded.

The second Spencer pulled back the shower curtain and stepped out onto the tile, Harriet was on him. She got behind him and wrapped her arms around his waist, grabbing his penis with both hands. Now her flannel-clad crotch was pressed against his naked, warm, and deeply bruised rump, as she masturbated him with her left hand and gripped the head of his shaft with her right hand, preventing his release.

"Don't fucking cum," she whispered dangerously in his ear, as he arched his back and bucked involuntarily, moaning from reactive pleasure.

She drew her hand up and down his shaft quickly, holding to the tight.

"Auaahh....oh man, Harriet....I've really gotta'...."

"Don't fucking do it," she warned him dangerously. He flailed in her grip gasping and screwing up his face. She massaged him for a bit longer and then deciding that she had deprived him of the pleasure for long enough, she released his tip, allowing him to ejaculate. He turned toward her and started nuzzling and kissing her neck, inching his hands slowly under the elastic band of her frumpy, pink and white striped flannel pants. She smirked as she felt his broad fingertips begin to brush her clitoris lightly. He mirrored the expression before kissing her on the mouth, flicking the tip of his tongue briefly between her lips.

Then, he grinned at her and said: "There's orange crap in your hair. How do you do that? Throw the nachos on your head?"

"Wouldn't you like to know."

Spencer grabbed a towel from the rack above the toilet and started drying himself off. When he was done, he walked back over to her and picked a piece of neon orange gunk out of her disheveled hair. Then he said: "You enjoy your shower, my cruel princess. I'm going to go about my butlerly duties of laying out your clothes and making breakfast."

"Good. Don't screw it up, "Harriet said, removing her flannel top and throwing it on the ground.

"Heheheheh...heh..." Spencer chuckled as he exited the bathroom. Harriet watched him leave with morose, bloodshot eyes, staring at him until the second that he was out of sight.

The door snapped shut. She disrobed and showered. Then, exited the bathroom, wrapped in a white towel. There were some folded clothes laid out for her on the edge of a freshly made bed. She walked over to them and unfolded them, noticing as she did so that Spencer had selected comfortable clothes for her: a pair of jeans, a lacey black top, and sneakers. It was far from the formal attire that she would have chosen for herself in this situation. Yet, when she thought about it, the restrictive heels and suit jackets that she had worn to the trial up until this point no longer seemed necessary. The next time the jury saw her, they would already have made their decision. The jury had seen her fancy clothes already and judged her for them. They had made their decision. There was no reason to be contentious of her appearance any longer, she figured. She might as well be comfortable.

Harriet dressed and tied her hair up in a ponytail. She walked through the next part of the day in a haze, interacting with other people on autopilot, while her brain screamed again and again: "This is the end. *This is the end.*" She made her obligatory appearance as Harriet Ross before the trial, assured people that she was not Justice Bitch, and corrected the fucked-up, incorrectly buttoned buttons on Gary's shirt, while he stood there like a zombie, barely able to keep his eyes open. Then, she went into the restroom and changed into her Justice Bitch costume. After all, it was Justice Bitch on trial, not Harriet Ross, and if she were found guilty, the judge would unmask her in ceremonial fashion.

The trial started again, for what would be the last time. The closing arguments were read. Firstly, the defense attorney's argument that another superhuman must have killed Finsveld and framed Justice Bitch. Then, the prosecutor's more likely and believable position that Justice Bitch was guilty. After this, the jury adjourned to deliberate the case. An hour or so passed and they all sat in silence. Harriet watched the clock on the wall, and her heart pounded in her chest. Then, the judge appeared to read the jury's verdict. Grim-faced and detached, he addressed the courtroom. Harriet sat in the front row, glancing around nervously, looking for Spencer. She could not find him anywhere. Perhaps he had not bothered to show up at all.

The judge's lips moved. Harriet could not bring herself to listen to him. His mouth made noises that she knew were words but they felt a thousand miles away. That was until he uttered the final words of his statement:

"Finds the defendant....guilty of murder in the first degree and sentences her to life in prison without the eligibility of parole."

The judges' voice burst through Harriet's detached haze with sharp, surreal, and jarring clarity. Finsveld's mother gasped her appreciation for the verdict and a couple of people in the audience applauded.

It was then that the lights went out. People shouted and fumbled in the dark. Confused and frightened by the sudden and jarring change.

"Heheheheh...." a sinister chuckle echoed throughout the room as though broadcast over a loudspeaker.

The judge shouted. There were some noises on the stand that sounded like a confused and violent struggle; knuckles hitting face; the elderly judge gasping as though the wind had just been knocked out of him. In the next instant, Harriet felt a man slip his arms around her. Then, he put his mouth close to her ear and whispered in a familiar voice: "Pretend like you're scared, ok?"

Now, Harriet understood what was going on. She let herself be led toward the stand. The lights flickered back on. Now, Spencer stood behind the stand dressed as Death Laser, holding Harriet close to his chest, like a hostage. The judge lay hogtied on the floor, with a strip of duct tape over his mouth.

"Did you really think you'd seen the last of me? *Death Laser?*" Spencer announced, addressing the courtroom. His brows drew taunt and his eyes began to glow crimson, "Stay where you are! Come any closer and I'll blow your heads off."

Gary staggered toward the stand and shouted in a disoriented voice, distorted by drug-induced fatigue: "What do you want? Just...just let her go, just tell me what it is and you can have it..."

"People of this courtroom, spread the word!" Spencer announced, ignoring Gary's plea for Harriet's release, "I have Justice Bitch and I will only release her for *ten billion dollars!*

Tell Reynolds Sanderland, tell Kathleen Love, tell all of the billionaires in California that might be interested in seeing her returned alive! Tell them that if I don't get my money in three days, I will *kill* the girl!"

Harriet let out a fake scream and pretended to struggle. Spencer put a hand over her mouth and pulled her closer to him, so that the back of her head was pressed tightly against his black leather-clad chest.

A man sitting near the back of the courtroom stood up and called Spencer's bluff:

"Hey, this is *bullshit*! Everybody knows that Justice Bitch has super strength! She could get away from you anytime she wanted to!"

"*Uh*...you don't know that! What if I have more powers than you know about? What if I have, like, the strength of ten thousand men or something! You don't know what kind of powers I have!" Spencer argued back, sounding annoyed and a little defensive.

Police sirens could be heard in the distance. The sound of them made the crimson lights in Spencer's eyes fade to brown as an involuntary wave of panic twisted his expression. He took Harriet by the hand and ran toward the side of the room, blasting a hole in the brick wall with a pair of crimson lasers and then darting through it. Harriet ran a few steps behind him, pretending to be dragged. She dropped the act the second they had escaped the courtroom and Spencer dropped her hand.

"Car...need a car..." he murmured in a panic, trotting around the courthouse parking lot and glancing at all of the locked cars. The distant police sirens were growing louder.

A man in his forties with silver hair and a grey suit walked quickly past them and toward what was presumably his car: a black SUV with chrome hubcaps and tinted windows. The man withdrew a ring of keys from his pocket, selected one, and hastily attempted to unlock the driver's-side door. Spencer darted up to him and snatched the keys out of his hand, then, phased through the car door, hastily jammed the key in the ignition, and peeled out of the parking space. He drove the black SUV up to the place where Harriet was standing, and unlocked the doors. The police sirens were getting louder. Harriet pulled the passenger's-side door open and jumped in the passenger seat. She glanced over at Spencer, who was sweating and breathing hard. He slammed his foot on the gas pedal and the car shot forward, over a patch of grass and raised cement. Then, he sped down the street, weaving between speeding cars and past various stop signs and red lights.

"This is..." Harriet murmured with disorientation as she watched the city buildings, cars, and pedestrians streak by. She felt as though she had just been swept away by a sudden and supernatural tide, "What just....what's happening?"

"We're going to make it. I know it," Spencer assured her, despite sounding unsure himself, "We just have to get as far away from here as possible, "They'll never find us"

"You had this planned all along, didn't you?" Harriet said, watching a fleet of speeding, flashing police cars approach in the review mirror.

"Uh...'planned' might be too strong a word," Spencer confessed nervously, as he glanced at the speeding police cars in the review mirror, "It's just...I couldn't...I'm a villain, ok? And villains...we don't let the things that we want slip away so easily."

"What are you babbling about?"

"Harriet, I...I don't *know* if you killed him or not. I mean...I know you say that you *didn't* kill him...but, *honestly*, if you *did* kill him, I definitely wouldn't care, like at all. It doesn't change a thing," Spencer said as he swerved left, narrowly avoiding being run down by an oncoming truck.

"I didn't kill him, you know," Harriet said.

"I *don't* know," Spencer replied as he swerved left, narrowly avoiding being run off the road by one of the speeding cop cars, "But like I said, it doesn't matter."

Spencer swerved to avoid another cop car that was attempting to run him off of the road and hit a telephone pole. The screech of crushing metal as the car ground to a halt filled Harriet's ears. The noise rang for a moment and then faded slowly to silence.

"Come out of the car with your hands up!" one of the policemen shouted. Harriet could see a wall of police in the rearview mirror, crouching behind the doors of their police cars, and aiming their guns in her direction.

Spencer obeyed the instructions, emerging slowly from the car with his hands up. Harriet did the same.

Spencer kept his hands up and started walking toward Harriet.

"Hey, what are you doing? Stop that! Stop that right now, or I'll shoot!" one of the police officers shouted.

Spencer grabbed Harriet by the arm and started running. She ran with him and pretended to be pulled. The fleet of police officers pelted them with a hail of gunfire but the bullets phased through Spencer, and bounced off of Harriet like harmless nerf balls. Spencer ran toward a nearby office building. Harriet ran after him, gunfire ringing in her ears.

Spencer reached the office building, which looked closed or abandoned. The parking lot was empty and the front door was locked. He phased through the front door and unlocked it, then, let Harriet in. She darted inside. He locked the door behind her, panting hard.

"So, what the hell are we supposed to do now?" Harriet said.

"I don't know."

"There's a lot of rooms in here...and the place seems to be empty....maybe it's being renovated...or something," Harriet mused, "Maybe if we hid in one of the rooms...they wouldn't find us. No...they'd just send dogs. Right. This is stupid. You should have just let them arrest me, Spencer. Then at least you could have had a life. Now, you've doomed yourself along with me."

"I was a wanted man, anyway," Spencer said, as they started moving down one of the hallways. There were cops outside, trying to kick in the door. The slamming noise and rattling of the door frame made Harriet and Spencer break into a sprint. They turned left and darted up a flight of steps.

"Yeah, but now they've got you," Harriet said.

"Nah. They haven't got me. They'll never get me. There's not a prison that could hold me...well, uh....at least I hope there's not..." Spencer said, scratching the back of his head nervously.

Harriet and Spencer ran down another hallway, turned right, and darted into an empty room. It was a large room filled with unoccupied cubicles.

"I think...maybe...this is a good place to hide," Spencer said.

"Sure, why not?" Harriet agreed.

The husky voice of a winded police officer came over the loudspeaker from outside: "Exit the premises immediately! This building is scheduled for demolition in one hour! And you have both been marked as a Boss Class threat to national security, that gives me the legal right to terminate your lives in the event of a confrontation!"

"Shit," Harriet muttered and she crouched down and hid in one of the cubicles farthest from the entrance of the room, "Now, they're going to try to kill us."

"They already tried, remember? The bullets?" Spencer said, crouching down and sitting on the floor next to her, inside of the cubicle, "They'll get tired of trying eventually."

"Or they'll succeed," Harriet said.

"This building is scheduled for demolition!" the police officer boomed from the loudspeaker outside of the building, "And you may have proved that you're bulletproof but that doesn't necessarily mean that you're *explosion* proof! If you're not out of that building in one hour, the demolition will go ahead as planned and you will *die*! So give up and come out with your hands up!"

"Fuck that guy. I ain't givin' up shit," Spencer said.

"Yeah, but, Spencer, what if we *die* in the explosion?" Harriet said with a hint of incredulity.

"They're not going to blow the building up. That's a bluff," Spencer said.

"Yeah, but what if it's not?" Harriet contradicted, "I mean, my life was kind of over anyway because of the prison thing, but you still had something to live for."

"I've given my life in service to you, my cruel princess," Spencer said, taking her hand in his, "It would be my honor to die in the line of duty....and besides, we're not going to die. Your super strength will protect you, and I can just hold my breath and let the explosion phase right through me when it happens."

"I guess there's a chance that will work," Harriet confirmed, "And as an added bonus they might assume that it killed us, making it much easier to get out of town."

"See," Spencer said, grinning, "It's going to work out."

It was then that Trauma's voice invaded both of their minds with furious incredulity: "What, *no*! That wasn't supposed to happen! You were both supposed to die! Here I've been waiting for you to die during this entire chase and....just, just forget it you scumbag motherfuckers might be a Boss Class threat to national security, but guess whose a *God Class* threat to national security? *Me*. And guess whose within my range of mental influence. *You*."

"Get out of my head, Trauma. If I see your fucking stupid face around here, I swear, I'll break your *other* arm!" Harriet shouted.

"Tsk, tsk, Ms. Ross. You should be more polite to God Class villains, otherwise....your little butler might not be in the state to hold his breath when that explosion happens."

"Where are you?" Harriet shouted angrily.

"Just outside, Ms. Ross. I've taken a little interest in your personal life, you see. I think someone with problems like yours could really use professional help, butler boy doubly so. He's a *real* head case. But that's ok. I am a therapist, after all. I can help him. I can help both of you."

"Get out of here! Get out of my head! I don't want *your help*! *We* don't want your help! Do you hear me?" Harriet shouted, standing up, as though to confront an invisible phantom.

"Harriet...who are you talking to?" Spencer murmured, sounding concerned.

"It's...." Harriet murmured, turning toward Spencer, but before her mouth could utter the word "Trauma" Spencer had collapsed onto the floor, twitching. His fingers flailed as though he were having a seizure and his eyelids slid shut, flickering every so often.

Harriet watched in helpless horror as Spencer's twitching subsided and he grew still, slumping against the back of the cubicle. Then, he curled into the fetal position and began sobbing loudly. Tears ran down his cringing face in streams. He whimpered and gasped for air between fits of undignified bawling.

"What the fuck did you do to him!" Harriet shouted. She heard Trauma cackling in her head and then his voice faded slowly to silence. Now Harriet was alone in a room, with a sobbing man, who was likely trapped in some kind of a vivid flashback. Harriet crouched down and observed Spencer's huddled, weeping body with concern. The man's dream-like state would certainly stop him from holding his breath when the building got demolished. If she did not do something to wake him up, he would certainly die.

"No...*no*....I'm soorry....just kill me! I deserve to die!" Spencer murmured pitifully between rattling sobs.

Not knowing what else to do, Harriet wrapped her arms around him and hugged his quivering body while he cried. This might have been a mistake, because as the skin on her arms, brushed against his, she felt her consciousness flicker and fade. Harriet collapsed, twitching and flailing her limbs, as she entered a dream-like state. Then, her body went still and her consciousness was forcibly dragged into Spencer's vivid flashback.

Chapter 30:
Spencer's Tragic Backstory

Harriet opened her eyes. She was in what looked like a middle-class suburb. The place contained a street lined on both sides with small, square houses. There were a pair of sidewalks on either side of the street, adorned with rows of tall, leafy trees.

Where's Spencer? I've got to wake him up before the building we're in gets demolished, Harriet thought as she glanced around at what looked like a deserted suburb. She spotted a pair of small, dark-haired boys walking down the sidewalk to her left. She ran up to them.

"Spencer? Spencer...is one of those kids you? You've got to wake up, Spencer!" Harriet shouted.

The boys ignored her and kept walking. She tried to get in front of them and impede their path but they walked right through her as though she were made of smoke.

"Whatever, Ronnie. I'm definitely going to win the talent show this year," said one of the dark-haired boys, the taller and, presumably, the older of the two.

"Yeah, I don't think so. Everyone knows your magic tricks suck, Spencer," Ronnie said.

"Oh yeah," said Spencer in a squeaky, prepubescent voice. He removed a length of rope from one of the pockets of his book bag, then, tied it around one of his fingers. "Well...does *this* suck?"

Spencer pulled on the rope and the loose knot untied itself, slipping off of his finger.

"Uh, *yeah*," Ronnie confirmed, "That's not even a trick. You just tied a rope around your finger and then untied it again."

"It is *so* a trick, Ronnie!" Spencer retorted angrily, "I'm going to be a great escape artist just like that guy on the TV who was handcuffed in that fish tank full of sharks but then instead he ended up sitting in the audience and was also dry somehow."

"Yeah, how are you going to do that?" Ronnie said.

"Well..." Spencer said, grinning, "Don't tell anybody this...but there's a Ross Foundation chemical plant near here. You know...that grey building next to the Pilot's Pizza?"

"Yeah."

"It's filled with this radioactive green stuff that's supposed to give people superpowers or something," said Spencer, "And they leave the door in the back, by the dumpsters, unlocked."

"Oooh, you're not supposed to go in there!"

"Shut up, Ronnie! I'm going in there. I'm going to swim in the radiation and be a great escape artist and no one's going to stop me. Not even you, you little turd!"

"If you go in there, I'm telling dad!"

"Go ahead, tell him. Rat me out. I don't care."

"Spencer," Harriet interjected hopelessly. "Can we stop this flashback bullshit now? You're about to get blown up, if you don't come back to reality soon."

The boys kept walking and ignored her. The memory sped up like a videotape on fast forward. Then, Harriet was thrust into a new scene. She blinked and glanced around. This was the inside of a chemical plant. Steel vats full of bubbling green liquid surrounded her. The walls were covered with metal tubes in some places, and, in other places, stacked high with metal barrels. The 10-year-old Spencer opened a door in the back and nonchalantly walked in. Evidently, this place was not well guarded.

Spencer walked to the edge of one of the vats in the floor, closed his eyes, and jumped in. He swam a few awkward laps, struggling against the thick goo as he moved, and then, pulled himself out of the vat again, spitting a mouth full of green liquid out onto the floor. His clothes and hair were slick with the foul substance but he grinned and wiped the slime off of his face with the back of his hand. Then, he knelt to retrieve something from his dry backpack, which lay on the floor, by the vat of chemicals.

"Ladies and gentlemen, how will he escape?" Spencer squeaked in his prepubescent voice. He withdrew a pair of handcuffs from the front pocket of his backpack, then, secured one of the cuffs experimentally to his right wrist. He held his breath, concentrating hard, and then, pulled on the handcuff. It phased right through his wrist and clattered onto the floor.

"Heheheheh...*wow*," Spencer chuckled, delighted that his plan to become a great escape artist instantaneously seemed to have worked. He held his breath and phased through the radioactive slime that still clung to him. It fell into a green pile on the floor and he was left completely clean, smirking as he retrieved his backpack, before exiting The Ross Foundation Chemical Plant just as nonchalantly as he had entered it.

The memory sped up. Harriet watched as Spencer walked home. The sky was dark. He returned to a little house in the suburb that Harriet had seen previously. It was on the corner of an intersection and had a red door. Its aluminum siding was tan and its shingles were brown. Christmas lights were hung over the awning on the front porch.

Spencer phased through the front door. Harriet ripped the door off of its hinges and followed him inside. Again, her actions went completely ignored.

A man who looked like the adult Spencer but with a potbelly, graying hair, and an extra twenty years or so hung on his face was standing in the living room. Harriet assumed correctly that this man must have been Spencer's father.

"Where the hell have you been, Spencer?" the man confronted Spencer angrily. There was a string of Christmas lights on the wall behind his head and a Christmas tree covered in tinsel, candy canes, and twinkling lights to his direct left.

"Nowhere," Spencer lied.

"Ronnie told me you went to The Ross Foundation

Chemical Plant," Spencer's father said in a harsh, accusatory voice.

"I didn't go to the freaking chemical plant, ok?" Spencer muttered back angrily. His brows drew taunt and his large, brown eyes, started to glow crimson.

"Did you mess with those chemicals, Spencer? Because your mother and I are fed up with you and all of your *bad behavior*! Here you're leaving the house at night and wandering around, *breaking* into buildings! And now you come home with glowing eyes and smelling like shit and orange juice, just like that fucking Ross Foundation plant they had to build here! That goddamn, billionaire-loving Republican governor had to shove in our neighborhood! But you couldn't just leave it alone! No, *no*! Why would you leave it alone? Why would you care about all of the times that I told you to leave that chemical plant *alone*! I can't take it anymore, Spencer! You're driving me *insane*!" Spencer's father yelled.

"Stop yelling at me!"

"Well, you can forget about going to that talent show!" Spencer's father yelled. "Unless it's to go to school, you're not leaving the house again for another month!"

"Shut up!" Spencer yelled angrily. Then, a pair of crimson laser beams shot out of his eyes and hit his father in the chest, slicing a large, bloody hole through his torso. The man choked and gasped, falling to his knees and spitting up blood. He clutched at the gaping wound in his chest, and then, shuttered and collapsed backwards onto the floor.

"No!" Spencer yelled, tears running down his young face as he ran toward his father. "*No!* Don't die! D-don't die!"

Spencer's little hands tried to shove the loose intestines back into his father's gaping torso wound. His father gasped and gargled his own blood, his eyes bulging with agony and mortal terror.

"Please....don't die....*d-don't die*....I'm soory!" Spencer bawled. His little hands were covered in blood now. He covered his cringing face with them as he sobbed.

A dark-haired woman with a plump, pregnant belly, appeared at the top of the steps and let out an ear-slicing scream. She was wearing a pink flannel nightgown and a pair of pink, fuzzy house slippers. Harriet assumed correctly that this must have been Spencer's mother.

"Oh my *God!*" Spencer's mother shrieked, "Howard? *Howard!*"

The woman screamed again and ran up to the man who lay dead and mutilated on the floor. She got down next to the dead man on the floor and wrapped his limp, blood-drenched body in her arms, trembling with grief-stricken sobs.

"I...I'm sorry, Mommy...." Spencer sniffled. He reached out to try to touch her arm but she recoiled from his touch.

"Spencer, what have you done!" she screamed, "Don't come near me! Don't you ever try to touch me again!"

"...Mommy..." Spencer sniffled reaching out to try and hug his mother.

"No! Get away from me, you *evil* little....little *thing*! I don't ever want to look at you again!"

Spencer withdrew from his mother and wept. Ronnie appeared at the top of the steps, his little face white from terror.

"D...Daddy?" the little boy stuttered.

"Ok, that is enough!" Harriet shouted angrily, "Trauma, where ever you are you better stop this shit right now! Do you hear me? I will find you and I will break every bone in your body if you don't stop this shit right now!"

"Mommy, what's wrong with D-daddy," Ronnie stuttered, tears streaming down his small face.

"Your brother *killed* him!" Spencer's mother howled.

Harriet got between the sobbing, 10-year-old Spencer and his mother. She seized the small boy by his shoulders and shouted: "Spencer you have to wake up! This is all some shit that must have happened like ten years ago! Right now, you're in a building that's about to be demolished, and if you don't regain consciousness soon, you're going to get blown up in to a million pieces! Do you hear me, Spencer? Do you understand?"

Harriet could hear her own voice becoming higher and higher pitched as she spoke, almost as though, with each breath, she were inhaling more and more helium out of a balloon. It took her a moment to realize that this was because her mental projection had, for some reason, devolved into a child.

She saw that her hands were tiny now; that the sleeves of her dress were puffy, and had a floral print, like something that her mother would have made her wear when she was young.

10-year-old Spencer looked at Harriet, noticing her in the flashback for the first time since her appearance: "....*Harriet*?"

"Yes, that's good! It's me. It's me, Harriet!"

"Harriet...what are you doing...in my p-parent's living room?" Spencer sniffled.

"We're not in your parent's living room! This is a dream! Or something like it...this is a trap created by Trauma!"

"What? Who is...."

Harriet grabbed Spencer by the shoulders and shook him again: "Wake up, wake up damn it! We might not have much more time!"

"I....I deserve to die, Harriet," Spencer sobbed.

"No you don't," Harriet said.

"I want to die...W-why won't you let me die?"

"Because, damn it, you're not allowed!"

She wrapped her arms around him and held him tightly. This seemed to calm him down. He sniffled and hung his head. Then, told her sadly: "I was about ten years old when it happened. I snuck into one of those Ross Foundation plants and took a dive in the radiation. My dad caught me coming home late and reeking with chemical smell, and he was mad and I mean...he should have been mad...he had every right to be. I shouldn't have been in that radiation. That was stupid. But then...I got really mad at him and I didn't know about the laser eyes thing at the time....or that sometimes it's hard to control when I get really mad. I only found out that I had the laser eyes....when I killed him. H...Harriet, I miss him so much!"

"Shh...it's ok, Spencer. It was an accident."

"But then...after I killed him....my mom never looked at me in the same way. She got really cold and distant. I mean...she'd buy me things sometimes but she'd always try to make me feel guilty about it, and she never let me hug her, and a lot of times, when I came into a room, she would just leave. She was never that way with my brothers, just with me...everything that Ronnie and James did was always the greatest thing ever, and nothing I did was ever good enough. It never even mattered how good I was at a thing and how much they sucked at it. It was never good enough for her. But then that might of been because after my dad died, we lost his income and he was young so he didn't have life insurance, so we got poor...but I missed him so much...I didn't even care about the house or anything. I just wanted him back." Spencer said.

"Oh Christ....I guess this is the shit you get when you do battle with a therapist," Harriet groaned, glancing at the imaginary clock on the wall. It occurred to her that she had no idea how much time had passed since entering this vivid flashback.

"Heheh...yeah..." Spencer said, "I really wanna wake up now, Harriet....but I....I don't think I can..."

"Try harder."

"He was a music teacher at Maplelake Middle school. Did I tell you that, Harriet?" Spencer said.

"No. You didn't."

"He could play every instrument you can think of so well. And he was really into classic rock. He taught me to play the guitar....and after he died, there was just this big room filled with all of his instruments and music stuff. It was all I had left of him. My mom wanted to sell all of that stuff but I wanted to keep it. And she made me feel really guilty about keeping it...but I still kept it."

"Wake up, Spencer. You can tell me about all of this stuff, after we're officially *not* dead," Harriet said, a little annoyed.

"I still kept it and....my mom wanted to get rid of me, I think. So after I got out of juvie, she sent me to band camp every summer. Probably so she wouldn't have to look at me...Then, one day, when I came home from a summer at band camp, for no reason at all, she got all happy and was happy to see me for once. Then, I was happy too because I wanted her to like me again," said Spencer.

"Well, at least your mother stuck around. My mother *left*," Harriet interjected.

"I'm sorry that happened to you, Harriet."

"Don't be. I don't even care. Don't even know why I brought it up," Harriet said.

"Anyway, she was all happy, right? And I was wondering why and hoping that it was because she liked me again. But, then...she told me that there was a cure to my laser eyes power. A doctor in New York was doing operations on superhumans with laser eyes and stopping or removing the ability. But this operation, required that the optic nerve in both eyes be completely severed, so all of this doctor's patients went permanently blind."

"That's horrible," Harriet interjected.

"My mother contacted that doctor right away, as soon as she learned his name and phone number," Spencer said.

"That bitch."

"But the doctor wouldn't do the operation on a kid. He told my mother that he could only do the operation on a consenting adult. So when I turned 18, she gave me an ultimatum, get the operation or get out. And I didn't want to go blind, so I left. She told me never to come back so I never did."

Now Harriet and Spencer appeared in the mental projection as adults again. Harriet was not exactly sure at what point in the conversation, this transformation had occurred.

"Great, ok? Can you please try to wake up now?"

"Hey, maybe therapy does work. I feel....*better*," Spencer said, "Ok, I'm going to try to wake up now. Ok....waking up....*waking up*..."

Spencer closed his eyes tightly and then opened them again as though willing himself to wake up. He blinked once, noting that they were still in the dream and then said: "Shit. I'm still asleep. Do you think this is a coma dream?"

"Spencer, shut up and start thinking awake thoughts! An explosion is about to happen, I think?" Harriet shouted.

"Awake thoughts...awake thoughts...awake thoughts..." Spencer muttered nervously.

In a desperate attempt to wake him up, Harriet grabbed Spencer by the collar and pulled him towards her, aggressively kissing him on the mouth. She let go of him and he staggered backward, grinning slightly. The flashback prison, however, had not been broken.

"Shit," Harriet muttered, "That always works in movies."

"Harriet, are we going to die?"

"No," Harriet said and then she corrected herself by adding, "Well, eventually, *yes*. But, goddamn it not today."

Harriet thought hard, trying with all she had to come up with a possible solution; the key that would unlock this nostalgic prison. She thought about the other times that Trauma had invaded her mind, in particular, the time that Trauma had impersonated her father.

"Why are you being all quiet?" Spencer asked.

"Um...." Harriet murmured, still thinking, "I think I might have an idea about how to get out of here."

She had seen through Trauma's disguise right away,

his demeanor was not quite right, but more than anything else it was the altered aura, which had alerted her to the change. Trauma gave off a unique aura, comprised of flashing and confusing electrical signals of a powerful magnitude, likely this was the result of his constant and powerful supernatural brain activity.

Harriet turned and walked away from Spencer, then, walked over to what looked like an older version of him; this was the image of Spencer's father, still dead on the floor. The fatal injury, which had been inflicted by Spencer's eye lasers, made Harriet a little nauseous when she looked at it. There were a lot of stringy insides hanging out of him and mushy, red, disgusting blobs that were no longer recognizable as organs. Yet this image gave off an aura of a powerful magnitude, no doubt, the signature of a God Class national security threat.

Harriet seized the dead man by both of his arms and lifted him off of the floor, shaking him aggressively.

"I know that's you, Trauma! Get out of here, Trauma! Get the fuck out!" Harriet screamed as loudly as she could, because this tactic had forced Trauma out of her thoughts before.

The dead man opened his eyes and cackled menacingly.

"Oh I'll leave," Trauma said with a smirk. "But not because you told me to. Only because I'm bored of messing with you now. You are powerless here, Miss Harriet Ross. And it's been over an hour, by the way. That demolition has already happened."

Harriet screamed and started pummeling the dead man with her fists. She felt his nose and facial plate splinter into a thousand tiny fragments. All of the dead man's teeth collapsed inwards, and then she was only punching what looked like a squishy, red puddle.

Harriet's eyes flickered open. She was in a dark place, covered in white dust and rubble. Her arms were still around the huddled Spencer. She could not see him in the dark, but she could feel him breathing and his heart beating fast against hers. He was alive. His aura alone could have told her that. However, it was too dark to know if he was injured.

"Spencer," Harriet murmured quietly, as though raising her voice might have somehow ripped any existing wounds asunder, "Spencer...are you hurt?"

"...Uh....no, I think I'm ok..." Spencer murmured back, "Are you..."

"No I'm fine...completely explosion proof, apparently," Harriet said.

"I figured you would be."

"Yeah, I did too."

"Do you think those cops are still out there?" Spencer asked.

"I'm hoping....that maybe they assumed we're dead and went home?" Harriet said.

"Yeah, that's what I'm hoping also."

"I'm going to toss some of this rubble aside and dig us out," Harriet said.

"I can just phase through," Spencer reminded her.

"Right. Then, I'll just dig myself out and you could phase through."

"Hey, Harriet?" Spencer said as Harriet stood, easily brushing boulders of drywall and metal beams off of herself as she began digging her way through the rubble. There was a small pocket of air around them, making it seem as though they had been imprisoned in a small, precarious cave.

"What?"

"Thanks for trying to wake me up," Spencer said.

"Well, I couldn't just let my butler get exploded," Harriet said as though this were the most obvious thing in the world.

Harriet did not need to see Spencer's face clearly in the darkness to know that he was smirking at her.

"You know, because I need somebody to get me

Danishes and shit and I'm much too important to do stuff like that for myself," Harriet added, in case Spencer decided to make too much out of her previous statement.

"So uh...all that stuff that happened in my head....that's uh...."

"We can talk about that later," Harriet said, "Right now we've got to get the fuck out of dodge.

Chapter 31:
In the Absence of Vice

Devin paced The Ross Manor, dressed as Freeze Out and chewing feverishly on the frozen cigarette in his mouth. The withdraw symptoms from his sudden and involuntary forced sobriety were still strong, and the desire to light up, shoot up, or snort up some kind of a mind-altering substance plagued him constantly. He scratched at the itchy, painful hole where his eye used to be, around the corners of a fresh bandage, picking at the plastic medical tape and cringing. Painkillers were completely useless to him anymore. Though he still carried a bottle of them in his pocket. The doctor, who the Jay Walker had forced to patch up Devin's battle damage, had prescribed him pills and they were supposedly powerful. Unfortunately, however, they were not powerful enough to override whatever super resiliency quality Devin had attained from his long soak in the radiation.

Devin walked down a long corridor, lined with onyx pillars and elaborate carvings of gargoyles devouring the flesh of ruined souls in ragged clothing. He walked toward a room near the end of the hall where he knew Miz Mayhem (otherwise known as *Bernice*) slept. She greeted him at the door with a wide grin. She was busty, blond, and wearing a long lacey, gossamer, white gown.

"Why might a gentleman call on me at this hour?" she inquired with a patronizing smirk.

"I..." Devin groaned through his considerable pain, "Fuck....I don't know, you're the only woman here aside from a couple of the lower ranking henchman, and when they tried to touch my ice dick, they all got mangled and mutilated by it like every other normal girl who tries to touch my ice dick anymore. So I was thinking...fuck it....Bernice is a superhuman, maybe if I touch her....she won't die, maybe?"

Bernice let out a long cold, cruel cackle. Then said: "You may be a handsome lad but you are like an angler fish,

213

luring women with your perfect face, and body, and laid-back California charm. You lure in the women, and then, you devour them whole. I should know, I am, in fact, a similar fish. But I see the pain in your face, you require a vice to be satisfied. It is unfortunate that those henchmen did not know the price of providing you this comfort."

"Well, mostly their hands just got burned and they ran away screaming. Not my fault FYI, they were all big groupies, frothing at the mouth to get a piece of that ice dick. Is it my fault that my dick is the greatest dick that there is, or whatever? So what if it's poisonous now, everybody still wants it, cause' I'm still a rock star and still the owner of the greatest dick on planet earth. And also probably other planets. If dicks exist there."

"You twenty-first century men are all so preoccupied with your own genitalia," said Bernice, "In my day, we didn't talk about such things in polite conversation."

"So who said I was polite?" said Devin, "Chicks go down hard on rock stars. So let's cut out all the pointless foreplay and just skip to the main attraction already. Maybe I won't freeze your skin off? Maybe you won't suck the life out of me? Let's make normal sex happen. The kind of sex that normal people have."

"Normal sex is overrated," Bernice quipped dismissively, "But I pity you, so I guess, ok."

"That's good enough for me."

Bernice opened the door to her room wide and Devin trudged in. He took the frozen cigarette out of his mouth and held it between his thumb and forefinger like a soon-to-be discarded lollypop. Bernice took the cigarette out of Devin's hand and stuck it in her own mouth. Then, she removed a pack of matches from the drawer of her bedside table, struck the match and lit the cigarette with it.

"You enjoying that?"

Bernice exhaled a puff of smoke.

"I prefer opium," she said, "Though it's been a while

since I gave that kind of thing up. Tobacco is a lot more...*filtery* then it used to be."

"Yeah, the filter will do that."

Bernice crept closer to him, her large, blue eyes half-lidded. She removed the cigarette from her mouth. Then, reached out to touch his muscular spandex-clad arms, her lips pursed. She attempted to kiss him, but instead, shrieked in pain as her lips brushed his. She recoiled, screaming and clutching her face. Her lips were now frozen, peeling and bloody. Strings of ruined flesh hung off of them in grotesque, worm-like runners. Streams of cold blood dribbled down her chin.

"Oops. My bad," Devin said, "Maybe this was a dumb idea. Anyway, can't you just suck the life out of somebody and fix it or whatever?"

"Damn you to hell!" Bernice cursed, clutching her ruined face.

She staggered back to the bed and sat down on the edge of it, breathing hard.

The room was quiet for a moment. A flame burned brightly, in the fireplace, on the opposite wall. Devin stared at it for a moment, and then, turned back toward Bernice.

"Yeah, maybe it was stupid to think that would work...I've been thinking about killing myself lately," he said quietly, "...How do you think I should do it?"

"It makes no difference to me," panted Bernice with as much indifference as she could muster. A wave of nausea came over her and she felt as though she were about to pass out.

"I've been thinking that maybe I'd jump from a high place...or that maybe I'd hang myself...but then maybe that stuff wouldn't kill me. Getting shot by the police didn't work. The only thing that can hurt me now is, like, other superhumans, apparently," Devin said, indicating his missing eye with a tap of his index finger.

"Yes, permanent battle damage is a real risk in any

physical confrontation," said Bernice, "It's not like these action movies that you twenty-first century men are so fond of, where the makeup artists don't even paint on the bruises."

"Whatever. I was fine before that *fucking dickhead* mutilated me!"

"Well, you *were* trying to kill him."

"And next time, *I will.*"

"All of this suicide talk is terribly unattractive, lad," said Bernice.

"Yeah, like I give a shit about what *you* think. I'm never gonna' fuck again, or get high again, or even have a cigarette again! What have I got to live for? Can you tell me that? I can't stand another second sober with my shitty self!"

"You'll get used to it," Bernice said, "I did."

"Oh, fuck you."

"And besides there must be a girl you can touch who won't be mutilated," Bernice said, the corners of her mouth curling slightly, "*Somewhere.*"

"Yeah, *where*?" Devin retorted a little sarcastically.

"Well....how 'bout that *Harriet Ross*?"

"You mean that evil bitch that Spanky Fuckerson's obsessed with? Yeah, she ain't my type," Devin said.

"Why should that matter? She's a girl you can touch who won't die," Bernice said.

"Huh...I guess I did touch her once...when we fought. And she *didn't* die," Devin contemplated, scratching his blond head, "...Or get mutilated....I've just got to pry her away from Fuckerson somehow," Devin contemplated this with a mischievous smirk, imagining the look on Spencer's face as he, Devin, made out with The Justice Bitch in front of him, "But then, who would want that doofus loser when they could be with *me*?"

"Exactly," said Bernice with a grin, "You're *Devin Forress.*"

Devin smirked, and, very much assured of his superior sex appeal, winked and pointed in Bernice's direction: "You know it, baby."

Chapter 32:
The Road

Harriet stared out of the tinted window of a large black truck as it rolled past palm trees and down the interstate highway. The truck was something that Spencer had stolen at the last rest stop, by sneaking the keys off of the guy that owned it, and then, phasing through the driver's-side door, while that same guy was distracted, wandering around the restrooms, and searching for his missing keys.

Harriet glanced over at Spencer, who was driving. His clothes and hair were dirty with drywall dust from the recent explosion. He had developed a dark, five-o'clock shadow.

"I've noticed that you always steal black cars with dark tinted windows," Harriet observed boredly.

"Yeah, those are rad," Spencer said.

"Sure, ok. But isn't that, like, a pattern that the police might pick up on?" Harriet said.

"Huh....I never thought about that before," Spencer contemplated, "Do you think we should ditch it and jump in some suburban house wife's minivan or something?"

"Then you would have stolen that guy's truck for nothing," Harriet said.

"Yeah, but, like, we're villains now, so who cares?"

"*I* care," Harriet said, "And who says that we have to be villains just because that's what society decided we are?"

"I don't know, *society*. And society sucks anyway. Who needs it?" Spencer said.

"Just because we steal things, doesn't mean we can't also give something back," Harriet said, "You know, use our superpowers to help humanity in some way."

"Humans are the worst. What've they ever done for me?" Spencer argued.

"Spencer, *we're* humans."

"I know. Isn't it terrible?"

"Well the last time I checked, you were still my butler.

So if I decide that I want to give something back to society. Then, you'll just have to assist me, won't you?" Harriet said.

"Well you've got me there, ma'am," Spencer said.

"And besides, didn't you say that you were a 'good guy' now," said Harriet.

"I don't know maybe I lied. Maybe deep down I'm just a bad person and that's all I'm ever gonna' be," Spencer said.

"I don't believe that that's true," Harriet said.

The car sped past rows of palm trees. The sun was setting in the distance. The street signs now indicated that they were leaving California.

"Anyway, I'll be glad to get far away from Trauma's range of mental control or whatever he called it. As long as that shithead stays in California at least I'll never have to relive that night again," Spencer said.

"You mean when you..."

"Don't say it, please...I don't want to think about it," Spencer said, sounding uncharacteristically melancholic.

"Fine. Let's brainstorm how we should use our superpowers to help people instead," Harriet said.

"Why do you care about helping people all of a sudden?" Spencer said.

"Uh? I've *always* cared about helping people," Harriet retorted, sounding very affronted. She crossed her arms and rolled her eyes, putting her bare feet up on the dashboard.

"Really, you could have fooled me....The world's turned its back on you, Harriet. You really should consider just going full villain already," Spencer said.

"So all that crap you said about how you're tired of being selfish and how you want to live for someone else. Was that just a bunch of bullshit? Or are you just a hypocrite?" Harriet said.

"Harriet...it's not like that..." Spencer sighed.

"Really, then what is it like?" Harriet challenged confrontationally, "Was there some truth to that or do you song writers just tell the prettiest lies?"

"Uh...maybe a little of both. I want to make you happy, Harriet. I don't really care about anyone else."

"Well, if you want to make me happy," said Harriet, "Then, you have to help me help people. That's a thing that I still want to do...you know with *violence and stuff.*"

"Ugh...fine," conceded Spencer reluctantly, "...Since you love *violence* so much."

"And helping people," Harriet added.

"Sure, whatever helps you sleep at night," said Spencer.

"What the fuck is that supposed to mean?"

"Uh...*nothing,*" Spencer retreated timidly. Then he forced a nervous grin, "So how are we going to help people, my brutal goddess from hell?"

"I...huh....I'm not sure. Maybe just when we see someone who needs help...we help them, maybe?" Harriet said.

"Great plan," interjected Spencer flippantly.

"Well have you got a better one?"

Spencer stretched and yawned, swiping drywall dust out of his bangs.

"I say we break into a mall after it closes and stay the night. I can break all of the security cameras. We can eat whatever food we want and sleep at the mattress store. No one will ever know we were there," Spencer said, "I mean, if we're going to be outlaws, why not enjoy it, right?"

Harriet reclined in her seat and shut her eyes, surrendering to fatigue as the sunset under a darkening sky.

"That sounds wonderful, Spencer," she murmured groggily before drifting into a shallow, uneasy sleep. Images of The Poltergeist's scuttling dolls, cackling and twisting their plastic heads unnaturally, plagued her nightmares.

Chapter 33:
A Sacrifice of Blood

That night, Spencer parked the black truck in an empty mall parking lot. Harriet watched through half-lidded eyes as he exited the car and trotted up to the side of the large shopping center building. He disappeared into the structure as his body made contact with a solid white wall. About an hour passed. Harriet played with the radio dial. The digital clock on the dashboard flashed unnaturally. She settled on a popular music station that was playing EAR MUTILATOR. Devin's scratchy voice sang to the tune of electric guitars about a celebrity drug party where lots of sex was happening. Though Harriet had no interest in the drug scene and couldn't really relate to the lyrics, she had to admit, the song was catchy.

Spencer returned to the car, grinning. Harriet turned the radio off, unlocked the door, and stepped out into the parking lot.

"I think I got all the security cameras," he said.

"No overnight security guards?" Harriet inquired skeptically.

"There was one guy who was like 80 but I locked him in one of the empty stores on the top floor."

"You're terrible," Harriet said.

"Yeah, I know."

"You do realize that people are going to figure it out that we were here, right?" Harriet said.

"Whatever, as long as we leave before the store opens, they'll never catch us," Spencer said.

"And locking that guy up there all night isn't really a very heroic thing to do," Harriet pointed out.

"Harriet, everyone thinks we're villains anyway. Why fight it? Let's just be villains. And besides, I gave him, like, a blanket and pillow and stuff. It's his job to stay up all night and do nothing. Now, he can just do that from a different room," argued Spencer.

"I'm not sure I'm entirely comfortable with this anymore," Harriet groaned, running both of her hands over her forehead in exasperation.

"Well, you are my hostage *so*...."

"Oh, shut up, and go unlock the mall already. You've already broken the ceil. We might as well do whatever we want now."

"Heheheh...*yes*! I knew you'd come around!"

They walked back to the building. Spencer phased through one of the doors and unlocked it from the inside. Harriet opened the door and walked in.

"I get the feeling that you've done this before," Harriet said.

"Yeah, a few times," said Spencer, still grinning and looking much more proud of himself than was probably decent.

They walked through an octagon-shaped food court and past a large, inert fountain, surrounded by short palm trees.

"Hey, do you think any billionaires will ever show up to try and pay your ransom?" Spencer said conversationally.

"Why should it matter?" Harriet said, sitting down on a bench near the fountain. "You didn't tell them where to bring the money and besides you can just steal whatever you want really easily anyway."

"I don't know. It would just be interesting is all," said Spencer.

"I've got news for you, Spencer. If you really *were* holding me for ransom, you'd be extremely *frustrated* right now," Harriet informed him grimly.

"Why? Don't you know lots of billionaires and stuff? What about that lawyer you used to hang out with? Wouldn't he pay 10 billion dollars to get you back?" Spencer asked.

"Gary doesn't have ten billion dollars," Harriet said, "He's only a millionaire."

"*Only* a millionaire?" Spencer parroted back incredulously. The way that Harriet talked about millions of dollars like it was chump change, was still surreal to him. He grinned and withdrew a hundred dollar bill from his front pocket.

"Check me out, I'm a hundred-aire" he bragged jokingly.

Harriet groaned and rolled her eyes. After the conversation they had had in the car, Harriet was in no mood to find anything that Spencer did or said in any way amusing. How could he not understand that no matter how society viewed her, she would always strive to use her superpowers for good? How could he not want the same thing?

"What about your mother, though?" Spencer said, "She'd pay the ransom, right? I mean, I know *she's* a billionaire. She's in Hollywood movies and stuff."

"Are you kidding me?" Harriet scoffed angrily, "My mother wouldn't pay your ransom, if your ransom was twenty minutes of her time."

"Um..." Spencer murmured awkwardly. Harriet's mood seemed to have darkened considerably. She glared at him as though prepared to backhand him across the face should he pursue the topic, "Sorry I brought it up then..."

Harriet spent the next hour or so, strolling around the dark and empty mall, as Spencer slipped through walls, unlocking stores and flicking on lights. Occasionally, he would snatch something off of a rack and put it on, or fold it up and carry it around with him under his arm. Harriet watched with a mixture of amusement and irritation as he snatched a leather jacket off of a rack in a department store, then, phased his hand through a glass case, which contained expensive designer glasses. He removed a pair of dark shades and put them on.

"I like sunglasses," said Spencer as he walked with Harriet from the department store, to a jewelry store near the fountain and the food court. "But they always get blasted to shit. I used to have a big pile of these in my car with the lenses melted out."

"Is that the fate of this pair as well?" Harriet predicted.

"Yeah, probably," replied Spencer with an indifferent shrug.

Spencer unlocked the jewelry store from the inside, and then, phased his hands through some of the glass display cases, grabbing fistfuls of diamonds and pearl necklaces, and then, draping them over Harriet's neck. Harriet glared at him as he did this. He ignored the expression and started clipping gold bracelets around her wrists.

"Before the alter of the goddess, the people lay a sacrifice of gold and silver and platinum and precious stones, hoping to quell her wrath," Spencer said, clipping a pair of diamond earrings to Harriet's earlobes.

"I'm not going to keep this stuff, Spencer," said Harriet with annoyance.

"Oh, *come on*? Why not? Why not just be a villain? You were born to be a villain. I can see it in your eyes."

"I mean, it's pretty. I can wear it while we're here. But I'm not taking it with me when I leave. It's way too conspicuous," Harriet said.

"The goddess has rebuked the sacrifice of the people. They stare up at her, trembling with terror as her volcano threatens to erupt, smothering their vital crops in molten ash," Spencer announced dramatically, bowing low before her.

"The goddess accepts only a sacrifice *of blood*," Harriet replied in a sinister tone, playing along.

Spencer got on his knees and bowed so low that his face touched the shiny floor: "Then on behalf of the people, my goddess, you may spill my blood until thou hath drunken thy fill."

What followed this conversation was a confused flailing of entangled limbs as the two undressed each other, hopped onto one of the benches near the inert fountain, and started furiously humping. Harriet dragged her long, sharp nails against Spencer's muscular, bare back again and and again, as he mounted her, kissing her neck, her breasts and her nipples. She felt something wet under her fingernails that was probably his blood.

"...Oh goddess of war and sex...I am unworthy of you..." he moaned stupidly, his breath hot against her ear.

That night, Harriet slept in the mattress store. After testing all of the mattresses and selecting what was, in her opinion, the most comfortable one, she laid down. She then ordered Spencer to go back to the department store and retrieve her the correct fitted sheets for it. He returned about twenty minutes later with sheets, a comforter, a tray full of Danishes from a snack pagoda, and some bottled water. Then, resumed his butler role as he proceeded to dress the mattress in the sheets and comforter, dump the Danishes on a silver plate, and serve them to her with a bow. He retrieved a large, golden harp, from a nearby furniture store, then, wheeled it to the edge of the bed, where he stood from a respectful distance and played a haunting melody. She ate a couple of Danishes and watched him play, grinning a bit as she did so. Classical music reminded her of fancy charity dinners and art exhibitions. It was a nostalgic and soothing sound, one that reminded her of her childhood and of her family, before her mother had fled to New York City and before her father had been killed in the accident.

She finished her meal and laid down under the freshly laid out blankets. The lights went out. She heard the mattress creak as Spencer stumbled into it. Then, found herself wondering how her life had become what it currently was. Is this what she was going to do for the rest of her life? Travel from state to state, running from the cops, breaking into stores and stealing things? Sure it was fun *now*, but after the thrill wore off, wouldn't it just become...*tiring*? How long could a lifestyle like that possibly *last*?

With that thought in mind, Harriet drifted into an uneasy sleep.

Chapter 34:
The Music Box

The sound of tinkling bells jarred Harriet awake. She sat upright and looked at the clock on the wall of the darkened mattress store. It was midnight.

"Spencer," Harriet whispered, roughly nudging his shoulder. He snorted and jerked awake, "Spencer, do you hear that?"

"...What?"

The tinkling bells fell suddenly silent.

"It sounds like...the music box that my mother gave to me before she left for New York," Harriet whispered fearfully.

"Harriet...I don't hear anything."

"It was playing a second ago," Harriet asserted.

"Maybe you were just dreaming."

"No, I definitely heard it. It was definitely playing...do you think that means...that something's here?" Harriet whispered.

"What you mean, like a ghost?" Spencer whispered back.

"I thought I told you that ghosts are stupid."

"Ghosts are stupid? You mean, like, the ghost that supposedly framed you for murder? Because from where I'm standing, that ghost is looking pretty smart right now."

"Ghosts are stupid forever and so are you," Harriet muttered in annoyance. She shut her eyes and went back to sleep.

In the morning, they left quickly, before the stores were opened. They took a few bags of beef jerky and potato chips with them as breakfast, and then, drove off. With the windows down and the radio turned up, they drove for hours through desert. Through a pair of Spencer's stolen sunglasses, Harriet watched miles of sand and cactuses roll by. Her long dark hair was jostled by the motion of the truck. The sound of her companion's well-trained voice, singing along to the radio filled her ears. During moments like this, when she was most at peace, Harriet's eyelids slid slowly shut and she dreamed of strange things.

Harriet dreamed of a wide green field, filled with white and pink teddy bears. The bears scuttled around like the Poltergeist's dolls, twisting unnaturally, stretching their fanged mouths wide, and lapping at air. The unseen music box played its familiar jingling melody. However, the song was different here somehow; creepy; off-key. A powerful wave of auras washed over Harriet. The auras were accompanied by a confusing torrent of terrified and pleading voices:

"Help us...somebody...please!"

"I have to get out of here. There must be some way out!"

"Dear Santa Claus, please bless mommy and daddy and daddy's new girlfriend, Helen. And please help Speckles get better soon and I want a Whoopsie Poopsie Potty Surprise for my birthday. Amen."

"For the love of god! No! NO! Somebody please help me!"

Harriet moved in the direction of the most terrified voices, the ones who screamed and pleaded for help without hope of receiving it, and with a level of desperation, which indicated starving and tortured minds. These voices suffered unduly in the forced absence of creative thought. They gasped and struggled against their restraints in some dark place. In some dark, moving place.

Some of them were foreign and spoke in languages, which Harriet could not understand but the meaning was never lost on her. They spoke in a universal language, a language of emotion, which could be felt and not heard. Harriet followed these voices, they grew stronger as she moved through the green field.

"Where are you?" Harriet asked through the veil of sleep, her voice distorted by fatigue, "Please. Show me where you are and I'll find you. I'll find you...where is that dark, moving place..."

A large teddy bear waddled up to Harriet in the green field and opened its fanged mouth wide to swallow her whole. Harriet opened her eyes. She blinked. The dashboard came into focus. The car was silent except for the whirl of the air conditioner. Harriet turned her head in Spencer's direction.

"Spencer..." Harriet murmured groggily, the dream still fresh in her mind. She could feel the cloud of auras still, "I want you to help me with something. There are some people out here...that I think need our help."

"What?"

"It's hard to explain. They came to me in a dream maybe?" Harriet said, "I think I can sense where they are...it's a...a dark, moving place. Like maybe a car or a...a van."

"It's a bad reason to risk being caught," Spencer replied.

"But playing around in a mall is a *good* reason to risk being caught?" Harriet muttered back.

"At least that was fun," Spencer said with a yawn. He slouched and a curtain of his dark hair fell over one eye, "This sounds like work."

"Whatever. You're my butler so shut up and obey me," Harriet grumbled.

"Of course, ma'am. Forgive my momentary lapse in decorum," Spencer replied with a grin, "I will be a soldier at your command, my goddess. For your amusement, I would lay my body down on your alter and be slaughtered."

"That's what I like to hear."

...

As the sunset, Harriet drove toward the swirling wave of anguished auras, which she perceived, throbbing and shrieking. They clawed and wept and starved reduced to animals in chains. Their presence grew clearer as she approached, made vivid by the strength of their emotions.

"They're in a van," Harriet said because at this point she

felt sure of it.

Then, she saw the vehicle. It was a large, white, unmarked van. The back windows were painted over so that she could not see inside.

"That's it," she said to Spencer, "That's the van."

She heard him snore in response and jarred him awake with a light tap on his shoulder, which caused him to groan and rub the spot she had touched, which was now purple with unintentional bruising.

Spencer squinted in the dark to see the van in the distance.

"That's it," Harriet said again. "That's the van."

"Ok...so what's the plan?"

"I was thinking....that maybe we follow it until it stops and then get inside," Harriet said.

"Sounds dangerous," Spencer commented offhandedly.

"It feels like the right thing to do."

Harriet followed the car for several miles. Then, it turned off of the highway and into a rest stop. A plump, balding man with a unibrow and a mustache emerged from the car. He was accompanied by a scrawny guy with a crew cut and a gold nose ring. Harriet watched the two from behind the tinted windshield of her stolen truck as they entered a large, stone building labeled "rest stop."

"Let's go," Harriet whispered the second that the two men were out of sight.

Spencer nodded, understanding what she must have wanted from him. He slipped through the side of the truck, darted across the dark parking lot, and phased through the side of the white van, disappearing inside. Harriet got out of the car and walked to the back of the van. Spencer unlocked the back of the van from the inside and let her in.

A wall of swirling emotions hit Harriet in the face as she entered the vehicle. She glanced around in the dark and saw between 15 and 20 women, chained together by their wrists and ankles. The women were dirty and bruised, their hair greasy, their eyes wild and terrified. Some were naked. Others wore dirty bras and undergarments.

"Oh...wow...shit...how'd you know they were in here, Harriet? You must be some kind of a telepath," Spencer murmured, "So, what are you waiting for...break the chains and set them free before those guys come back."

"No," Harriet said.

"What?"

"No. I can do better. They must be taking these girls someplace. Like a human trafficking ring or something. If we stay in the van...it'll lead us to more of them."

"So I guess we're ditching the truck then?" Spencer said.

"Yeah," said Harriet. Then, she unbuttoned her shirt and threw it on the floor, revealing the lacy black braw underneath. "Take your clothes off."

"Uh...*what?*"

"We can hide in plain sight, as merchandise," Harriet said, with a sinister grin. "Then, when they least expect it, I can break my chains off and you can phase through yours. Then, we can just run around and free every sex slave they have."

"Goddamn this is terrifying."

"Whatsamatter? Are you a *chicken*?" Harriet said, with a smirk, arching one of her eyebrows at him as she unzipped the fly on her jeans and discarded them, revealing a pair of black bikini briefs underneath.

"Psh...no," Spencer said, unbuttoning his black and grey plaid flannel shirt and discarding it on the floor. "Human traffickers are dumb," He discarded his jeans on the floor, revealing a pair of white boxer shorts, "Probably."

Harriet walked over to one of the dirty, huddled women on the floor and pulled her wrist and ankle restraints open with a loud *clank*. They broke easily, as though made out of a hard, burnt cookie. Harriet moved to the next captive, and freed her from the restraints in the same way. The two women ran to the doors at the back of the truck and escaped into the parking lot. Harriet did not have time to worry if they would be noticed, or if their presence at the rest stop would alert the two men driving this truck that something was awry. She quickly snapped the restraints shut over her own wrists and ankles. Spencer followed her example, snapping the remaining wrist and ankle restraints shut, and then, phasing through them so that he appeared to be trapped just like the other passenger in the van were.

The two men returned to the van. Harriet could hear their muffled voices. She could feel their tainted auras, sopping with an alarming amount of corruption, and malice. Suddenly, all fear had left her. She was filled with a maddening bloodlust; a desire to eradicate her opponents with gruesome force; to rip their faces from their skulls, and then, shove the clods of bloody face meat down their throats until they choked to death on their own shredded flesh. She imagined herself do this as the van rolled; as the scantily clad women murmured in foreign languages; as Spencer whistled nervously, and leaned into her. His pale skin felt cold against hers; his aura betrayed a fear that his face hid well, at least in this dark place.

After some time, the van stopped. Harriet heard footsteps. Then, the doors on the back of the van were pulled open. The fat man with the mustache and the skinny man with the nose ring stood there for a moment and surveyed their merchandise with amorous grins.

"There's supposed to be 15," said the fat man to the skinny man.

The skinny man nodded, and paced the rows of captives as they stepped out of the van and into the larger building that the van was parked inside. It looked like a warehouse, with a high ceiling, grey, water-stained walls, and dilapidated floors. A line of chicken wire cages packed with scantily clad women and girls stood at the center of the room. The skinny man stopped in front of Spencer, looking skeptical. He crouched down slightly, to get eye level with this

231

suspicious male captive, and squinted.

"Is this a....*guy*?" the skinny guy murmured suspiciously, as though perhaps someone had purposely snuck a rock in with his bag of popcorn. The skinny man glanced back at the fat man, as though to confirm that Spencer's presence there was not, in fact, some kind of a mistake.

The fat man shrugged and said gruffly: "Different strokes for different folks."

The skinny man grunted with indifference and then resumed counting his acquisitions. The fat man paced the rows of bound captives, looking them over, as though to appraise their value. He stopped in front of Harriet, his tiny, beady, bloodshot eyes, glistening with delight.

"She's a pretty one," he said, his voice almost sticky with accumulating drool. His fat fingers moved slowly in the direction of her crotch. "She'll fetch a good price."

Spencer glared at the man as he moved closer to Harriet, grinning amorously, inching his hand slowly toward the front of her underpants, clearly with the intention of molesting her. Before the man's hand could so much as make contact with her skin or the elastic band on her underpants, however, Spencer had phased through his restraints and put himself between them.

"What the fuck?" the fat man growled, now staring down Spencer's glowing red eyes. In the next instant, before the fat man had a chance to react, Spencer had dug his fist into the man's chest, phasing through the clothing, skin, fat, muscle, and bone. The fat man gasped, choking up blood; his beady eyes bulging from his skull. Spencer's fingers closed around the man's beating heart, and then, he wrenched the organ free from the fat man's body with one swift, gruesome motion. A torrent of blood exploded from the gaping wound left in the fat man's chest, and he fell to his knees, gasping his last breath as Spencer held out his still-beating heart, grinning and cackling like a madman. His face and body were covered in blood, and his eyes glowed crimson.

"H...holy shit," the skinny man swore and then he turned to run. Before he could escape from the room, however, Spencer shot him in the back of the head with a laser. The skinny man's skull exploded into a thousand bloody fragments and he collapsed onto the floor, dead.

Harriet pulled off her restraints, smirking at the mutilated corpses of her slain opponents. She darted around quickly, pulling the restraints off of the other passengers of the vehicle. Then, got to work, tearing open the surrounding chicken wire cages. Her super strength made this as easy as tearing the plastic rings which hold soda cans together. Men with guns entered the room and opened fire. The bullets ricocheted off of Harriet and phased through Spencer. One of the bullets hit a flat-chested girl (who was probably about 13) in the head. She fell down dead in a puddle of her own blood. Harriet screamed and ran at the gun-wielding men, unaffected by the bullets, she tore their limbs from their torsos, and their heads from their necks, ripping strips of skin off of red, glistening muscle and snapping bones like sticks of chalk. Spencer blasted at the gun-wielding men with his eye lasers, blowing their heads off of their necks, and blasting large seeping holes in their torsos. For a short time, the air was thick with squirting blood, and the agonized shrieks of terrified henchmen in the moments before they were taken by death.

Soon a pile of dead sex traffickers littered the floor. The room was silent except for the panicked murmuring of terrified women.

"Don't be afraid!" Spencer announced to the human trafficking victims as they shrank away from him and Harriet, looking fearful and cautious, "We're not going to hurt you! We're here to set you free!"

"I don't think that all of them speak English," Harriet said, seeing that many of the women reacted to Spencer's statement with confusion and bewilderment. She got to work tearing open the remaining chicken wire cages.

Spencer breathed hard and then collapsed against a wall, running his bloody hand against his face.

"You ok?" Harriet asked him as she ripped the final cage asunder. A group of confused, scantly clad, women stumbled out.

"Fine...it's just...it's been a while since I've killed someone."

"How do you feel?"

"I feel...*pretty good*, actually," Spencer said with the shadow of an exhausted grin. "I feel like...we did a good thing today."

Harriet walked to the edge of the room, grabbed a fistful of drywall, and then, ripped it away with one swift, violent motion, tearing a large, jagged arch in the wall. There was grass on the other side of that arch, and the light of dawn. Women and girls poured out of the building and escaped into the world. Spencer crept up behind Harriet and rested his chin on the top of her head.

"Now, those girls will have a chance at a decent life. I'm really glad we did this," he said.

"Yeah," said Harriet, the memory of her first kill still fresh in her mind; the look of terror in his eyes; the way that his arms snapped off of his torso like dry twigs. It had been the first time that she had ever unleashed her full power without restraint. Surreal and intoxicating, the experience was one of the most gratifying in her life, "Me too."

Chapter 35:
The Dark Presence

At The Ross Manor, Jason stared down at the skin of the hollow, eyeless face, which he held clutched in his hands. It stared back up at him with a blank expression. The hollow, dark holes, where this victim's eyes used to be, were black mirrors. In them, he could see the possibilities which lay before him.

At the moment, Jason was sitting in a high-backed green armchair, by the fireplace, in the library. The light of the nearby fire danced across his bare face, casting a collage of odd shadows. The moonlight, which came in from the skylight overhead, cast the entire seen in a soft blue glow.

Jason turned the skull-less skin in his hands and examined it with interest. He examined the sunken face, searching for any lingering humanity in it. Who had this man been before his untimely demise? How had Crunchy Toast Muncher selected him as the subject of this gruesome taxidermy?

Jason smirked as he contemplated how *hardcore* this was. Wearing the skin of his enemies into battle would surely mark him as the most terrifying villain in the city, and possibly, *the world*.

Ha, he scoffed inwardly, *I'd like to see the motherfucker who could out-villain me now! Whose that motherfucker. Nobody, that's who. And soon, the entire world will bow before me...I will soon rule the pitiful normals, uncontested!*

Jason grinned at the gruesome face skin in his hands, and then, he thought, without meaning to: I wonder if this guy will haunt me?

Come to think of it, there had been some odd occurrences in the manor recently; strange little things that Jason sometimes noticed out of the corner of his eye. A quiet, tinkling, laughter that might have just been some punk henchman pulling a prank on him, sometimes rang in his ears, at times when it was quiet and he thought he was alone. Creepy messages, written on the mirrors in shaving cream and lipstick, sometimes appeared. They usually said something like: *Get out, leave now*, or, *if you stay here, you will die*. Sometimes the messages were more threateningly specific, and said things like: *You're a fool, Jason Walker, and soon the house of my ancestors will run red with your blood*.

Messages like this made Jason think that, perhaps, all of this bullshit was being perpetrated by Harriet's ex-villain boyfriend, who could walk through walls and had infiltrated Jason's lair before without any trouble.

At times when it was quiet, and Jason heard that wicked little tinkling laugh, he would call out into the darkness, confronting the presence (which he assumed was Spencer Tuckerson), out of frustration: "I know you're there, you stupid fucker! …Hiding in the walls like a coward…if you really want the house back then *come out and fight me!*"

Usually, these kinds of outbursts were greeted with silence. Some times, however, the mysterious presence would respond by flickering the lights, or changing the TV station to channel 666. Despite the mysterious intruder's best efforts to scare him, however, Jason was not superstitious and understood that every phenomenon, which he had witnessed, was just a stupid parlor trick. Every surreal occurrence, which had taken place, could have been easily explained by a superhuman, with the power of telekinesis or invisibility. However, Jason was never successful at catching the intruder, and despite his best efforts, could not seem to discover its true identity.

Tonight, however, as the mysterious intruder crouched behind Jason, poised to strike, everything that Jason thought he knew about his own superiority and the nature of the universe in general, was about to be resolutely contested.

As Jason sat by the burning fireplace, in the library, a door creaked open and Trauma entered. Jason slipped the hollow skin over his mask-less face. The much older man approached him with respectful and submissive poise:

"Jay Walker...I've come to ask you uh...about my salary...I wouldn't want to bother you with all of that kind of stuff. You know, since taking over the world is our primary objective and everything. But, I've got bills. And rent is due."

Jason scoffed openly at this request and then responded: "Ha! Salary? Yea, I don't think so. You're my *slave,* remember? If I had to pay *everyone* I enslaved with mind control, I'd go broke."

"Perhaps consider a more lucrative business model?" Trauma interjected with a well-practiced therapist-like friendliness.

"*Shut up,*" Jason shot him down caustically. He then considered the eerie presence that he felt in the room with them and decided to mention it: "Trauma...have you...noticed anything strange in the manor recently?"

"No more strange than usual."

"No flickering light, creepy, shrill laughter, messages on the bathroom mirrors? Nothing like that?"

"No."

"What about dried-up dead people and skeletons in the mirrors and bathtubs...just for a second...and just out of the corner of your eye," Jason insisted, scanning the darkened room with suspicion as he spoke.

"Jason, as a therapist, I've got to say, you're starting to concern me," Trauma replied measurably.

"Enough of this 'as a therapist' crap! Do you notice it or don't you!" Jason shouted in frustration.

"I don't believe in ghosts, Jason."

"Neither do I, but that doesn't mean we don't have a problem! Someone is doing this! But *who?*"

"Hmm...now that I think about it...I have been hearing some strange laughter lately. But...in a house full of villains and henchman...that could have been basically anybody. Perhaps your imagination is getting the best of you."

"Don't talk to me like I'm crazy, Trauma. I'm *not* crazy," Jason growled, standing up.

"I'm just saying...it's not unusual for people under a lot of stress to..."

"You don't believe me, do you?" Jason shouted angrily.

"Jason, I..."

"I'll prove that it's real if I have to! I'll call it out!" Jason shouted.

"Calm down, please. It was not my intention to challenge you," Trauma interjected measurably.

"I call you out, motherfucker!" Jason screamed as he paced the room, "Reveal yourself! I call you out! If you're really the hot shit you think you are, stop playing these games and come strike me down!"

The fireplace went dark and the chandeliers overhead flickered. Shrill, distorted laughter filled the room and then a deep, distorted voice replied quietly: "Well, if you insist...I've grown bored of playing with you...and I've already given you more than enough chances to leave of your own free will."

Jason searched the dark room for the owner of this deep, distorted voice, but found nothing. As the intruder continued to speak he felt around in the dark for the contours of an invisible foe. The voice, however, did not seem at all concerned that it would be discovered before it was ready to be discovered.

"You can still relinquish what is rightfully mine..." the voice continued theatrically, "Free of the violent death...witch you temp with every petulant breath. I will give you a final warning *now*... Leave this place, release the minds that you have stolen, repent your sins, and live out the remainder of your life as a man of honor and virtue. Do this and you may go in peace, for I am a dark and brutal creature of violent justice, the dark empty nothing that you know only in the pit of your soul...a demon, which has risen from the pits of hell...so that only the *truly wicked* shall know my wrath."

"Yeah, yeah. End the monologue already so that I can fucking kill you and make your head into a mask," Jason growled threateningly and then he boasted, "Hear that, you stupid fucker? No creature *alive or dead* is a match for my power!"

A creature made up of swirling, black rags appeared near the ceiling, illuminated by the light of the moon, overhead. It had the appearance of an ephemeral wraith, with a white, porcelain mask for a face.

The walls started to bleed. Jason called his top-ranking henchmen to the battle through telepathy, and they darted toward the room. The Poltergeist hovered overhead, perhaps waiting patiently for them to arrive.

Jason grabbed a yellow notepad from his breast pocket and scribbled a few hasty words on it. Then, held it up for The Poltergeist to read. To his surprise, however, The Poltergeist read the words aloud with derision but continued to hover, completely unaffected:

"You will land and bash yourself in the head until you are incapacitated from head trauma," The Poltergeist read, and though not a fleck of its skin was visible beneath the mask and flowing robes, Jason could hear the smirk on its face in that mocking tone it spoke with. It was clear to him, even through the high levels of distortion; the shrill squeaks and buzzes and clicks of static that seemed to always be present when it spoke.

In frustration, Jason grabbed a nearby desk lamp and threw it at The Poltergeist's head, but it passed straight through as though the creature were made of smoke. Miz Mayhem, and Freeze Out entered the room. The Poltergeist floated down to the floor, as if to greet them.

The two villains charged at it but all of them passed through its body without damaging it at all.

"Read its mind, Trauma! Find out who it is and how it's doing this!" Jason demanded.

"I...I can't," Trauma replied, sounding

uncharacteristically shaken, "I can't read its mind... I...I can't read *anything*..."

"What?"

"It must be shutting off my powers somehow," Trauma said.

Jason watched in horror as all of his henchmen attempted to use their powers on his adversary, but failed. Miz Mayhem's touch did not suck the life out of it. Freeze Out aimed his ice breath in The Poltergeist's direction, but again, nothing happened. The temperature in the room had not dropped with his presence as it usually did, and his skin was slowly regaining its former California tan.

Realizing that their efforts were in vain, the villains relented. The Poltergeist stood before Jason, unchallenged and Jason's underlings merely stood in a ring; surrounding the creature; eyeing it with apprehension.

"What are you waiting for? *Kill it!*" Jason commanded. However, his underlings did nothing. He insisted once more: "I don't care if you *all* die! I don't even care if that thing even *can* die! I gave you an order and you *must* obey! Kill that thing or *die* trying!"

Again, Jason's henchmen did not respond. They merely stood there and looked at him. The Poltergeist laughed a shrill little distorted cackle, which filled the vast room and reverberated off of the walls.

It wafted over to where Freeze Out was standing, and brushed his blond bangs away from his sun-kissed forehead in what was almost a paternal gesture. Freeze Out stared at the thing with an expression that was a mix of terror and incredulity, but did not dare retreat from the touch, for fear of insulting the monster.

"No longer will you answer to The Jay Walker. By my hand, you have all been freed from his power *now and forever*," The Poltergeist announced, withdrawing its gloved hand from Freeze Out's head and rising back into the air, "Flee this place, *now*, or face my wrath! Remember always that it was I, The

Poltergeist, who freed you from your mental servitude!"

Trauma, Miz Mayhem, and Freeze Out watched the creature with awe, hardly daring to believe what they had just heard.

"...There will come a day...when I will call upon you to do my bidding, and so your lives are spared. Leave! *Now!*" The Poltergeist shouted.

With these words, Trauma, Miz Mayhem, and Freeze Out fled the room.

As the door shut behind them, a dark figure entered from a shadowy corner of the room. He stepped into the light, and was revealed to be a thin, balding man, with a grey mustache, who wore a butler's uniform. It took Jason a moment to recognize this man as Reynolds Sanderland, the former lover of William Fredrick Ross and the rightful owner of The Ross Manor.

"Well," Reynolds said to The Poltergeist with a thick and pompous British accent, "Let's get on with it and kill him already."

The Poltergeist advanced on Jason and Jason backed up against a wall, his eyes growing wide with fear.

"W-who are you," Jason stuttered out of desperation, as the thing grew closer still.

"I am the voice of damned souls, the harbinger of doom, the dark hand of *justice,* come to drag the ruined souls of the damned back to the pits of hell," The Poltergeist replied cryptically.

The walls bled more violently now. A few ugly plastic dolls with twisted-up faces rose from the shadows and started crawling up Jason's legs.

"Oh shit, oh shit, oh shit, you don't want to kill me, man!" Jason whaled as the plastic creatures started to crawl up his arms, "You-you can *use* me! Yeah! I've got some really good mind control powers! Don't waste my potential! I could be a useful tool for your dark crusade! I'm really like a God, man! I'm like a fucking *titan!*"

"Know that before God and before the creatures of hell, that you are *just a man*," The Poltergeist hissed darkly. Then, as though having been triggered by those words, each of the plastic dolls withdrew a small knife from its open mouth and stabbed Jason in the throat. Jason choked and fell to his knees, rivulets of blood poured out over his Adam's apple and stained the yellow police tape sash he wore red.

Reynolds and The Poltergeist watched Jason for a few moments as he writhed on the floor, and then, finally, stopped moving. The dolls scurried away to hide again, in the dark corners of the room. The Poltergeist walked over to Reynolds, pulled back its white, porcelain, mask, and then, kissed him passionately on the mouth. The Poltergeist withdrew, and pulled the mask back on, for once, speaking with a voice that was free of distortion:

"It's ours, my love. It's finally *ours*."

Chapter 36:
The Impending Hoarfrost

Exhausted from a sleepless night, Harriet and Spencer spent the rest of the day in a hotel room. Harriet closed her eyes. The sound of Spencer's haggard breathing faded. She opened her eyes. Now, she was standing in a long hallway of The Ross Manor, dressed in a frumpy pink flannel nightgown and a pair of pink bunny slippers with black button eyes. Crunchy Toast Muncher appeared at the end of the hallway. Harriet walked slowly towards him, unintimidated by the creepy bread-shaped mascot head, which masked his expression.

"Justice Bitch," the villain addressed her in a thick German accent. He removed the mascot head and revealed himself to be Vigo VonCrucible.

"Vigo VonCrucible?" Harriet murmured stupidly as she recognized the eccentric artist by his wild, dirty blond curls, striking green eyes, and large, circular glasses.

"...Dee shrink he says dat you are a low level telepath. Hear me, Justice Bitch, you must hear me. Dee Jay Walker he will not help me. He is a vile brat who will taste like the rarest veal, seasoned with victory and vengeance. I will not lie to you, I am a bad man. But you are a hero. You must help me. You are the only one who can help me. You must help me free my son."

"Free your son?" Harriet repeated nonplused, "What on earth are you talking about?"

The walls around them started melting as though made from thick oil paint caught in a torrential downpour.

"It's coming..." VonCrucible murmured creepily. There was true fear there in his crinkled green eyes, "We must talk quickly. If eet knows that I am talking to you, it will be prepared. It hates you, Harriet. Eet will come for you, I

243

imagine...after it's finished preparing whatever scheme eets cooked up...and when it finally does..."

VonCrucible put his hands on Harriet's shoulders and lowered his head. Harriet cringed but there was something in the man's voice, a profound and genuine desperation, which made her suppress her instinct to recoil.

"You must find a way to set him free," VonCrucible finished in a tone of deadly seriousness. His face had started to melt like wet paint in a rainstorm, so that now he resembled a frighteningly disfigured abstract blob, "Do that and I will be eternally in your debt."

It was then that VonCrucible opened his fanged mouth wide and quickly swallowed Harriet whole.

Harriet opened her eyes. The dark hotel ceiling stood above her. She could feel the heat of Spencer's breath against her neck as he exhaled in his sleep. Harriet reached out in the dark and touched his hair. He twitched in his sleep and made a small noise in his throat but did not wake up. The memory of Vigo VonCrucible's voice echoed in Harriet's ears: "It will come for you...and when it finally does...you must find a way to set him free."

What exactly had VonCrucible meant by that? Was this dream another real world cry for help, like the wave of human trafficking victims' pleas she had heard the night before? No. It couldn't have been. That dream had felt more like picking up on a concentration of powerful emotions, the desperate prayers of a group of people who had no idea that she existed. No. VonCrucible seemed to have been communicating a message with clarity and intention. Had VonCrucible contacted Harriet intentionally somehow? Or was this just a meaningless dream? A random assortment of thoughts generated by her weary brain to confuse and astound her?

Harriet stood up and paced the hotel room, frustrated by her inability to decode VonCrucible's cryptic message. What was the mysterious force that VonCrucible had alluded to? In what way was VonCrucible's son, Benjamin, 'trapped'?

And even if Benjamin were in some way 'trapped', Benjamin was a passive-aggressive jerk, who had gone out of his way to make her feel unwelcome in Viola's social circle, and also, probably a traitorous villain in disguise. Why would she want to help him anyway?

In the morning, Harriet exited the hotel room and walked out into an abandoned courtyard. It was unseasonably cold. Harriet wrapped her bathrobe tighter and wrapped her arms around herself. Long, glistening icicles dripped from the awning, which ran the length of the row of hotel rooms. Frost dotted the cracked and taped windows. The courtyard's dirty, green pool was frozen solid. Harriet could sense a presence and turned to slip back into the hotel room before whoever it was could catch a glimpse of her and recognize her as the notorious murderer that she was believed to be.

A cold hand tapped her shoulder before she could escape back into the building.

"Harriet Ross," a laidback California draw greeted her.

She turned and saw Devin dressed as Freeze Out. One of his eyes was now covered by a white eye patch with a blue-silver star on it. Devin shrugged and then finished his greeting: "*Heey.*"

"Freeze Out?" Harriet murmured in confusion. Her hands clenched into fists and she took a step forward, prepared to pummel his pretty face into mush should he attempt to attack her.

Devin put his hands up to show that he was not carrying any weapons and shook his head quickly.

"I'm not here to fight. I just wanna' talk," he said in a measured tone.

"Yeah, you just want to talk? Is that why you tried to kill me the last time you talked to me?" Harriet said, unconvinced.

"Psh. Whatever. I'm sure I couldn't kill you if I tried. No, I said that to fuck with Spanky. I never wanted to kill you, Harriet. In fact, I'm here to help you out."

"How did you even find us here?" Harriet asked, crossing her arms and scowling as she shivered in Devin's supernaturally frigid presence.

"What you think, so like, you're going to just release a bunch of half-naked chicks out into the streets and nobody's gonna' notice? That shit was all over the news."

"And that told you to come here?" Harriet interjected with some concern. If Devin figured out that she and Spencer were staying here, then who else might have figured it out?

Who else might be following us? Harriet thought suddenly, her heartbeat picking up slightly, *Crunchy Toast Muncher? The Poltergeist? The police?*

"Well, on the news, they said that the scorch marks on the side of the building were probably left by a superhuman with some sort of laser powers, and that the wounds on the dead guys looked like lasers…so, I figured, based on that, that you two were probably somewhere in the area. And the band stayed in this hotel once when we were doing a gig, so Spanky would know about it," Devin said.

"What, are you *serious*?"

"I may be a fuckin' swole-as-hell, blond-ass ex-professional pretty boy, but I'm not as stupid as you might think, Harriet," Devin said with the kind of sly, sideways grin that could make any hormone-addled teenaged groupie drop her panties for him: "Now, let's talk."

"Ok, fine. I'm listening. But make it quick. It's *freezing* out here," Harriet said, rubbing her hands together. She could see her hot breath visible against the cold air.

"I wouldn't have gone through the trouble of hunting you down, it's just that I hate to see a woman trapped in an abusive relationship is all."

"What are you even talking about?"

"You and Fuckerson. It just makes me sad. Wake up, Harriet. Look around you," Devin extended his arms for a moment to indicate their surroundings. The abandoned hotel courtyard was dirty and dilapidated. In places it was covered in crude scrawling, gang signs, and bubble spray paint letters, "He's reduced you to living like a criminal in a fucking slum."

"Well, it's better this than prison, and besides," said Harriet and then she grinned and added with a bit more affection than she had intended, "Spencer's learned to serve me well."

"Oh, you think that just because he lets you smack him around a little that *you're* in charge. Can't you see? That's what he wants you to think. He's manipulating you. He's been manipulating you this whole time," Devin said.

"Shut up. No he's not," Harriet scoffed jovially.

"Who do you think killed Martin Finsveld?" Devin announced darkly. The smirk slipped off of Harriet's face as she was forced to consider the question.

"It wasn't you, right? I know that," said Devin, "So then who was it? Think about it, Harriet."

"No..." Harriet murmured back in willful disbelief, "No. *He wouldn't.*"

"Spencer told me that he was planning to murder that fat guy...when I was locked in that piranhas room," Devin said, referring to a time, during Spencer's career as a villain, when he had kidnapped Devin and locked him in a room full of piranhas.

Harriet could not be sure whether or not what Devin had just told her was true. Had Spencer really confessed his plans to trap her in a relationship by framing her for murder to Devin during that kidnapping fiasco? Given the fact that Spencer had stooped to some criminal lows in order to get Harriet's attention as a nemesis, a devious plot to trap her in a relationship was certainly not out of character for him. Harriet did not want to believe it, but given Spencer's behavior in the past, it would be foolish not to take the possibility seriously.

Devin stretched and yawned boredly. He could tell that his previous statement had shaken Harriet's faith in Spencer by the look on her face. It was a look of anger at her lover's betrayal.

"He told me everything about it, like he thought he was *so* clever..." Devin continued, "That he was going to murder that annoying Finsveld guy and then frame you for it, so that you'd have to be his girlfriend forever and never leave him. It would have been pathetic if it hadn't been so *fucking disgusting*."

"Well...that *does* sound like him," Harriet muttered under her breath, remembering the chaos and destruction that Spencer had caused in his crusade to win Harriet as a nemesis. The possibility that she had been tricked filled her with rage and indignity.

"You said at the court hearing that Finsveld stole your identity and credit cards?" Devin said.

"Yeah."

"Well, Martin Finsveld didn't steal those things from you. Obviously, *Spanky did*," Devin said with complete and resolute conviction, "He did it so that you'd go up to Martin's apartment and confront him. Then, after you left, he slipped through the wall of Martin's apartment and murdered him so that it would look like you did it."

"No...it couldn't have been. It was the Poltergeist..."

"The *who*?"

"The Poltergeist."

"Think about it, Harriet. There is no Poltergeist. That's probably just one of his fucking aliases or something. Then he gets to save your life and be the hero when the fucking normals, who already hate you, try to lock you away in prison for the rest of your life. Then, you have to run away with him. Then, you can't ever leave him because you need his powers to keep stealing shit and getting away with murder."

"But The Poltergeist has powers that Spencer doesn't..."

"You *don't know* what kind of powers he's got. He could be hiding all kinds of powers. Remember? He said it himself, at the hearing."

As much as Harriet hated to admit it, this was the only

explanation that made sense. And at made complete, *perfect* sense. What other explanation could there have been?

"My God..." Harriet said, covering her face in her hands as the realization finally dawned on her, "It *really* was him."

"You see, Harriet. I'm not the bad guy here. *He* is," Devin said. Then, he stuck his hand in his pocket and withdrew a silver skull-shaped lighter. "I don't need this anymore," Devin said, handing Harriet the lighter, "Why don't you take it. You know...so the next time you've got that motherfucker tied up, you can douse him with gasoline and set his loser ass on fire."

Harriet hesitated for a moment, looking over the gift with suspicion. Then, she took the lighter out of Devin's outstretched hand.

"Thank you," she said.

"Something to remember me by," Devin said, "In case you ever get tired of his bullshit, you know, in case you ever want your fuckin' dignity back or whatever. If that happens then come find me. I'll help you out."

Lighter in hand, Harriet returned to the hotel room intent on grabbing her clothes and the few possessions she had left that actually belonged to her, before quickly leaving. It was not her intention to confront Spencer. She did not want to look at him or speak to him. She wanted to shrink away from him, without a word. She wanted to rebuke his touch, the way his mother had, on the day that the radiation had changed him. She knew him well enough to understand, that this, her indifference, would hurt him more than anything else she could say or do.

However, Harriet's emotions got the best of her. When she saw him, sitting on the edge of the bed, half-dressed and grinning at her like a lust-drunk fool, she could not help but confront him. She walked up to him, looked him in the eye, and growled:

"I know it was you."

"What?" Spencer replied, genuinely confused.

"*You* murdered Martin Finsveld, didn't you?"

"Huh?" Murmured Spencer in reply. He spotted the silver skull lighter in Harriet's hand and his tone switched from confused to angry, "That's *Devin's* lighter. Have you been talking to Devin? What did he say to you?"

"He told me *everything*," said Harriet dangerously.

Spencer's eyes lit crimson as his brows drew together.

"Whatever he told you," Spencer growled furiously, "It's a lie."

"You murdered him, didn't you, Spencer? And then you framed me so that you could be the hero and I would have to run away with you. You did it so that I'd have to stay with you...no matter what."

"It's a lie. Devin's a fucking liar. Everybody thinks he's a great guy just because he's blond and can *barely* play the guitar but he's a lying sack of shit and.....and I don't want you talking to him anymore," Spencer said, in a voice quivering with repressed rage. Then, he bit his lip until he tasted blood to maintain control of his emotions and his eye lasers.

"Whatever, asshole. I can talk to whoever the hell I want," Harriet said, "And now that I know the truth, that you fucking ruined my life, I am fucking *done*! I don't care if I *am* a wanted criminal now! I'm not staying here another second!"

Spencer sat back down on the bed and covered his face with his hands. Then, said sadly: "Harriet....please..."

"And don't try to find me, either! I don't ever want to see your face or hear your voice again!" Harriet yelled.

Spencer had covered his face with his folded arms and was not looking at her. His shoulders trembled slightly.

She grabbed an arm full of her clothing, and then, stomped out of the hotel room, slamming the door behind her.

Chapter 37:
The Men of the Black Mask

Since Harriet's abduction, Gary had become depressed. He worked infrequently, and spent much of his time in front of the television, watching the news. The mystery of Harriet's conviction and subsequent disappearance had piqued the media's interest, drawing attention to Gary's failure as a lawyer. Footage of him, incoherent, disheveled, and falling asleep towards the end of the trial was played frequently. Late-night talk show hosts made jokes about Gary's incompetence as a lawyer, painting him as a shameful buffoon and a blight on his successful family's otherwise spotless legacy.

Still sluggish and loopy from the effects of his medication, Gary had grown accustomed to visiting Dr. Meredith every Saturday to share his anxieties and woes.

"Everyone thinks she's dead....she must be dead, right?" Gary said to Dr. Meredith one Saturday, "But I don't know in what way to be sad, right? Because is she dead? Or is she out there somewhere...*ignoring me*?"

"Sounds as though you're experiencing a bit of ambiguous grief," reflected Dr. Meredith, the lenses of her large glasses flashing under the light which hung over her desk

"I just....I don't know...."

. . .

One day, as Gary approached the steps leading up to Dr. Meredith's office, he was stopped by a man with a scruffy beard and a baseball cap.

"You should do yourself a favor and stay far away from this place," the man offered as friendly advice, "That Dr. Meredith is not what she seems."

"Don't be ridiculous. Dr. Meredith is my friend," Gary

251

staggered and slurred through the haze of his medication. He was very annoyed that this man had dared to question Dr. Meredith's honor.

"Ha! That's the funniest thing I've ever heard in my entire life! Do you have any idea *who* she is?" the man scoffed cryptically before resuming his stroll.

Gary dismissed this warning as the ravings of some dirty, possibly homeless vagrant and continued his sessions with Dr. Meredith. Despite the professional nature of his relationship with the woman, he had to admit that he was developing a bit of a crush on her. She was elegant and worldly in demeanor, always dressing in long, floral skirts, lacey shirts, and colorful, button-down sweaters. There was something about the calm, emotionally-measured, way that she spoke. It was soothing, like the sound of soft waves lapping again and again against the shore.

One day, as he was speaking to Dr. Meredith, Gary shared his frustration with finding work as a lawyer, after his heavily televised disgrace in Harriet's highly sensationalized trial.

"Nobody wants to hire me anymore," Gary told Dr. Meredith. Dr. Meredith stared back at him from behind her desk and nodded calmly, "Everyone thinks that I'm just a big joke."

Dr. Meredith smiled subtly and then said in a calm, soothing voice: "I don't think you're a big joke, Gary."

"You don't?"

"Of course not," Dr. Meredith said, "You see, Gary, a wise man knows that he knows nothing. If you were truly a fool, you would tell me only positive things about yourself. The fact that you are critical of yourself tells me that you are intelligent and that you have the capacity for growth."

"You really think so?"

"I wouldn't say it if I didn't believe it to be true," Dr. Meredith said, "In fact, as luck would have it, I am looking to hire a lawyer. Now, I don't usually approach clients with these kinds of offers, Gary. But I'm willing to make an exception for you."

"You are?"

"Yes," Dr. Meredith said. She handed him a business card, "I'm sure you've heard of our organization. It's called The Men of the Black Mask."

"Wait...isn't that....*a cult*?" Gary muttered, shocked to discover that Dr. Meredith was affiliated with a shady organization like The Men of the Black Mask. Gary remembered a young man who had been brainwashed by The Men of the Black Mask. His parents had come to Gary's office and wept, telling him that their son had been branded, starved, and severely beaten with a metal cane. This abuse had taken place during a long "initiation period" at an isolated outpost. The Men of the Black Mask, however, had many powerful lawyers working for them and would not allow this battered "henchman in training" to return to civilian life despite his parents' pleas for his release.

"You want me to become some sleazy cult lawyer?" Gary said to Dr. Meredith with a mixture of apprehension and disbelief.

"We're not a cult. We're an organization, which distributes highly-trained mercenaries to powerful individuals in need of military-grade protection."

"...That sounds just like something a cultist would say. Everyone knows that The Men of the Black Mask is a cult that hangs around universities recruiting impressionable young guys to work as henchmen for slave labor wages," Gary argued.

"Sensationalized media lies. We are not a cult. We are an organization, which distributes highly-trained mercenaries to powerful individuals in need of military-grade protection," Dr. Meredith repeated, "Our bodyguards and mercenaries undergo an intense training program. Starvation and physical pain are part of that program. These are conditions that our soldiers may encounter in the field. That is all."

"Huh...well....*I guess* maybe that makes sense," Gary conceded hesitantly.

"As I'm sure you've probably gathered by this point, we do face our share of legal problems. We also have a bit of an image problem. I was very hopeful that you might help us with that, Gary. What do you say, Gary? Will you help us? Will you be the star player of our prestigious and respected legal team?"

"Um...."

"There's no need to rush, of course, take all the time you need to decide," Dr. Meredith said, leaning in uncomfortably close.

"I *um*..." Gary murmured. He could smell the flowery and woody notes of Dr. Meredith's perfume; see her blue eyes through the thick wall of glass which divided him from them. *Is The Men of the Black Mask really a cult?,* he wondered. *Or an intensive training program with an unfair reputation?* Dr. Meredith's close proximity mixed with the dampening qualities of his medication made these questions hard to rationalize.

"I...I need to think about it..." Gary said a little unsurely.

"That's understandable. As I have said, take all the time you need," Dr. Meredith said. She took a business card out of the top drawer of her desk and then handed it to Gary, "But I do hope you'll stop by our compound for a free information consultation to learn about our organization and the ethics for which we stand. I think that you'll find that our bad reputation is unfounded and that we are a welcoming and constructive group. Just listen to our presentation. I think you owe it to yourself to get both sides of the story...before turning down what could be the most important move of your career."

"Right, of course, thank you," Gary said, pocketing the business card.

"So, I'll see you there then?" Dr. Meredith asked.

"Yeah," said Gary, now convinced that he should at least give the organization a chance to tell its side of the story before deciding not to represent it, "You'll see me there."

Chapter 38:
After Harriet

After Harriet left, Spencer was overcome by a crippling sadness, which manifested itself in the form of a joyless, stabbing ache. Now the prize that he had fought so hard for was gone and he was left alone in the ruins of an empty and meaningless life.

After some time, Spencer emerged from the hotel room, disheveled and unshaven, with bloodshot eyes. He wore a crumpled white T-shirt and black cargo pants. The weather was warm and the sky was very blue. It did not match his mood at all. This irritated him. Silently, he wished for Lightning and for a downpour that would soak his hair to the roots and his clothing to the skin.

He walked through the abandoned hotel's empty and dilapidated courtyard, past the green pool, and a few broken, boarded-up windows. He slouched and put his hands in his pockets, staring at his feet.

"Oh my gosh—*buddy*!" a familiar voice squealed excitedly.

Spencer looked up and was surprised to find a pretty girl, with long, auburn hair, grinning at him.

"Janet Laxley?" Spencer murmured in surprise.

"Oh my gosh, Spencer Tuckerson? I never thought I'd see you again," the girl said excited, beaming with joy, "Yeah, It's me, Janet? Don't you recognize me?"

Spencer grinned, remembering his old friend and said in a warm voice: "Well, sure. I remember you."

"Ooh, we have to catch up! Tell me everything that's happened since high school," Janet said.

Spencer walked with Janet fora while. She was in college and spoke to him about college life; about her classes and professors; about her dorm room and the laundry machine in the common area of the dormitory building. She talked about her friends, her textbooks, and her favorite TV shows. She was not exactly the Janet that Spencer remembered, however. There was something different about her that Spencer could not quite explain. Perhaps it was that she had grown more mature. Perhaps it was that his memories of her had dulled with time.

"I'm really glad we got to see each other again!" Janet said, grinning. She had walked with Spencer down the sidewalk and to a shopping center parking lot. "My car is parked here somewhere. Ooh, there it is!"

Janet pointed to a black SUV with dark tinted windows. She walked towards it.

"Come with me," she said to Spencer as she withdrew her keys from the pocket of her cherry red handbag.

"Uh...sure," Spencer said with a grin, "But I just got out of... like a really intense, serious relationship. *So...*"

"You need time to heal. Yeah, I get it," Janet said. Then, she surveyed Spencer with a lustful gaze, leaning against the side of her SUV, "It's just that, it's been so long! What has it been like, two years?"

"Yeah."

"I didn't want to say this but you look like you really need a hug. Do you mind if I hug you?" Janet asked innocently.

"Uh...sure," Spencer said.

Janet leaned into him and wrapped her arms around him, squeezing him tightly. For a moment, he relaxed, feeling better; feeling as though there was a future without Harriet, in which he could be happy and loved. It was in that moment, when he was most relaxed and at peace, that Janet Laxley jabbed him in the neck with a hypodermic needle. His vision blurred and he fell where he stood. He was unconscious before he hit the asphalt.

Janet giggled and then started laughing in a different way, in a deep, throaty masculine way. She grew taller, and her long, auburn hair grew dark, slinking back into her skull as she transformed into a scrawny, dark-haired man, with a stern, serious face. He wore a limo driver's black uniform, with a pair of dark sunglasses, a pair of black gloves and a flat-topped, chauffeur's hat.

The limo driver's cell phone rang and he withdrew it quickly from his front pocket, answering it in a cold, deep, serious voice.

"Boss," he said to the person on the other side of the phone, "You will be pleased to hear that I have secured the bate."

"Excellent," the voice on the other end of the line replied quietly, through the man's Bluetooth earpiece, "You've done well, Catfish."

Catfish grabbed Spencer's limp body and with some difficulty, lifted it, and dumped it into the trunk of the car. He returned to the driver's seat of the SUV. Through the Bluetooth earpiece, he heard his boss cackling maniacally.

"Are you sure this'll work, boss?" Catfish asked as he pulled out of the parking space and drove away.

"Oh, this'll work," the voice on the earpiece asserted sinisterly, "That scumbag bitch will come for him and when she does...the walls will run red with her blood! *Haaahaaaahaahaaahaaaaaa!*"

Chapter 39:
Flight of The Poltergeist

Day became night. Harriet walked on the side of the road, through desert, past cactuses and distant rock formations. She was distressed. She could not help but think about everything that she had lost. Her family, her friends, her good reputation, her code of ethics, The Ross Manor, and now her treacherous ex-butler. It was all gone now and she was alone and directionless, wandering through the rubble of her ruined, once-fabulous life. She did not know what to do or where to go and so, without thinking about it, she continued to walk.

The night grew darker. Harriet became tired and sat down to rest. Without meaning to, she collapsed onto the sand and fell asleep.

Harriet opened her eyes. The distant chime of her mother's music box had torn through her dreams and jarred her awake. Its eerie tinkling bells wafted over the sand, causing Harriet's heart to race with apprehension. Was someone there?

Harriet stood up and wandered in the direction of the noise. It grew louder as she walked towards it. Then, she spotted it in the distance: her mother's pink and gold music box.

The small, hexagon-shaped music box lay open in the sand. The ballerina doll, at the box's center, danced and twirled as the eerie song continued to play. Who had put the music box out in the sand and where were they now? Who had turned the gold knob under the box, and let loose that creepy, depressing melody?

Harriet knelt in the sand, and picked up the music box cautiously, snapping it shut to stifle the noise. She could hear her own heart beating against the sudden silence. She put the music box down in the sand where she had found it, noticing as she did so that there was a large, old-fashioned video camera, from the 90's, laying nearby it. Harriet grabbed the camera and stood. The camera was charged and on. The plastic screen on the side of it was open and the image of a gaunt figure in a long, shredded, black cloak, and a white porcelain mask was frozen on the screen. The figure was creepy, Harriet supposed, because she could not make out its face or expression. The mask covered the figure's face from forehead to chin and its eyes were lost in dark oval shadows. The dark rags that it wore covered every patch of skin.

Harriet pressed the play button on the camera and the video un-paused.

The masked figure let out a shrill, high-pitched cackle.

"Tick tock, you mother fucking whore...." the masked figure murmured quietly. Though Harriet could not see the figure's face, she could hear the grin in its voice, "I am the darkness, the emptiness, the hand of death, and the champion of lost voices who scream for vengeance from their shallow graves."

The figure floated slightly. The torn tendrils of its dark cloak floated around it, standing out in stark contrast against its pure, white mask.

"I am the keeper of the gates of hell; the lord of the rotting and of the damned. Those too foolish to fear me will find that their disrespect comes at a steep price," the masked figure announced in a shrill, distorted voice. The camera moved with the masked figure as it floated upward. An elaborate metal device became visible in the darkness. It appeared to be a vertical meat grinder, with whirling circular blades, and a slow-moving apparatus for feeding meat into the blades. A limp man with a burlap sack over his head was tied to the machine in a standing position, with his feet together, his arms pulled straight and his hands tied up over his head.

"You will come here and fight me, Justice Bitch. Or I will grind his flesh until he bleeds to death, Just like I did with Martin Finsveld," said the masked figure. It floated up to the bound man and removed the burlap sack from his head so that Harriet could see his face. Harriet felt her heart rate pick up. The masked figure's captive was Spencer. He slumped against his bonds, clearly unconscious and inert, "Except, *much slower*...since you dumb, scumbag, lowlife motherfuckers *love* pain so much. And *don't worry*, he won't wake up and escape, I drugged him to make sure that he stays put until he's been ground into hamburger meat. *Haahaaahaaahaaaahaaaaa!*"

Harriet twitched as she noticed the meat grinding device jerk slowly upward. With time, Spencer's bound hands were growing gradually closer to the whirling blades.

"Of course, if you don't show up, I'll still have plenty of fun watching him get ripped apart. But how about instead...we make this interesting. I'm at The Ross Manor, in Daddy's wine cellar. Tick tock, Justice Bitch. The hand of death beckons. Come play with us in our realm of horrors."

The video cut to static. Harriet dropped the heavy camera in the sand and darted down the street and back toward the city. Sensing a presence, Harriet ran and ran until she finally reached The Ross Manor. She tore at one of the gray, stone walls and ripped a hole in it, bounding inside.

Harriet glanced around her quickly. She was in a dark room. There was a tall cage in the corner of the room, next to a tall, black onyx door with a skull for a handle. A huddled figure, dressed in green, lay in the fetal position, at the center of the cage. He stood up and staggered into the dim light cast by the hole that Harriet had torn in the wall.

"Benjamin?" Harriet murmured with disbelief.

Harriet recognized the prisoner as Benjamin VonCrucible by his curly brown hair and striking green eyes. He was dressed in the same green hat and suit that he had worn as Green Lightning during Sexy Rad Super Pals excursions.

"W...who are you?" Benjamin replied in a thick German accent. He seemed confused that Harriet seemed to know who he was, "Are you a hero? P-please, you must help me...dee Poltergeist, she is crazy!"

"The Poltergeist is a she?"

"Yes....unless the girl who tortures me is *also* a puppet. I cannot be sure...." Benjamin said.

"Well, I'm sure this whole story is really interesting and confusing and everything," said Harriet in a quick, worried voice, "But I really don't have time for this. I've got to stop someone from being ground into paste...then I'll come back to save you, and hear your tragic backstory and everything, ok?"

Harriet turned from the cage and ran toward the door, leading out of the room.

"Wait!" Benjamin yelled before she could leave.

Harriet turned back around and looked at him.

"Let me go first, please! I can help you!"

Harriet walked back to the cage, put her hands on the bars, and attempted to snap them free, but they stayed in place almost as though they were just ordinary bars and she was just an ordinary woman.

"It's...*not working*," Harriet said with a mixture of fear and disbelief, as she discovered that ripping the cage open was, in fact, physically impossible.

"It's The Poltergeist...," Benjamin said, "She can produce an electromagnetic field dat makes strange things happen. Dees energy, she can use to suppress supernatural abilities in other superhumans. She can also split her consciousness into two pieces and control another human like a puppet. Dat is why she keeps me alive. I am her puppet. I have been since she kissed me."

"What?"

"That's how she does eet, you see. That's how she possesses a body. She can move corpses and inanimate objects as well. She can move all kinds of theengs. This is all I can tell you about her. She ees very dangerous. More dangerous than me, even. You will likely not return alive. Go with God, Hero."

"Thanks for the info," Harriet said quickly, "I'll come

back for you, if I survive."

"And if I survive, you must let me paint you," Benjamin invited flirtatiously as Harriet darted away, through the door and out into another dark room.

Little plastic baby dolls, with long, ratty hair, crawled up and down the walls like spiders. Their heads turned around and around, and their mouth's opened wide, as they made unnatural noises and spat blood in Harriet's direction. A few of them landed on Harriet's head and tore at her hair. She tried to pull them off but they were surprisingly strong, and clung to her with hallow plastic fingers, weighing her down and scratching painfully against her scalp. She grabbed one by its ratty hair and pulled it off, flinging it across the room.

A man appeared at the end of the hallway. In the darkness, it was difficult to tell, but Harriet thought she recognized the wrinkled face and bald head of Reynolds Sanderland. Despite the fact that he was now retired, for some reason, he was still wearing his butler's uniform. Despite the suspicious circumstances, however, Harriet was very glad to see him.

"Reynolds! She called to him. What are you doing here? What has the poltergeist done to you?"

The man stared at her in a cold, indifferent way, and then, withdrew a gun from the inner pocket of his black vest, firing off six shots. Harriet ducked to avoid them. Reynolds threw his now empty gun down and it clattered against the floor. He withdrew a long serrated knife and charged at her with the weapon drawn, prepared to run her through with the blade. Harriet screamed and ran in the opposite direction. As she was running, she glanced behind her and saw that Reynolds' face had started to decompose. Flies buzzed around his swollen, discolored head and trickles of blood spilled from his gasping mouth. The corpse's foot caught one of the scuttling dolls and he tripped, falling face-first onto the cement floor. He dropped the knife. It clattered onto the floor and slipped away. Now Harriet was cornered at the end of the hallway. The corpse rose to his feet and groaned, dusting debris off of his black vest and pressed slacks.

"It's no matter," the corpse said in Reynolds' voice, "I expect the boss will want to kill you herself, anyway. She might be angry if I finish the job for her."

"You're not Reynolds Sanderland," Harriet accused angrily, "*Who are you?* Where is *the real* Reynolds Sanderland?"

Reynolds threw back his head and laughed a cold, deep laugh that was very unlike the laugh that Harriet remembered.

"Why, Miss Ross, I thought you'd *never* notice!" he said as he began to transform, from an old butler into a young limo driver with dark hair. Harriet watched with amazement as his wrinkles faded, and short dark hair sprouted from his shiny dome.

"You're...the *limo driver*!" Harriet realized with a start, recalling the man who had driven her around for years in her father's personal limo, the man whose name she had never bothered to recall, and the man whom Reynolds had always referred to condescendingly as "Jack."

"I have a name Harriet. I've always had a name, whether you thought it was important enough to remember or not. But that's not the point right now. Because *now*, I go by a stage name....that's *much* easier to remember. It's *Catfish*."

"Whatever, *Jack*. I don't have time for your fucking backstory, ok?" Harriet muttered angrily, thinking of Spencer as he moved slowly toward those rotating saws.

"Fuck you. Do you think I give a shit if Death Laser gets killed?" Catfish swore. "I was never supposed to be a limo driver, *ok*! I...was supposed to be..." Catfish paused for dramatic effect and then finished dramatically: "*an actor*! I wanted to be the greatest character actor that's ever lived, and now, thanks to the radiation, *I am*!

"Great. Ok. Awesome. Good for you. Now what the

fuck did you do with Reynolds Sanderland?" Harriet muttered with some frustration. Catfish was blocking her path with his body, and she was afraid if she tried to scoot around him, that he might punch her in the face. In her current state of powerlessness, any hit she took would likely be a brutal and damaging blow.

"Reynolds Sanderland is *dead*," Catfish announced dramatically, "He died in the car accident along with your father. I survived the accident, disposed of his body and assumed Reynolds' form. You see, I'd heard rumors that Will was secretly doing the butler, and that he was planning to leave him the estate. So, by taking Reynolds' form, I was able to snag billions of dollars worth of inheritance."

"I knew there was something wrong with him. You were him the whole time, weren't you?" Harriet accused.

"Yes. Guilty as charged," Catfish replied with a smirk.

"So then, who is The Poltergeist? Why are you working for her?" Harriet demanded with genuine curiosity.

"She's an old friend," Catfish replied, "And actually the reason, why I came to work for your father in the first place. You see, The Poltergeist has always hated your father, and she's always hated *you*. She's been planning this for a long time."

Feeling confident, Catfish leaned against one wall of the hallway and smirked at her. Harriet was growing frustrated and angry, as she imagined Spencer getting shredded to ribbons while she listened to every longwinded backstory in the building. Seeing that Catfish had grown relaxed and confident in her relative powerlessness, Harriet seized her opportunity to strike while he had his guard down. She quickly ripped one of the clinging dolls from her hair and threw it at Catfish's head. He screamed and attempted to dislodge the thrashing monster. While he was distracted, Harriet quickly darted past him and into one of the many doors which lined the hallway.

She entered the next room, quickly descending the

steps, which led to the wine cellar. She heard the door close and lock behind her. A shrill, cruel cackle reverberated off of the walls. Then, crimson streaks began to seep from the edges of the ceiling and into sticky pools around the edge of the floor. Harriet spotted the meat grinding apparatus. Spencer was still unconscious and bound to the apparatus, rolling slowly closer to rapidly buzzing blades.

The shrill voice cackled again.

"Without your super strength, there is no hope of setting him free," the voice whispered.

"Come out and fight me!" Harriet yelled, remembering what Benjamin had said about The Poltergeist's abilities. If the Poltergeist's electromagnetic waves were suppressing Harriet's powers, then there was an easy solution to this problem. Harriet would just have to kill the Poltergeist, thereby stopping the electromagnetic waves and restoring her own super strength. After that, she could tear open Spencer's metal restraints and rescue him from the meat grinding machine before he was killed.

"I am the bleak inevitability of fast encroaching death, the sick, primal fear, which exists in the heart of every child..." The Poltergeist whispered back.

"I don't care how many nicknames you've given yourself! You're still just a human! Fight me if you think you're so fucking great!" Harriet yelled.

"Well...if you insist..." The Poltergeist whispered quietly.

The Poltergeist rose from the floor to stand between Harriet and the meat grinding machine. She appeared as a dark figure in a white porcelain mask. Harriet watched in amazement as The Poltergeist cackled and rose slowly higher, hovering a few feet above her in the air. The tendrils of The Poltergeist's shredded black robes wafted around her like long, flatworms, expanding to fill the corners of the room.

The Poltergeist cackled again, and then, dived at Harriet like a bird, busting her nose with one gloved fist, and then, floating back into the air before the other woman could retaliate. Harriet breathed hard. Hot blood poured out over her gasping mouth and quivering chin. The Poltergeist circled her like a vulture, cackling confidently.

"Who are you, anyway? Why are you doing this!" Harriet yelled. She glanced at Spencer's limp form as it rolled closer to the rotating blades. She did not want to think about what might happen if this fight was drawn out too long.

"I told you who I am..." The Poltergeist whispered creepily.

"I want to know who you are *for real*!" Harriet yelled. Then, she ripped the remaining doll from her head and threw it at The Poltergeist's face. The Poltergeist dodged the flailing object easily, by tilting her head slightly to the right as it whizzed by. "Is this because we stayed the night in the stupid hotel room you were squatting in? *Get* over yourself!"

"No, Harriet. I've hated you my entire life...ever since I was a little girl...." The Poltergeist uttered quietly. She threw off her mask, revealing the face underneath, which was very pale with white blond, nearly non-existent eyebrows. A cascade of platinum blond hair exploded around her head and wafted around her like the tendrils of her dark clothing.

"Lilly?" Harriet murmured in disbelief, as she recognized the true identity of The Poltergeist at last.

Lilly swooped down and clocked Harriet in the face again before shooting back into the air. Harriet felt a few of her teeth loosen and tasted blood. She put her hands up in a probably useless attempt at defending herself.

"But...I don't understand," Harriet muttered with genuine confusion, "I just met you pretty recently...how could you have hated me since you were a little girl?"

"Allow me to explain," Lilly whispered, sinking back to the floor, so that she and Harriet were eye level. Over Lilly's shoulder, Harriet watched as Spencer rolled slowly closer to the whirling blades. A trickle of sweat rolled across Harriet's forehead as she imagined how his body would be mangled if she did not find a way to defeat Lilly soon.

"My biological father," Lilly proclaimed, raising her voice aggressively, as she advanced on Harriet with her fist's raised, "Was *William Fredrick Ross!*"

"*Bullshit*," Harriet muttered caustically, crossing her arms, "My father was gay. Ask anyone. He was fucking the butler."

"Well, actually, he was *bisexual*. And he also fucked the maid. He fucked a lot of maids actually." Lilly corrected, "And one of those maids was my mother. After I was born, she quit her job and moved in with my stepfather. We lived happily for about eight years after that. But then...my parents ran into some money trouble. So my mother stupidly threatened to tell your evil, greedy father, who had every fucking thing in the world, that if he didn't help us out...that she would tell his wife, *your mother*, about their affair...and about *me*. This was a deadly mistake."

"You know what, why don't you finish your fucking sob story after you *let Spencer go*?" Harriet interrupted desperately. She saw the rotating blades of the meat grinder nearly brush the knuckles of Spencer's hands and cringed.

"I'm not letting him go," Lilly said with a smirk, "He's an evil piece of human garbage. And I intend to fucking kill him."

Harriet screamed and flung herself at Lilly, violently punching and kicking every inch of her that she could reach. Without her super strength, however, Lilly was more than a match for her physical power. Lilly easily flung Harriet off of her and wafted back into the air.

"To shut them up, your father hired Crunchy Toast Muncher to kill my parents," Lilly continued. I watched him turn them into bread statues and eat them in front of me. Then, he told me who sent him, as though that would make me hate him less for it. That's why I made his fucking evil son, Von Dali, my puppet. Haaahaaaahahaaa....that's why I stab that little fucker under the clothes with needles whenever

I get a chance. Of course, I can't fake a German accent to save my life, so it was much easier to just make people believe that he'd taught himself a perfect American accent. Then, all I had to do was pronounce myself 'reformed' and vawlah, perfect puppet! Could you even tell that when you were talking to him, you were really talking to *me*?"

Harriet was only half listening to Lilly's angry rant by this point. She watched helplessly as Spencer rolled closer to those whirling blades. Then, she darted over to the meat grinder and desperately attempted to pull off the metal restraints. But there was nothing she could do. Without her super strength, it seemed, there was no way to free him. The blades sliced his knuckles and blood began to pour slowly down his arms. Harriet wept as she began to pry uselessly at the metal restraints, which bound his ankles.

"You're a fucking monster!" Harriet shrieked as blood poured down Spencer's muscular arms in slow rivulets. The buzzing saws covered his white shirt in angry red splatters.

"Can't you see, Harriet. I'm not the bad guy here. *You are*," Lilly said as though this were a simple fact that should have been obvious to everyone, "It's your fucking selfish, elitist, entitled bullshit that's making the world burn. The Ross Foundation destroys families and ruins lives. I'm doing the world a favor by getting rid of people like you."

Lilly floated back down and Harriet charged at her, intent on strangling her dead. She balled her hand into a fist and struck the other women in the face. Lilly staggered backward, spitting blood in Harriet's face and smirking.

"You got to live your perfect little fucking life in that goddamn mansion, going to fucking celebrity yacht parties, and eating rare truffles that cost more than an entire fucking house...." Lilly whispered dangerously, dodging a second and then a third clumsy blow from Harriet's flailing fists, "Meanwhile..."

Lilly aimed a kick at Harriet's shin, which Harriet dodged clumsily. Harriet staggered backward, nearly tripping over her own feet.

"...I went to a foster home that was set up like a fucking roach-infested barracks, with ten other kids living there," Lilly whispered. She grabbed Harriet's neck and started strangling her. Harriet gasped and clawed at Lilly's white hands against her throat. "Where my foster mother made me work like a slave for a crust of bread and her pedophile boyfriend molested me."

Harriet gasped and as she managed to pull Lilly's fingers off of her throat.

"So that's why you want to kill Spencer? Because you had a shitty childhood? How does that make any sense?" Harriet rasped, clutching her damaged throat.

"I don't owe you an explanation, you evil bitch," Lilly whispered, "You broke my doll. So, I broke your *fucking dildo*."

Lilly pointed at Spencer's limp form hanging off of the meat grinding apparatus. His gory, shredded wrists gushed blood as he slowly rolled into the whirling blades.

"Now he's a like a vibrator with the rabbit snapped off, a fucking useless, damaged piece of shit for you to *throw away*," Lilly hissed viciously.

Harriet reached her hands into her pockets and slouched, defeated. As she did this, she felt the cold surface of Devin's silver, skull-shaped lighter. Her hand closed around the object slowly, and suddenly, she had an idea. She walked up to Lilly slowly, while the other woman was distracted, cackling maniacally and pointing at Spencer's bloody, mangled wrists. Harriet snuck up behind her, flipped open the lighter, and set a lock of Lilly's wafting blond hair on fire. In an instant, the flames had spread, engulfing her entire scalp. She screamed and dropped to the ground, shrieking and flailing her limbs as her hair burned and her scalp was scorched black.

Her screams faded suddenly to silence as she vanished. Harriet returned the lighter to her pocket, and then, bounded over to the meat grinding apparatus, where Spencer was still bound. She felt her strength return to her and the glow of Spencer's aura filled her consciousness. She could sense it. He was still alive.

Quickly, Harriet tore Spencer free of the device. She could feel his chest heaving and his heart beating as she set him down on the floor and tore his shirt off. She then tore the shirt into strips of fabric and wrapped his mangled wrists tightly, staunching the flow of blood. She sobbed as she did this, because both of Spencer's hands were now gone. They had been ground to slush by the whirling blades.

She picked him up and carried him, cradling him gently in her arms, as she sobbed and staggered away from the still whirling meat grinding apparatus.

Chapter 40:
The Aftermath

Spencer opened his eyes. Blinding white lights disoriented him, and he blinked rapidly, attempting to clear his vision. He sat upright abruptly, glancing around the room and breathing hard. He was in a stark white hospital room, with a powder blue curtain encircling it.

"...Whatssthisplace?" he slurred disorientedly. Then, he became very dizzy and lost the will to sit upright, slumping back down onto the hospital bed.

Harriet rose from the chair at the corner of the room, where she had been sitting, and walked up to him. She was wearing a short, curly red wig, a sunhat with a broad brim, and a pair of oversized sunglasses. Her face was bruised and swollen to the point of being barely recognizable.

"...Harriet...." Spencer murmured groggily, when he noticed her standing there. "What happened to your face....who did this to you?"

"Shh..." Harriet whispered, brushing a strand of his shaggy black hair over one ear, "My name is Charlotte right now..."

"I'm....*really confused.*"

Harriet pulled her chair to the edge of Spencer's bed and described everything that had happened while he had been drugged unconscious, excluding the detail about his hands being ground to slush.

"I feel kind 'a sleepy...." Spencer interrupted.

"That's probably the morphine," Harriet said, alluding to the IV drip sticking out of Spencer's arm.

"So then...what happened....after you pulled me off of the meat grinder?" Spencer asked.

"I pulled the bars off of Benjamin's cage and set him free. Which...I really hope wasn't a mistake since he's not *technically* reformed. That was just a thing that Lilly made him say when she was him.   Then, I carried you to the nearest hospital. Which luckily, wasn't that far away. My face was so busted up from the fight that the doctor's didn't recognize me, which, I guess, is a good thing, because otherwise I'd be running from the cops right now. Then, they wheeled you into surgery and I went out and bought the shitty disguise that you're currently looking at. I called Gary and told him about the Poltergeist murdering Martin Finsveld, and he said that with the tape of The Poltergeist confessing to the murder, and the murder weapon that she left in the wine cellar, he might be able to clear my name. They declared a mistrial because of my abduction, and also for lack of competent council, because Gary was a drugged-up mess the whole time, so thanks for that, Gary. Hey, maybe he's a really good lawyer after all? The next trial's bound to go better."

"That's....great news..." Spencer interjected weakly, the shadow of a smile twitching the corners of his mouth.

"I'm sorry I thought you were the murderer, by the way," Harriet said.

"That's ok..." Spencer replied, smiling sluggishly, "If I were you I probably would have thought it was me too. I mean...after all of that other stuff I did to get you to notice me."

"And if you don't want to be...you know...my butler anymore. I understand," Harriet said.

"Heheheh..." Spencer chuckled, "I still live to serve you, my angel from hell."

He turned toward her and extended an arm to touch her hand. Then, he discovered, with a look of terror, that his arm now ended in a bandaged nub. He held his arms up and stared at both of his bandaged nubs with his mouth agape. What little color he had drained out of his pale face.

"I'm sorry," Harriet said with profound sadness, "I was a little late."

Spencer collapsed back onto the hospital bed and tears poured down his cringing face, as he began to sob loudly. Overcome by grief and pity, Harriet lay down on the hospital bed next to him and draped an arm over his quivering body.

"...I....I'm useless to you now, Harriet...I'm just a burden....I'm a cripple..." He wept.

"Shh... that's not true..." Harriet whispered in his ear. She smoothed back his hair, and then, wiped the tears off of his cringing face with both of her thumbs. She pressed her lips against his and kissed him deeply.

"I...I'm never going to play the guitar again...or...or....cook again...or...or reach out and touch your breasts with my fingertips....or reach out and touch *anything* with my fingertips...." he wept, and then, shuttered and sobbed as something else occurred to him. "Harriet, I *literally* can't wipe my own ass now! Harriet....*I*....I think....I think I might actually....w...want to die..."

"Well, you don't get to die," Harriet said a little angrily, "I told you, you're not allowed!"

"I don't want you to feel like you have to do anything for me, Harriet," Spencer said, "But I know that you will...because you're too good for your own good and I know you won't listen. You'll waste your time trying to help me because you feel sorry for me. But that's not what I want for you, Harriet...I never wanted that for you..."

Spencer stood up and the thin white blanket fell off of him. He looked pale and sickly in his blue hospital gown and, under the bright, white lights, his skinny, white legs trembled and his knees buckled as though he were about to collapse onto the ground.

"I'm going up to the roof," he said in a hollow, resolute-sounding voice.

"*Why?*" Harriet demanded angrily. Tears gathered in the corners of her eyes.

"I'm going to look at the city one last time...and then, I'm going to jump," Spencer said.

"No you're *fucking* not," Harriet growled.

"You're not going to stop me."

"No!" Harriet shouted.

———

"Yes."

"No!"

"I've made up my mind."

A pair of tears rolled over Harriet's face and she shouted desperately: "S...*Safe words are dumb!*"

"This is for you, Harriet."

With those words, Spencer staggered through the blue curtain, which encircled the hospital room, phasing through his IV. Harriet followed him. He increased his pace. She darted after him. He phased through the door to the stairway at the end of the hall. She opened the door and bounded after him. He scaled the steps quickly and made it to the roof of the building.

Harriet emerged at the top of the steps, hyperventilating, and clutching her side. The sunhat and curly red wig tumbled off of her head. She left the disguise on the ground and walked over to the place where Spencer was standing, near the edge of the roof. There was a mesh link fence there, presumably to stop people from jumping.

"Don't do this, Spencer," Harriet said, hunching forward and gasping for air.

Spencer had his back turned toward her and was looking out over the city skyline. The sun was sinking low in the sky. It painted the rooftops in shades of orange, purple, yellow, and fuchsia.

"Please...I don't want to see you die...," Harriet gasped.

"Then don't look."

"Don't do it, Spencer."

Harriet reached out and grabbed him by his forearm, holding on tightly. He turned around and stared at her face with dead-looking bloodshot eyes.

"I *love* you, Harriet," he told her. He lingered there for a moment to stare into her eyes, and then, she felt his arm phase through her hand. He turned away from her and jumped through the wire mesh fence, over the edge of the building.

Before she knew what she was doing, Harriet had

ripped the wire mesh fence down and jumped over the edge of the building after him. As she was falling, she did not have time to wonder why she had done such a stupid and crazy thing. She was going to fall with him and die or shield his body from the impact of the fall with her own body. *One of those things is going to happen*, she thought, reaching out to wrap her arms around Spencer as he fell. *One of those two things...* She closed her eyes and waited for a wall of hard concrete to crush her body flat.

The impact never came. Harriet opened her eyes slowly; cautiously. The lights of the city still twinkled far below, but they were no longer hurtling closer. Still clutching Spencer tightly against her chest, Harriet glided forward through the air. A strange weightlessness had come over her, along with a dream-like euphoria. Spencer breathed hard, and then, chuckled in a relieved and nervous sort of way. His muscular arms and bandaged stumps had wrapped themselves around Harriet, and clung to her tightly.

Harriet flew higher into the night sky over the tops of buildings, racing cars, crowded streets, and busy sidewalks. There were too many flying superhumans active in the city for anyone on the ground to pay much attention to her.

"This is....*amazing*..." Harriet murmured as she watched the city glide by underneath of her.

"Could you really fly this whole time?" Spencer asked her weakly.

"I didn't know until now. It's never occurred to me to jump off of a building before!" Harriet shouted happily.

She flew fora while, watching the lights, the flashing billboards, and the speck-like people. She moved through clouds, exhilarated by their cool bursts of condensation. She spiraled and turned onto her back, staring up at the stars and the moon, which was large and yellow, tonight; very close to full. Spencer hung limply in her arms occasionally letting out a nervous chuckle. She did not know if he was enjoying this or not and, by this point, did not really care. She laughed like she was insane and shot forward into the sky, her dark hair twirling around her as she pirouetted like a jubilant child.

Spencer laughed along with her and then he said:

"Harriet?"

"Yeah?"

"...I'm sorry that I tried to kill myself."

"That's ok." Harriet said as she glided back toward the now distant hospital building.

"I promise that I won't ever try to do it again," Spencer said, with a smile, "...I don't want to give up anymore...I want to get better."

"Great because I want you to be my butler!" Harriet exclaimed jubilantly, "Not for play but for real! You know, like, with a salary and stuff?"

"Can you do that?"

"Sure, now that I know Reynolds is dead, The Ross Manor legally belongs to me. Jay Walker is dead. I heard it on the news today, and The Poltergeist and Catfish are on the run, so that takes care of *those* irritating squatters. It legally belongs to me now, I can do whatever I want with the manor! You know, like hire the guy that I'm screwing to me my butler!"

"Shouldn't you give that job to a guy who went to school for it or something?" Spencer said.

"No, I'm giving it to you because you're my friend! And besides, I can pay for you to go to school, if that's what you want!" Harriet said. She reached the top of the hospital building and floated down onto the roof, landing on her feet. A network of spider web cracks sprang up around her at the point of impact, leaving a pair of shallow, foot-shaped, craters in the hospital's rough, cement roof.

Chapter 41:
To Be Continued...

Time passed. Harriet spent her days in Spencer's hospital room. There was a small, white television in the corner of the room, which received only ten channels. It buzzed inanely in the background, mixing with Spencer's sedative-induced snores and the chattering of hospital personnel behind the blue curtain.

Harriet spent her nights in Gary's apartment, not as his girlfriend but as his platonic friend, who happened to be female. He had an expensive place, of course, with big rooms, and perfect new appliances, but it was also masculine, Spartan, and sparsely furnished; with white, empty walls, ugly, sharp angles in the architecture, and blinding fluorescent lights. The apartment looked more like a picture in a furniture catalog than it did a home and stood in stark contrast to Viola's cluttered and eclectically furnished living space.

Gary spent little time in his apartment, and Harriet saw him rarely. She spent her evenings staring at a blinding white ceiling, wondering if the police would find her and Gary would be arrested for harboring a fugitive.

Time passed. As Spencer's injuries started to heal, he spent more of his time conscious and cognizant. During this stage of his recovery, he was given to voluntary inertia and long, listless silences often punctuated by grief-stricken fits of hysterical sobbing. Harriet lay next to him in the hospital bed and spoke to him in a quiet, soothing, voice, holding his quivering body close to hers and awkwardly petting his muscular arms.

"Shh...it's going to be ok..." Harriet whispered quietly.

Spencer exhaled slowly and murmured in reply: "No, it's not."

"Shh...things are going to get better I promise..."

"No they aren't..." Spencer replied, sounding broken and sober, "How are things going to get better? I don't have fucking *hands*...."

Time passed. Gary kept Harriet up to date on news about the police investigation into the reopened Finsveld murder case.

"There was a police raid of The Ross Manor after your encounter with The Poltergeist," Gary said one evening as Harriet stood in Gary's kitchen, watching a TV dinner spin around and around in the microwave, "They've just released their report actually and it's really good news for you."

Harriet tore her gaze away from the timer on the microwave and looked at Gary, who loosened his tie and grinned tiredly.

"They found Finsveld's DNA on the murder weapon, along with a number of fingerprints and a few long, blond hairs now identified as belonging to Lilith Harrison, a.k.a., The Poltergeist," Gary informed her.

"Well, that's good news," Harriet said, brightening a bit.

"But it gets better," Gary announced, his tired grin broadening slightly. "Apparently, Lilith kept souvenirs of her murders...a handful of Polaroid photographs were found at an abandoned hotel room, where she had been staying. Apparently, she dropped them or forgot to take them with her when she fled. So, anyway, some of the photographs that were found...are of her brutalizing Martin Finsveld. And in some of the photographs... she's not wearing her mask. That combined with the fact that she confessed to the murder on the video that you found, will likely shift police attention to finding her rather than recapturing you. Or rather, looking for you. Since officially, you're on file as having been kidnapped, whatever the public may suspect."

"That's great news," Harriet said.

"It is, isn't it?" Gary said, exhaling with relief, "I can do it now...I know I can. I can get you acquitted for the murder charge. Then, everyone will stop treating me like a big, stupid joke. People might even say that I'm a better lawyer than Everett."

"Not Everett," Harriet teased as the microwave beeped and she removed her scalding meal with bare, burn-proof hands, "He's a legend."

Gary laughed and proclaimed happily: "Yeah, well, not for long. When this case is through, *I'll* be the legend. Seriously though, I'll be stealing Everett's clients left and right. No one will want him as a lawyer when they could have *me*."

Time passed. Spencer's condition improved. He spent less of his time sleeping and crying and more of his time spouting dramatic monologue for Harriet's benefit.

"...I don't deserve you, Harriet," Spencer said as he lay next to Harriet on the hospital bed, draping one handless arm around her shoulders and kissing her affectionately on the neck again and again, "...Seriously though, you're the only person in the world that gives a crap about me...and without you. I would have nothing…and I would be nothing. I am unworthy to lick the dirt off of the heels of your boots, let alone kiss you. Let alone run my fingers through your hair and gaze upon those beautiful, perfect breasts. Before I was your servant, I was nothing."

"Ugh...creative people tell such pretty lies," Harriet groaned with a mixture of annoyance and sedate contentment. Spencer's melodic voice had lulled her into a relaxed, near-sleep state. Harriet stared up at the white squares of the hospital drop ceiling, and grinned tiredly. Spencer's lips tickled her neck and she let out a reflexive giggle, rolling onto her side and staring into his large, brown eyes, with a lusty grin.

"It's not a lie, Harriet," Spencer said, very seriously, "The privilege of serving a woman like you is the very highest honor....just....don't give up on me please. I can be useful to you again."

"Yeah, you better be if you know what's good for you," Harriet teased, leaning in close to kiss him on the lips.

Harriet's cell phone rang. She rolled over and grabbed her handbag off of the bedside table. Then, removed her cell phone from the front pocket and answered it.

"Harriet? It's Gary," Gary's voice informed her very seriously.

"Hey, Gary," Harriet said. Spencer's lusty grin sank into a dour scowl as she uttered the other man's name.

"I'm just calling to tell you that the police have captured The Poltergeist," Gary informed her, "She's currently in custody."

"Thanks, Gary. That's great news," Harriet announced excitedly.

Later that day, Viola visited Spencer's hospital room, to offer her condolences as well as a large basket of fruit and cheese. She wore her long, sea-foam green dreads in pigtails and was accompanied by her new boyfriend, the podiatrist. The podiatrist was a tall, good-looking, and conservatively-dressed man with short, dark, and neatly parted hair. His caramel complexion and racially ambiguous features made it difficult to tell if he was Indian, Middle Eastern, Pilipino or some combination of all three.

"Steve and I just wanted to drop by and say that we're sorry you lost your hands," said Viola to Spencer, sounding a little more cheerful than she had intended to.

"Thanks, Viola," Spencer said, sounding drowsy from the painkillers but still grateful for the company.

"And Harriet," Viola said, turning toward Harriet, who was sitting in the corner of the room, wearing the red wig and large sun hat as a disguise, "I just wanted to say that I'm sorry I doubted you."

"You don't have anything to be sorry about, Viola," Harriet said, "I mean, if I was you, I would have thought that I murdered Finsveld too. Also, thanks for letting me stay at your place for so long. I promise I'll pay you back for whatever rent I owe you as soon as I stage an escape from my 'kidnapper' and claim my inheritance."

"Yeah, and for that chair you broke when you were whupping Spencer's ass in the kitchen," Viola snorted jovially.

"Oh *wow*...so...." Harriet murmured awkwardly. Up until this point she had chosen to believe that the sex games that she played with Spencer were not so blatantly obvious to everyone, "About that...."

"What, you think that's a secret? Don't think I haven't noticed all the damage ya'll were doing to my apartment with your Gomez and Mortisha type relationship," Viola said, grinning. She laughed and elbowed the podiatrist in the side as though to cue him in on a joke, "But seriously, pay me back whenever you can. The costume shop chain is doing really well now. We just opened a third location. We even just put out a local commercial. Steve, say the thing that you say in the commercial."

"At Masky's Halloween..." the podiatrist began awkwardly and with as much enthusiasm as a man rereading a list of groceries in order to clarify that no revisions are in order.

"We've got all your costume needs!" Viola finished with a flamboyant shout.

The next day, Spencer was released from the hospital. Not wanting to impose herself on Viola (who was living with the podiatrist now) or Gary (who flatly refused to let Spencer live at his place for any length of time), Harriet rented a small and modest apartment. Here, Spencer continued to recuperate from his grievous injury, as Harriet tended to his physical and emotional needs.

Time passed. Gary spent much of his time in the office or cavorting with Dr. Meredith and her legal team. Harriet spent some of her evenings watching TV on Gary's 92-inch flat screen, while waiting for the Masky's Halloween commercial to make an appearance. One day, Gary returned to the apartment, grinning, and looking very proud of himself.

"The jury read their verdict for the Martin Finsveld trial today," he informed Harriet as he straightened his glasses with one quivering hand. He behaved as though the words that he was about to say were struggling to escape his mouth prematurely and against his will, "...And *guess what*?"

"What?"

"...I actually did it. They found you not guilty of the murder of Martin Finsveld. Harriet, you've been acquitted," Gary said with some elation as he removed his tie and threw it down on the floor.

Harriet smiled and stood up.

"So...does that mean?" she murmured, hardly daring to believe her luck.

"That's right. You're no longer a murderer in the eyes of the law...and since Death Laser kidnapped you, they can't say that you tried to evade arrest. If I were you, I'd just turn up at a police station one day, and tell them he let you go."

"You really are a good lawyer, aren't you!" Harriet shouted in elation, running over to Gary and embracing him.

"No longer the worst Goldstein," Gary bragged proudly.

Harriet spun with him in her arms, and before she knew what was happening, he had leaned in and kissed her. Harriet froze. She could feel Gary's tongue in her mouth, lapping at the edges of her teeth awkwardly. She backed away and Gary withdrew. He could tell by the look on her face that something was wrong.

"I don't understand," he said, sounding genuinely confused, "I...I thought you'd be happy."

"Uh...well....I am happy but....Gary, I just don't know if I'm ready for us to be. You know, a couple again," Harriet said awkwardly, suddenly very aware of the silence in the room. The buzz of the television seemed one thousand miles away.

"What? Why not?"

"It's just like college. We date and we break up. We date and we break up. It's beginning to make me think that...maybe this just doesn't work," Harriet said.

"What do you mean?" Gary asked her with incredulity, a little indignantly.

"You broke up with *me*, remember?" Harriet said with some frustration.

"Well, yeah, but that's because you were being too bossy and controlling," Gary told her as though this should have been obvious, "You're being way less of a bitch, now."

"I don't want to change Gary. And I don't intend to change just to be with you," Harriet stated bluntly.

"What are you still seeing that 'butler' of yours?" Gary muttered, "I don't know if you've noticed this or not but he's a worthless loser. And he's using you for your money. Can't you see, Harriet? He's going to drag you down."

"He's not a 'worthless loser.' He's my butler and I love him," Harriet muttered back defensively.

"Oh, I see how it is. After all we've been through, you love *him*?"

"Don't act like you're entitled to a relationship just because you did stuff for me," Harriet grumbled.

"Well, I'm sorry, Harriet."

"You should be sorry."

"Yeah, Harriet. I'm sorry. I'm sorry I'm not edgy and alternative and play the guitar! I'm sorry that I'm not a freak in the bedroom! I'm sorry I work for a living instead of stealing money from charities! I'm sorry that I'm not *stupid enough* to blindly agree with everything that you say!"

"Whatever, asshole, I'm out'a here."

"I'm sorry I have a brain in my head and the sense I was born with! I'm sorry I went to Harvard instead of living in my mom's car and sitting under a bridge, begging for quarters! I'm sorry I don't let you treat me like shit and then pretend like I like it and like it's ok!"

"Well, if I treat you like shit, then why are you still trying to date me?"

"I don't know! I just…I just always hoped that someday you'd be different. That you'd grow up a little and get easier to deal with and less of a…"

"A what, Gary?"

"Less of a…a bossy bitch."

"Yeah, but that's the thing, Gary. I don't want to be with a guy who wants to change me," Harriet explained with a mixture of incredulity and irritation, "I'm bossy and I'm a bitch and that's me, that's just part of *me*. I am who I am and if you don't like that, then you don't like me. I don't want to be with someone who doesn't like me."

"Oh...right, I guess that makes sense," said Gary sounding let down, "I...I don't know what came over me...I do like you, Harriet...but I guess...I understand what you're trying to say. I can respect that point of view, I guess." He held out his hand for Harriet to shake, "Friends?"

Harriet extended an arm and shook Gary's hand.

"Friends," she confirmed with a smile.

Time passed. Harriet turned up at a police station and pronounced herself "escaped" from Death Laser's nonexistent secret lair.

The Poltergeist was convicted of first degree murder and sentenced to life in prison. She revealed the location of Reynolds Sanderland's body during a police interrogation. After the body was exhumed and identified, Harriet received her 10 billion dollars worth of inheritance and became the majority stockholder of The Ross Foundation. She did not move back into the manor right away, however, because Spencer hated having the servants everywhere, and said that they made him feel like he was living in a public boarding house. Instead, she celebrated her victory by purchasing a new, large, flat screen, television for the apartment that she had been staying in with Spencer. Then, by furnishing the previously modest apartment with very expensive furniture. Then, by paying Spencer's hospital bills. And then, by paying for his prosthetics.

After the bandages were removed from his stumps, Spencer tried a number of prosthetics, ranging from the more cosmetic variety, which resembled plasticized human hands, to the more functional and less aesthetically pleasing variety.

After some experimentation, Spencer settled on a pair of metal hook hands that he could use to grasp and manipulate objects. He spent hours practicing with them and, over time, taught himself to perform steadily more and more complex tasks.

Spencer learned fast, and before long, he was picking up objects, opening containers, and dressing himself without any trouble at all. His mood improved dramatically, as he began to regain his independence.

Despite this, however, Spencer's hook hands made it impossible for him to play the vast majority of musical instruments with any degree of skill. It seemed that metal hook hands could not match the speed, accuracy, and dexterity of ten long fingers dancing over guitar strings or piano keys. This limitation depressed Spencer. At times, Harriet noticed him staring at his old guitar with a dead look in his eyes. His silence spoke of a sadness more profound than tears could express; of a powerlessness in the face of the plans of a cold and unfeeling universe.

One day as Harriet was reclined on the couch, in the living room, pouring over a book entitled: Deprogramming Mind Control Victims, she glanced up from the pages and spotted Spencer hunched over the kitchen table. He had that dead look in his eyes that he got sometimes when he was staring at musical instruments that he no longer had the capacity to play, or when he was listening to the radio and an EAR MUTILATOR song came on. He had a mostly empty six pack of beers with him and he was drinking what remained of it. Harriet put the book down, stood up, and walked over to the place where he was sitting.

"Hey, are you ok?" Harriet inquired softly. She sat down next to him and extended an arm, brushing strands of his black hair behind one ear. He did not look at her. Instead, he stared at the drink in his hand, brought it up to his lips, and drank deeply.

"Yeah..." he said, sounding distant and detached. He gulped down the remainder of his beer, and then, dropped the empty can on the floor. Its metal surface bounced against the kitchen tiles with an impotent *clank*, "Wait thas a lie...," He slurred drunkenly and then he corrected himself, "*No*..."

"I'd join you, but alcohol has no effect on me anymore," Harriet commented conversationally, "...You know, I don't think I've ever seen you drink before."

"Thaats...because...because *I can't* drink," Spencer slurred, "I mean...I *can* drink... physically...I can get drunk...but I *don't* drink because...because..."

Spencer hesitated, the red lights in his eyes had ignited and were building in strength. He wavered slightly in his chair as though forcing back vomit.

"Because....then I sometimes lose control," Spencer finished, steadying himself against the side of the table. The crimson lights in his eyes burned brighter, and then, a pair of lasers shot out and blasted a hole in the drywall, at the other end of the apartment, while at the same time, demolishing the sofa. Spencer sniffled and a pair of tears rolled down his face as the crimson lights faded to brown, "*Fuuuck*...like *that*..."

"Hey, it's ok...I'm rich. I'll just buy another one," Harriet crooned in an attempt to comfort him.

"You're sweet, Harriet..."

"Well, I don't often hear myself described that way," Harriet said with the shadow of a smile, "You're being a really naughty butler right now, by the way. Hey, are you even old enough to drink?"

"...I turned 21 last week," Spencer informed her.

This simple fact stated so plainly was shocking news to Harriet. It had not, until this point, occurred to her just how much time had passed since she'd met Spencer.

"What, It was your birthday? Why didn't you say anything?" Harriet asked.

"I didn't want to make a big thing out of it. No one's celebrated my birthday since I was like a little kid. Not since....you know..." Spencer said.

"Oh...that sucks," Harriet said, feeling a sudden and

unexpected spasm of pity for Spencer. She remembered the face of Spencer's mother in Trauma's supernaturally vivid flashback; her furious scowl; the way she'd recoiled from her young son as he'd reached out to her for comfort and screamed that he should never touch her again.

Harriet inched closer to Spencer, put her arms around him, and leaned into him. He was quiet and still for a moment, and then, she felt his muscles relax. She snatched the unfinished beer out of his hook hand and put it back down on the table.

"Shhh...no more of that," she whispered in his ear, as she saw that the alcohol was doing nothing to improve his mood, but merely making him sick and more prone to destroying her furniture.

"Yes, mistress," Spencer replied obediently.

Harriet leaned close and kissed Spencer on the lips. He pressed back and retaliated with a lot of sloppy drunk tongue.

Harriet pulled away and wiped the slime off of her lips with a grin.

"You know, given your recent destructive behavior. I think you're deserving of a punishment," Harriet whispered with a lusty smirk.

"What's my punishment...oh dark tormentor from hell....oh goddess, mean angel, baby demon face...God, you're so cute. Hurt me. Please," Spencer slurred drunkenly, staggering to his feet and bowing before her, nearly falling on his face as he attempted the feat.

"You're punishment is that you get to fuck me," Harriet said with a grin, thinking that a bit of carnal pleasure might do something to cheer Spencer up.

"It is my privilege to pleasure you, oh cruel one," Spencer said, taking her hand in his and kissing it on the knuckle, "...I'll get a condom."

"No condom this time," Harriet said, "Your punishment is that you get to fuck me without a condom. I'll just take one of those morning-after pills or something."

"You're too nice to me, Harriet. You should be stricter," Spencer protested.

"Just do what I tell you and shut up," Harriet muttered with some annoyance.

Harriet stood up and pulled Spencer over toward the ruined sofa. Its cushions had been charred black, and, in some places, reduced to piles of smoking, shredded foam. She lay down on the piles of foam chunks and shredded black fabric, and waited for him, staring at him through half-lidded eyes as he clumsily attempted to remove his black jeans with drunk hook hands.

With some effort, he managed to pull his jeans down and they fell to his ankles. He stepped out of them and walked over to Harriet, now naked from the waist down. She parted her legs, inviting him to enter her. She closed her eyes and felt the cold metal of his hook hands against her skin, the length of his erect member brushing her clitoris. She reached out and gripped his bottom with both hands as he entered her. The damage left from the numerous spankings he had previously endured had healed, and in its absence, the man's behind was white, round, soft and cool to the touch. She ran her hands along his backside as he thrust into her, gripping him firmly as he kissed her neck again and again. He moved in an id-driven, dignity forgotten way, moaning and shuttering, proclaiming his love drunkenly between pleasured gasps.

When he was finished, he pulled out of her and staggered to his feet, grinning stupidly. He bent down in a clumsy attempt to redress himself. Harriet smirked evilly and then smacked him once on his bare butt while he had his back turned to her.

"Ow!" he yelped in surprise, rubbing the reddened spot on his ass where she'd slapped him.

"That's for ruining my sofa, you drunk jerk," Harriet said with a grin.

"...I deserve so much worse, oh cruel goddess," Spencer

said.

"Yeah, well your punishment's not over," Harriet said.

"It's not?"

"No," said Harriet, "The rest of your punishment is that we're going to celebrate your birthday."

"Noo...it's too mean..." Spencer complained drunkenly, he staggered and struggled to dress himself with the hook hands.

"Shut up. It's happening," Harriet said.

"You're a creature from hell!" Spencer complained. His pants were still down and he struggled to slip his metal hooks through the belt loops, slipping and staggering several times.

"And there's going to be cake and presents and balloons and all that other crap. Whether you like it or not," Harriet announced.

"I'd rather get the thumbscrews..." Spencer muttered, finally managing to pull on his pants, and then, stumbling back over to the kitchen, where he clumsily plopped his ass into one of the kitchen chairs and then slumped over onto the table, "So dizzy...." he moaned, and then, he fell asleep. Harriet watched him for a moment and smiled. He snored and his tight, gray band shirt rose and fell along with his back as he breathed.

In that moment, Harriet was happy as she had not been for quite some time. So happy, in fact, that for a moment she was not threatened by the intensity of her affection for this unusual man. Nor was she infuriated by how this reluctant fondness had grown and grown out of control and without her permission. Instead, she was enveloped by a profound and overwhelming infatuation that had snuck up on her and quickly robbed her of her senses, like a pickpocket in a crowded subway.

She left the apartment to get some cake and a present for Spencer. Despite his drunken protests, Harriet believed that Spencer must have been deeply hurt by not having his birthday acknowledged by his family for so many years. This was likely a symptom of their disconnection from him after the accidental death of his father. After witnessing this traumatic event firsthand, Harriet understood the mental anguish that had plagued Spencer since childhood, and she wanted to comfort him, to make him feel important and special, and, most importantly, to show him that life did not have to be all terrible just because he was irreparably mutilated now. She searched for a present for hours, driving to many stores, often asking the clerks cryptic questions like: "What do you buy for a man who has no hands and is basically insane?" It was not until she entered a music store on 5th street, that this question yielded a satisfying response.

"How about this harmonica, you can wear on your head. It's hands-free," the man behind the counter at the music store replied.

"That's perfect. Wrap it up. I'll take it," Harriet said excitedly.

That night, while Spencer slept off his drunkenness, Harriet laid awake and stared at the ceiling, grinning, and imagining the look on Spencer's face as he discovered that there was still an instrument left that he could play without his hands. The next morning, she got to work, making plans for the birthday celebration that she would force on Spencer after he recovered from his hangover. She ordered a cake, decorated the apartment, wrapped the harmonica, and dressed herself in a sexy, slinky skirt that showed a lot of her cleavage. She was so preoccupied by all of those activities, in fact, that she forgot to take the morning-after pill.

About the Author

Hello, My name is Coyote Paria and I am the person who wrote and illustrated this book. I am an artist, an indie game designer, and a writer of science fiction and fantasy novels. I love pastel watercolors, animation, every art supply ever, comics, fandom, and storytelling in all of its forms.

If you are a fan of my particular brand of weirdness, you can follow me on Twitter and Instagram (@CoyoteParia) for news and updates about my upcoming novels, videogames, and creative projects. You can also vote on future book covers, or tell me how much you loved or hated this book directly. I read all mail, from everyone, all of the time.

Frustrated by the fact that this book is a sequel?

Want to figure out exactly what's going on here?

Read about how it all began in

Justice Bitch by Coyote Paria.

www.ingramcontent.com/pod-product-compliance
Lightning Source LLC
Chambersburg PA
CBHW060406260626
47160CB00006B/2457